Jaded

ANNE CALHOUN

BERKLEY SENSATION, NEW YORK

THE BERKLEY PUBLISHING GROUP
Published by the Penguin Group
Penguin Group (USA) LLC
375 Hudson Street, New York, New York 10014

USA • Canada • UK • Ireland • Australia • New Zealand • India • South Africa • China

penguin.com

A Penguin Random House Company

JADED

A Berkley Sensation Book / published by arrangement with the author

Berkley Sensation Books are published by The Berkley Publishing Group.
BERKLEY SENSATION® is a registered trademark of Penguin Group (USA) LLC.
The "B" design is a trademark of Penguin Group (USA) LLC.

For information, address: The Berkley Publishing Group,
a division of Penguin Group (USA) LLC,
375 Hudson Street, New York, New York 10014.

ISBN: 978-0-425-26512-3

PUBLISHING HISTORY
Berkley Sensation mass-market edition / February 2014

PRINTED IN THE UNITED STATES OF AMERICA

10   9   8   7   6   5   4   3   2   1

Cover art by Dan O'Leary.
Cover design by George Long.

This one's for Kari and Anji: moms from the playground turned best friends, helping me keep it together since 2009.

As always, for Mark.

ACKNOWLEDGMENTS

I could not have written this novel without the able assistance of librarians in Nebraska and South Dakota. Special thanks to Peg Williams of the Potter County Library in Potter County, South Dakota, and Barbara Hegr of the Morton-James Public Library in Nebraska City, Nebraska. Their insights into the daily routines and unique challenges facing rural libraries (and communities) fueled this novel, and I thank them for their time and generosity. Robin Rotham also provided insights into small-town life. Any mistakes are my own.

Jill Shalvis reminded me that sometimes old-school methods work best. Megan Mulry was her usual dazzling self, flinging plot ideas and character insights like holy water.

1

ALANA WENTWORTH LOCKED the front door to the Walkers Ford Public Library with one thing on her mind: Chief of Police Lucas Ridgeway.

She gave the brass door handle an absentminded tug to make sure it was secured before setting off at a brisk walk down the traditionally named Main Street. Lucas usually got home a few minutes after she did. With any luck she'd have just enough time to put on the opposite of her librarian clothes, a primly buttoned silk blouse and cashmere cardigan over a tweed skirt. The blue scoop-neck T-shirt with the rosettes, her 7 For All Mankind jeans, then she'd put a little extra oomph into her makeup. Figure out her strategy before his truck pulled into the driveway next door to hers.

A quick glance at her watch told her she'd left herself just enough time to get ready, but not enough time to talk herself out of what she planned to do.

She stepped lightly in the shallow depressions worn into the marble steps by thousands of residents, and turned for the house she rented from Lucas. Spring had taken a firm grip on the region. The business district's beautification committee spent the day hanging planters full of impatiens from the green-painted light poles, set out the half barrels spilling over with tulips and crocuses, and hung the banner announcing the upcoming Spring Fling Carnival in a few weeks' time. Alana noticed the hardy spring flowers only when a sharp knock on the Heirloom Café's front window snapped her out of her reverie. Fifteen-year-old Carlene Winters, dressed in her green uniform, waved brightly and hurried to the café's front door.

"Hi, Miss Wentworth! I just wanted to say thanks for the recommendation. I started *Pride and Prejudice* last night, and I can't put it down."

"You're welcome," Alana said. "I really have to—"

"The language was a little tough, but I totally got that Mr. Darcy was being mean to Lizzie," the girl continued. "He says there aren't any pretty girls for him to dance with, but she's more than pretty. She's funny, and she laughs at herself. That should count for something."

Dear God. Normally she'd love to talk to Carlene about all the intricacies of Darcy and Lizzie's courtship, but not tonight, not when she wanted to start a courtship of her own. Or something resembling a courtship, in a way. In a very indirect way. "It should," Alana agreed rather desperately. "I'm sorry, but I have to get home. Come by the library tomorrow and we can talk about it then?"

"Sure! Have a good night."

An image of Lucas from last Sunday flashed into her mind. He'd caught Alana in her thin robe and nightie, scampering barefoot down the driveway for her Sunday morning tradition of reading the *Trib* in bed with a pot of coffee and jazz on in the background. Dressed in jeans, hiking boots, and a hunter green fleece pullover, he'd loaded his retired service dog, Duke, into his truck for *his* Sunday morning tradition of a long hike. As usual, he'd looked unflappable during the embarrassing encounter, but when she reached the safety of the stoop and looked back, he was still watching her.

The look in his dark chocolate eyes had sent heat flickering through her despite the early morning chill. Even now, two days later, her nerves still held the charge of that look.

"I hope to," she said to Carlene, then set off again, impatient with the delay, but mostly impatient with herself.

Once again she'd left something important until almost the last minute. Well, this wasn't the last minute. The last minute would be two weeks from today, when her contract with the town of Walkers Ford ended and she left to drive back to Chicago. But her habitual distraction and procrastination meant yet again she was scrambling to do something she'd always meant to do, then didn't.

Like work in a public library, the goal she'd set when she got her MLS then let slip through her fingers after graduation. The whole point of this diversion was for her to learn to be more proactive in her life, to make things happen rather than letting them happen to her. Including Lucas Ridgeway, assuming he had no objection to being one half of the oldest cliché in the book, a whirlwind affair between a repressed librarian and a cop.

She hurried down the street to her rented house as nature put on a show in the expansive sky at the end of the street. There was the Hanford house five doors down, then there was nascent twilight streaked with the sunset's reds, oranges, and pinks. It should have clashed horridly, but the prairie sky wore the colors with a magnificent lack of concern that reminded her of her sister, Freddie. Freddie wore jeans, ballet flats, and a faded blue button-down shirt in front of fifty thousand people, and within minutes #preppiestyle trended on Twitter all over North America and Europe.

Nothing ever happened to Freddie. Freddie made things happen. Their mother often complained that one daughter got all the initiative and the other got all the absentmindedness.

She hurried up the driveway, trying to remember if the shirt with the rosettes was in her dresser or on the closet shelf, when Lucas's police department Blazer passed her and pulled into the driveway next to her. The transmission ground when he shifted into park and cut the engine.

Too late. The story of her life, but she resisted the urge to write off the rest of the night. Instead, she climbed the front step and waited, pretending to thumb through the mail while she watched him greet Duke, his Belgian Malinois. Maybe it was the untempered affection he had for the dog that tugged at her heart. He hunkered down to scratch the dog's throat and whisper *You're a good boy, yes you are* into his upturned muzzle. Duke spent his days on the screened-in front porch of his house next door. Every time Lucas came home, Duke pranced and danced, rubbed his white-furred snout against Lucas's legs, his fawn-colored tail wagging frantically. The raw blast of emotion from the dog and Lucas's gentle scratching tightened Alana's throat every time she saw it.

Tonight was no exception. When the reunion ended, Lucas got to his feet, then glanced her way. He wore a navy suit and a gray tie, with his badge and service weapon clipped to his belt.

"Evening, Chief," she said.

"Ms. Wentworth," he replied.

The way he said her name shouldn't have made her heart beat a little faster, but her name on his lips always did. She could salvage this, still get a few minutes to get ready. "I wonder if you'd have a moment later tonight," she said. "The bathroom sink isn't draining properly."

"It's not the kitchen sink this time?"

"Sorry, but no," she said.

He looked at his watch, a no-nonsense Timex. "I've got a couple of minutes now," he said. "I'll get my toolbox."

Damn!

Alana carried her bags inside, turning on lights as she moved from the kitchen through the dining room and down the short hall to the bedroom she used as an office, where she dumped the bags, then continued down the hall to her bedroom. The house was lovely, with gorgeous hardwood floors, walnut cabinets built into the corners of the dining room, brick molding, and charming window seats in the three bedrooms. When she first looked at the rental property, Lucas had told her his grandparents lived out a seventy-year marriage in the house. Love seeped from the woodwork and floors to give texture to the light that poured through the picture window overlooking Mrs. Ridgeway's famous rose beds. Chief Ridgeway had scrupulously pointed out the house's defects—leaky windows, ancient plumbing, and a kitchen straight out of the 1970s—but to Alana, bundling up during the winter was a small price to pay for the chance to see those roses bloom in the spring.

After opening the kitchen door, she poured herself a glass of wine, turned on NPR, and more attentively sorted through her mail. The stack included the usual bills as well as invitations, personal notes, and birth announcements on Crane's finest paper. She slit open the formal announcement of an upcoming party honoring her stepfather's contribution to efforts to ameliorate global poverty. Her mother had set the date for the celebration months earlier, but receiving the formal invitation made it all real. Alana's time in Walkers Ford was almost over. She should start packing, another task she was putting off, but she'd brought so little with her. A few hours one evening and she'd be ready to leave.

Lucas knocked at the kitchen door with the Maglite she recognized from the sports bag he carried to and from work each day. Glass of wine still in hand, she crossed the kitchen and let him in.

"You're still dressed for work," she said, stating the obvious. He'd left the gun and badge in his house, though.

"Town council meeting tonight," he said as he turned sideways to get past her. He carried an old-fashioned wooden toolbox in weathered gray. A hammer and a neatly organized set of wrenches lay on the top shelf, other tools stored in the compartment underneath. His broad shoulder brushed hers as he managed to avoid hitting her knees with the toolbox.

Every cell in her body lit up, and heat bloomed on her cheekbones. His gaze, normally so controlled, flicked down just enough to let her know he saw the blush. Silence. The air between them heated.

"I'll just . . ." he said with a tilt of his head to the bathroom.

"Of course," she replied, and stepped to the side to let him down the hall.

Her experience with Marissa Brooks and Adam Collins a few weeks after she had arrived taught her about small-town values, and gossip. After a tragic accident in high school, Adam Collins left town to join the Marine Corps. He returned to Walkers Ford a distinguished veteran and rekindled his relationship with Marissa, setting off a firestorm of gossip. Alana couldn't just start up a torrid affair with a small-town chief of police. Yet she wondered how to tell him in no uncertain terms that she wanted to go to bed with him and stay there until she couldn't remember her own name, preferably without sounding like a shameless tart.

A sophisticated woman would know how to go about this. Freddie could probably do it while polishing the paper for an international conference on human trafficking that Alana had researched and outlined for her two weeks ago. But Alana wasn't Freddie, or her mother, or her stepfather, the former senator Peter Wentworth. In a family characterized by brilliance, wit, and a talent for far-reaching policy development, Alana was quiet, observant, content with the background. *Just stand still and smile*, her mother used to say with resignation. *You have such a pretty smile*. So her pretty smile graced the walls and corners, first of school dances and mixers, then college parties, then cocktail parties and receptions when she went to work for the Wentworth Foundation.

But not even time spent on the edge of the limelight matched the long, heated moments when Lucas Ridgeway gave her his full attention.

"It's a budget meeting," he said as he set down the toolbox. He shrugged out of his suit jacket and draped it over the linen closet's doorknob.

"Oh. Of course." Mayor Mitch Turner had asked her to update the former library director's proposal to renovate and upgrade the town's library, presumably to round out the town's annual budget meeting.

The tiny, rose-pink bathroom was barely large enough for her to dry off after a shower. Lucas could brace one shoulder against the wall and rest his palm on the mirror opposite, something he'd done the day the pipe draining the shower cracked and leaked peach-scented water into the basement. He'd been cursing steadily and quite prolifically under his breath then, but not tonight.

He yanked the stopper free and peered into the drain. "It's clogged."

"I could use a drain cleaner."

"It'll eat right through the pipes," he replied. "They're seventy years old. Some weekend soon I'll replace the drain line and the P-trap. Maybe that will help. In the meantime . . ."

He handed her the flashlight, then stretched out on his back and wedged his torso into the cabinet under the sink. One hand fumbled in the toolbox. He lifted his head to better see, banged his forehead on the cabinet, and grunted.

"Sorry," Alana said hastily, and shone the light on the offending pipes.

It took only minutes to clear the pipe, then reattach the stopper to the drain lever, each stage punctuated by curt instructions given by the big male maneuvering in the small room. He twisted, his legs pushing against the opposite wall so his knee pressed into her shoulder.

"Do you wash your hair in the sink?" he asked.

"No," she said, pulling a handful forward to consider it.

It was thick and poker-straight, cut in a bob that swung just below her jawline. Its only redeeming characteristic was the natural, pale blond color. Freddie bemoaned her regular appointments with Chicago's best hair salon to maintain the same shade. "There's just a lot of it."

"I can see that," he said to the interior of the cabinet. His dress shirt pulled free from his pants, revealing the waistband of his dark blue boxers. A thin line of hair ran from his navel into the waistband. Muscles flexed as he tightened the joint, and with each moment the scent of male skin and laundry soap permeated the air.

Don't let this chance slip through your fingers.

According to the thriving small town gossip, he wasn't seeing anyone, which gave her an excellent reason to use what she'd heard described as the oldest technique in the book to get over what happened with David. She was going to get under Lucas Ridgeway. Tonight. A single, uncomplicated interlude without any awkwardness because he'd leave for the town council meeting.

She should probably attend, too. Mrs. Battle, a lifelong Walkers Ford resident and her assistant at the library, would be there, providing continuity to the permanent hire, assuming the city council ever got around to choosing one. The relationship between the previous library director, the former police chief, and the fire chief was contentious at best. Efforts to usher the library into the digital age had stalled while Mrs. Battle struggled with cancer, and gone dormant in the months Alana served as the temporary library director while the council slowly weeded through applications.

Ushering libraries into the digital age was her research focus during her master's program. At his request, she'd given Mayor Mitch Turner a fairly lengthy document outlining a wide variety of possible approaches to upgrading the library. It was an interesting challenge. The library, built with money donated by Andrew Carnegie in the early 1900s, was a beautiful old building dangerously near the point of being irreparable. Something would have to be done, soon, although she assumed the something would be done by whoever they hired full-time. . . .

But she had no long-term business in town. She'd committed to a short-term contract, which extended month after month as the council dickered over who to hire.

The wrench thudded back into the toolbox.

Stay focused.

"Do you want a beer?" she asked.

"Yeah. Thanks."

In the time it took him to extract himself from his contortionist's position under the cabinet, she went into the kitchen and snagged a bottle from the fridge. Back in the tiny bathroom she handed him the bottle. He twisted the cap off and tossed it on the counter, then tipped it back. His throat worked as he swallowed. Her heart skittered in her chest.

Then he turned sideways to step through the door just as Alana made the same move. They ended up chest to chest in the narrow door frame, her breasts brushing that rock-solid chest with each breathy inhale. An electric charge sparked between them, heating the air as she looked up at him. He didn't move closer, or take her mouth. He simply stayed a breath and a heartbeat away, like he was waiting for her to close the distance.

She went on tiptoe and brushed her lips against his, slow and hot, striking sparks. One arm tightened around her waist, pulling her against his body as he leaned back into the frame, adding to her breathlessness. He wasn't like any other man she'd kissed. He let her lead, waited for her tongue to touch his before responding, somehow both completely male and completely available to her all at once.

"What are we doing, Alana?"

She grew bolder, drawing back to nibble at the sensitive corner of his mouth, pressing herself against him, and felt his erection thicken against her lower belly.

"Okay," he said with a growl, and backed out of the doorway and down the hall until the backs of his legs hit the boxy arm of the sofa. He tipped backward. She landed on top of him, forcing a grunt that became a groan as they shifted up until his head lay against a red throw pillow. The vivid color softened his brown eyes, or maybe that was the simmering heat radiating from his big body. She wove their legs together, gripped the armrest over his head, and kissed him through the groan into hot, sexy demand. He looped one leg over hers and rubbed his erect cock against her hip and belly.

Her hands found his lower abdomen, warm skin and ridged muscle that sent a hot zing along her nerves. She looked down. His pants had ridden down again, revealing the erection straining against the waistband of his boxers. She loosened his tie, pulled it free, and dropped it on the floor. Starting with the lowest button on his dress shirt, she worked her way up to his throat, then spread the fabric wide. He looked at her, his body bared to her, his gaze unapologetically, unashamedly sexual.

And for good reason. He was built, ripped, whatever the current slang was for not an ounce of fat under skin stretched over workout-honed muscles. She looked him over, her fingers winding in that tantalizing line of hair.

"That doesn't tickle?" she asked.

His abs tightened but his smile loosened. "Not enough to distract me from how close your hand is to my cock."

Heat flared in her cheeks. "Very close," she said as she trailed the tip of her middle finger down the chestnut brown hair, then squeezed the hard shaft straining against his zipper. A few moments of one-handed work, all very slow and awkward and yet somehow sexy, and she'd unzipped his pants, then tugged the fabric to the tops of his thighs. He didn't help, just lay there, the fingers of one hand tangled in her hair while the other flexed on her hip, and let her strip him.

The combination of utter availability and remoteness was so hot.

Then hard hands closed on her ass. "Take this off," he growled as he worked the hem of her sweater over her hips.

"Why?"

He looked at her, the gold flecks in his brown eyes glowing in the lamplight. "Because I like watching you blush."

"That's a relief," she said as he tugged the cashmere sweater over her head. Static electricity lifted her hair in a wild nimbus. He smoothed it down again, hands cupping her ears as his gaze traveled from her eyes to her lips, then to her throat and the tops of her breasts. "I do it all the time," she added breathlessly.

"All the time?" he asked, as if he hadn't noticed.

She nodded.

"Show me."

THE WAY ALANA Wentworth blushed damn near slayed him. Every. Single. Time.

Blushing usually meant innocence, but the combination of soft hands on his body and the heated slide of her tongue banished any illusions he had about sheltered librarians. The color on her cheeks darkened from the pale shade of his grandmother's Pierre de Ronsard roses into Fragrant Cloud, a color he would associate forevermore with arousal.

He waited a long moment, letting the heat coursing down his spine show in his eyes, until she kissed him again. Her lace bra chafed his chest. Her nipples pebbled as the kiss extended, her tongue rubbing seductively against his before she nipped at his lower lip. He reached behind her and unfastened her bra. The sweet, hot pressure of her breasts made his heart pound. He shifted and tightened one arm around her waist while cupping her breast in his other hand. Her thigh pressed hard against his erection, and for a few moments he indulged himself in the tantalizing, erotic tease of making out on the couch, lips pressed together, tongues sliding. Her hair tumbled on either side of his face, snagging on his five o'clock shadow.

Duke barked. Hands firmly gripping her seriously luscious ass, Lucas paused to listen.

Alana halted her progress down his throat. "What is it?" she murmured.

The last time a woman purred into his ear that plaintively he'd been deep inside her, moving slow and hard and steady.

Duke barked again. Lucas recognized the yelp. It meant *Hey, Tall Guy Who Brings Food And Walks Me, there's someone here! Come see! Come see!* The dog, a cheerful, people-loving, retired K-9 member of the Denver PD was Lucas's polar opposite.

Whoever it was, Lucas was ready to shoot them first and ask questions later.

Another bark. Alana lifted her head and peered in the direction of his house. Since they were in her living room, all she could see was a wall of bookshelves, but he got the idea. He relaxed his grip and groaned low in his throat. "Someone's at my house."

That got an unexpected reaction. She sat up, snagged her bra and sweater, and all but levitated backward into the bathroom, where, based on the sounds of lace and silk against skin, she was dressing like a teenager whose parents had come home without warning. For his part he sat up slowly, rubbed his face with both hands, then stood to button his shirt. Tucking his shirt back into his pants only confirmed how frustrated he was. He took a deep breath, thought about cold nights in cold cars staking out cold-hearted criminals.

Not working. Blood thumped slow and hot in his veins as he plucked his tie from the floor and stuffed it in his pocket.

"Lucas?"

Mitch Turner. Lucas blew out his breath and thought about blizzards on the high plains.

Alana reappeared beside him, arms tense with the effort of holding the toolbox. "Here. This will . . . I'm sure it won't look like . . ."

He took the box before she dropped it on her bare feet, but didn't move. "Hey. We're two consenting adults."

"I know . . . it's just . . . you have a position to maintain in the community, and I'm not . . ."

Was that some kind of code for *I don't want anyone to know what we were doing*? He lifted the corners of his mouth in what passed as a smile for him these days. "Relax. I'm fine. You're fine. It's all fine."

"Mayor Turner's waiting for you!"

He felt his brows furrow. She didn't seem like the type to get freaked out by a small-town mayor. "It's still all fine," he said.

She breathed in, smiled back at him. "Okay. Good. But—"

Next door his screen door slammed. "Lucas? You around?"

"We'll talk," he said, and headed for the kitchen door.

The door closed behind him. Still gripping the toolbox, Lucas rubbed the back of his neck and took a deep breath.

Where in the hell did *that* come from? Alana always seemed too—he hated to say innocent because a decade on the Denver PD and five years on the DEA task force had trampled any notions he had of innocence, but that was sure what it seemed like. She blushed, for God's sake, and she did it a lot. She'd blushed as she signed the rental agreement on the house next door to him, and Lucas hadn't been able to get the memory out of his mind. It was so completely small-town librarian, which she wasn't, and so innocently sexy.

He was beginning to suspect she wasn't innocently anything.

He knew she watched him, but the only time she ever

said anything was when something broke. Then after he'd gone over and fixed whatever it was, she'd turn on a throaty jazz singer, hand him a drink, and struggle to make small talk. Which was strange in itself. In his experience, women as polished as Alana knew what they wanted and how to ask for it, but Alana turned pink every time she had to ask him for anything.

And yet she'd come on to him tonight. And he'd let weeks of celibacy dictate his response. She was an enigma he'd have to figure out later—after they finished what they had started.

He inhaled deeply, reaching for his composure, trying to reroute blood from his cock to his brain. Then he crossed their driveways to his house. The purple-blue twilight carried the scent of a greening prairie and texture of starlight. Maybe he'd take a couple of days off and go rock climbing in the Black Hills. It had been years since he'd been cranking, long enough for memories to fade.

He'd go. After Alana left. Just in case she wanted to take what happened tonight to its natural conclusion, then maybe do it again.

That's an excuse, and you know it. You're procrastinating.

For a very good reason . . .

"Hi, Mitch," he said to the man standing on his front porch. He was small and slight, wearing jeans, boots, and a jacket. His gray hair, maintained every week by the barbershop Lucas visited quarterly at best, was neatly parted and combed.

"Lucas." Lucas climbed the stairs and opened the porch. "Some guard dog you've got here," he said. Duke leaned against his leg, eyes closed in satisfaction as Mitch scratched the sweet spot behind his ears.

"What's up?" Lucas asked. He opened the front door and walked inside. Mitch and Duke followed but stayed in the living room as he stowed the toolbox in the hall closet.

"I thought we'd head to the meeting together," Mitch said.

Lucas narrowed his eyes at the mayor. Maybe Alana was more savvy than he thought, because Mitch played the political game with the ruthlessness of a Washington insider. Most of the time he went to council meetings on his own. There'd been a small but noticeable spike in burglaries lately, which meant that the discussion about renovating the library would face opposition from people more concerned with public safety. While Mitch wasn't one to sell his seed corn to pay for the harvest, he'd been pretty tight-lipped about why he hired Alana temporarily, or how committed he was to a large-scale library renovation. Tonight he wanted to show up with the chief of police by his side.

"What are you up to, Mitch?"

"Just wanted some company." Mitch unwittingly copied Alana's move and glanced significantly at the living room wall. "Problem next door?"

Lucas kept his face blank. "Just seventy-year-old plumbing," he said noncommittally.

"You should replace it, or just sell the house."

"I'll replace it when Alana leaves and I renovate the kitchen," Lucas said, "but you keep extending her contract. Are librarians that hard to find?"

"The right one is," Mitch said easily. "Look how long it took me to hire you."

Lucas called bullshit on that one, because Mitch took exactly two minutes to offer Lucas the job when he called to ask about it. At the time it seemed like a good career move that just might save his marriage, too.

He'd been wrong on both counts.

"Let's go," Mitch said. "We can talk on the way."

Once the meeting started, Mitch morphed into Mayor Turner in formal business mode and ran efficiently through the agenda. A few minutes after the meeting started, Alana slipped into the back row of the high school auditorium, still dressed in her work clothes. Lucas had his moment in the spotlight addressing the burglaries, reminding people to lock their doors and report anything suspicious. Alana picked up a handout discarded by local rancher Jack Whiting, and paged through it, seemingly half listening to the various line items and totals. The general rustling of people slipping into spring jackets and tucking handouts into purses and coat pockets halted when Mitch spoke.

"Ms. Wentworth, I read through the information you compiled on the options and costs around renovating the library. Would you run through the situation for us?"

Clearly surprised, Alana got to her feet. When she moved, her perfume drifted into Lucas's nose, straight to his back brain. Not possible. They were thirty feet apart, maybe more, but there it was. It took a moment, but he realized her perfume was on his skin.

"As you know, the building's in dire need of renovation," Alana said. "The plaster needs repairing, and the brickwork and roof are long past their best days. The Carnegie libraries are a national treasure. It would be an absolute shame to lose that building. The budget for books is adequate, but the shift in technology to e-books and e-readers means making a commitment to new technology. The computers are adequate, for now, which means in a year they'll be hopelessly obsolete."

"And what exactly do you recommend?"

Alana blinked, and Lucas's radar went off. Mitch was up to something the contract librarian didn't know anything about. "I didn't . . . that is, all I did was update Mrs. Lancaster's proposal to incorporate current digital strategies. But the real question that must be addressed before any renovations or shift in fund allocation occurs is what purpose does the library serve in the community? Without an answer to that question, you can't direct the funds you have to best meet your needs."

Don Walker, the local bank owner and spokesperson for the fiscally conservative segment of the town spoke.

"Ms. Wentworth, we barely have the money to do that, let alone upgrade computers or repair a hundred-year-old building."

"I've applied for a variety of state and federal technology grants," she started, but Mr. Walker cut her off.

"We're not in the business of supporting national treasures. What percentage of the community uses the library?" he asked. "We've got high-speed Internet access now. Based on what I've heard from Chief Ridgeway, we need to upgrade the police department's vehicles and consider making David Wimmer a full-time officer. You're asking us to commit a fairly sizable investment into a resource that, as you said, is well on its way to become obsolete."

"That's not what I said at all," Alana replied. "Libraries become more relevant, not less, as information is digitized and democratized. Nearly a quarter of the county's residents live below the poverty line. Those who can afford the service have high-speed Internet access. Many in Walkers Ford and the surrounding county cannot. Access to information is one of the greatest divides between rich and poor in this country. I think we'd all agree that poverty fuels crime."

"Don's got a good point," Mitch said. "We've got an expert here, and it doesn't cost us anything to work up a proposal. Ms. Wentworth, why don't you put something together for the renovation project, talk to people, give us something to work with? Present it in a couple of weeks, just before you leave. How does that sound?"

As one, the audience turned to look at Alana. Her mouth opened, then closed, then opened again. "I could do that," she said.

"Good," Mayor Turner said. "I'm calling a special session in two weeks. Ruth, make sure the meeting announcement is posted in all the appropriate places, and book the auditorium. Talk to Ms. Wentworth about the A/V setup she'll need for the presentation. Folks, if you have any questions or ideas, feel free to contact Ms. Wentworth. For any other business, you can contact me, or any of the council members, or Chief Ridgeway."

Mitch's final comment meant Lucas was surrounded by people with questions about the break-ins, information about suspicious activity occurring down every remote dirt road in the county, and a whole slew of other questions. He glanced past Don Walker's shoulder at Alana, who was similarly surrounded. Mrs. Battle, the former English teacher who'd come out of retirement to work part-time at the library, stopped to talk to Alana before leaving.

Alana looked over Mrs. Battle's head, straight at him. Electricity sparked along the invisible connection between them, an involuntary tug of attraction he hadn't felt in a long, long time.

Ever so slightly he lifted one eyebrow at her. *Later?*

She gave him a compact shake of her head, just enough to indicate *Not now*, and loosen her hair from its mooring behind her ear. The shiny blond strands slid forward in slow motion, setting off a sympathetic flex in his fingers as the nerves remembered the sleek feel of her hair between his fingers, the curve of her hips in his hands.

If secrecy mattered to her, they could work something out. She'd leave in a couple of weeks, which was plenty of time for him to explore every nuance of her blushes. Hell, thanks to the plumbing, they had a good cover story to explain him in her house.

Based on their chemistry, he had even better reason to be in her bed.

2

SEXUAL FRUSTRATION RUINED sleep.

Cell phone firmly in hand, Alana scuffed her feet into her slippers and pulled on her robe over her cotton nightie, then shuffled down the hall and into the kitchen. Sunshine poured through the window over the sink, glinting off the worn gold rim of her Syracuse University coffee mug as she got the mug from the cupboard, then ran water into the electric kettle. No chamomile or herbal teas this morning. Today was an Earl Grey Breakfast Blend day, probably two cups. She found her strainer in the drying rack, added the loose-leaf tea and set it in the teapot, and stared at the kettle. Little bubbles but not boiling. Cream. She needed cream.

"You're such a librarian," she mumbled.

When the water reached boiling, she poured it over the strainer and pulled her phone from the pocket of her robe while she waited for it to steep. Where was Freddie this week? The last time she'd talked to her sister, she was preparing for a three-week trip to South America. The Women's Development Network annual meeting was being held in Sao Paolo, which meant site visits to various local organizations funded by the Wentworth Foundation, appearances on local television programs, meetings with politicians and dignitaries, and banquets. Lots and lots of banquets. If the devil himself took a few minutes to create Alana's special, personalized version of hell, a conference and all the meetings scheduled around it would be an apt description.

Freddie thrived on it. Freddie was probably already awake, or perhaps hadn't gone to bed.

She tapped through to her sister's mobile number and pressed Call.

"Where are you, and when are you coming back to work?" her sister said without preamble.

"I'm in the kitchen, and soon," Alana replied. Lucas's grandmother's kitchen, to be precise. Beulah Ridgeway had had her kitchen gorgeously renovated in 1970s avocado and orange, and fashion hadn't quite circulated back around to the '70s yet.

"The one with the orange and green floral wallpaper and the fridge like the one in our cabin when we were kids?"

"It's not so bad when you get used to it. The window faces east, and I'm watching the sun rise over the backyard. Where are you?"

"Do you mean which continent, which city, or which hotel?"

"All of the above."

"South America, obviously. It's Wednesday, so this must be Chile. I'm in Santiago, in the restaurant of the Hilton, attempting to get coffee from people who seem no more awake than I am."

Chile meant she was behind Walkers Ford. "What time is it?"

"Five in the morning. I need coffee. My brain feels like it was removed from my skull with a dull ladle. Disculpe, señor. ¿Me puede dar una taza de café, por favor? Gracias."

Coffee took Freddie from high-functioning to superhuman. For not the first time, Alana wished her stomach tolerated the acid, because on her best day she didn't process the world like Freddie did.

"How's the conference going?"

"Fine," Freddie said. "But next month's conference in New Delhi still needs work. I need the research on programs to increase the literacy rate for girls in rural areas. Your replacement—"

"Denise."

"—Does not possess your gift with academic databases. When are you coming home?"

Denise didn't know Freddie's brain, what she'd read, what she wouldn't read, what interested her. "In two weeks, as we've discussed."

"Just before the Senator's banquet."

"As we've discussed," Alana repeated. "Why don't we call him Peter?"

"Because Mother called him the Senator when we were growing up, and while we found him intimidating as children, we now find it amusing. *Practice your piano, Frederica. The Senator will want to hear your first Chopin piece. Stay out of the Senator's way, Alana, dear,*" she said, mimicking their mother's precise intonation. "Ah. Gracias. Eres mi salvador."

Alana lifted the strainer from the pot of tea and waited while the last drops plunked onto the surface of the liquid. "Have you seen Toby lately?"

"I was able to squeeze in a quick visit while they played in Mexico City."

"How's the tour going?"

"Brilliantly. They've sold out every venue. Next year it's stadiums. I'm not sure when we'll fit in the wedding, but fit it in we will."

Her sister met Toby Robinson at a star-studded foundation event in New York City the previous year. After a whirl-wind romance that led to pictures in the society pages of the *New York Times*, the *Washington Post*, and the *LA Times* (coverage suitable for the socialite philanthropist stepdaughter of a former senator), and the glossy pages of *People*, *Hello!*, and *US Weekly* (dating tattooed, dreadlocked lead singer and songwriter for an English band rooted in the visceral music found in the world's slums) Toby proposed onstage at Wembley Stadium as they closed out the final concert of last year's tour. The video went viral before the final encore. The publicity for the foundation went a long way toward soothing their mother's horror that her older daughter, a graduate of Miss Porter's, Stanford, and Yale who had the ear of powerful people on five continents, was marrying a rock star who hadn't finished high school.

"Have you set a date yet?"

"If only it were that easy," Freddie said, uncharacteristically wistful. "I mentioned to Mother I'd love to have a small ceremony in his parents' garden in Stoke-on-Trent. It's a gorgeous garden, full of roses, enclosed by this stone wall built from rocks his ancestors took from the fields hundreds of years ago. Just us, family, a judge. Cake and champers. And the graves of the plague victims from 1666."

"You can't exactly uninvite the plague victims," Alana said. "And what does Mother think of that?"

"Having lost the opportunity to barter me off to an eligible up-and-coming politician, Mother sees the wedding invitations as legal tender. The last time we talked, she'd pared her list down to six hundred and forty-three."

"Six hundred guests?"

"On our side, Lannie. On our side alone."

"Does Toby know six hundred people?" she asked, envisioning a balanced ceremony, twelve hundred white chairs aligned in rows, Freddie's side crammed to overflowing, Toby's side populated by his parents, his sisters, the other band members/wives/children, and Toby's personal assistant.

"By a conservative estimate, he knows six *thousand*

people, but only considers about twenty of them close enough to invite to our wedding."

"I'm sorry," she said.

"So am I. Did you call me for a reason?"

"I went to the town hall meeting last night."

"You hate politics. You also hate meetings, crowds, and potentially contentious situations. This is why you're my research guru, and I do the meetings."

"The library budget was on the agenda."

"Don't tell me they cut it. Please do not slash the last remaining hope I have for the future of our country before I have another pot of coffee."

"Actually," Alana said, "they asked me to come up with a proposal for updating the library. I mean, I know how much the library means to the community, but they asked *me* to do the proposal."

"And why wouldn't they? You are the research librarian for the Wentworth Foundation."

"It's not research. It's a proposal and a presentation."

"To all eighteen residents of Walkers Ford, South Dakota?"

Alana rolled her eyes. "Nineteen. Lisa Sturdyvent had her baby last week. Michael Christopher. Seven pounds, eleven ounces. Mother and baby both healthy."

"Well, then. A buzzing metropolis."

"Don't make fun of this, Freddie. This matters here. I don't want to mess it up."

"I'm sorry, Lannie," she said, her voice gentling. "What do you need?"

"I can do the research. It's the proposal I've never done."

"It's simple. Do the research. That part you know. Then go through the research, identify the best solution, then anticipate objections, and counter those in the proposal. A good position paper is as much persuasive as it is factual. Surely you've read the position papers we craft after you obtain thousands of pages of data for us."

"Of course," Alana said, stung. "I've just never written one."

"I'll send you some of the shorter ones from the foundation's infancy, when we weren't getting invited to sit at the big-boy table. Oh, this is brilliant!" Freddie had picked up Toby's slang, but stopped short of imitating his accent. "This will be good training for you. Then when you get back you won't have any reason to object to taking on a larger role in the foundation."

She didn't want a larger role in the foundation. She liked the role she had. For the most part. She liked getting staffers what they needed, spending hours trawling through databases and archives, considering a problem from as many different angles as she could. She didn't like moving on to the next problem, then the next one, constantly skimming the surface. But when she sat at her family's table at a conference, or heard stories from people helped downstream by the changes the foundation affected, she really liked what she did.

"It's a situation with no real world impact," Freddie went on, by this point talking as much to herself as she was to Alana. "It's the perfect rehearsal."

"There's actually quite a bit of real world impact," Alana said.

"Of course, but not your real world," Freddie said smoothly.

Santiago, New Delhi, or Budapest weren't actually her real world, either, but Alana didn't have enough tea in her to argue with a caffeinated Freddie. "It's a key resource in the community and Chatham County. When a town this size makes a financial commitment like this one, the ramifications, the impact is enormous."

"I understand." Alana heard her sister's fingernails against keys. "You should have left two months ago. You can't let local politics delay you."

The council couldn't agree on a direction for the library,

let alone make a personnel decision. But with the upcoming banquet and Freddie's wedding, Alana had to leave in two weeks.

"Build strategy on research," Freddie continued. "Base the proposal and execution phases on that research. Keep it rational, fact-based, unemotional, fiscally beneficial. Lead with the blindingly obvious. By the time you're proposing a solution, they're so used to nodding their heads that they just keep nodding. I'm sending you documents and the tip sheet we give interns when they're drafting papers for us. Sent."

Alana watched as the notification materialized on her phone. "You've had some of that coffee."

"Most of the pot. Conference folk are late-nighters. If I want to get anything done, I get up early."

"So you're running on five hours of sleep?"

"Four. I'll sleep on the plane tomorrow. I'm flying to Sao Paolo, and Toby's flying down to meet me. I want to be rested for the reunion."

Alana smiled. "Sounds like a good plan."

"This won't delay you leaving Walkers Ford, will it?"

"No. The mayor asked for the proposal in a couple of weeks, right before they make a decision on the new library director."

"He's neglecting to get buy-in from key stakeholders," Freddie said immediately. "Won't the new director want to develop the proposal?"

"I made that point. He said he thought the new library director would appreciate coming to a fresh start, but I'm not so—"

Freddie had moved on. "And you'll be home for the banquet."

"Yes, I'll be home for the banquet."

"Do you need a date?"

That casual tone meant that Freddie knew something Alana didn't. "No. Why?"

"Are you bringing someone?"

"I repeat: No. *Why?*"

"Because Nancy said Mother said the Senator said David said he was bringing Laurie. You remember Laurie. She likes to name-drop senior faculty from Harvard's government department and White House staffers she knows from her internship."

Alana sipped her tea and tracked the gossip chain. Nancy was Mother's assistant. Mother was Mother. The Senator was the Senator. David was Alana's ex-boyfriend, the Senator's latest golden boy, and Laurie was an intern, hired fresh out of the Harvard School of Government after a stint at McKinsey and Company, and already proving indispensable in ways Alana never had.

"You might want to bring someone."

"David's welcome to bring whomever he chooses. I'm fine going alone, as I did before David and I started dating."

"You're not seeing anyone there, are you?"

A song lyric popped into her brain: *I kissed a cop and I liked it* . . . She'd had all the experiences available to a graduate of a girls' boarding school and a women's college, so the song's original lyrics weren't nearly as risqué as kissing the chief of police of Walkers Ford, South Dakota. The image of Lucas Ridgeway, sprawled on her sofa sent heat flickering along her nerves. It was nine o'clock in the morning, too early for longing. Longing was for evenings, for seductions, for dinners and candles and sofas and *please God* beds.

Dating was for Chicago.

Her body fervently ignored that rule. "I'm not dating anyone here," she replied.

"Good. No entanglements. No complications."

"Entanglements? You're marrying a global brand who's on tour eight months out of the year."

"Our lives and ambitions fit together," Freddie said serenely. "It's not complicated at all."

"What about when you have children?"

"God invented nannies, tutors, and private jets for a reason."

"You want your children to have the life we had?"

"Why not? They'll be Wentworth-Robinsons, and if you thought being a Wentworth came with responsibilities, being a Wentworth-Robinson means global opportunities and global obligations."

Alana turned to look out the kitchen window at the grass greening up in the backyard, the vines twining up the picket fence. Nannies and private jets . . . or a swing set. A wood one with a slide would look perfect next to the garage. Maybe a sandbox. She'd always loved the sandbox. The sandbox was a local thing. Not a global thing.

The door slapped closed on Lucas's front porch. Suddenly aware not only of the heat simmering deep in her belly but of her robe open over her thin cotton nightgown, Alana turned to look out the screen door.

Lucas, wearing a uniform shirt, jeans, and boots, stood on his step. The early morning sunlight highlighting the planes and angles of his face only served to accentuate the lines on either side of his unsmiling mouth, the seemingly permanent furrow between his eyebrows. Despite the gentle, early morning sunlight, he slid on a pair of wraparound shades, gave her a short nod, and got into his Blazer.

Alana resumed breathing again. Two weeks. Just over two weeks to write a proposal and go back to Chicago different. It wasn't much time, but if she played her cards right, two weeks could be an eternity of heated nights.

"I have to go. I need to send Mother yesterday's briefing. The Senator's on his way here. Do not get yourself ensnared in any . . . snares out there on the prairie. Love you."

"Love you, too," she said absently.

Lucas gave her another nod, then backed out of the driveway. Released from that intense stare, Alana rinsed out her mug. If she felt this frustrated after a night dreaming heated, unfulfilling dreams about Lucas, would the converse be true if she actually slept with him? Would she sleep well, body and mind satiated?

She intended to find out.

ALANA LIFTED ONE shoulder to keep her tote bag and purse in place as she locked her front door. In her peripheral vision, she saw Lucas's police Blazer parked in the driveway, but she wasn't going to glance over at his house. The lock was tricky. She had to lift the key just so while holding the doorknob toward the frame, so locking the door required all of her attention.

Or so she told herself.

Refusing to get caught sneaking sidelong glances at Lucas's house like a lovesick teen had nothing to do with it. Besides, nothing had happened last night. Okay, a little something happened before the town meeting, but a whole lot of nothing happened afterwards. It would have been too obvious to leave with Lucas. Walkers Ford's citizens had welcomed her with open arms, then with casseroles and cookies and invitations to attend church. This wasn't Chicago.

She got the door locked, more out of habit than necessity, and set off down the sidewalk into the heart of the town. She knew nature existed, of course, but watching spring bloom in Walkers Ford continually amazed her. Trees bereft of buds a week ago now held a haze of that gorgeous spring green shade, full of promise and hope. Daffodils bobbed lazily in the planters lining Main Street, seeming to say good morning. She took a couple of pictures with her phone's camera and sent them to Marissa Brooks's e-mail address. Last fall the lifelong resident of Walkers Ford had left town to fulfill her dream of living aboard a sailboat, and she'd taken former Marine Adam Collins with her. They were sailing across vast expanses of open ocean, so Adam

insisted on state-of-the-art communications technology.
Even in Hawaii Marissa would enjoy seeing pictures of
spring blooming on the prairie. As she typed up the email,
Alana walked past the gas station and volunteer fire department to the Heirloom Café.

"Morning, Alana," the waitress called. "The usual?"

"Please," Alana said. She set her bags down at the end
of the counter and scanned the national news on her phone
while she waited for her morning oatmeal. The *New York
Times*, then the *Trib*, then the political blogs all got a quick
skim before the waitress set a to-go cup of oatmeal in front
of her, the lid to the side. Alana handed over a five and
poured syrup on the oatmeal, then fitted the lid to the container before shouldering her bags again.

"You could make that at home for a quarter," the waitress
said.

Alana took the change and left a dollar on the counter as
a tip. "It's a bad habit," she said with a smile. "Besides, who
would keep me up to date on the gossip?"

Her pace of life didn't seem to allow for cooking. She
perpetually ran late, often grabbing a bagel for breakfast,
then a sandwich for dinner from the same deli that sat
between her apartment building and her family's offices.

"You're the gossip today," Peggy said.

Alana blinked. "I am?"

"People have opinions about the library, and no one knew
Mayor Turner'd asked you to redo the proposal," Peg confided, then hurried off with her coffeepot to the other end
of the counter.

Neglecting to get buy-in from key stakeholders, Alana
thought. This could be a problem.

Tote and purse back on her shoulder she walked through
the chilly, damp spring air to the library. A hundred years
of traffic had worn depressions into the marble steps leading
up to the double doors, and they could be slick when wet.
Today several plastic grocery sacks clung to the bottom step.

Alana opened the doors, left her bags and breakfast on the circulation desk, hurriedly swallowed a couple of bites of her breakfast. Experience taught her that she'd be on her feet and running the moment the library opened, which meant eating on the run.

She turned to go back to the front door, intending to remove the old wooden book drop box from the door and sort the after-hours returns, but ran smack into a gray sweater. Startled, she gasped and stepped back, hand clasped to her chest.

Stereotypical librarian. You have to stop doing that if you want to go home different.

Behind her stood a boy she'd never seen before in her life. He was caught in that awkward phase somewhere between teen and man, his height exacerbated by a frankly skinny frame, with reddish brown hair and blue eyes. His gray sweater was misshapen from washing and wearing, and his jeans barely skimmed the tops of his sneakers. His face was white with cold.

One eyebrow lifted, and a mocking amusement filled his eyes. "Sorry," he said.

"I wasn't expecting anyone," she said. "We're not open yet."

He looked around the building like he'd never seen it before. "I'm not here to check out books," he said.

Alana composed herself. "How can I help you?"

"I'm here for community service."

"What kind of community service?"

The mocking expression sharpened. "The kind of community service you do when you get busted for stealing. A hundred hours at the library. Ridgeway set it up."

"*Chief* Ridgeway, and I have no idea what you're talking about," she said.

"I bet you don't," he said, his gaze skimming her.

Alana drew herself up to her full five feet nine inches in three-inch heels. "I beg your pardon," she said.

His shoulders crept up toward his ears. "Sorry, ma'am," he said.

She nodded at the wooden book drop attached to the unopened front door. "Remove that and set it on the table while I call Chief Ridgeway and find out what's going on."

He slouched off toward the front door. Watching him carefully, Alana picked up her cell phone and considered it. Lucas Ridgeway, her landlord, had given her a cell and a home number, but this was chief-of-police business. She dialed the department's main number and got the station's secretary.

"Hi, Mary," she said. "It's Alana Wentworth calling from the library. Is Chief Ridgeway available?"

"He just walked in. Hold on a second."

At the bawled *Chief, it's the librarian, line two,* Alana held her phone away from her ear.

"Ridgeway."

"Chief Ridgeway, did you forget to tell me something yesterday?"

"Why are you calling me Chief Ridgeway?"

Heat flared in her cheeks. "Because this is an official call from the library director to the chief of police," she explained.

"Said library director and chief of police were officially half-naked on your couch," he said.

She was no good at this. Was he flirting, or making a simple statement of fact? He made it nearly impossible to tell, his tone of voice, deep, slightly raspy, and yet somehow emotionless. "Tell me you have your door closed," she hissed, keeping one eye on the kid. After some fumbling, he'd managed to disengage the heavy box from the door and was now carrying it to the wooden table along the windows.

"Okay, but I don't."

She drew in her breath.

"I do have my door closed. You're blushing again. I can hear it."

"You can't possibly hear me blush."

"Sure I can," he said.

The still unnamed teen dropped the heavy box on the table. The crash rattled the windows and made Alana jump. "There is a young man here who claims he was arrested for theft, and you sent him here to do community service," she whispered into the phone.

A pause, then a muffled *dammit*. "I did forget to tell you something yesterday," he said.

"Who is he?"

"That's one Cody Burton, caught red-handed stealing from the market. Because it was his first arrest, the judge agreed to counseling and a hundred hours of community service."

"Here?" she hissed.

"There."

"What on earth am I supposed to do with him?"

She heard a door slam and the sound of something hitting the desk top. "Put him to work. You said at the town hall the library needed repairs."

She looked around the building, at the cracked plaster, the windows in their original frames that either wouldn't open or leaked cold air in the winter and hot air in the summer, at the worn marble floor, the tarnished signs indicating the bathrooms and meeting room, at the oak shelves in desperate need of refinishing. "He's sixteen years old."

"Seventeen. He's lucky to get community service. He should have gone to jail."

She blinked at that brusque assessment. "I don't have any supplies. What could he possibly know about that kind of work?"

Lucas's shrug was audible. "No idea. Might not be a bad thing for him to learn."

"Who's going to teach him? I can't unstop my own drain."

"I have to go," Lucas said.

She stared at her phone, which was flashing a call time

of just over a minute, then looked at her new assistant. Cody Burton was pulling books from the overnight returns box and stacking them on the table. He was tall and so painfully thin Alana could see the bones of his shoulders jutting through his sweater. She slipped her phone into her purse and walked over to the table.

"Why aren't you in school?"

"Suspended," he said.

"For?"

"Two weeks."

"I meant, what did you do?"

Cody just shrugged and continued to stack books, his defensive demeanor shattered by the loud rumble of his stomach. He had cheekbones like cliffs to go with the prominent shoulder bones, but he didn't stop removing books from the box. Alana considered him for a second, then went to the circulation desk and picked up her oatmeal. Without a word she set it on the table next to him.

The color in his cheekbones darkened along with his pale blue eyes. She thought he'd refuse the offering, so she spoke hurriedly.

"I wasn't prepared for you, so give me a little while to think about what you'd be able to do for the library. Do you have a form to track your hours?"

He pulled two sheets of paper stapled together, folded into quarters, from the back pocket of his jeans and handed them to her. Alana walked once again to the circulation desk, sat down, and smoothed open the papers.

Cody Mitchell Burton, she read just below the county court's seal. Birth date. An address on a county road. A chart with columns for the date, start and end time, and her signature for each day. Easy enough, if she knew what to do with him.

She risked a glance at the table. Cody had his back to her, his shoulders hunched over. His hair curled into the fraying collar of his sweater.

The oatmeal was gone from beside the box.

It was a breakfast perfectly suited to a sedentary librarian a little worried about weight gain as she approached thirty, but probably a drop in the empty stomach of a reed-thin teenage boy. As she watched, he bent over to place the container at the bottom of the plastic-lined trash can next to the table, taking care not to make a single sound, no mean feat in the empty, echoing library. Alana glanced back down at the paperwork in front of her and waited until Cody lifted another handful of books from the box.

"Looks simple enough," she said as she approached the table.

This banality didn't even get a shrug. She held the sheet out to him.

"You're not going to keep it?"

"Your hours, your responsibility," she said.

His long, thin fingers closed around the paper while his eyes dared her to say anything about the oatmeal. She prayed her own stomach would stay quiet, then added a second prayer that Mrs. Battle hadn't eaten all the cereal bars stored under the microwave in her office.

Give him something to do. Anything. "You can start by reshelving those books," she said. "After that, please sweep the entry, run the sweeper along the runner protecting the hardwood floors, and water the plants."

He looked at her, mocking challenge twisting his lip. "How do I know where they go?"

"I know the librarian at the high school teaches you how to use the Dewey decimal system," she countered.

"I must have missed that day."

"I'll give you a quick tour," she said, and led him away from the large paneled front doors. The interior didn't lack for light, as big triptych windows, framed in oak with smaller windows above, opened to the main room. A small fireplace framed in brick with a charmingly carved mantel above set off the reading space by the windows. "Periodicals," she said, gesturing at the oak magazine racks and the spindles holding the weekly newspapers from Brookings and Sioux Falls. "Children's section, then hardback fiction on the shelves, with paperbacks in the racks. Nonfiction is housed at the back," she said, pointing at the taller stacks in the darker rear of the building, then widened the sweep of her arm to include the balcony running along the side of the building. An oak railing theoretically kept people from falling to the main floor, but the wood had weakened over the years, and now Alana brought down reference materials herself. "Our reference section."

He looked around, taking in the green paint that probably looked fresh and inviting when it was originally applied decades earlier but had faded to something not out of place in a hospital. Air huffed derisively from his nostrils.

"This *is* your library," she said, tightening her grip on her temper. "The town funds it for everyone in the community to use."

"This is the first time I've set foot in this building since the tour we took in fourth grade."

Inspiration struck. A nonuser from Generation Z required to spend time in the library was the perfect focus group. "No time like the present," she said. "After you've finished with the morning tasks, I'd like you to sit down and make a list of the things you could do for the library during your community service time."

He looked at her. "You're not going to tell me what to do?"

Only if I have to, she thought. "I might, but I'd like to know what you think we need and what you can offer. After you shelve the books. And clean the bathrooms."

As she watched, he examined the books' spines and sorted them into the appropriate stacks. Through the front window Alana watched Carmody Phillips park her minivan. She moved slowly up the steps, a plastic laundry basket full of picture books braced against one hip, her baby girl on the other, and her toddler holding on to the laundry basket as they made their way up the steps.

Alana held open the front door. "I remember when she was just a newborn," she said with a smile.

"Eight months old yesterday," Carmody said. "And growing fast."

"She certainly is. Let me get that for you," Alana said, and reached for the basket.

THE SIGHT OF Alana, dreamy-eyed and wearing a nearly sheer cotton nightie as she drank her tea and talked on the phone was a good way to start Lucas's morning. The phone call reminding him that he'd flat-out forgotten to tell Alana about Cody Burton prompted him to consider exactly how much he'd changed since his days with the DPD. When he started out with DPD a kid like Cody would have been on his mind constantly.

Not anymore.

The call from dispatch about a break-in ended all thoughts about Cody Burton.

He braked the Blazer to a stop in front of the weathered farmhouse and slid out of the truck. Gravel crunched underfoot as he shifted his jacket back from his right hip and approached the front door. The screen door, worn gray by years of wind and snow and summer heat, was closed, but the interior door stood open. His hand tightened reflexively when a gnarled hand appeared, then pushed open the door.

"They're gone," Gunther Jensen said.

Hand still on his weapon, Lucas stepped through the opened door and scanned the wreckage of the old man's living room. "You check the cellar?"

"No," Gunther said, white-knuckling the railing on the porch. "The stairs bother me some."

Lucas could see a twin mattress stripped of its sheets and shoved awkwardly into the corner. Gunther probably moved downstairs after his last fall. "Sit down. I'll take a look around," Lucas said. "Stay here. Don't touch anything."

Old habits died hard, so he released the snap and kept his hand on the Glock's grip as he climbed the stairs. The board creaked under his feet, alerting anyone upstairs to his presence, but something in the house's shocked stillness told him whoever had trashed the seventy-nine-year-old widower's house while he was visiting his sister in the county home was long gone.

He checked the four equally wrecked bedrooms, closets, and bathroom, then opened the narrow door to the sharply pitched stairs leading to the attic. A thick layer of undisturbed dust covered each riser. No one, including Gunther, had gone up there for some time, but Lucas still put his back to the wall and edged up the narrow stairs. He peered cautiously over the landing and found nothing more threatening than an ancient dressmaker's dummy and a hundred years of Jensen family history crammed into boxes, crates, and trunks. Cobwebs covered the dust. No one had been in the attic in decades.

Sneezing once, he retraced his steps and did a quick check of the cellar, which was in much the same condition as the attic, except it smelled of damp and mildew. "Whoever did this is gone," he said to Gunther.

"They got my wife's jewelry," Gunther said. He pointed at a small mahogany box, and his hands trembled, although whether from Parkinson's or shock, Lucas couldn't tell. "She didn't have much. I buried her with her wedding ring but kept the engagement ring. The diamonds weren't more than chips shaped like a daisy. These days the gold was worth more than the diamonds. Thought I'd give it to my granddaughter for her sweet sixteen next month. But they took it."

Lucas remembered the ring, so similar to the one his own grandmother had lost. As a boy he'd rashly promised her he would find the ring for her, spent hours digging for it in the backyard. Even now when he worked on the plumbing, he automatically kept an eye open for the glint of gold or light refracting off a tiny diamond, insignificant by today's standards. Even though his grandfather replaced the ring with an anniversary band, Lucas never stopped looking. Then he got busy in Denver, and finally accepted that the ring was gone forever. Sometimes lost things weren't meant to be found again.

He'd been a cop too long to make those kinds of promises. Instead, he stepped forward and clasped the man's shoulder. Gunther nodded twice, then seemed to steady himself. "Mind if I take a look in your medicine cabinet?"

As he suspected, Gunther's supply of pain pills for his herniated disk was missing. Determining what else was missing from the wreckage took an hour. He righted the furniture and straightened what he could while they searched. In the end, the thieves had made off with jewelry, the old man's laptop he used to e-mail his grandkids living in Sioux Falls and Minneapolis, and a stash of cash they'd found in the freezer.

"Who would do this?" Gunther said.

The old man gave money to anyone who asked, so Lucas wondered the same thing. "Have you had anyone working around the house lately?" he said neutrally.

Gunther stared out the window, his hand hovering over the wooden box's mother-of-pearl inlay. "Cody Burton needs service hours at the high school. He walks over and helps me download audiobooks."

Suspect number one. Lucas nodded, but watched Gunther's expression close off. "Anyone else?"

"I hired your cousin to take down the storm windows and turn over the garden," Gunther said slowly. "She showed up last week, looking pretty bad. I couldn't pay her much."

Suspect number two. *Looking pretty bad* meant Tanya had found a new source for the prescription painkillers again, and using again meant she needed money. He tried to feel something at the news—anger, regret, sadness, but discovered Tanya'd used up her allotment of empathy a long time ago. Or maybe he just didn't have anything left to give.

"So they were both in the house at some point in the last couple of weeks."

Gunther nodded. Dusting for fingerprints was pointless, unless they found someone else's. Not his cousin's, and not the kid he'd sent to the library staffed by a shy librarian for community service.

"I need to get back to the station," Lucas said. "Don't touch anything until I send someone out to dust for fingerprints. You still attend First Lutheran?" When Gunther nodded, Lucas added, "I'll call Pastor Theresa. She'll get the youth group out here to help you clean up."

Outside the house he stood, hands on hips, and surveyed the prairie rolling away to the horizon. When he was a kid he'd spent summers in Walkers Ford, and thanks to a functioning Chevy Camaro and a steady supply of Tanya's friends, he knew the surrounding landscape pretty well. When he returned as chief of police, he spent long evenings driving the county roads with a map, marking off farms and ranches, abandoned buildings, homes. So he knew that due south of the Jensen place lay the double-wide trailer that was home to Cody Burton's mother, three younger half brothers, and his brother, Colt, who'd been released from the state penitentiary in Sioux Falls a couple of weeks earlier.

He'd sent Colt away for burglary. Unlike on television shows where cops had to troll the world looking for perps, in reality, most crimes were committed by people close in relationship or proximity to the victim. The Burton trailer clung to a wide swath of exposed prairie less than a mile away. Tanya's ramshackle house hunkered by the creek that ran past Brookhaven, the sprawling, grand old house he still thought of as Marissa Brooks's place, just over two miles north as the crow flew.

No time like the present to do the job. He drove first to the

Burtons' and banged on the door. The trailer's metal skirt, rusting and loosened from the boxy structure, vibrated in counterpoint to his fist, but he didn't let up. No way in hell someone wasn't home. Eventually, Colt Burton opened the door.

"What do you want?"

Stale beer and body odor hung around Colt like Pigpen's dirt cloud as Lucas peered around him into the trailer's dimly lit interior. "Courtesy call," he said. "Someone broke into Gunther Jensen's place this morning."

"Wow, Chief, you're worried we're next?"

Lucas ignored the sarcasm. "Mind if I take a look around?"

Colt leaned against the door frame, a good eighteen inches higher up than Lucas. "Got a warrant?" he drawled.

"Not yet."

"Get one and come back."

"I'll do that," he said easily. "Who's home?"

"Mom's sleeping. The little kids crawled into bed with her to watch TV. You know where Cody is," Colt said, then shut the door in his face. Lucas got back in the Blazer and drove over to his cousin's house. He knocked on the weathered door, watching it rattle in the frame as he did.

No answer. One good shot with his fist would splinter the rotting wood around the lock, but once again, he refrained. Either the Burtons or Tanya had both motive and opportunity, but an arrest wasn't enough. Convictions counted. He'd stop by again later.

Back in the Blazer and headed into Walkers Ford, Lucas mulled over the break-in. Until recently, crime in Walkers Ford had run more to alcohol—underage drinking, driving while intoxicated, accidents—and dog problems of the loose and/or barking variety. The social fabric of a small town policed as effectively as he did. Neighbors looked after one another, kept an eye on each other's kids. Life as the Walkers Ford chief of police was exactly the break he needed after a decade in Denver.

Then J&H Industries, the manufacturing plant on the county line, had lost a major defense contract and scaled back to two shifts, with the corresponding eddies into small businesses supported by those workers. Convenience stores, cafés and restaurants, gas stations were all directly affected by fewer people driving to and from work. Shops noticed a decrease in sales. People worried about feeding their kids and paying bills sometimes turned to drugs for relief.

Sometimes they took what they needed from someone else who had it. Like Gunther Jensen, a retired farmer making ends meet on Social Security.

Lucas drove past the library on his way into town. On impulse, he pulled into the parking lot and climbed the stairs to the front door. Through the leaded-glass windows he saw Cody, a can of Pledge in one hand and a dust rag in the other, carefully wiping down the woodwork around the front windows.

Alana stood in front of one of the library's public access computers, guiding a patron through using a search engine. She wore a knee-length skirt made of brown fabric that looked like it would be rough to the touch, a cream sweater that hit at her hips and was belted around her waist with a very thin brown leather belt. The outfit was sophisticated, clearly expensive, and worn with a confidence only big-city money brought. But while the way her skirt clung to the curve of her ass when she leaned on the elbow-high counter made his pulse pound, it was the bright interest in her eyes as she explained the nuances of Google-fu to Mrs. Finley that tightened his heart in his chest.

He opened the door. Cody steadfastly ignored him, but Alana's gaze flicked to the door to see who the newcomer was. Her eyes widened when she saw him, and she excused herself.

"Yes, Chief?"

He lifted his eyebrows, just as a test. As expected, she

blushed, just a faint hint of pink, but enough to remind them both of unfinished business.

Relenting, he flicked a glance in Cody's direction. "How's he working out?"

"Considering he's been here for all of three hours, fine. Why?"

Her stomach growled ominously, loud enough for the mom sitting in the children's book area to look up in surprise. "I'm going to grab some lunch. You want to come along?"

She looked around the building. Mrs. Battle, the former library director who'd come out of retirement at seventy-seven to help Alana, held a book at an odd angle and peered at the call numbers on the spine, then shelved it just as the phone rang. Mrs. Battle beat Alana to it, and another mom with kids came through the front door. "I can walk over to Gina's with you," she said. "I can't stay away for long."

"Fair enough," he said.

"Chief Ridgeway and I are going to walk over to Gina's and talk about Cody's community service," she said to Mrs. Battle. Lucas wasn't thrilled with the way she made this sound all professional, nothing personal. "I'll bring back lunch. Minestrone soup?"

"Yes, please," Mrs. Battle said. "Take your time."

Alana disappeared into the office to grab her purse. Once down the steps, she shouldered the enormous bag and set off down the sidewalk. He didn't have to ease up on his stride so she could keep up. She gave him an expectant glance as they crossed Main Street. "I just came from Gunther Jensen's place. It was broken into this morning while he was visiting his sister at the nursing home."

"That's terrible," she said.

That was life. That kept guys like him in enough work to last a lifetime. "They wrecked it pretty badly, took some jewelry, a laptop, some cash." He waited while she processed this. "Gunther lives about a mile from Cody's place."

She stopped in the middle of the sidewalk and looked at him. "Cody was waiting outside the library this morning. He was nearly blue with cold. I'd say he'd been outside for quite a while."

"He have a car?"

"I didn't see one in the lot," Alana said.

So the kid probably walked the six miles from the trailer to the library, a long trip in the cold damp spring air, but staying out of jail was a good motivator. If he'd even spent the night at home. He could have been outside all night, except his clothes were clean, if worn and a size too small. "Okay," he said, filing the details away.

He held the door to Gina's Diner for her. Everyone noticed them walk in together, but conversation didn't stop. He was her landlord, and everyone local would know about Cody's arrest and community service. That and their public-service roles were enough reason for them to be together, if anyone asked, which would keep her happy.

Gina slid the plastic menus back into the caddy when he said they were getting food to go. He ordered a burger and fries. Alana ordered lasagna, two cups of minestrone soup and extra rolls, and two slices of pecan pie.

"Mrs. Battle loves pecan pie," she confided as she dug in her bottomless pit of a purse for her wallet.

"I've got it," he said, and handed over cash for the meals and a tip.

"Thank you," she said.

"Did you skip breakfast?" he asked when Gina brought out two white sacks of food.

"I gave my breakfast to Cody," she said.

He just shook his head at her naiveté. Defensive color stood high on her cheekbones, or so he thought, until she added, "Let me make you dinner tonight. As a thank-you for lunch."

It wasn't defensive color. It was nerves. The shy librarian was asking him on a date. A quiet date at her house. A quiet, private date at the house where she had kissed him, and something about the secrecy rubbed him the wrong way. This wasn't who he was, a man who did things on the sly for any reason at all.

"Sure," he said.

"Is six too early?"

"Six is fine," he said.

"You can bring Duke over if you want," she said with a smile. "I promise I won't ask you to fix the bathroom sink again."

3

ALANA STOOD IN the pasta/canned goods aisle of Hooper's Market, an empty plastic basket in one hand and her phone in the other, waiting for her e-mail to download. When the wheel stopped spinning, she knew why it had taken so long. She had e-mail from Marissa Brooks, which meant pictures.

Hey, Alana—

Thanks for the picture of the Main Street planters. I always knew spring had arrived when the planters went out. Are the prairie crocuses blooming? Has the council hired a replacement director?

I'm sending pics in return. We're a couple of weeks out of San Diego. I'll be in touch soon.

Marissa

No. Not yet. She was due to leave in less than two weeks, and Mayor Turner and the council still hadn't agreed on a candidate. Mrs. Battle could run the library, but with her macular degeneration she wouldn't be able to for much longer. She had trouble seeing titles or author names on the spines of books, much less the various screens for the online catalog and check-out system.

She scrolled through the pictures and thought about hot breezes, the restless waves, and time to do nothing for weeks on end. Initially Marissa's e-mails had been full of sailing details, but after a while they grew shorter and shorter while including more pictures. It was as if time and space, wind and water and love, soothed something edgy inside her, and a calm spaciousness opened up in its place. The last picture was of Adam, tanned to a deep brown, wearing cargo shorts and flip-flops, his feet braced on the captain's chair, a bottle of beer in one hand, a smile full of love and laughter and contentment on his face.

This trip had been good for both of them.

The next e-mail was from her sister.

Lannie,

1. Did you get the docs I sent?

2. We're having fun in Sao Paulo and by fun I mean we haven't left the hotel room in two days. After Israel-Palestine style negotiations between Mother and Toby it looks like London is the wedding location. See attached list of location possibilities. Mother prefers Westminster Abbey. Ignore contacts on websites; list of real contacts (aka people who would like to have Mother owe them a Really Big Favor) also attached. Please research availability and get back to me.

3. Stay out of snares.

4. Pics!

Love, Freddie

The list of real contacts included two members of Parliament, an undersecretary in the Home Office, and a bishop in the Church of England. Alana scrolled through the pictures. Her sister looked beautifully content, her hair a wreck around her face, snuggled under Toby's muscular, tattooed arm. She shifted her grocery basket to the crook of her elbow, hit Reply, and went to work with both thumbs.

Freddie,

1. Docs received. Am working on proposal.

2. Need at least three days to pull together information. No wedding in the rose garden?

3. AM NOT GETTING ENSNARED.

4. Is the tattoo of Thor's hammer on Toby's neck new? Mother will not be pleased.

Love, Lannie

A shopping cart bumped into her heel as she clicked Send. She looked up to see it steered by a small boy. "Apologize to Miss Wentworth," his mother said firmly. The boy ducked behind hair that hung in his eyes, but repeated the words before zigzagging the cart after his mother.

"I'll get out of the way," Alana said with a smile, then stepped to the side. What a metaphor for her life, getting in the way of elementary-school-age kids who steered a shopping cart with more purpose and passion than she lived.

Her game plan hadn't changed. Get under Lucas Ridgeway. She hadn't done it last night, but she'd do it tonight. She'd put off returning to Chicago for as long as possible, and she wasn't going home the same person she was when she'd left. That would make this nothing more than wound-licking hibernation, not a tactical reinvention.

She would go home different. She would.

She plucked pasta from the shelf before heading for the produce department. There she sniffed and squeezed tomatoes, then added a cucumber, cherry tomatoes, a red onion, spicy sausage, and feta cheese to her basket. She had the spices she needed at home. The meal she intended to cook wasn't very fancy. Pasta with homemade Bolognese sauce, a loaf of French bread slathered with butter and garlic, and a salad. She already had ice cream and fudge sauce for dessert. The next time she had him over for dinner she'd make a trip into Brookings and pick up something more interesting.

Think optimistically. There will be a next time. With that in mind, she added a box of dog biscuits to her basket.

The checkout clerk rang up the groceries while Alana bagged them into her reusable sacks for the walk home. Freddie's reply arrived when she got home.

2. No wedding in the rose garden.

4. Tattoo is new. Mother will shit a brick, but see #2.

3 DAYS???!!!! Tomorrow? Pretty please?

She debated leaving her work clothes on, but the tweed and wool felt too warm for the warm spring air. She started the sauce simmering, e-mailed the contacts on Freddie's list, then changed into a pair of dark jeans and a fitted long-sleeve V-neck T-shirt in a periwinkle her mother assured her matched her eyes. Back in the kitchen, she stirred the sausage, added it to the sauce, and turned down the heat to let it simmer while she went outside to examine the rose bed in the dwindling light.

Green stalks emerged from the dirt, straining toward the white trellis, but weren't quite long enough yet to need the support. Something in the wild tangles of thorny stems and canes worried at her soul, so the previous fall she'd read up on winterizing roses, then carefully pruned the bushes, sprayed them with dormant oil spray, dug trenches in all the beds, tipped the canes into the trenches, then covered them with soil and pine needles. A few weeks ago, she had removed the blankets and bags of leaves and replanted the bushes, then fertilized and mulched the bushes. New growth emerged nearly every day, but she wouldn't be around to see the first bloom.

Lucas pulled into the driveway. Alana felt her cheeks heat, but threw him a smile over her shoulder.

"Hey," he said.

Duke hustled down the steps, his tail spinning like a propeller. Once again, Alana watched the reunion, the muted play of emotion on Lucas's face, Duke's adoringly upturned muzzle. Lucas looked tired, but not physically tired. Bone-weary, the kind of exhaustion that came from deep inside, not from whatever Walkers Ford was throwing at him. A shiver of sympathy resonated inside her. She knew that feeling. Knew it well.

Emboldened, she rose from her crouched position and stretched until her back popped. "I've got spaghetti sauce simmering," she said. "We can eat in an hour or so."

He straightened his shoulders. "Great. I'm looking forward to it."

She continued to redistribute the mulch. The downspout emerging from the back of the roof needed to be reconnected; the spring rains pushed the mulch away from the foundation. Lucas emerged from his house, Duke on his black leash at his side. Somehow putting the leash on Duke changed his entire demeanor, as if the old dog remembered his former work, how important it was. He trotted with more purpose beside Lucas, who was now dressed in jeans and a navy blue T-shirt that made his brown eyes even more vivid.

"Do you know what these are?"

He strolled over to stand beside her, then unclipped

Duke's leash. "Country Dancers. Gram planted them on this side of the house because they don't need as much sun as other hybrids. You didn't have gardens growing up?"

"Of course we did. We also had gardeners."

In invitation she opened the screen door to the kitchen. He reached over her head to hold the door for her and she stepped inside. With a click of his tongue, he told Duke to clamber up the two cement steps, then waited for the dog to hoist himself inside. He sniffed desultorily at the cabinets, then the baseboards, then slumped down on the floor under Lucas's chair.

"Smells good," Lucas said as he eased into one of the two chairs at the kitchen table.

"Nothing fancy," she replied. "Pasta with homemade Bolognese sauce. I hope you like sausage."

"I like anything I don't have to cook," he said.

She got a beer from the fridge and handed it to him, then poured herself a glass of wine and sipped it while water ran into the stockpot to boil.

"I didn't think you'd want Italian again after having that big lasagna for lunch."

Alana felt her cheeks heat beyond what could be explained by a warm stove. "I didn't eat the lasagna," she admitted.

"You gave it to Cody."

She nodded. "The only people I've seen with cheekbones like that are the models working in the fashion industry," she said. "I want to feed them, too."

One corner of Lucas's mouth lifted, but otherwise, the regular rise and fall of his chest under the blue T-shirt was his only response.

"What exactly did he do to earn a hundred hours of community service at the library?"

"Shoplifting," Lucas said.

"What did he take?"

"Three boxes of cereal bars and a bag of M&Ms."

Alana felt her jaw drop open. "What?"

Lucas just shrugged. "Ron Pinter wanted to press charges," he said. "He thinks Cody had been doing it for a while and getting away with it."

"I would think the correct response would be twenty hours of community service and perhaps some contacts with social services. Food insecurity is a very real problem—"

"Pinter talked to the judge."

"And you didn't make a different recommendation?"

His expression closed off even more. "Sometimes the only way people learn is to face serious consequences."

"I get the M&Ms, but why would he steal cereal bars?"

He shifted on the chair, then took another swallow of beer. "The dad took off before I came back to Walkers Ford. He's got three younger brothers under the age of five. They're actually half sibs, and their father left after three kids in three years. They've been on and off welfare until their mother got a second-shift job at the plant. His older brother Colt is heading down the petty loser path. He's on parole. The cereal bars are probably easy for the kids to eat while he's at school and his mom's asleep."

She made a little sound to indicate she'd heard him, and continued stirring the sauce. Small bubbles were forming at the bottom of the stockpot, and Lucas was silent, still. She'd seen this in volunteers or staff at nonprofit organizations all over the world. The world's deep needs attracted people with an incredible capacity for compassion, but if they weren't properly nurtured and rested, they cycled from enthusiasm through anger and frustration into emptiness. *Compassion fatigue* was the term psychologists used. They exhausted themselves caring so much about systemic problems that were inherently difficult to solve. A sabbatical could help, but that wasn't an option for a small-town police chief. What did Lucas do to rejuvenate?

This was basic research, figuring out what questions to ask.

And you're curious.

"How long have you been back in Walkers Ford?"

"About three years."

"And you were in Denver before that?"

"I grew up there. My dad moved out of Walkers Ford to go to college and never came home. Met my mom at the Rocky Mountain Music Festival and that was that. He played drums in a really bad band, and she fronted a much better one."

Okay, she could do music. "What do you play?"

"My iPod." He didn't smile, but his brown eyes held a touch of humor. "I'm tone deaf."

She laughed. "Me, too. Well, not quite tone deaf, but I can't sing. My mother finally gave up on the piano lessons when I was fifteen."

"You didn't like them?"

"I wasn't good at it, so there wasn't any point in continuing."

His gaze narrowed. "But did you like it?"

She shrugged. "I enjoyed it when I could play for myself. My sister's brilliant at the piano, though. She won a national music competition when she was seventeen. A cell phone rang when she sat down to play, and rather than Chopin's Tarantella Op. 43, she riffed from the ring tone through Chopin into Lionel Hampton's *Flying Home*. She got a standing ovation from the judges."

"Older or younger sister?"

The sheer novelty of meeting someone who didn't know all about Freddie made her smile. "Two years older. Her name's Freddie."

"Alana and Freddie?"

"Frederica."

He lifted his eyebrows.

"Mother chose the names from her most distinguished ancestors. As women really didn't play big roles in public service until the last couple of decades, we got feminized versions of male names. Freddie calls me Lannie, but she's the only person who does." She smiled wryly as she dropped a thick handful of spaghetti into the boiling water. After a not-so-covert glance at the span of his shoulders, she added a second handful and stirred the water.

He smiled, but didn't add anything. "The sauce smells good."

"Thanks." Okay. They'd covered when he returned to Walkers Ford. The next logical question was why.

"Tell me about you, Alana Wentworth."

His asking about her wasn't in her plan. She blinked, then moved to the sink to run water in a bowl for Duke. "Surely you did a background check before I moved in," she said.

"Actually, I didn't," he said. "Women who move to small towns to work as librarians and drive Audis are usually pretty safe risks."

"Especially when they're living next to the town's chief of police."

He tipped back his beer. "It's not like on television, where one quick search performed by a quirky genius gives me your entire history down to your shoe size in third grade. I could get your criminal record from the national database, but that's it."

He wouldn't find what brought her here in a criminal history check anyway, and not even in Google search results, unless he knew how to dig. She didn't expect cops to be hyperparanoid, but somehow Lucas's remote bearing struck her as odd. "I'd figure you for the curious type," she said.

"Why's that?"

"Cops are like librarians," she said. "We know things other people don't know. I know, for example, that as we increase microfunding for women's businesses, their standards of living increase, birthrates drop, and their children are more likely to attend school. You know things about people they may not want other people to know. Like Cody's family history."

Silence behind her. When she turned to him, his face was entirely blank. Maybe he wasn't curious about anything. Except he had asked about her.

"There really isn't much to tell," she said.

"So let's start with why you took the contract job."

This part was easy enough. She slowly stirred the sauce, inhaling the scent of tomato, basil, and garlic, melding with spicy sausage. "I wanted a change of pace."

"Moving from Chicago to Walkers Ford for a change of pace is like throwing a speeding semi into park."

"Denver to Walkers Ford was about the same," she observed.

It was his turn not to answer.

"It's not forever," she said, when he obviously wasn't going to respond. "I went to library school intending to be a librarian. Instead I went to work for my stepfather. This is a sabbatical, of sorts."

"I hear you on the phone when I get home late," he said.

"I'm still working for my sister," she admitted, "so I end up on calls at odd hours."

"Doesn't sound like much of a sabbatical," he said.

She shrugged. "It's just easier to get Freddie what she needs than trying to train someone else to do what I do. I wasn't supposed to be gone as long as I have been."

Nina Simone's sultry voice drifted from the living room, where Alana had put her iPod on the speaker set. Perfect seduction music, sophisticated, raspy longing melding with the Bolognese as she set the platter of spaghetti, the sauce, bread, and the salad on the table between her place and Lucas's. His fingers brushed hers when he passed her the bread, warm skin against hers, his knees bumping into hers under the table.

But he didn't back up, so she didn't either.

"You want to know what I think happened?"

"Sure," she said.

"People don't move to small towns, even temporarily.

They leave them. Sometimes they come back to raise kids here. Usually they come back because they're running away from something."

"That's what you think I'm doing?"

He used his spoon to twirl his spaghetti onto his fork and ate the mouthful before he answered. "It's good," he said.

"Thank you," she said.

"I'm not sure. You don't seem like someone with something to hide."

"I made a mistake in Chicago," she said.

"Because?"

Because one of these things wasn't like the others. One of these things didn't belong in the perfect political picture, and that thing was me.

"It's a long story," she said with a smile as she speared some arugula and feta.

"People say that when what they really mean is 'I don't want to talk about it.'"

"It's in my past," she said. "This is my present."

"Will he be in your future, when you go home?"

"No," she said firmly. "He will not."

Nor will anyone like him, because I'm going to learn how to deal with men.

Flushing to the tips of her ears, she looked up at Lucas, and found him eyeing her across the steaming Bolognese.

Oops.

"You're tricky," she said. Her small-town police chief had questioning techniques from Denver's interrogation rooms.

"I can't see you making a mistake in your work, let alone one bad enough for you to essentially flee your hometown."

"Making a mistake with a man, however, that you can see?" She'd intended the words to come out liltingly, and they did. Mostly.

"Don't let my amazing powers of deduction overwhelm you. There's only two areas of life where people make bad mistakes. Work and love."

Which one brought him here, she wondered.

"Did he hurt you?"

"Is a cop asking or the man I invited over for dinner?"

"Same person."

There were so many ways to hurt a person, she realized. So many. She set her fork down, and thought about the simplest way to explain what had happened between her and David. "It was a misunderstanding, and partly my fault. My boyfriend asked me to marry him in a rather spectacular proposal, and I said no."

"You didn't want to marry him. How is that a mistake?" His expression sharpened. "Unless you decided you did want to marry him, and that's the mistake."

"No! I didn't want to marry him. I just . . . couldn't figure out how he'd thought I did want to marry him."

Lucas lifted an eyebrow. "Go on."

"I went to an all-girls boarding school through high school. A women's college after that. While most girls were learning to flirt, or at least getting comfortable with boys, I was learning Latin and reading my way through the library. I'm not . . . savvy," she said.

"That explains the kiss for fixing the sink."

"In a manner of speaking, yes."

He put down his fork and swiveled sideways to brace his back against the wall and his forearm on the back of the chair. Eyes heavy-lidded and knowing, he looked at her. "Tell me what you want."

His voice held an air of command that sent heat flooding into her cheeks, but she didn't look away. "Is it that simple?"

He shrugged as he trailed his fingers through the moisture condensing on his second bottle of beer. "Yeah."

"I want to put him behind me."

"Okay," he said.

Her cheeks heated. "I shouldn't have kissed you," she said. "Becoming intimate confuses things. I'm leaving. We shouldn't . . . I don't want . . ."

To hurt you was the unspoken end to that sentence, but the mocking amusement that filled Lucas's eyes stopped her from finishing it. Of course she wouldn't hurt him. She'd never seen a woman leaving his house in the morning, or coming over for dinner and a movie, but she wasn't naive enough to think that meant Lucas was celibate. He spent nights away. Not many, as he obviously didn't like to leave Duke alone. This man was too potent to be going without sex, and darkness clouded his eyes too frequently to think he'd get hurt.

As if he heard her mind turning this over, he said, "I'm not going to get hurt. Stop thinking about what you don't want to do, and tell me what you do want to do."

"I want to finish what we started last night."

"Too general," he said bluntly. "Be specific."

The blush heated her cheeks as she looked at him. His five o'clock shadow dusted his cheeks and jaw like dark sand, and as time slowed and heated between them, she found she could name one very specific longing.

"I want to know what your beard feels like against my lips."

He tipped his head in a c'mere gesture. With Nina Simone playing in the background, Alana got up from her chair and circled the tiny table. He adjusted the chair so she could straddle him, and straddle him she did. His thighs shifted under hers as she gently brushed her fingertips over the scruff. Nerve endings ignited in the wake of the soft, rasping sound of skin over bristle.

Pressing her hips to his was intimate. Simply spreading her legs to do just that was even more intimate. But the most intimate thing of all was touching his face with her fingers. His eyes darkened, but he didn't move. One arm rested on the table. The other lay across the back of the little rolling cart that held her cookbooks. His legs sprawled into the narrow strip of linoleum between the table and the counters, his bare feet nearly to the baseboards. She couldn't look directly into his eyes without her face heating unbearably, so she restricted herself to little glances, her gaze flicking from his flat abdomen to his throat to his eyes, then down to where her thumb grazed his full mouth. Her heart pounded slow and hard against her breastbone as she stroked from cheekbone over stubble to his jaw, then brushed her thumb across the spot where scruff met the edge of his lower lip.

The muscles in his face slackened just before his tongue touched the tip of her thumb. Her heart skittered against her ribs, then settled. Kissing his mouth suddenly seemed like too much too fast too soon, so she angled her head and bent to brush her lips over his cheek.

More nerve endings lit up, this time in her lips. A sweet heat ignited along her jaw. Never before in her life had a man like Lucas Ridgeway wanted to kiss her, let alone wanted her to kiss him.

Is that what this was? Could she call the brush of lips on skin a kiss? Hesitantly, she touched the tip of her tongue to the bristly hairs emerging from his cheek. His breath stopped, just for a moment, just long enough for his thighs to tense under hers.

He liked that. He liked what she'd done, so she kept on doing it, mouthing her way to his jaw, using teeth on his chin just to hear the rasp before she gathered her courage and lifted her mouth to his.

He didn't shape his lips to hers, or try to take control of the kiss, but his body grew taut under hers as she nibbled and licked her way around his mouth, luxuriating in the paradox of rough scrape and soft heat. His breath heated her lips, somehow trickling along her nerves to her nipples, then lower to pool in her belly.

When she lifted her head, his eyelids drooped, and a heated flush stood high on his cheekbones. "How did it feel?"

"Scratchy." She stroked her own lips with her index

finger, feeling how the stubble brought heat and tenderness to the surface of the skin.

A corner of his mouth lifted. "I can go shave."

She shook her head slowly and felt her hair slide free from her ear as she did. "I want to know how it feels other places," she said.

The hand resting on the kitchen table flexed, then he exhaled and it relaxed. Trapping her gaze with his, he palmed her ass and snugged her up against his erection. One hand still cupping his jaw, she steadied herself on his shoulder and bent to kiss him.

Chemistry incinerated the air between them. It was hot and sliding and wet, but better than the slick stroke of his tongue on hers was the way he didn't rush things. He sat back, his hand flexing on her hip, yes, but he simply sat there and let her kiss him. Slow and not at all sweet, not until she nipped at his lower lip. Then his hand slid into her hair, gripped the back of her head, and held her for the same treatment.

Lightning flashed from her mouth straight to her sex. She jerked back to stare wide-eyed at him, but his hand stayed on her hip and head, his brown eyes unrepentant. The message was clear: she wasn't going anywhere, and she better be ready to take whatever she dished out.

"More," she breathed.

With a twist of hips and shoulders he surged to his feet and pressed her into the narrow space between the fridge and the door to the dining room. She wound her legs around his hips and her arms around his neck, the better to revel in the sensation of his arm under her bottom and that delicious, sensitizing scruff against her mouth.

When her hands scrabbled at the back of his T-shirt, he leaned into her, using his chest to keep her in place and reached back to haul his shirt over his head, then drop it to the floor. Greedily she skimmed her palm up his ribs, feeling bone and muscle shift as he ground against her.

A car door slammed across the street. Lucas dragged his mouth from hers and peered over his shoulder at the screen door. "Better take this somewhere more private."

His voice was a low rumble that rasped like velvet against her nipples and sex. "Agreed," she whispered. She expected him to set her on her feet, but instead he carried her down the short hallway to her bedroom. Again, she expected him to put her down, but instead he bore her backward onto the bed. The sensation of hips between her legs, a warm, lightly furred male chest and broad shoulders looming over her, and those deep brown eyes sent a kick of arousal against her chest.

"Tell me what you want now."

WHEN ALANA'S EYES widened, Lucas gave himself a hard mental shake.

Slow down. Forget that it's been months since you had sex. It's only been a couple of days. Maybe even a couple of hours. This woman thinks she can hurt you. That's how inexperienced she is. She can't see who you are, what you are. If you rush her into anything she's going to furl up like a flower.

Alana had covered the bed with an old-fashioned chenille spread tucked over the pillows. Spring twilight darkened outside the windows, casting soft shadows over the dresser and the cedar chest at the foot of the bed. Roller shades with beaded fringes covered the windows. In an effort to make a house with a frankly ugly kitchen more appealing to a tenant, he'd stripped the wallpaper before she moved in, and painted the walls a soft white. The room felt old-fashioned, delicate, much like Alana.

The contrast between ladylike furnishing and demeanor and the tension thrumming between them seeped into his veins to pool in his cock.

He didn't add words to the heated air quivering between

them. He just let the silence stretch between them, let her decide. He knew how to wait out suspects. Some days he felt like if he never had to speak another word, he'd be good with that. Words didn't fix anything, and more often than not, he found the wrong ones.

He made a conscious effort to dampen his usual intensity, breathing slow and deep, forcing his hands to relax on her hips, leaning back imperceptibly. He also knew how to use his body to intimidate and coerce, and while turning it off wasn't easy, he tried. His reward was the slow seep of trust and arousal back into Alana's face. The muscles around her eyes relaxed as her lids drooped, and her mouth softened into a fullness he found sexy as hell. She rarely wore anything more than a lipstick one shade darker than her lips. Damned good thing, too, because she had the kind of wide, full mouth men dreamed about.

She peered up at him through soft black lashes. "Anything I want?"

No way in hell could this woman come up with something he wouldn't do, so he nodded without reservation.

"Lie down."

The . . . request? Hardly. Command? Demand? Instruction? A little of all three? . . . surprised him when not much surprised him anymore. He tried to remember the last time a woman wanted to work him over, and failed. He tugged the spread down to the foot of the bed, stacked the pillows, then stretched out on his back. The light from the dim reading lamp beside the bed gilded her bobbed hair as it slid forward, but rather than hiding behind the curtain she tucked it behind her ear.

For a split second she studied him. An odd mix of emotion flickered through her eyes, hesitation and nerves blending into a need that would have knocked at his heart if she hadn't told him flat-out that she wanted to get over a mistake. No problem. If she wanted to go home with a sabbatical fling behind her, he could do that.

Then she straddled him, planted her palms on either side of his head and kissed him. It was hot and wet and sliding, pure visceral demand. A bolt of electricity splintered inside him, and he wrapped one arm around her waist while the other cupped her skull. Her tongue slid into his mouth, rubbed against his. He growled and fisted his hand in her hair at the same time he tightened his grip on her waist, pulling her tight against his erection.

Easy . . .

But she rocked against him, the movement hard and slow, just like he liked it, and *easy* incinerated in the heat combusting between them. He used his grip on her hair to tug her head back and expose her throat. Lifting his head, he nipped and licked and nuzzled his way along her jaw to her pulse point. A faint scent rose from her skin, and it was all he could do to refrain from biting the town's librarian in a place not even a turtleneck would hide the mark.

"Jesus," he muttered.

She tugged her head free from his grip and straightened her elbows to loom over him. Shiny hair clung to her flushed cheeks, and he took a primitive satisfaction in the fact that her sexy mouth now crossed the line into provocative.

The corners of her lips lifted, telling him she not only knew what he was looking at but why. Once again, he exhaled long and slow, fighting to keep control.

When she bent and put that mouth to the hollow between his collarbones, his hard-won control slipped a little more.

No expectations. Just take what she's giving you. Don't ask for more. Hope is what burns you. Not disappointment.

"I want to taste you," she said.

His heart stuttered in his chest before he answered. "Be my guest," he said roughly.

She put her lips back to the hollow, slowly, thoroughly exploring the landscape of his chest and shoulders with her mouth. He took in the arched line of her spine, the flare of her hips in jeans until he couldn't take any more, then closed his eyes. The blunt-cut ends of her hair added texture to the soft, wet kisses, while the contrast between trailing hair and her teeth made him tense and grunt.

"Too much?" she asked, concern in her eyes.

Fuck no. He managed to filter his response to a curt, "No."

"Good," she said, and shifted down, nuzzling into the mat of his chest hair, then the line disappearing into the waistband of his jeans. She sat up, straddling his thighs, and tucked her hair behind her ears.

He knew what was coming next. She'd unbutton his jeans. Instead she trailed her fingers over his hip bones, sending another flare of heat to his cock.

"I've never actually seen these muscles defined before," she said.

Suits with desk jobs had no reason to work out enough to get that kind of muscle. In Denver, he had had good reason. Sure the chief and the mayor developed high-level strategies to combat gangs and drugs, but strategy didn't mean shit at two in the morning when it was him and a tweaker. Strength and smarts lowered the odds he'd get zipped into a body bag. In Walkers Ford, he'd increased his odds of dying of old age, but old habits died hard. All he had left of the life he'd imagined for himself was Duke and his workout routine.

In response, he linked his fingers behind his head to elevate it and nodded at her. "See something you want?"

She smoothed her fingertips inward from his hip bones. The muscles contracted and her gaze flashed up to his. "Does that tickle?"

"Not hardly," he replied.

Confidence renewed, she slid her fingers into his waistband and began to work open his button fly. The backs of her fingers brushed his erect cock with every movement, and his heart pounded hard and slow in his chest. No flirting glances, no teasing looks through that sexy hair, just a businesslike stripping that left him with his jeans trapping his legs and his cock straining up toward his navel.

She stopped and peered at him. Her fingers toyed with the hem of her blue V-neck, but he stopped her. "Only if you want to," he said.

Her shoulders relaxed. She pulled the T-shirt up and off, then dropped it on the floor by the bed. She wore a pretty lace bra in a shade of cream very close to her skin color.

"It's going to be hard to walk into the library knowing you're wearing something so sexy under your clothes," he said without moving.

And there it was, the blush he dreamed about, blooming on her collarbone as she ducked her head and reached behind her back to unfasten her bra. The lace dropped away, rasping against his cock as she dropped it beside her shirt.

She looked so mysterious wearing only spring twilight and a blush. Her nipples hardened under his gaze, but he stopped himself from reaching for her. Intentionally or not, she rewarded his restraint by leaning forward to lick a path from the base of his shaft up to the tip.

A low growl rumbled into the air. For a split second he wanted to roll her, spread her, and fuck her, but pride and intuition kept him to nothing more overt than a tightening of his interlaced fingers. He could hold out against this, and that smart little voice in his head, the one he always honored, told him she needed this.

Don't worry. You're going to get yours.

He shut off the more cynical voice in favor of concentrating on the sensation of Alana's hand wrapped around the base of his shaft while her lips closed around the tip.

"Oh, fuck," he said.

And there went his filter. Her tongue sought out the bundle of nerves just below the tip, teasing and flicking before she took him deep enough for her lips to meet her fist. The resulting combination of hot wet mouth and tight squeeze was enough to make his hips buck. Keeping the tight suction she moved slow and purposefully, as if her purpose was to drive him fucking insane.

"Stop," he bit out.

Her little hum of protest vibrated down his shaft to his balls. Breaking his promise to himself, he reached down and wove his fingers into her hair and tugged. Breaking contact, she looked up at him. Her eyes were glassy, the blue stormy dark and unlike anything he'd seen before.

"I'm gonna come if you don't stop," he said. "Is that what you want?"

She blinked, and a bit of awareness returned. "No," she said.

She scrambled off him. He shucked his jeans while she did the same beside the bed, her movements jerky and endearingly awkward. Biting her lip, she yanked open her nightstand to remove a box of condoms. An unopened box of condoms. While she tore into thin cardboard he stared unabashedly at the slim curve of her hips and the triangle of pale blond hair at the crux of her thighs.

"Yes, I am really a blonde," she said without looking at him.

"I didn't doubt it," he replied, amused.

One condom gripped firmly in her hand, she straddled him again, her hair swaying as she did. She opened the packet. He gripped his shaft and pulled it away from his abdomen, but let her roll down the latex without his interference. As much as he wanted to cover her fingers with his, to guide her hand down to his balls and the sensitive patch behind them, he held off.

Next time.

If there is a next time . . .

There's so going to be a next time, because if this is all she wants, that's great. It was all he had to give.

She wrapped her hand around his and centered herself over his erection. The pause before she lowered herself went on long enough for him to drag his gaze from the vision of her hand, his hand, his erection, and the damp, mysterious curls a mere inch away from his shaft.

"I want to ride you," she murmured when his gaze met hers.

The words nearly disappeared into the deepening night and the fog of lust clouding his brain. "I want that, too," he replied. "So bad."

She sank down, her hand leaving his to brace on his hip bone. He kept his wrapped around the base of his shaft, preventing her from taking him in fully, until the sensation of wet heat working the head of his cock drove him to grip her hips and guide her down.

Her eyes closed and a very faint, high-pitched noise escaped her parted lips. It took every ounce of willpower he had left at his disposal to keep his hips still and relax into the pleasure, the sheer, undiluted pleasure of being inside her. She shifted a little, tensing and releasing around his cock until he was settled exactly to her liking, then braced her hands on his shoulders and lifted her hips. He flexed his hands, part urging, part guiding her back down.

"Oh," she said. "Oh, that's good."

He growled his agreement, then growled again as she found a rhythm she liked, slow, steady, stretching time like taffy. Each downstroke firmly embedded him inside her, but she didn't rush. Slow went with gentle and hard with fast, but Alana disconnected the two, keeping the pace torturously even and wickedly hard. His hands slid up her torso to cup her breasts, but she didn't speed up. Instead, and oh, this was new, this was different, this made things a thousand times hotter, he felt her inner walls undulate around him as he rolled and pinched her nipples.

He'd thought he would treat the librarian like a well-bred lady, but she was taking him apart, muscle from bone, brain from defenses.

"Jesus," he ground out. Air huffed from his lungs when she straightened and put the heel of her hand against his sternum. He lifted into her next gliding, quivering stroke and she cried out, her head lolling back on her neck.

The urge to bite that pale, slim throat roared along his nerves, but he held off, held off, because a hot red flush climbed from her collarbone over her fluttering pulse into her cheeks. Oh, Jesus, that was hot. That pushed him right to the edge, his balls tight, release seething in the tip of his cock, sweet heat and primitive pressure barely lashed down until . . .

She cried out again, the sound redolent with helpless release. The rhythmic clench of her walls around him, the defenseless droop of her shoulders combined to push him over the edge. Blackness swamped him as he jetted into her.

When he could see and think again, he opened his eyes to find Alana slumped above him, eyes closed, purely satisfied female slackening every line of her body. He'd done that to her. Him. He wrapped his arms around waist and shoulders and rolled her onto her back.

Her eyes flew open and she gave a startled gasp. Not bothering to explain what he couldn't understand himself, he gripped her hair to expose her throat, then set his teeth to the soft hollow under her jaw.

She quivered under him, and the soft sound she made, all purring surrender, rippled through him. He felt himself start to soften. Reluctantly he pulled out, then walked down the hall to the bathroom, where he cleaned up. When he came back into the bedroom, she'd pulled the sheet and blanket up to her chin. He found his jeans and shorts, and stepped into both at once.

"Something tells me I've underestimated you," he said as he buttoned his fly.

"How so?"

"You wanted this for a lot longer than the last couple of days. I thought maybe you were scared."

Her skin pinkened again. "I said I wasn't savvy. I'm experienced enough to know better," she said cautiously. "I wasn't sure it was a good idea."

"Felt like a damned good idea to me," he said, and put

his hands on his hips. She didn't fuss or fidget under his gaze. "What do you think about renovating your kitchen?"

She blinked at the abrupt change of subject. "It's your house," she pointed out.

"You're living in it," he replied. "Never mind. I'll tackle it between tenants."

"I've already cost you three months you could have spent renovating," she said. "That would be fun."

"You've never renovated anything before, have you?"

She shook her head, a smile curving her kiss-swollen lips. "Not fun?"

"Depends on your idea of fun."

"It sounds interesting," she offered.

"I can go with that. Another chance for you to tell me what you want," he said.

She blushed, and her hand tightened on protective cotton and chenille armor, but then she climbed out of the bed, took her robe from the hook on the closet door, and wrapped it around her body. "We just established that I don't have any experience with renovations," she said again as she tightened the belt.

"You're better with decorative stuff," he said vaguely, looking around the bedroom. She hadn't done much, but what she had done made the room look soft and homey. Feminine without froufrou shit, and somehow right for the house. His grandmother would have approved.

"All right," she said.

"Saturday," he said decisively.

"The library's open until one. I'm free after that."

She followed him into the kitchen where he plucked his T-shirt from the floor and pulled it on. Duke, still sprawled under the table, lifted his head to peer inquiringly at Lucas. He clicked for him and the old dog scrambled to his feet.

"Is Cody working Saturday?"

She nodded as she began clearing the dinner dishes. "He wants to get his hours in as quickly as possible."

"Good." He gathered the bread platter and her wine glass and set them on the counter. "Look, don't get too close to him. You're thinking about what you can do to help him. The answer is nothing. Just stay out of it."

She gave him a smile that said she'd do whatever she damned well pleased, but covered it with a polite, "I've got it. Thanks for coming over."

"The house doesn't have a dishwasher," he said.

"I don't mind at all," she replied, "I think Duke's ready to go."

"Thanks for dinner," he said.

4

LUCAS RIDGEWAY LOOKED good in pink.

Alana's cheeks flushed as she walked from her house to the Heirloom for breakfast, more than the damp spring air could explain away. But remembering Lucas's tanned face and hair-roughened body against her pale pink sheets sent electric heat flashing along her nerves.

Really good. Dark and rough and at her disposal in a way she never would have expected. He was constantly in motion, assessing, thinking, analyzing. His gaze stopped moving only to take in details, then move on. The spur-of-the-moment suggestion to renovate the bathroom was a case in point. Lucas didn't like to sit still. Grass didn't grow under him. She didn't think he'd have the patience to sit still as stone while she lost herself in his textures and tastes. Stubble against her lips. A trace of salt on his abdomen. The thin skin of his shaft on her tongue.

Looks like there was one area in his life where Lucas knew how to slow down.

Lucky her.

She didn't feel that she could turn down his request to renovate the kitchen, though. Spending nights and weekends picking out wallpaper or paint and a new vanity with a big tough guy used to getting his way would be a good learning experience, maybe even better than spending nights in his bed.

She hauled open the door to the Heirloom Café with a little more force than necessary. A big, satisfying meal followed by an hour in bed with a big, satisfying male had combined to make her sleep like a baby. The bell over the door clanged rather than jingled, and heads swiveled to look at her. She smiled, then headed for the counter, mentally prioritizing her day. In addition to the library, Mrs. Battle wanted to talk strategy for the renovation proposal, and Freddie needed the position paper from the human-trafficking conference two years earlier—

"The usual?" Peggy asked.

"Yes, but would you add one of your skillet platters to the order? Also to-go."

"You want home fries or hash browns?"

She remembered Cody's cheekbones, the pale skin, his frame that bordered on skeletal. "Home fries, and toast, and a side of sausage, please. And juice."

"Did you miss supper last night?" Peggy asked as she clipped the order to the wheel above the counter and spun it to face Eugene, the cook.

"I'm picking something up for a friend."

"Your friend wouldn't be Chief Ridgeway, would it?"

Alana felt her eyes widen. "No. Why would you think that?"

"Because Mrs. Denison across the street saw him go into your house around seven and not come out again until nine." Peggy gave her a broad smile. "He was barefoot, she said. And he took Duke with him."

She can't tell you had sex last night. You showered and washed your hair and put on fresh clothes, and that possessive bite to your neck—that was a purely animal reminder that no matter if I was on top, he was still in charge—didn't leave a mark. "Chief Ridgeway wants to renovate the kitchen before I leave so he can rent it again as soon as possible," she said, striving for a casual tone. "I've already been here months longer than we'd planned. He came over at suppertime, so we ate and talked about the project."

"Oh," Peggy said, deflated. "Not very exciting."

"I'm a librarian. Nothing exciting happens to me." *Except last night. Last night a tall, dangerous, remote man walked barefoot into your kitchen, then into your bed. Except it's technically his bed.*

Desire flashed low and white-hot in her abdomen.

"Take a seat," Peggy said. "The skillet platter will be a minute."

She sat down and picked up a copy of the local newspaper a previous customer had discarded in the rack by the door and skimmed the headlines. Peggy set a plastic bag containing a Styrofoam box, her bowl of oatmeal, and two shrink-wrapped packages of plastic utensils on the counter a few minutes later.

"Where is Gunther Jensen's house?" she asked before Peggy could inquire into Alana's breakfast companion.

"Out Route 46," Peggy said.

The same road listed as Cody Burton's address on his community-service paperwork. While she could find nearly any address in Chicago using the house numbers as her only reference, she was lost when it came to the numbering systems used on hundreds of miles of county roads. But if Cody lived anywhere in the vicinity of Gunther Jensen, that explained Lucas's visit to the library, and the tension in his shoulders last night.

Alana paid Peggy, accepted her change and left a tip, then set off for the library. Cody was waiting for her, sitting with his back to the door at the top of the steps, forearms dangling over his knees. He wore jeans, worn sneakers, a gray hoodie and a jacket unzipped over the hoodie. His nose was red with cold, but more telling, the nail beds of his long, thin fingers were purple.

"Good morning," she said pleasantly as she climbed the stairs.

He peered up at her when she reached the top stair. "You don't know that," he said.

"I'm an optimist," she replied. "Scoot over."

He did her one better, scrambling to his feet to loom beside her while she juggled her bags and unlocked the front door. Once inside, she went straight to the office and shed bags, coat, and scarf. Cody lifted the wooden return bin from the back of the door, stacked the books on the circulation desk, then stood outside the office door, silent and brooding. The boy could brood like nobody's business, she thought. I'm not prepared to deal with a teenage boy. Teenage girls she understood. Grown men were mysterious enough. Adolescent boys might as well be from another planet.

While her laptop booted out of sleep mode, she pulled the Heirloom Café bag to her and removed her oatmeal, then the skillet platter. Cody's shoulders straightened and a dull red heat suffused his cheekbones.

"I need to run antivirus updates on the computers," she said, without looking at him. "Remember the boxes I showed you in the basement? I need those unpacked and stacked. Thank you."

With that she slid past him and headed for the row of computers. For a long moment Cody didn't move, something she knew only because all she could hear was her heart thumping in her ears and the whir of a computer's hard drive coming to life. Then, a rustle of denim and the rasp of the leather and wool of his letter jacket. The squeak of Styrofoam. The sound of the basement door opening, and closing.

Good.

In between booting up the computers and running the antivirus software updates, she finished off her oatmeal.

Just before the library opened, she walked down the stairs into the basement. Cody had five of the boxes unpacked.

"I didn't know how you wanted the books organized, so I grouped them together like they were in the original boxes."

She walked over to the table. "This is fine. I need to go through them and see which ones have any value in the resale market."

"Resale value?"

"There are people who make a decent living going around to sales and auctions finding books that are rare or desirable," she said. "There's no reason why the library can't do the same."

He eyed the books stacked on the table, then the boxes in the room. "How do you know which ones are worth something?"

She showed him the app on her phone that allowed her to enter the ISBN and see what the prices were on various online sites. "Forty dollars," she said after she scanned a book. "It's not much when you need to repair the roof and add a sewer line, but it's more than we had. The buyer pays for the shipping, too."

Cody hefted a copy of a book containing Leonardo da Vinci's drawing and sketchbooks. "How much is this one worth?"

His voice was too casual to be casual. She entered the ISBN and waited for the data network to crawl along the Interwebs and produce an answer. "Oh, not much," she said. "Just a few dollars. Why?"

"Can I buy it?"

This from a boy who didn't have the money to buy breakfast. "Just take it," she said gently.

"Thanks," he said, as if the word didn't sit easily in his mouth.

"How about if I leave you my phone and you check them for me?"

He hefted the phone, then slid her a look. "How do you

know I won't download a bunch of porn and spend the day watching it?"

"Because my data network is so slow that you'd die of boredom," she said with a smile. "And this conversation is inappropriate."

Another flush. "Sorry, Miss Wentworth."

She turned to leave.

"You don't have to buy me breakfast. I eat before I leave home."

Pride rather than truthfulness motivated the words. "Of course, but I don't like to eat in front of someone who isn't," she said simply.

"I don't care," he said.

"But I do."

Back upstairs she vacuumed and swept. The computer was up and running, so she checked in and reshelved returned DVDs and audiobooks, which were in high demand. Mrs. Battle was due to work today, so she would reshelve returned books while Alana helped the library's visitors, worked on a blog post detailing upcoming releases and asking for the community's input into which ones would be purchased, and checking the Facebook and e-mail accounts.

Mrs. Battle arrived just before noon. Alana went downstairs to find Cody working his way through the books. The edge of one table held a few books while a larger section was stacked back in the boxes.

"I've found a few worth some real money," he said, without looking up from the phone. "Most of them are junk."

She walked over to one box, crouched next to it, and picked through the selection. "It was worth a try," she said.

"Your mother sent you an e-mail with the subject line DO NOT IGNORE THIS EMAIL and someone named Frederica e-mailed six times. Your battery's almost dead."

She'd forgotten about the notifications on her phone. Cody slapped the hot phone into her outstretched hand. Alana opened the e-mail app and saw the e-mails queued up.

"Do you always ignore your mother's e-mails?"

"Not always," Alana said as it opened. *Just when she's e-mailing about her plans for the party she'll throw when I return to Chicago, or asking when I want to start work again, if I need a vacation from my vacation, and how exactly do I feel about David dating Laurie?* Alana couldn't think about that. She had a kitchen to renovate, the town's police chief in her bed, Freddie's wedding to plan, and a proposal due in less than a week.

And a sullen teenage boy talking to her. A boy who, other than answering direct questions, hadn't said one word. She tapped back to the home screen. "I need you upstairs."

He snagged the book of sketches and followed her up the stairs. Back on the first floor, she made sure he saw the half sandwich sitting on her desk, then she went back to circulation. A few moments later, he emerged from her office. "What now?"

"You can read *Alexander and the Terrible, Horrible, No-Good, Very Bad Day* to the preschool kids, or you can shelve magazines," she said, half joking.

With a cocky grin, he said, "I don't need the book." Alana nearly gasped *Wait!* but bit back the word at the last minute. She should know better than to make jokes like that.

Some of the mothers looked a little taken aback at the idea of having a juvenile delinquent read to their children, but others took the opportunity to browse the popular-fiction rack themselves. Cody settled himself onto the low stool, his knees nearly in his armpits, gangly elbows perilously close to pigtails and cowlicks. One of the little kids giggled at this awkward stork impression. He drew the chalk easel to his side and started drawing. Within a couple of minutes, the kids were clustered around his feet, practically in his lap as he quickly drew, erased, and drew again, illustrating a story about a truck trying to deliver tomatoes to a store. He did voices for the truck, named Growler, and the tomatoes, who didn't want to go to the store and be made into sandwiches. They wanted to throw themselves at things, people, trees, other trucks, which sent the kids into a fit of giggles.

Mrs. Battle set a stack of paperbacks on the circulation desk. She wore polyester slacks, a print blouse, and a cardigan. Her glasses were perched on her nose, and the chain got caught in her collar. "Well, that's unexpected," she said.

Alana watched him a moment longer, then turned to Mrs. Battle, who had her head cocked at an odd angle as she studied the Dewey decimal sticker on the book's spine. "I get the same problem when I need a new prescription," she offered.

"A new prescription won't help," Mrs. Battle said matter-of-factly. "My eyesight's getting worse. I have an appointment tomorrow to see a specialist in Sioux Falls. I'm going to have to reschedule, though," she said. "My neighbor fell yesterday and isn't up to driving me."

"What time is the appointment?"

"First thing in the morning."

The older woman's lips were firmly pressed together, holding in tears. In the story nook, Cody drew Growler convincing the tomatoes to throw themselves at the wall above a big vat to be made into pizza sauce.

"I've been meaning to run to Sioux Falls," Alana said. "How about if we drive down together?"

"You don't need to do that," Mrs. Battle said firmly.

"I'd like to," Alana replied. "It would be a big help for me. We're so busy, we don't have much time to talk about the proposal. We can talk on the way there and the way back."

"All right," Mrs. Battle said.

"I'll pick you up early," Alana said.

In the story nook, Cody dusted off his hands. The little kids whined and one lurched forward to tug the leg of Cody's jeans. "More Growler!" he demanded imperiously.

"I can't, buddy," Cody said. "I've got to get back to work. But if you come back tomorrow, I'll tell you another story about Growler. Next time he delivers pumpkins."

He threw Alana a defiant look that made her smile. If Cody thought that reading to little kids was the best part of this job, he could have it.

Cody strolled over to the desk, the first real smile she'd seen on his face. "That was fun."

"The kids loved you," Alana said. "Nice job."

He shrugged. "No big deal. Want me to sort some more books?"

"Yes, please."

She scrolled through Freddie's e-mail again, which was asking for a slightly different angle on the literacy issues. Her mind wandered between the conferences she'd attended, the conversations in the identical hotel ballrooms about global literacy efforts, and Cody's take on story hour. Lights went on in little eyes when he told Growler's story. It was a sweet moment, one that made her heart lift a little. Good for Cody, good for the kids, good for the moms watching. But she knew her place, and it wasn't here.

ALANA CLOSED THE library's front door and locked it. Mrs. Battle clocked out just after three, but Cody hung around after Alana pointed out that as long as he wasn't in school, he might as well make a dent in his community-service hours. Arms laden with her purse, tote, and laptop bag, she opened the back door of her A4 and set her bags on the backseat. After a deep inhale, she took off her coat as well. Late afternoon spring sunshine gilded the tops of the trees and cast long shadows on the street, and the air held a faintly sweet scent she didn't recognize. After a few moments, she decided it was the smell of blossoming, sap pulsing through winter-iced trees to produce and unfurl buds. Spring in Chicago had a smell all its own, but spring was far too delicate to overcome concrete and exhaust.

The scent would be even stronger when she got out of town, which was exactly what she intended to do. Lucas wanted her aesthetic opinion on the kitchen, and she didn't want to tell him that decorating wasn't her strong suit. Her mother did all of that and went for ultramodern. But Lucas's tiny jewel of a house deserved a better kitchen than the one it had. It was small, yes, but the right countertops, perhaps some built-in shelves in the wall behind the door, and a brighter color scheme would make the space feel airy, even beautiful.

With that in mind, Alana planned to make a pilgrimage of sorts to Brookhaven, form and function and beauty rocking tranquilly on the rolling prairie a few miles outside of town. Marissa Brooks had restored the grand house in a way that honored its period feel without sacrificing modern conveniences and comfort. She'd been to Brookhaven almost weekly since Chloe Nichols had bought the house and opened a yoga studio and retreat center, and Brookhaven's new owner had become a friend.

She carefully backed out of the library director's parking space and turned right, heading for County Road 12 and Brookhaven. On the edge of town she passed Cody, walking along the shoulder, hands shoved in his pockets, the book tucked under his arm. As she approached, he turned and stuck his thumb out. She pulled over next to him and rolled down her window.

"Hello, Cody."

His wary expression closed off. "Keep driving, Miss Wentworth."

"I'm going to Brookhaven," she said. "Your house is on the way."

"It's a couple of miles out of your way. I'll catch another ride."

If this boy walked home from town, he'd burn off all the calories from lunch and then some. "A couple of miles isn't much," she said, and reached across the car to open the door. "Get in."

"No, thanks."

"Get in or I'll tell Chief Ridgeway you're hitchhiking. Which is illegal in South Dakota." Or so she hoped.

"It's not illegal."

"Then it's just stupid."

His eyes narrowed and a dull heat a completely different shade from the healthy color of exercise in fresh air crept up his face. "I can take care of myself," he sneered.

"I'm sure you can," she lied. "But today I'm going to give you a ride home because I'm going that way anyway."

"And you'll rat me out to Ridgeway."

"*Chief Ridgeway*, and yes I will."

He jerked the door open and thudded into the passenger seat, muttering something under his breath Alana chose to ignore. She checked her mirror and merged back into traffic.

"Fasten your seat belt, please."

After a moment's hesitation he did, his expression sullen. Hands fisted in his coat pockets he stared out the window, keeping his face turned away from Alana. Content to ride in silence, Alana drove through the deepening twilight, bypassing the turnoff for Brookhaven on County Road 12 and continuing another mile east.

"You know where you're going," Cody said.

"I've driven the bookmobile when Mrs. Battle has a doctor's appointment, so I learned some of the country roads," she explained. Suddenly Mrs. Battle's willingness to give up bookmobile duty made more sense.

He snorted, and turned to look at her. "You drive the bookmobile," he said.

The bookmobile was in a renovated school bus. "I do," she replied. Technically, she should have a commercial driver's license to drive such a large vehicle, something she hoped would escape Cody's attention, but if she didn't make the weekly rounds to the four other tiny communities in the county, the residents went without books. Not to mention the hassle of extending loans due to expire. "As long as I don't have to back up, I'm fine."

A single light in the distance grew larger, then resolved into two windows in a double-wide trailer. Cody didn't say a word as she turned into the rutted tracks forming the driveway. Weathered skirting sagged from rusted bolts, and the television blasted from the interior, loud enough for Alana to hear it through the screen door and inside the heavily soundproofed Audi. A plastic turtle sat off to one side, sand and a scratched plastic shovel spilling onto the grass.

Cody fumbled along the arm of the passenger door until he found the correct button to unlock the door. Three little kids piled out of the trailer's door, tumbling down the rickety steps and swarming around her car. He shoved open the door and swung out those long legs, the light from the open door cutting his cheekbones into unnatural angles.

It was a long, long walk from this house to the library.

The five-day forecast flashed in her brain. She stopped him with a hand on his arm. "I can come pick you up tomorrow morning," she started. "The low tonight is—"

He shook her off and got out of the car. "Not necessary," he said.

"Cody—"

"Just go."

She expected the door to slam with enough force to rock the car on its axles. Instead, it closed gently, almost respectfully. He picked up two of the kids under one arm and hoisted the oldest into the other. Each of the kids got a kiss.

She shifted into reverse and backed down the ruts, the car jouncing as she did. Cody stood in the darkness beside the rectangular light cast on the dirt in front of the door, watching her go. Only when she was back on the road did he climb the steps and open the screen door.

She backtracked to Brookhaven. The house loomed black and angular against the twilight sky, a swath of stars spread over the prairie as she drove up the wide, arcing driveway to park in front of the grand double doors. She paused for a moment. This was the kind of house she was supposed to live in, grand enough to make a statement about the position she was supposed to have in the world, big enough for the role she was supposed to have as the highly educated, capable-in-her-own-right political hostess for David. It was beautiful and stately and perfect for a Wentworth, exactly the kind of house she'd go home to when she went back to Chicago. If she felt more at home in the tiny house she rented from Lucas than she did in Brookhaven, much less Chicago or the Hamptons or Nantucket, she could fix that. She could learn to make Chicago and the Wentworth Foundation her home. After all, no one would really trade the life of a Wentworth for the life of a small-town librarian.

Like Lucas's grandmother's roses, carefully tended and nurtured in harsh conditions, she would bloom where she was planted: in Chicago, in a hundred years of family service, not in Walkers Ford, South Dakota.

Brookhaven's new owner, Chloe Nichols, had moved right in and opened the retreat center, where residents could come and stay for any length of time from overnight to several months. At the moment, only the upstairs bedrooms were available, but Chloe had plans to build small cabins in the meadow that sprawled from the backyard to the creek running through the property. She had slowly but surely made her mark on the big house. Carefully piled stones lined the driveway, and the sailing ship figurehead was gone from the third-story balcony, replaced with a string of Buddhist prayer flags. Wind chimes sounded above the entryway. Alana rang the doorbell, not sure who would answer. Chloe had three retreatants at the moment, but Chloe herself pulled open the door. Her dark brown hair was pulled back in a simple ponytail, and she wore yoga pants, thick socks, and a green fleece pullover zipped to her chin.

"Come in, come in," she exclaimed, leaning in for the cheek kiss Alana automatically returned. "How are you? Would you like some tea?"

"I'd love some," Alana said, and followed Chloe through the main room to the kitchen.

One of Brookhaven's unique architectural features was Japanese-style sliding walls. Chloe had closed off the great room to form a meditation-and-yoga studio space lit by south-facing floor-to-ceiling windows. A scattering of zabutons and zafus ringed the simple bench where Chloe led guided-meditation sessions, and at the other end lay yoga mats, blocks, and bolsters for yoga classes. Alana got the sense that the house found these changes amusing, rather like a dowager duchess supremely confident in her status and therefore utterly unconcerned with changing fashion.

The kitchen, however, was a gorgeous homage to the house's heritage. Marissa had included modern conveniences like granite countertops and stainless steel appliances, but she'd kept the cabinet doors and the original slate floors.

"Do you mind if I take a look in the servants' quarters?"

"Not at all," Chloe said as she ran water into an electric kettle.

Alana stepped through the connecting door into the empty space. Chloe was living in the master suite, but until she built her cabins on the meadow, was renting the servants' quarters to a long-term residential student. Marissa had painted the kitchen cabinets a soft gray with pink undertones that reminded Alana of sunrise over London. She'd used brushed silver handles, but Alana thought Lucas's kitchen would look prettier with gold. So much light streamed into the room. Hints of gold would pick up the sunlight and make the room feel bright, open, welcoming.

Back in the kitchen, Chloe was opening a cabinet. She removed a gleaming Japanese teapot and two ceramic cups. "So why the sudden interest in my kitchen?" she asked as she arranged everything on a mother-of-pearl-inlaid tray.

She'd claimed Brookhaven with ease, Alana noticed. My kitchen. "Lucas wants to redo the kitchen in the house I'm renting and asked me for input. This is the nicest kitchen in the county, so I thought I'd start here."

"Some of the houses on the golf course have gorgeous kitchens," Chloe pointed out as she offered Alana a wooden box containing a selection of loose-leaf tea pouches.

"I don't have much time. Lucas wants to buy supplies tonight. Anyway, those houses have a cookie-cutter feel to them," Alana said, looking around again. She chose a pouch of white orchard tea and handed the box back to Chloe. "Marissa had a gift. In Chicago she had owned her own design firm."

"New York, too," Chloe admitted. "Where is she now?"

"She left Hawaii a few weeks ago on her way to San Diego." She focused on Chloe, pouring water over the tea leaves. "So. Tell me the latest."

Single women who relocated to rural areas were a rare commodity, and one in high demand with farming or ranching bachelors. Chloe was slender, lithe, with big brown eyes and a wide-open smile, one on display as she set a cup in front of Alana. "The latest is Henry Marsden."

"I don't know him."

"He ranches a few miles out of town. We've been out three times in the last two weeks."

"And?"

Chloe's brown eyes sparkled over her tea. "Not so fast. Your turn."

Alana shrugged. "I had Lucas over for dinner."

"And?"

"And . . ."

Both dark brown eyebrows lifted toward her hairline, a question Alana answered with a nod. "It's about time."

"It's a mistake," Alana said. "I'm going home in a few weeks."

"So? Why does that make it a mistake?"

Because in Alana's experience, the kind of shell Lucas carried around formed over an unshakable piece of grit in the soul. Even the wounded ones could still get hurt.

Mistaking her silence for confusion, Chloe went on. "He's hot," she said, using her right hand to tick off points. "He's single," she said, adding her index finger to her thumb. "He's right next door. He's a cop."

Alana stopped her. "Don't say it."

"You're a librarian."

"We're a cliché."

"Nothing wrong with being a cliché." She sipped her tea, then lifted her pinkie finger to complete the list of five reasons why Alana should make a mistake with Lucas. "And it's not really a mistake if there're no consequences. Which there aren't, because you're leaving in a few weeks."

Somehow it didn't seem that simple. "That's all very true," Alana said. "How's business?"

Chloe pursed her lips. "Good. I'm talking to organizations in Brookings and Sioux Falls about using the house for company off-sites, and to churches and spiritual directors who need space to run weekend retreats. I can pay the mortgage coaching disillusioned corporate employees looking for somewhere to strategize about their next steps, and I've got regulars coming to yoga classes. That's enough."

Alana thought about her mother and stepfather's definition of *enough*. Once Freddie married Toby, her mother's expectations would turn to Alana in a way they never had before.

"Are you happy with how things are turning out?"

"I thought I wanted a big life. Money, power, prestige,

influence. Turns out I'm happy with a very, very small life that's saturated with meaning." Chloe set her empty cup down. "Let's take a look through the rest of the house. Every room is so unique, and you never know when an idea will strike your fancy."

5

LUCAS BROUGHT THE Blazer to a halt in front of Tanya's cabin. Her rusted-out Ford pickup sat at the end of the ruts serving as a driveway, but that didn't mean she was home. Last he heard, the truck needed a new transmission. Smoke was rising from the chimney, so odds were better she was home. Or she might be out tramping along the creek winding through the prairie waves toward Brookhaven, deceptively small on the horizon, all straight lines and sharp angles against the spring blue sky. The moment Tanya stopped loving the outdoors was the moment Lucas checked her into a treatment center. Again. Because treatment didn't work the first time, or the second time, or the other times she tried on her own and Lucas wasn't supposed to know about.

For the moment, however, Tanya got up, got something to eat, then walked. But as nothing changed, the need for the drug would simmer, then seethe in her system, and by night she'd be high again.

Lucas stepped onto the splintered porch, noted the muddy boots with gray wool socks tucked into the shanks next to the door, and red-and-black wool jacket hanging from a hook screwed straight into the cabin's wall. He knocked, automatically scanning behind him while he waited for Tanya to open the door.

Her dishwater blond hair hung in lank strands around her face. She'd forgotten to shower for a few days, not a good sign, but her pupils were the correct size for the sunshine flooding into the cabin from the big windows overlooking the creek. She was barefoot, but he could see the imprint of her hiking socks in the skin of her feet. "Hey, Tanya," he said.

"Hey, Chief," she replied.

The dig stung. "Put your boots on," he said. "We need to talk, and it's too cold for you to stand out here without shoes."

"You can come in," she said liltingly.

Fuck this attitude bullshit. "Can I?" He held her gaze until it dropped. "I don't want to arrest you today, Tanya. Put your boots on and come outside."

She slammed the door behind her, movements jerky as she yanked the socks from the boots and stuffed her bare feet into them. Thumbs hooked in his jeans pockets, he waited for her on the grass beside the dirt road leading to the cabin.

"What do you want?"

He studied her again in the bright light of day. Not strung out enough to have trashed Gunther Jensen's place, but he had to ask. Blood was blood, but crime was crime, and he worked for the citizens of Walkers Ford.

"Someone broke into Gunther's house yesterday. Trashed it pretty thoroughly and took some cash. And his wife's engagement ring he had planned to give to his granddaughter."

Shock widened her eyes ever so slightly, a sight that eased his heart just a little. Addicts gone too far to recover didn't care about anyone else. Compassion lived somewhere deep inside the bitter woman standing in front of him. "Was he home?"

"No. He was visiting Betty in the nursing home. Do you remember where you were yesterday?" Blacking out happened frequently to prescription drug addicts.

"Of course," she said, just indignantly enough to sound hurt. Then the penny dropped. "You thought I did it. Because I did some work for Gunther, and I'm an addict and a user."

He didn't deny it. "His Percocet's missing."

"Fuck you, Lucas Ridgeway. Fuck you to hell."

She spun around, but he grabbed her arm. "I had to ask. And if the roles were reversed, you'd have to ask, too."

The look she slid him, sharp with pain and bright with tears, made him look away. Because she'd wanted his job. Years ago, when he was eighteen and she was fourteen, all she'd wanted was to become chief of police of Walkers Ford. She'd gone to Denver for college the same year he graduated from the academy. In the fall of her sophomore year, she tried to break up a fight in a bar she shouldn't have been in, in the first place, and got her elbow broken in two places. She'd pushed her recovery too hard, too fast, requiring a second surgery. Even after months of physical therapy, she didn't have the mobility she needed to pass the physical entrance exams for the academy. Then she got hooked on the prescription painkillers. He'd gotten busy at work and fallen head over heels for Leanne. He was struggling to find time for a relationship, let alone his cousin. Not even knowing one of Denver PD's brightest prospects could save her. All her hopes and dreams died that night.

He stared at her, making the connection for the first time that she was around Alana's age. Twenty-eight. Twenty-eight, too thin, frequently dead-eyed and always bitter.

"You never used to be mean," she said.

He let her arm drop. She rubbed her elbow significantly, but wouldn't meet his eyes.

"I didn't break into Gunther's place," she said.

"Okay," he said.

"I didn't."

"I heard you the first time."

"You have a hard time believing me when I tell you the truth."

When he'd come back to Walkers Ford, she'd said she was clean; instead, he figured out she was getting pills from multiple doctors in four different counties. He'd called every doctor, clinic, and hospital in a two-hundred-mile radius and warned them not to prescribe for her. When she found out, she'd screamed at him for an hour. All he'd done was drive her to get drugs from illegal sources.

You've lied to me too many times trembled on the tip of his tongue, but he held it back. "How're you doing?"

She wrapped her arms around her torso and looked off into the distance. "Now this is a social call?"

"I still care," he said.

"You used to care. Now you say it's caring when you dial it in from Mars on a tin can attached to a piece of string. A kid died, Lucas. Big deal. Gangbangers die all the time and cops don't shut down over it. They deal with it and move on. That's the job. Dad said you don't have the heart for police work."

That should hurt. It was supposed to hurt, and at one time, it would have hurt. "I would have said you didn't have the heart for it, either."

He just stared at her until she dropped her gaze. "I'll pay for treatment again."

"I've got money," she said.

"From where?"

"Mack Winston's taking people hunting again," she said. "He pays to use the land. My kind of work. I don't do a goddamn thing, and I get paid."

Back in the day, Tanya could run a six-minute mile. Back in the day, she'd turned every head in the precinct when she came to visit him. Back in the day, she'd do field-hand work during the day, stay out most of the night, then get up the next morning and do it all over again. She was built for work, hard work requiring muscle and brain. She was built to be a cop, and instead she walked the prairie and slept the day away and burned her brain cells with OxyContin.

"Did you see anything while you were out walking yesterday?"

"Near Gunther's? No. I went the other direction, towards Brookhaven. I'm not using," she said, looking him straight in the eye.

A lie, or she would have let him into the cabin. Which meant he couldn't trust that she hadn't broken into Gunther's house, either. Frustration and regret cemented together in his gut. He put his hands on his hips and looked away. Nothing with Tanya was easy anymore. Nothing.

"Anything else?"

"You need anything?"

The words were out before he could stop them. She looked him over, taking in the badge on one hip, the gun holstered on the other. She would know his handcuffs were in a case at the small of his back. Standing in front of her wearing the signs of her shattered dream made the words a slap in the face.

To his utter shock, she didn't launch herself at him, something she'd done when the drugs poisoned her system. A little smile, all the more devastating for the self-mocking edge to it, broke his heart. "Nothing you can give me, Lucas."

Resignation was worse than her fury. He nodded toward the pickup. "How much to fix the transmission?"

"It's fixed. I got it back a couple of days ago. I wasn't kidding about Mack." She shot him a glare, then turned and headed for the cabin. "Go away, Lucas. I didn't steal from Gunther Jensen, and I don't need anything from you."

Fuck. Fuck it all. Lucas hauled open the Blazer's door and thought about how good it would feel to pound on something. He picked up his cell phone and dialed the library.

"Walkers Ford Library, this is Alana. How can I help you?" The hint of laughter that lay under the pleasant words was a sound he hadn't heard in what felt like a lifetime.

"Is it okay with you if I start demo on your kitchen tonight?"

A pause.

"It's Lucas."

"I know it's you," she said, and even over the phone line he could hear her cheeks heating. "You sounded . . . never mind. You don't have to ask. You're my landlord, the chief of police, and the guy I'm sleeping with."

"None of those things give me permission to be in your house without your consent."

"Go ahead. I have to run an errand after we close. I'll be back at the house in a couple of hours."

That would give him plenty of time to take measurements. "We'll get supper in Brookings."

"Brookings?"

"The location of the nearest home-improvement superstore," he said. "Normally I'd shop local, but after the hardware store in town closed, that's the best place to buy supplies."

"Right. Of course. I'll see you back at the house."

Back at the house. She didn't call it "home." She didn't even call it "her house." She called it "the house" or "his house." Because home was in Chicago.

He parked in his own driveway and greeted Duke. "Hey, buddy, you have a good day?" he crooned as the dog pranced and snuffled between his legs. A gentle scratching of Duke's hindquarters sent fur flurries into the air. The dog was losing his winter undercoat. Lucas snagged the stiff-bristled brush and smoothed out his coat while Duke stretched.

Inside his house he changed into work jeans, a long-sleeved T-shirt, and work boots, then grabbed his toolbox from the porch and crossed their adjoining driveways. As they had every year since his grandmother passed, the shoots and stalks extended from the carefully mulched beds lining the side of the house. The bushes grew on their own, a tangle of branches and thorns he'd let run wild. The year after his grandmother died, Mrs. Battle had come over and dealt with the beds, but last spring she'd had trouble shaking bronchitis.

His grandmother had welcomed him, the odd child out in a family of musical free spirits, because he cared about what she cared about: people, a place, a community. His grandfather and Uncle Nelson took him hunting, hiking, rock climbing. All his grandmother wanted was for him to take care of the house, the town, his family.

He'd failed her in every possible way, and her house was a silent reminder of promises broken, lives ruined.

Big-city girl that she was, Alana locked the house every time she left, so he used his keys to let himself in. Duke followed gamely at his heels, sniffing around until he lost interest, and settled under the kitchen table. Lucas set the toolbox on the linoleum and studied the house. He spent a fair amount of his career going into people's homes and looking around. Serving warrants, searching for contraband, it all came down to finding out someone else's secrets. But this house didn't have any secrets from him. He'd spent summers in the room at the end of the hall, eaten more meals in this kitchen than he had in the house he had shared with his ex-wife.

Including a simple meal shared with Alana before a rather complex round of sex.

He looked around. The little shelf his grandfather had built for his grandmother now held African violets and a couple of pictures of Alana with a blond woman he assumed was her globe-trotting sister. The drop-leaf table was pushed against the wall and wiped clean. Salt and pepper shakers shaped like roses clustered in the middle with a sugar bowl. Opened mail was tucked between the shakers and bowl, a square letter mailed in the kind of thick envelope his ex had insisted on for their wedding invitations.

He opened a compartment in his mind and shoved his curiosity in with everything else he felt, but the shift in the house intrigued him. Observing the differences between the house his grandmother kept and the one Alana kept was scientific. Data gathering. Not emotional.

Note, for example, the books stacked by his grandmother's chair, like they were when she was alive.

He flipped on the kitchen light. The cabinet doors were the original beadboard but painted in a green that reminded him of hospitals and retro television shows. The handles were a darkened iron. The counters were forty years old, and despite his grandmother's care, marred with scratches and burns that came from making three meals a day, seven days a week. The wallpaper was faded yellowish and decorated with green and orange flowering vines that repeated in the linoleum. Both of those had to go, too.

It wasn't the decorations that made it feel like his grandmother's house. It was the care Alana took of it. The wood gleamed, the windows shone, and the grout looked like she spent an hour each weekend scrubbing at it with a toothbrush and bleach. Maybe she did, despite working thirty hours a week in the library and who knew how many more for Freddie and her family.

He'd spent enough time fixing Alana's sink lately to know that this wasn't going to be an easy project. The sink didn't have any shut-off valves attached; in order for her to have water in the bathroom he'd have to install those . . .

He was standing in the tiny room, notebook in hand, developing a plan when the back door opened. "Hello?"

"In here," he called back.

The sound of bags hitting the kitchen table, then her heels against the hardwood as she walked down the hall. The scent of her, spring air, a layer of faintly floral perfume over a more fundamental soap and heated female skin, reached him before she did. Then she peered around the doorjamb.

"Hi."

"Hi," he said. "Duke didn't give you any trouble."

"No," she said. "He lifted his head and looked at me, then laid it back down and grunted. When I come back in my next life, I want to be that dog."

He felt the corners of his mouth lift, a totally unexpected response. "He worked hard for eight years as a police dog. He's earned a rest."

The humming noise she made in response slipped over his nerves like velvet. "I'd like to change before we head out."

"Sure," he said, forcing himself not to look up from his notebook.

"I need the bathroom to take my makeup off," she said.

Startled, he turned sideways and slipped past her. Like the first time they brushed up against each other in this doorway, his chest brushed her breasts. Unlike the first time, he went from aware of her to desperately aroused in a split second.

She bit into her lower lip but firmly shut the door behind him. He went into the kitchen and sat down at the table. Thinking through the renovation would take his mind off a quickie before running into Brookings.

Only a few minutes later, she came back down the hall wearing slim jeans, a white T-shirt, and a fitted cardigan in a blue that matched her eyes. She'd taken off her makeup and wore glasses. Chic, blue-rimmed glasses, but glasses to be sure. He couldn't speak for the rest of the species, but he would totally make a pass at this woman in glasses.

She offered him another quick smile as she wrapped a scarf around her neck, then slipped her feet into the flat black shoes by the kitchen door. "I'm ready."

Lucas looked down at his jeans and gray T-shirt, both faded to near white. For a second, he contemplated changing, but discarded the idea. Alana always looked like that, and when he was off-duty, he always looked like this. This wasn't a date. They weren't a couple. He had no reason to put on nicer jeans or a button-down shirt when they were going to a home-improvement superstore, and he'd probably end up loading building supplies into his truck.

"Let's go," he said brusquely.

ALANA SPENT THE first half of the drive into Brookings watching the sunset transform the prairie into rolling green gilded with reds and oranges. The wide-open expanse of grassland changed constantly, the wind and sky conspiring in ceaseless shifts, cross-hatching and patchworking.

"How was your day?" she asked Lucas. She had to make conversation, knew how to do it, but she hated to break the warm silence in the truck's cab.

"Fine."

She glanced over at him. The last rays of sun filtered weakly through the truck's windows, picking out hints of red in his hair and the five o'clock shadow on his cheek, and highlighting his firm lips. He drove with one wrist on the top of the steering wheel, the other hand on the gearshift.

Was she supposed to dig deeper? Sometimes when David was in a mood, she knew to keep asking questions, but Lucas seemed too straightforward for that. She tucked her hair behind her ear, and returned her gaze to the window. He shifted in his seat.

"How about you? Cody give you any trouble?"

"No," she said. "He did everything I asked, perhaps not cheerfully but at least without fussing. He's sorting books for me. I want to figure out which ones have some resale value. Then he read to the preschoolers during story time."

Lucas turned to look at her, one eyebrow cocked. "He read to little kids."

"He told them a story and drew illustrations in real time on the chalkboard," Alana said. "He used voices for all the characters, too. It was almost performance art. Surprised?"

"Nothing surprises me anymore," he said. "I went to see my cousin today."

The non sequitur startled her. It was her turn to make a noise that passed for a comment in the hopes that he'd continue.

"She's an addict."

This was news to Alana. The prairie might stretch to the horizon, but Walkers Ford held the craggy terrain and hidden crevices of small-town secrets. "I didn't know," she said. "I'm sorry."

"She lives less than a mile from Gunther Jensen."

The puzzle pieces clicked together, connecting Cody to the crime to his cousin. "That can't have been easy."

"It wasn't."

What to say now? Ask him whether or not his cousin had anything to do with the break-in? Ask him how he felt? Ask him something else? Sit quietly?

"What did she say?"

He turned and looked at her. "You can't trust an addict."

Wrong question. "But . . . you must know her."

"She's lied to me before." Another mile passed before he spoke. "I don't think she did it, but I don't know. Ten years ago, no way she'd do something like this, or lie to me. Now? I don't know."

She used the reflection on the windshield from the setting sun to study him covertly. Carved from granite would indicate rigidity, immovability, a hardness meant to be admired or appreciated, but the skin and muscles of Lucas's face were too taut for that. Instead, they looked like they'd been schooled into immobility. That was the difference. He still felt the pain and sorrow he saw on a near daily basis, but he'd taught himself to show no emotion. Maybe the renovation project would give him the break he needed, a chance to work on something tangible, with visible progress, to combat the ugliness in the world with a bit of beauty.

They pulled into the home-improvement superstore's parking lot. He eased his long legs out of the truck immediately, but she rummaged through her purse to make sure she had her tablet, only to find him at her door. He opened it, then offered his hand to help her out.

She blinked, then set her hand in his. "Thank you," she said, and slid to the ground. Her hand stayed in his for a very brief moment, rough and warm and shockingly possessive, providing the right amount of support to help her keep her balance as she got out of the big truck. There was nothing tentative about this man. He knew exactly who he was, where he belonged, what he was about.

She knew none of those things about herself, but maybe some of his purpose would rub off on her in the next few weeks. Literally. Tonight, after dinner.

He stayed close as they crossed the parking lot, whether out of a totally unexpected chivalry or training, she didn't know. But a delicate, potent trill of desire shivered through her as his big body moved beside her, his hand at the small of her back, his shoulders blocking the last vestiges of the setting sun.

They walked through the sliding doors. He steered her down the main aisle, through the lighting fixtures, and back to the cabinets department. She pulled out her tablet and woke it up, then logged into the store's free Wi-Fi.

"I went out to Brookhaven and looked at the two kitchens Marissa renovated out there. She did a nice job of keeping the house's original ambiance while integrating all the modern conveniences. Then I browsed through Pinterest and other sites, getting a feel for what's possible."

He bent over her shoulder, studying the pictures as she swiped through them. "No one's trying to modernize the 1970s," he noted.

"Not yet, anyway. Do you want a retro feel, one that plays off the house's original kitchen, or do you want something new and modern? You could remove the cabinets, but I'd keep them because they've got those gorgeous beadboard doors and I'd refinish them, or even paint them. Cream would be perfect. That would make the room feel so much bigger and brighter, regardless of what color you painted the walls. Updating the hardware would add visual interest, and save some money. I'd pick something in a bright brass or gold, because that room gets so much gorgeous light. I'd do a jade paint, or even a sage. A soft green would flow beautifully into the living room. Tiling the backsplash from the cabinets to the counters would make it much easier to clean. If we went with a more muted paint, we could choose a complementary tile color and insert bright accent pieces . . ."

Her voice trailed off because he hadn't said a word. The silence stretching between them allowed for a flush to climb into her cheeks. This wasn't her house. As much as she loved the house, with its polished walnut floors and clever little shelves, it was Lucas's house, not hers. "I'm sorry," she said gently. "I was just thinking out loud."

"That's why I invited you along," he said. "Left to my own devices, I'd paint it white, put in white appliances, and go with basic oak cabinets."

"That would look all right, too," she said.

He quirked an eyebrow and one corner of his mouth. "You blush when you lie, too."

"I told you I blush all the time," she retorted.

"And now I believe you."

"I'm no design expert, but white will wash all the warmth out of the room," she said. "That said, it's probably the most generic solution, if you want to keep renting the house."

"No possibility of offending a prospective tenant," he said.

"But no character," she finished.

He gestured vaguely at the picture on her phone. "Do what you think best suits the house. I'm going to look at PVC." He hooked a thumb over his shoulder in the direction of the actual plumbing.

She wandered into the paint section and got a few small containers, a pale yellow, a sage green, and a blue the shade of the prairie sky in winter. Then she wandered into the fixtures aisle and chose three different handles for the cabinets. Her tasks completed, she went into the plumbing section to look for Lucas, but he was nowhere in sight, so she fell back on her default time killer. She found the books section and started browsing.

The store had a nice supply of gardening books geared to South Dakota's extreme climate shifts. Temperatures routinely dropped to below zero for weeks at a stretch in the winter, and topped out around a hundred in the summer. "Humid subcontinental climate," she muttered to herself.

A book focused specifically on roses caught her eye. Remembering the recalcitrant Country Dancers, she picked it up and started paging through it. Twenty minutes later Lucas rounded the corner, sheets of paper flapping from his hand. "Somehow I knew I'd find you here," he said when he saw her sitting on the floor, the book open on her lap, her tablet beside her. "That took longer than I thought it would."

"No worries," she said absently, then looked up at him. She intended for her gaze to go from the open book to his face, but somehow the trip up took longer than she planned. He had such long legs, the denim of his jeans fitting snugly to his thighs. They rode low on his hips, seemingly held there by his hands. His gray T-shirt made his brown hair glint in the lights, and soft strands curled against his collar. He needed a trim, she thought, but oh, how she'd regret losing any of that thick soft hair. It felt like silk against the sensitive inner flesh of her fingers while she kissed him.

Heat crackled between them before he blinked and shut it down. "What's that?"

Not trusting her voice, she held it up so he could see the cover.

"I'm pretty sure Gran had that one," he said.

"Really? She had books?"

"She had hundreds. I figured with a librarian moving in I needed to clear the shelves. Her books are all in boxes in the basement," he said. "We can look through them later."

"I thought it was strange she didn't have any books in her house, with all those shelves," Alana said from her seated position. "But you don't have to put books on shelves."

"She loved books," Lucas said bluntly. "Books and her house and roses and her kids and grandkids, and Walkers Ford."

"I can tell," Alana said quietly. "It's in every room in that house."

"Get what you need?"

"I grabbed a few paint samples. We can test them out on the wall to see how they look in the natural light. I also got these," she said, and held out the three door pulls she'd chosen. "Do you hate any of them?"

Three seconds to scan the options. "No."

"We'll take them home and try them out once you paint the cabinets. You can return the ones that don't work."

He looked at her. "This isn't a one-and-done trip, is it?"

"It can be," she hedged. "White paint. White appliances."

"No character." He gave a resigned little grunt. "I'll pay at the register. We pick up the plumbing after we pay."

He held out his hand and effortlessly pulled her to her feet. It was a talent of his, guiding people from one position to another, from one frame of mind to another, and his touch was no less potent when it happened under horrid fluorescent lighting in a home-improvement superstore than it was in her kitchen.

Flustered to the point of blushing, she set the book back on the rack, then walked with him through the checkout and back to the truck. He drove through the parking lot to the sheltered overhang. While they waited for the handcart loaded with plumbing supplies, he stared straight out the windshield.

"It doesn't matter why, but that blush gets me every time," he said.

The words were largely emotionless but slightly puzzled, as if his reaction surprised him. She turned to look at him.

He looked at her, his face still devoid of expression, but heat simmered in his brown eyes, now the color of melted dark chocolate.

"Oh," she said.

The clang and bump of the handcart across the threshold splintered the tension into shards. Bill of lading in hand, Lucas opened his door and got out, leaving her to take a deep breath to slow her racing pulse. She'd expected the longing to lessen, that the tension and nerves and eagerness and anticipation leading up to their first sexual encounter would dissipate after the first time. Familiarity bred contempt, or at least comfortable awareness.

It hadn't, a fact that rewired her understanding of desire. Now she knew. She knew the hard planes of his naked torso, knew how her body quivered around his as he slid inside her, knew that maddening, compelling, sparking arousal that built with each stroke. Visceral heat flashed like a strobe light in her breasts, deep in her sex.

The tailgate clanged shut, then Lucas's door opened with a "thanks" called to the retreating employee. "Dinner?"

"Yes, please," she said automatically.

"Preferences?"

She liked that he asked. "The Copper Rock?" she offered. The classic American menu offered burgers, sandwiches, and steaks as well as a nice wine list and a large selection of beers. The brick walls and casual atmosphere fostered a relaxed meal.

He shifted into drive and headed into the Brookings historic district. They found a spot on the street. With the sun down, the air held a distinct chill, and she wrapped her sweater more tightly around her body as they stepped onto the sidewalk.

"Hold on," he said, opened his door again, and reached into the truck's backseat. He came back out with a fleece-lined jacket and held it open for her.

"We're twenty feet from the door," she said with a smile.

"You might get cold inside," he said, and gave the jacket a gentle shake.

The soft fabric smelled like him, like male skin and sweat and the greening grass of South Dakota's spring. She felt mildly ridiculous, but slipped her arms into the sleeves anyway. The warmth engulfed her as they crossed the sidewalk. He opened the door and let her walk through first. The host seated them in a quiet booth away from the bar, leaving them with the menus and a promise that a server would be with them shortly.

She opened the menu and shrugged out of the jacket, but draped it across her legs for the warmth as she considered the offerings. Dating conventions suggested she get a salad, but she'd given most of her lunch to Cody. Decision made, she closed her menu.

"That was fast," he commented.

"I've eaten here a couple of times on dates," she said.

His head came up. "Dates?"

Her mother's wince flashed in her brain, but she held her head high. "Dates. You find that surprising?"

"No," he said.

"It's not surprising I said it."

"It's honest," he said. "No one seriously, though."

"It didn't feel right," she said. "I'm not staying."

"That wouldn't matter to most men," Lucas said easily.

"It matters to me. It wouldn't be fair for me to date them knowing I'm leaving at the end of the contract. I don't want to hurt anyone's feelings."

"And yet here you are with me."

Their server showed up with glasses of water. "Are you ready to order?"

"I'd like the pulled pork sandwich, with fries," Alana said.

"The Copper Rock burger with Swiss," Lucas said, then flicked a glance at Alana. "Wine?"

"Beer, actually. Goes better with the pork."

Lucas added a beer to that order. After collecting their menus, the server left, leaving Alana with a choice. If she wanted to go back to Chicago different, she needed to have this conversation.

"Here I am with you," she said. She couldn't tell if that amused him, offended him, or didn't matter at all.

"What keeps you so busy in your off-hours?"

"Good question. I was a research analyst for the Wentworth Foundation."

"Which is . . ."

"It's a think tank, a nonprofit economic research foundation focusing on global initiatives," she said, reciting the tagline from the website.

One eyebrow lifted. "In English?"

"The policy analysts need research to write their papers. I compile policy papers, research, legislation, newspaper and magazine articles, that kind of thing."

"How did you end up doing that?"

Another little smile. "My stepfather is Peter Harrison Wentworth."

"The name's familiar," he said as the server set their drinks on the table.

"The former senator."

His eyebrows lifted over the glass of beer. "No kidding."

"No kidding. He decided not to run for reelection after he was diagnosed with Parkinson's, but he wanted to stay involved in public policy. His choices were become a lobbyist, which he found personally abhorrent, or do something like this."

"Why won't you go back to work there?"

"I could," she said. "I probably will."

"Does this have something to do with the mistake?"

"It has everything to do with the mistake," she said, then changed the subject. "What brought you from Denver to Walkers Ford?"

His expression closed off again. "A mistake of my own."

"Personal or professional?"

"Both."

She sipped her beer. "We don't have to talk about it."

He shrugged, as if making mistakes was no big deal. "I was on the DEA task force in Denver. My ex-wife wanted a husband who was there, emotionally and physically. When the job in Walkers Ford opened up, we moved here. I thought a slower pace of life would give us a chance to work on our marriage, but all it did was wedge dynamite in the fault lines and blow it apart. She filed for divorce eight months later."

The frank assessment made her blink. "I'm sorry."

He swallowed another mouthful of beer. "So was I."

"How long have you been divorced?"

"Two years. Your turn. Tell me about the mistake."

How to characterize David? "He started as a program manager for the foundation. It's a part-time position that runs for a specific duration and gives people exposure to the behind-the-scenes workings of a foundation, and a chance to network. He was bright, ambitious, outgoing, with a real gift for connecting with people. He wanted to run for office, make a difference. The Senator knows everyone, and I mean everyone, in Washington and appreciates ambition, so when David came on board, they got on like a house on fire. Suddenly he was at the office full-time, going to meetings with the Senator, coming over for dinner for strategy sessions. I liked him. He was charming. Easy to be with. He always had something to say.

"I'm not sure how we started dating. I think I needed a plus one for a banquet or something, and they're not my favorite way to spend an evening. He made them easier. After that we just . . . I don't know. We'd get dinner, or see a play on the weekends. He was just there." At work, at home, in her bed.

"What happened?"

Alana got out her phone, logged in to the restaurant's wireless, and went to YouTube. "That's my sister's engagement," she said, and offered the phone to Lucas.

His dark hair gleamed in the low light as he watched
Freddie's big moment play out on a stage at Wembley Stadium in London. Toby's band had just finished the last
encore when he called Freddie out onstage. She wore fitted
jeans, a pair of Chanel ballet flats so old they were clearly
vintage, and a button-down shirt Alana remembered from
high school, and she was clearly, beautifully stunned. Flashbulbs were going off all over the stadium as Toby went down
on one knee, opened a ring box, and asked Freddie to marry
him. According to the tabloids, people two miles away could
hear the cheer that went up when she said *yes*.

"Freddie Wentworth is your sister?" Lucas said. "You
never said anything."

"I'm a little fanatical about her privacy, and my own."
Alana retrieved her phone. "And this was my proposal."

The scene was vastly different, a political fund-raiser
given in Chicago for a presidential candidate on the campaign trail. The Senator and her mother had arranged for
Paul Simon to play. At the end of the set, David, who was
acting as the emcee for the night, called her up onstage.
Mildly bewildered, she went, but the other shoe dropped
only after she was in the spotlight. The rest of it seemed to
happen in slow motion. She didn't need to see the video to
know what was happening. The memory was burned in her
brain, and the reaction of anyone watching spelled out the
whole humiliating incident, moment by moment.

On screen, David proposed.

Lucas's eyebrows lifted slightly.

In the video, Alana shook her head frantically.

Lucas winced.

Silence fell in the room. A nervous laugh and some
coughing before the singer, in an act of generosity Alana
would remember for the rest of her life, said something that
deflected the audience's attention, causing the lighting person to switch the spotlight back to him.

"Ouch," Lucas said.

Alana remembered the moments backstage not with her brain but with her body. The way she'd been shaking, fury and humiliation burning David's cheeks and eyes. Her mother's utter disbelief. Her own fury rising when she realized her mother and David had cooked it up together.

The next day the librarian LISTSERV she belonged to contained a post about the contract job in Walkers Ford. Her family had fought her departure, but she'd stood her ground.

"I'll quit," she'd said. "I can either keep working for you from Walkers Ford, or I will quit and do this on my own."

"You don't know what you want," her mother had said impatiently. "You never have, so don't be ridiculous. David is perfectly suited for you."

In that moment, one single thought had surfaced in her brain. She'd *never* known what she wanted. That had to change. Now. She'd just chosen to set her own desires aside for the greater good of the family; the foundation; in some ways, the world. But knowing her mother thought she wanted, or deserved, a pale substitute of Freddie's international moment burned like acid in her throat.

"I didn't mean to humiliate him," Alana said hastily. "I really didn't. But I wasn't ready for that. We'd been dating for a few months, and I had a good time with him, but I had no idea he was thinking about getting married. I certainly wasn't thinking about getting married."

"I got that, yeah," Lucas said.

She smiled at his deadpan humor. But with the initial burst of enthusiasm and defiance behind her, she'd slipped back into her old routine. She loved the library work, spent her nights doing Freddie's research, and never really cut the velvet ribbons tying her to the foundation, to her old life.

Until she realized that if she didn't go after Lucas, she'd go back to Chicago exactly the same as she was when she left. Decisions weren't easy, or her strong suit. She just followed where Freddie led, and for the most part, she was happy to do that. She had the kind of life people dreamed of having, making a difference on a large scale, jet-setting around the world, rubbing shoulders with rock stars and billionaires and policy makers at every level.

So why did she feel so ridiculously happy sitting across from Lucas at a restaurant in Brookings, South Dakota, discussing kitchen renovation plans?

Don't think about that. You're going home. You said you were going home. You've made commitments there. You can't leave your family. Freddie depends on you, and the work matters. You don't really have a reason to stay.

"So that's my bad breakup," Alana said briskly, retrieving her phone. The memory didn't just sting. It burned. "He proposed. I said no. My mother was so disappointed."

Lucas's brow furrowed. "You're not your sister. I don't know you all that well, but you don't seem like the type to want a big production for anything that intimate."

She blinked, because if he'd figured that out, he knew her better than most of her family. "After that, all I knew was that I needed to do something different. Be different. I needed time to regroup."

"Walkers Ford, the halfway house for people needing a second start," he said, startling a laugh out of her. "I hope it goes better for you than it did for me."

Time to change the subject. "How long will it take to renovate the kitchen?"

"A few weeks. I can move the fridge into the living room, but there's nowhere else wired for the stove unless I move it into the garage."

"So no cooking, unless I microwave and use paper plates. I'm leaving in a few days anyway."

"I can wait. This is going to be a hell of a mess."

The corners of her mouth lifted. "No, if you're okay with it, I'm okay with it. It's your house, after all."

"But you're living in my house."

Such simple words, with so many nuances to them. She did live in his house. She slept in his bed, and Walkers Ford was his town. Mr. Walker might own the bank, and Dave Miller might be the school superintendent, and a husband-and-wife team might be the doctor-pharmacy team, but this was Lucas Ridgeway's town. He protected the residents, their property, their sense of safety.

A delicious shiver of possession danced up her spine. She was accustomed to belonging somewhere. She'd always belonged to the Wentworth family, but always by accident. Born to her mother and father, part of the package when her mother married the Senator, part of the team at the foundation. But no one possessed her. No one reached out and claimed her. Of course in the twenty-first century, women didn't want to be claimed. They built careers, made their own money, raised children on their own, planned for their own retirement.

Given a little time, she could probably come up with a less politically correct ambition, but she really, really wanted to belong somewhere, to someone. Because there was a difference between being part of a package deal, and belonging.

"I like being in your house," she said.

His gaze somehow both sharpened and heated. "Keep going."

"I'd like to be in your bed."

"I can arrange that."

6

LIBRARIANS KEPT SECRETS. They heard odd stories, got requests that ranged from reasonable to wildly inappropriate, and like cops, they learned not to bat an eyelash. But keeping the arousal humming under her skin from heating into a radiant aura visible in the spring darkness took every bit of her professional demeanor.

And then some.

Lucas backed into her driveway. "I'll unload this," he said as he shifted into park in front of the single detached garage.

"I'll help," she said.

"Go inside," he said, his brusque tone refusing her offer of help.

The interior light faded, leaving them in darkness. Moonlight washed the planes of his face in pale light. Her gaze skipped from his eyes, shadowed in darkness, to his mouth. Trusting the darkness to hide them from the neighbors, she reached out and brushed her fingertips over his full lips.

"I have something in mind for that mouth," she said.

She felt more than saw the sudden tension in his body, then his lips parted ever so slightly, and his exhalation drifted over her fingertips. "Go inside," he said against her fingertips, this time lower, rougher. A completely different meaning.

She slid out of the truck, crossing paths with Lucas in front of the truck as he went to open the garage. Duke trotted out of the screened-in porch and was waiting for her at the kitchen door, his front paws on the top step, his tail wagging. She let him in and gave him a dog biscuit. He settled under the kitchen table.

She walked down the hall, into the bedroom, where she set her glasses on the nightstand and draped her sweater over the end of the spindle bed. There was no point in emphasizing the cliché. Her T-shirt and jeans weren't sexy, but they weren't unattractive, either. For a long moment she debated where to stand, or sit, the sounds of Lucas unloading the truck, faint but purposeful. But when the tailgate clanged shut, she stripped back the chenille spread and top sheet, then scrambled onto the bed and sat in the middle, cross-legged. It was almost a relief not to have to figure out what someone else wanted. This was about what she wanted.

And Lucas didn't seem to object to giving it to her. Lucas Ridgeway had lied to her. He'd said he wasn't going to get hurt by their secret affair, but she wasn't so sure.

His sneakers didn't make much noise against the floors, but she could hear him approaching. He appeared in the doorway, all broad shoulders and lean hips in his T-shirt and jeans. She liked that he didn't change, that he didn't pretend to be anything other than what he was. He was unlike most of the other men of her acquaintance, who needed to establish who they were through words. They used volume, both sound and content, to create an outline of a man. They used degrees, dropped names, touched on all the high points—education, travel, connections, work—to paint a desirable picture. Lucas Ridgeway just was.

Her mouth went dry at the memory of his hard-muscled torso.

He didn't close the door or speak as he took two steps into the room, put one knee onto the bed, then bore her back onto the mattress. It was a clean, unconscious move. Knee on the bed, left hand bracing his weight, his right arm coming around behind her shoulders to control her descent. She ended up flat on her back with him lying half on top of her, his knee sliding between hers. She inhaled breathily, and good thing, because when his mouth came down on top of hers, she forgot all about breathing.

He kissed her, lips soft but demanding as they slid against hers. Automatically she opened her mouth, but rather than his tongue she felt a smile against her lips. "Patience is a virtue," he murmured, giving her vibrations when she wanted slick heat.

"I don't feel very virtuous at the moment," she said.

"This is a problem?"

"It's . . ." He used the edge of his teeth along her jaw to the soft spot just under her ear. "It's . . . different."

"That was the goal, right? To be different."

Never before in her life had a man explored the sensitive skin below her ear so thoroughly. She made a little noise, part desire, part assent, part plea, and felt an answering rumble of a chuckle deep in his chest.

"You said you had something in mind for my mouth."

Heat swept through her, shock at her bold words blending with the arousal at hearing them repeated back to her. She arched under him. "This is good," she said. "This is what I had in mind."

Another chuckle. He straddled her and braced his weight on elbows and knees, trapping her without giving her the delicious pressure of his weight against her. He nipped at her earlobe, breathed a heated exhalation against her ear, then kissed his way back to her mouth.

This time his tongue rubbed against hers. She writhed under him, lifting until her breasts, then hips, brushed his hard torso, then subsided back against the bed. His mouth left hers to trace over her chin and down her arched throat to the hollow between her collarbones. Alana wrapped her fingers around his upper arms and dug in her nails as he kissed the skin not covered by the neck of her T-shirt, nuzzling it aside. Desperate for his touch, she reached down and peeled off her shirt. Without further prompting, he kissed and licked his way to the tops of her breasts, careful to lavish attention on exposed skin only.

The concept of a tease clarified in her mind. With a low moan she undulated under him as that wickedly talented mouth skipped over the front clasp of her bra to work over her ribs, then her stomach, exposed above the waistband of her jeans.

He lifted again, dropping another kiss on her mouth, and this time it was pure, hot desire. Slick and hot and wet, nearly carnal in its intensity. She slid her hands under his T-shirt and dug her fingernails into the ridge of muscle on either side of his spine.

"Easy," he growled.

"Impossible," she gasped in return.

His hair tumbled forward, tangling with his eyelashes as he surveyed her. "Take these down," he said, using his chin to edge her bra straps toward her shoulders.

She removed her nails from his back and put her fingers to the front clasp.

"No," he said. "Just the straps."

Sensation shivered over her skin as she trailed her fingers along the upper curves of her breasts to the straps and urged them off her shoulders. The fabric covering her breasts loosened slightly. Lucas kissed his way down the memory of the bra strap, using his rough chin to push the cup to its limits. His scruff gently abraded her skin, a shocking contrast to the wet heat of his mouth. She moaned.

The plea implicit in the sound didn't stop him from doing the same thing on the opposite side. She gripped his arms and trembled under him, her nipples peaked against her silk bra.

"Now," he said.

Under his heavy-lidded gaze, she unfastened the clasp and drew the thin silk to the side, revealing the tight tips. When he bent and took one between his teeth to lave it with his tongue, she looped her leg around his and tried to pull him down. He laughed at her efforts and moved to the other breast. Both tips were red, swollen, and wet by the time he moved down her breastbone and over her belly.

She watched him, idling her fingers through his hair.

"Now these," he said with a nod at her jeans.

She unbuckled her belt, opened the fly, and shimmied both denim and silk down to the tops of her thighs, but his legs straddled hers, preventing her from getting them all the way off. He took in her exposed hip bones and the top of her mound, then bent to her mound and slid his tongue into the soft folds. Intentionally or not, he grazed her clit and she quivered under him. Then he levered back up and kissed her mouth. She tasted herself on his tongue, and slid her fingers into his hair to grip the back of his head and hold his mouth to hers.

"Remember what I said about patience?" he asked.

The sound she made was positively carnal and held an edge of desperation. That was the only explanation for the way she pushed, *pushed* at his head to force him back down her body. He took his time, let her feel the strength of him at her command as he once again retraced his path along jaw, throat, collarbone, sensitive nipples, belly. Taking his weight on one elbow, he tugged her jeans down far enough for her to kick them off and spread her legs.

"No more teasing," she said.

He bent and circled her clit with his tongue, the movement steady and firm. He didn't rush her to climax, made her wait as the pleasure built and built, tight and hot and undeniable. Her fist tightened in his hair as release crashed through her.

She subsided into the bed, her muscles trembling with

aftershocks as Lucas opened her nightstand, sheathed himself. Without preamble he slid into her, and she cried out as his thick shaft stroked over hypersensitive nerves and set off another wave of need. She wound her arms over his shoulder blades and her legs around the backs of his thighs as he withdrew and plunged in again. It was hard and fast and a little rough, each thrust forcing a hot little cry from her throat. To her utter shock, another climax detonated deep inside. As her nails dug into Lucas's spine, he growled, plunged deep, and shuddered as he came.

He eased down against her, sweat slicking the contact between their bodies. "You okay?" he rumbled.

"Fine," she said, then cleared her throat, said it again, and added, "Why?"

"I was pretty rough at the end."

"I liked it," she pointed out.

"Just checking."

"You didn't mind that I . . . wanted that?"

He sat back on his heels, disengaging their bodies and establishing some distance in one movement. "I found it incredibly hot that you not only wanted that, but told me you wanted it."

A little smile ghosted across her lips. "Just checking," she said.

Aside from his opened jeans, he was still dressed, so cleaning up was a simple process. She tugged her bra off and pulled up the sheet and spread to ward off the evening chill.

"I'll start tear-out this weekend," he said. "I'll start in the basement, replacing the plumbing."

"All right," she said. "I dropped Cody off at home earlier today. He's pretty isolated out there."

His head came up. "I know you mean well, but take it easy with Cody, okay?"

"I don't know what you mean."

"He's a kid on the poverty line, with no real future, and

he knows it. Just get him through the community service. That's all you can do right now."

"You're the one who sent him to the library," she pointed out. "You must have thought the experience would be good for him."

"I thought it was the least-risky place to send a kid caught stealing. Do him a favor and don't get too involved."

He strode down the hallway. Moments later she heard him click for Duke, then the dog's nails on the linoleum and the screen door closing.

"Like you?" she said.

HE WAS IN over his head.

Unlike many of his law-enforcement counterparts who linked their egos and professional identities, Lucas was perfectly willing to admit when a situation was spinning out beyond his control. He was so in over his head. On the surface, everything was perfect. She was beautiful, intelligent, a slow, fierce burn in bed, and didn't want so much as a date, let alone a commitment.

They'd hired her temporarily while they conducted a search for a new librarian. She'd thrown herself at a problem without hesitation, but it was nothing more than academic, a quest to get results. Building renovated, computers upgraded, future secured. He knew the type, had worked with them in Denver. He'd married one, a person who came through with plans and programs and never stopped to count the human cost. His wife had left Walkers Ford for exactly that reason. It was too personal, too intimate, too much history and connection to stand.

Life was breaking free again, free from the frozen earth of winter, free from the blizzards and howling wind and the long, dark nights.

There was one person in town he could count on to compartmentalize life. He poured the remainder of his pot of coffee into an insulated travel mug, pulled on his ball cap, clicked for Duke, and headed for the Blazer. The drive didn't take long, just past Main Street into the newer subdivision, and then he was in his uncle's driveway.

He knocked on the door and found his uncle up and dressed for the day. Regulation haircut, belt and shoes polished, khakis pressed, shirt tucked in. "Lucas, my boy," he said amiably. "What brings you by?"

"I need to make a run into Brookings. Want to come along?" he said.

"Is this family business or police business?"

"Police," Lucas said.

The old man's shoulders squared up. "Let me get my jacket," he said.

Ten minutes later they were on their way out of town. "What's going on?"

Lucas explained about the break-in at Gunther's house. "You've got a contact at the Brookings PD who knows something about the drugs?"

"I want to hit the pawn shops, see if anyone's pawned the ring."

Silence from the seat next to him.

"It was his wife's," Lucas said.

"And this is the best use of your time today."

"It's one way I'm going to use my time today," Lucas said. "You talked to Tanya lately?"

Nelson flexed his hands on his thighs, the knuckles swollen and angry. Crippling rheumatoid arthritis had forced him to retire before his time. "No. I told her the last time she relapsed, we were done."

"I saw her a couple of days ago," Lucas said.

Nelson, no fool, snorted. "She's what, eight-tenths of a mile from Gunther's place? That was the right place to start."

"She looked okay," Lucas said, even though it wasn't true.

"She let you into the house?"

Lucas was silent.

Nelson shook his head. "Weak," he said.

Lucas wasn't sure if Nelson's flat summary was directed at him for not forcing his way into Tanya's cabin, or at Tanya for becoming an addict. Or both. "She says she didn't do it."

"Of course she says that. Two most frequently heard phrases from my daughter. *I didn't do it. It wasn't my fault.*" He looked out the window at the rippling prairie grass, cross-hatching in the wind. "That girl never did learn to take responsibility for her choices."

"I went to the Burtons, too."

"Hmm. Which one?"

"I arrested Cody for shoplifting a few weeks ago. He's doing community service at the library."

"Following in his brother's footsteps, I assume," Nelson mused. "I put him away three, no four years ago, when he broke into the pharmacy."

Twenty-two years old and a felony conviction that would stay with him for the rest of his life. "He got out a few weeks ago. I called his parole officer. He's checked in regularly and is looking for a job."

"Where's he living?"

"At home."

With Cody, and the three younger siblings, and the mother, working the second shift at J&H.

"That's a lost cause," his uncle said finally.

"I don't know about that," he said. "Colt had been in and out of juvie by the time he was Cody's age. So far Cody has stayed off my radar."

"Maybe he's just better at hiding what he's doing."

Lucas thought of Tanya, how well she'd hidden her drug use, right up until a random drug test at the academy turned up positive for painkillers. He could follow Nelson's train of thought. If Tanya could hide drug use from her father, the chief of police, and from Lucas, who, by that time, was rolling onto the DEA task force in Denver, then Cody Burton could hide whatever he was doing from an overworked mother.

Or maybe Cody Burton felt like he didn't have any other option.

They pulled into the first pawn shop's parking lot. Duke's ears swiveled forward alertly, but he made no move to jump out of the truck when Nelson got out and followed Lucas into the shop. The place was brightly lit, jewelry, guns, and electronics displayed in cases and in locked cabinets.

The guy behind the counter wore a navy blue polo with the shop's logo stitched on the chest and a wary expression. He lifted his eyebrows in greeting. "Morning, officers," he said.

Lucas identified himself as he pulled out an enlarged picture of Gunther's wife's hand. "Anything like this come in recently?"

The clerk took the picture and studied the ring. Even enlarged it was difficult to see the details, the diamond chips that disappeared into the white gold. "No," he said finally, and offered the page back across the counter. "I'm not sure we'd even take something like that on pawn. It's small. People today want bling. Flashy."

"Keep it," Lucas said as he wrote his cell phone number on the bottom of the page. "If you get something like that in, call me."

"You got it," the clerk said, "but this ring isn't worth the cost of gas to drive down here from Walkers Ford."

"It is to the man whose wife wore it for sixty-two years."

The clerk shrugged, apparently unimpressed by a six-decade marriage.

They repeated the same conversation with only minor variations at three other pawn shops, then drove through for a fast-food lunch, eaten in the truck on the way back to Walkers Ford. Lucas shared half his French fries with Duke, still sitting alertly in the backseat.

"You're not supposed to reward K-9 animals with food," Nelson muttered.

This was true. The dogs were rewarded with play for a job well-done, not treats. "He's not working. He's retired," Lucas said. "Do you have any idea what Gran did to get the roses along the east side of the house to bloom? The stalks come up every year, but the buds don't bloom."

"No idea. Why?"

"Alana's been asking about them. I didn't pay attention while Gran was alive, and I packed her books away when Alana moved in. I thought you'd know."

"Nope. What do you think about spending the money to fix up the library?"

There was no love lost between Nelson and Mitch Turner. Lucas knew Nelson would rather run naked through the town square than call the mayor and ask about the budget. "I think we've got a shrinking tax base and a growing crime problem," Lucas said. "Alana's updating the proposal."

"Whatever it is, it's too much," he said, and looked around Lucas's aging truck.

Lucas didn't argue with him. He drove the Blazer because he spent less time out on patrol than his officers did, but they needed a new vehicle, upgrades to the computers and cameras in the existing cars, and that was just the top of his list.

"I hear you've been spending time with the librarian."

"You know about the plumbing in that house," Lucas said. "The kitchen's a liability. I'm going to renovate before the next tenant moves in. She's doing me a favor letting me work on the house while she's still in it."

Nelson just gave him a look. "That's one mistake you can't afford to make."

His uncle's voice was oddly gentle under the gruff. "There's no mistake to be made," Lucas said.

"She's a consultant," he said. The way he said it equated the word *consultant* with *vulture*.

"I know that."

"Even if she was hired, she's not local. She doesn't know the community like you do."

Nelson underestimated Alana's ability to dig out, assimilate, and use information. She didn't know Walkers Ford like he did, but that wasn't necessarily a bad thing. For better or for worse, she wasn't paying attention to the way things were done, the habits and silos they all occupied. She saw the community in a completely different way, an analytical way that left no room for emotions, feelings, networks.

"She's leaving," Lucas said.

That was indisputable fact. She had a job to go back to, in a city famous for art, music, and theater. Family. Work that spanned the globe. He shifted uncomfortably in his seat, glad to see the exit for Walkers Ford. "I'm not making a mistake."

You are, he thought unsentimentally. *You're making a mistake. You know it, and you're going to do it anyway. Because knowing something's doomed to fail never stopped you from trying. You're a professional at tilting at windmills. Because you like jousting.*

The thought made him laugh. Nelson and Duke both looked at him curiously, but he didn't explain.

"This was a waste of time," Nelson said.

"Grammie died wishing she had her engagement ring back."

"You always were soft. You can't find every lost puppy or engagement ring."

He knew very well what he couldn't do, but Nelson's cynicism was getting on his nerves. "Little things matter," he said when he pulled into his uncle's driveway. "You need to go see Tanya."

"Why?"

"Because she needs you. She needs her father."

"She's twenty-seven years old and she's got nothing to show for the air she breathes. No degree. No badge. No real job. All she's done with her life is waste every chance she's ever been given, and she's had too many chances. I don't know what she needs, but it's not a father."

"Dad doesn't agree with any of my choices," Lucas said, "but I still talk to him."

"You're a man. You take responsibility, do a hard job not many people can do. All she has to do is quit using and get a job. That's not too much to ask."

Is that all it took to deserve the air he breathed? Because it didn't feel like enough. "Nelson," Lucas said.

"She's an addict and a user. She's the cancer that happens when the schools and the library fails. That's why you have a job. Someone has to cut out the cancer." Nelson shot him a glare. "You learned your lesson in Denver. We can't afford for you to forget."

Lucas felt his jaw tighten. "I haven't forgotten," he said.

"Good. Do your job. Forget about the things you can't control."

Back ramrod straight, Nelson slammed the door closed and stalked up to his front door. Lucas backed out of the driveway.

7

ALANA'S PHONE RANG while she and Mrs. Battle were
merging onto I29, headed for the eye doctor in Brookings. She answered it with the hands-free button on the steering wheel.

"Hi, Freddie," she said.

"Why do you sound like you're at the bottom of a big
tin can?"

So much for German engineering. "I'm in my car, with
Mrs. Battle. We're on our way to a doctor's appointment."

"I hope everything's all right," Freddie said, her voice
shifting smoothly from imperious sister to solicitous spokes-
woman for the Wentworth Foundation.

"I'm fine," Mrs. Battle said. "Just getting old. Your sister's driving me to the eye doctor."

"I can call back another time," Freddie said, which was
thoughtful, but doubtful.

"Do you mind?" Alana asked Mrs. Battle.

"Not at all."

"Is this wedding stuff or work stuff?" Alana asked.

"A little of both. I need you to dig around and get me
everything you can about the situation in Andhra Pradesh.

I'm getting a very pretty, whitewashed picture from the undersecretary to the junior minister, and you know how much I hate that."

"Got it," Alana said.

"Any word back from the wedding locations?"

"Nothing yet, but I only sent the e-mails six hours ago. Patience, Freddie."

"I don't have time to be patient," her sister said rather nonsensically. "Toby's planning tour dates for next summer."

"I asked about April and early May," Alana said.

"Oh. Good. All right. That's all I needed. Drive safely. I hope you get good news, Mrs. Battle."

"I'm going to have to get a shot in my eye every three months," Mrs. Battle said. "That's the good news."

"Well, you've got a positive attitude," Freddie replied.

"That I do."

After she hung up, Mrs. Battle looked at Alana.

"I think sometimes she calls just to hear my voice," Alana said apologetically.

"That doesn't surprise me," Mrs. Battle replied. "I used to call my sister for exactly the same reason. What are you doing here?"

Funny, Lucas asked the same question every other time they talked. "The contract position came up at a time when I needed a break. I'm leaving at the end of the month, but before then, I want to get this proposal ready to go."

Mrs. Battle lifted her eyebrows at her. "Nelson Ridgeway was a hard man. He saw approaches like libraries and schools and social programs as doomed to failure."

"With all due respect to the former chief, he's wrong," Alana said. "Will you help me develop the proposal? What happens after that is outside my control. But I want to give Walkers Ford the best possible plan, so the new librarian has something to stand on when she tries to get the funding to go ahead."

Over the next forty minutes, they developed a plan of attack—who to include in the discussions, how to approach them, and when. "I think we should include Cody, too," Alana said.

"Are you sure about that?"

"He's bright, he's creative, and he's the town's future," Alana said. "Outside of his art classes, the school hasn't engaged him. We need to find something that does, and we have nothing to lose. It makes me think about the technology needs. Maybe we can get equipment that would support start-ups and seed entrepreneurial business."

"That would be tremendously helpful," Mrs. Battle said.

Alana remembered Mrs. Battle's kids spread out all across the country, the grandkids she rarely saw. "I don't think we can stop the people we love from leaving," she said quietly. "But I do think we can make it easier for them to stay, or to come back."

"To what?"

"Jobs where they work from home. Jobs they create. A well-educated workforce with a great work ethic is an entrepreneur's dream. There is no reason why someone from Walkers Ford can't be that entrepreneur."

"Not to be rude, but why do you care?"

Alana considered her words carefully. "Anything worth doing is worth doing well," she said. "It makes no difference whether the task is preparing materials for an international conference or proposing a major renovation to the Walkers Ford Public Library."

"That's a very vague answer, young lady."

"Mrs. Battle, I'm thirty years old." And I'm secretly sleeping with your chief of police, so I'm not a lady, either.

"And I'm seventy-seven, which makes you a *young lady* and me an *old lady*. Answer the question."

"I left Chicago under difficult circumstances," she said finally. "I would like to go home changed."

"No one comes to Walkers Ford to be different."

"I did. But," she said, thinking of Marissa and Adam, "this place seems to have a powerful effect on people."

They rode in silence for a few minutes. Then Alana said, "Nelson Ridgeway is Chief Ridgeway's . . . ?"

"Uncle. His father's brother. You're living in his mother's house."

"Oh. Why didn't he inherit it?"

Mrs. Battle smiled. "Lucas's grandmother thought it should go to Lucas. She thought he needed a place he could go to get away from his life in Denver. He loved coming there every summer, and she loved having him. I think she was trying to stop him from becoming like his uncle."

THEY WERE THE first appointment of the day at the eye doctor's. Alana waited outside until the exam was over. The doctor opened the door and invited her inside. "You're her granddaughter, right?"

"No, just a friend," she replied hastily. "I'm not sure I should be in there."

"She asked for you, so that's good enough for me," the doctor said.

Alana took careful notes while the doctor explained the aftercare instructions, then helped Mrs. Battle into her jacket and out to the waiting room. She made another appointment.

"We'll have to find someone to drive you down next time," she said lightly as she backed out of the parking lot.

"Don't you worry about that," Mrs. Battle said. "You've got plenty on your plate as it is."

She sounded exhausted. "I'm taking you home," Alana said. "There's no need for you to come in to work today. Cody and I can handle it."

"I think that's for the best," the elderly lady said. Both of her eyes were closed, including the one covered with gauze.

"I'll bring you some lunch."

"You don't need to do that."

"I know," Alana said, "but you know I can't eat the whole soup and sandwich from Gina's by myself."

She was fairly sure this wasn't what Freddie meant when she cautioned Alana against getting entangled, but entangled she was.

THE TOOLBOX IN one hand, Lucas used the other to open the door to the cellar. Alana ducked under his arm, flipped on the light switch, and walked down the stairs. Duke followed her down, his tail wagging at the prospect of a new place to explore. Lucas inhaled. No mold. The room was chilly, as the earth held on to the remains of the cold air, even as spring gained a hold aboveground.

He set down his toolbox by the pipe draining from the sink into the sewer, then headed for the main shut-off valve and switched off the water coming into the house.

"It's chilly down here," Alana commented, rubbing her arms. She wore jeans and a thin T-shirt again, this one printed in swirls of grays and blues.

"You don't have to hang around while I'm working," he said.

"I wanted to go through your grandmother's books. If you don't mind," she added hastily. "I'm curious to know what she did to get those roses to grow and bloom."

He gestured at the boxes neatly lining the wall. "Help yourself."

She pulled open the flaps of the box and began extracting them, studying them attentively before setting them aside. He turned off the water and drained the pipes, then applied a wrench to the aging joints. For a few minutes they worked in silence.

"How's Cody working out?"

"Fine," she said. "He's an interesting kid. He reads to the

kids at story time, but he doesn't use the library's books, which Mrs. Battle finds rather scandalous. He drags the easel over to the front window and draws them pictures as he talks. The kids are utterly entranced by him."

"That doesn't surprise me," Lucas said.

"Why not? These are all novels," she said and closed up the box.

"Cody probably does the bedtime routine for his little brothers. I doubt there's a book in the trailer."

"So he makes one," she mused. "It's not the story the kids like. It's the way he draws while they're watching. He's making magic, right there in front of them."

Lucas yanked free a length of copper pipe and dropped it to the floor with a clatter. She opened another box, then made an interested noise. "Found them," she said.

He focused on the pipes. After a few minutes of silence, he looked over to find her sitting on the floor, going through his grandmother's gardening books. The covers were beautifully drawn roses twining along the dust jacket, not the glossy pictures covering today's books.

"She wrote notes," Alana said.

The delight in her voice made him pause. "That's good?"

"Oh, yes. Marginalia. It's becoming a subject matter in its own right. The study of what a book's owner wrote tells you as much about their thought process when she was reading as the content of the book itself. You have the text, which is an insight into the writer's mind, then the notes, which are an insight into the reader's mind as she reads and reflects on what the writer wrote. I love marginalia."

"It's messy."

"One friend of mine would study marginalia in used textbooks. If the previous owner took good, legible notes, she'd buy that book rather than a clean copy."

He barked out a laugh, then turned to look at her. She sat on the floor, her back to the boxes, the book balanced on her knees. "Ethical cheating?"

"She considered it a strategy for success, but yes, I suppose so." She began reading. "Why roses?"

"What?"

"Why did your grandmother grow roses? It's not an ideal climate for them."

He went to work on another locked joint in the pipes. "She liked a challenge," he said finally. "Every year it was a battle between her and the roses, and the climate. Some years the heat or the wind won, but most years she did."

"She sounds tough."

"She was determined to make her part of the world more beautiful."

For a few more minutes they worked in silence. Alana removed gardening books and stacked them in a neat pile on top of a box, then quickly skimmed the contents of the rest of the boxes. She crossed the small space to stand next to him.

He gave an internal groan. "You found the photo albums."

"I did indeed," she said. "Is this you?"

He looked down at the picture of himself as a teenage boy. Shirtless, tanned, and wearing a pair of jeans with two inches of the elastic band of his boxers visible above the waistband of his jeans, he had one elbow braced on the roof of his car and the other on his hip. A smile split his face.

He hardly recognized the grinning, shaggy-haired boy in the picture. "That's me. Uncle Nelson and I had just got the car running. I was a couple of weeks away from going home, and the deal was if I got the car running, I could take it with me."

"Sounds like fun."

"I thought it was a sweet deal until I realized my dad and Uncle Nelson cooked up the plan to keep me from spending the summer parked on the county roads in the backseat of a girl's car," he said.

This time she laughed as she flicked him a glance. Her glasses were still perched on top of her head, holding her hair back from her face. "But did it work?"

"Until I got the car running," he said. "I had two weeks to go until I went home, and I made up for lost time in those two weeks."

"Anyone I know?" she asked without looking up.

Absolutely.

She turned another page. "It's none of my business."

"It was just high school parking," he said. "You know what it's like."

"I don't actually. I went to a girls' boarding school, then a women's college." She flashed him another smile, this one complete with the blush staining her cheeks.

Sometimes her innocence astonished him. Who blushed while talking about a high school rite of passage? "You've never been parking."

"Not with a boy, no," she said in a distracted little voice, her attention seemingly focused on the photo album.

His heart stopped in his chest. He felt like a bird flying solely on expectations then crashing into a freshly cleaned pane of glass. Because if she hadn't parked with a boy, then . . .

Heat soared into his cheekbones, prickled along the back of his neck.

She flicked him a glance, then laughed—*laughed*—at him. "Look who else can blush."

"Um . . . does that mean—?" he said.

"Yes," she replied. "I'm such a cliché," she said, then turned another page and pointed. "Who's this?"

Butter wouldn't melt in her mouth. He looked at the pretty blond girl on the page, her hair a tumbled mass of curls, her skin tanned and healthy, her eyes clear and unclouded. Her smile lacked the twist of bitterness that had crept in between her second and third rehab stints. She looked like she'd march out of the picture and smack someone around, and make them like it. "Tanya."

Her eyebrows lifted, nearly sending her glasses down to her nose. "Oh. How stupid of me. Of course it is."

"Don't bother," he said, cutting her off. "That was before she started using."

Alana went back to the gardening books, and he went back to sealing the pipe. A tense silence ensued and he wondered when that boy lost the ability to charm a woman into the backseat of a car, or bed, rather than just making himself available for a one-night stand, or a series of them.

"What's this?"

He glanced down at the page she was reading. She pointed at a tiny pencil drawing of a rose blooming around a small stone. "That," he said as he turned back to the pipe, "is a drawing of Gran's first engagement ring. She took it off all the time because the bud would get crusted with pie and bread dough. She'd tuck it in her apron pocket, then put it back on when she was finished. One day when she went to put it back on, it was missing. They looked inside, outside, nearly tore the house apart looking for it, but they never found it."

"How sad!" she exclaimed.

He looked at the drawing. "I promised her I'd find it. On rainy days we'd have a treasure hunt in the house. She'd hide things for me to find, the silver candlesticks, her spoon collection. When I found them I'd take them back to the blanket fort in the living room. When I got older I took off all the baseboards, just in case the ring slipped between the cracks, look for it when I weeded the garden through the summer. It just disappeared."

"You tried," she said softly.

He shrugged. The memory felt distant, like someone else made that promise, searched that hard for something long gone. "I didn't find it."

"But she knew you cared that she lost it, and was sad about it. Did they buy a new ring?"

"Money was always tight, and she still had her wedding band. Grandpa bought her a ring for their fiftieth."

"That's lovely," she mused.

The ring discussion sparked another thought in his mind. He set the wrench in the toolbox and reached in his back pocket. "Does this look familiar?"

She pursed her lips and studied the picture. "That's Gunther Jensen, right?"

"Yes, but not the people. The ring on her finger."

Alana tipped her glasses from her forehead to her nose and examined the picture more closely. "It's a daisy. A really tiny daisy."

"It's the ring that was stolen when Gunther's house was broken into. His wife's gone, but he had planned to give it to his granddaughter for her sweet sixteen in a few weeks."

Another small hum to indicate she'd heard him. "I haven't seen it before," she said.

"Keep your eyes open."

"Why? You said it was stolen."

"I went to pawn shops in Brookings today. None of them had it, but all of them said they'd think twice before they took something like this on pawn. The resale value was almost nonexistent, because the diamonds are so small."

Alana peered up at him through those blue-rimmed glasses. "It's a charming ring," she said staunchly.

"It's out of style."

"According to men who staff pawn shops," she pointed out, amused. "Why do you think I'll see it?"

He didn't respond, but her intelligence headed the list of things he liked about her.

"You think Cody did that. You think Cody broke into Gunther's house and stole this ring, and when he can't pawn it, he'll hold onto it."

She wasn't asking a question. She was stating facts that transformed her from a rather sweetly shy woman to a staunch defender.

"I don't know," he said. "There's too many mouths to feed in that trailer, and his brother's home with a felony conviction under his belt. He'll have a hard time finding a job."

"Cody's certainly not eating enough," she said, as if that made him less likely to steal, not more.

"Cody's a kid in bad circumstances. He'll try to do the right thing until he doesn't have any more options. Then, who knows what he'll do?" He sighed. "I'm not accusing him. I'm just asking you to keep your eyes open. You see more of those kids after school than I do. Maybe you'll see it on a girl's finger, or in someone's bag."

"I'll pay attention," she said.

"Come on a ride along with me," he said.

"Why?"

"Because if you're renovating the library, you need to see more of Walkers Ford and the county than just the route between the house, the library, and the Heirloom. You need to see the darker side of this town."

"All right," she said. "When?"

"Tomorrow night. Days are boring."

8

THE SILENCE IN the library was oddly expectant, different from the relieved quiet that settled after closing. Not even Cody's presence changed that. Phone in hand, Alana shrugged purse, tote, and plastic take-out bag from the Heirloom onto her desk while Cody removed the wooden drop box and quickly sorted the books onto the cart. In an unspoken agreement, Cody took the Styrofoam box containing his breakfast and headed down the stairs to sort books in the basement. He paused in the doorway, box in hand, and said, "Thank you."

The quiet words, buttressed by pride and offered with humility, diverted her attention from the list of links for reception sites she'd compiled in an e-mail. "You're welcome," she said.

The tips of his ears turned a dull red. "The little kids aren't so little anymore. They eat more than they used to, but Mom's hours were cut at the plant. Colt's home, but he hasn't found a job yet."

Her throat tightened. "I'm sorry," she said inadequately.

He shook his head. "We'll figure something out," he said. "We always do."

She found when she lifted the lid from her oatmeal that she'd lost her appetite. In the hopes that if she distracted herself she'd regain her appetite, she dropped the last link into the e-mail on her iPhone and clicked Send, then shrugged out of her jacket. Freddie had asked for recommendations for movers to get her furniture and clothes moved to Toby's flat in London.

Intending to hand off her phone to Cody, she followed the narrow staircase to the basement. In the small room the books were now sorted into various stacks: Give Away, Sell. The unsorted stack shrank nicely every day Cody worked. "Here you go," she said, and offered Cody the phone.

"Thanks," he said.

"What are these?" she asked as she shifted a stack at the back of the table so she could read the spines.

"Ones to sell," he said without looking up from the phone.

His voice was too noncommittal. As if he didn't care that she'd looked at the stack. But she was becoming an expert in noncommittal responses that were truly unemotional, and Cody couldn't quite match Lucas's even tone. "Oh. Good."

Upstairs she powered up the computers, then she opened the link to the resale market Cody set up online. Three, no, four pages of books were listed, and nearly a page of sales came up. They'd need to get to the post office in the next day or two.

On a whim, she searched for one of the titles in the box in the corner. A list of used options appeared on the screen, but the cheapest price was a seller with no ratings, located in South Dakota, open for just a few days. Chalkart was the seller's name.

Oh, Cody.

Alana rubbed the base of her thumb against her forehead, then clicked on Chalkart's other books for sale. They matched the titles in the innocuously invisible stack, as well as several others Alana remembered from her initial survey of the boxes. She pushed her glasses up on top of her head and rubbed her eyes.

Mrs. Battle pulled open the library's front door. "There are three universal truths to life," she said precisely as she crossed the marble floor. "Death, taxes, and the trash that remains behind after the Walkers Ford baseball team wins an away game. Send that boy outside to pick up—what's wrong?"

She joined Alana at the computer. Alana tilted the screen down and toward the shorter woman. "I don't know what I'm looking at," she said.

Alana clicked back a couple of screens. "These are the books we're selling online."

"Yes."

"And these are the books matching a seemingly innocent stack downstairs that we should be selling online but are instead being sold by a brand-new retailer who lives in South Dakota and calls himself Chalkart."

She expected exclamations of disbelief and righteous indignation. Instead the elderly woman's face sagged a little before she spoke. "Oh."

"I don't know how to handle this."

"Obviously, the right thing to do is to call Chief Ridgeway and tell him Cody is stealing from the library."

"Is that the right thing to do? I mean, I know that's what I *should* do. But . . . is it the *right* thing to do?"

Mrs. Battle's cornflower blue eyes held a hint of doubt. "You're the library director. That's your decision."

It was her decision, at least for a few more days. She had options. She could turn a blind eye to Cody's theft and let whoever the mayor hired deal with the problem. He needed the money. But so did the library foundation, and in the end, it was wrong.

She looked at the clock. They had fifteen minutes until the library opened. "You're here early."

"We need to talk about the final proposal. I have garden

club this afternoon, then a doctor's appointment, after which I will need to lie down. You're delaying."

Alana straightened her shoulders. "No, I'm not."

She took the stairs more slowly this time, walking past the Styrofoam container in the trash can just inside the door. Cody turned as she walked in, and the smile he flashed her nearly broke her heart.

"We need to talk upstairs," she said.

The smile dimmed a little, but he followed her up the stairs. When he crossed the floor to stand by the computer, she held out her hand. The smile flicked off, then back on. He gave her the phone, but the smile disappeared when he saw the seller page on Amazon.

Shoulders hunched, chin dropped, mouth compacting back to sullen. The movements were so small and so telling. To cover her own disappointment, she skimmed through the history on the phone's browser. Three books uploaded to the library's sale page. Two uploaded to Chalkart's page. The two least expensive of the five books, she noted. Honor among thieves.

"Explain this," she said.

"You said our taxpayer dollars paid for them. You gave me one."

"Yes, and after you left, I deposited the book's value into the library's fund," she said. "Money from sales should go to the library, to the community. Not to benefit one person."

Or three little kids who don't get enough to eat? She didn't ask what he would use the money for. She knew. *Food insecurity* was a phrase she knew well, but only from program descriptions. Now food insecurity stood in front of her. See also: *angular* and *bony* and *skeletal*.

"I didn't steal the books to buy food," he said defiantly. "The kids get enough to eat if I don't eat, and I don't need to eat."

The combination of bold-as-brass defiance and outright lies shocked her. "What did you steal them for?"

"None of your fucking business."

"Language," Mrs. Battle said, but it was halfhearted.

"Are you going to call Ridgeway?"

"*Chief Ridgeway*, and I haven't decided," she admitted.

Cody's mouth clicked close when he simultaneously realized his fate had not in fact been decided and his attitude wasn't doing him any favors. Alana gave him a short nod to indicate approval, then handed back the phone. "I expect the following to occur in the next ten minutes: you will close down Chalkart's shop. You will transfer those books to the library's account. You will continue to sort books. Understood?"

"Yeah," he said.

Mrs. Battle inhaled sharply. Alana just lifted her eyebrows.

"Yes, ma'am," he said.

"Better."

"What about Ridg—Chief Ridgeway?"

"I'll let you know when I've decided."

Cody slunk off down the stairs just as the first mother and toddler group came through the front door. Later, after she'd reheated her congealed oatmeal for lunch, she went downstairs. Cody shot her a look seething with both fury and wariness under his tousled wreck of chestnut hair, so she didn't bother with idle chatter. "If you didn't intend to buy food with the money, what did you intend to buy with it?"

"Nothing."

"You can tell me. I won't tell anyone else."

Silence.

"You're not the kind of person who steals for the thrill of it."

Silence.

"Are you buying drugs?"

He shot her a look full of bitter humor. "I'm not stupid. I've watched my brother fuck up his life. I can't afford to do that. I fuck up, and Mom and the little kids end up on welfare, or in foster care."

"What, then?"

She just sat there, watching him, knowing he couldn't leave without her permission, hating that she used that to hold him, knowing Cody hated it, too. She breathed slowly and evenly, making peace with the anger and frustration simmering in the room.

"You don't know what it's like."

"Try me."

"I hate this place. I don't fit in here. I hate football, basketball, baseball, wrestling, and track. I hate parties. I hate that my brothers are living in a trailer that's got so many cracks in the walls snow blows in five months a year. I hate that my mom's stretched so thin, and my dad's gone, and people look at me like I'm a freak. But mostly I hate that there's nothing I can do to change any of those things."

His voice had risen through this speech, his hatred a palpable thing in the room, emotions battering at Alana. "I know what some of that is like, but not all of it."

His gaze flicked scornfully over her. "What do you know about any of it?"

The story about slipping on the parquet and falling on her fanny during her coming-out ball wasn't appropriate here. He was a child, not her friend, so all she said was, "I know what it's like not to fit in. Tell me what you'd buy with your ill-gotten gains."

"I was lying about not needing food. Or clothes."

They would find a way to deal with that. "What would you buy for you."

"Paint," he said.

Her brain raced through iterations of Cody attempting to start a house-painting business. Small-business funding. Grants. A mentor? Too bad Marissa was half a continent away. She and Cody would get along like a house on fire.

"Charcoal," Cody continued, and her brain screeched to

a halt. "Pastels. In a dream world, I'd buy a Mac and as many programs for artists and graphic designers as it would hold. High-speed Internet access. The moon will fall out of the sky before any of that happens, so I'll take the old-fashioned supplies. If I had a car, I'd go to Brookings and steal them, but I don't have a car, or money for gas. It's a bitch to steal gas. I've done it, but newer cars have those gas-tank flaps that you have to release from inside the car."

"We can't fault your resourcefulness," she mused.

He looked up, resignation clear in his gray-green eyes. "Are you going to tell Chief Ridgeway?"

She should, for so many reasons. It was the right thing to do, given that Cody was already doing community service for theft. It was the right thing to do because she and Lucas were more deeply involved than she'd anticipated, and Lucas the man wouldn't take well to her withholding information from Lucas the cop.

Who was Lucas the man?

"Not at present," she said.

"Going to blackmail me?"

"It's called a second chance," she said quietly. "Do you want it or not?"

He looked down between his arms, braced on his knees, then up at her. "Yeah," he said. "Yes, ma'am. Thank you."

"Don't thank me yet. I want a quid pro quo."

His eyebrows arched alarmingly. "Whatever that is, I don't have one."

"I want a favor in return. I want you to write the section of the proposal outlining what the library needs to be useful to young people in town."

"Sounds like school." He looked at her. "You're going to call Chief Ridgeway if I don't, right?"

"No," she said calmly. "I'm not."

"Fine. I'll do it."

Later in the day, when Mrs. Battle's shift ended, she came into the library director's office. "You did the right thing,"

Mrs. Battle said. She struggled to find the sleeve of her wool coat, and Alana reached around to help her.

"Out of curiosity, what do you think Chief Ridgeway would have done?"

Mrs. Battle fussed with her scarf. "The boy I knew growing up would have done one thing. The chief of police, I'm not so sure I know. He's filling his uncle's shoes very ably."

"I saw pictures of him as a teenager last night," Alana said. "He was working on the kitchen plumbing while I went through his grandmother's books. I found photo albums."

"He was an astonishingly good-looking young man," Mrs. Battle said matter-of-factly. At Alana's surprised look, she added, "I'm seventy-seven, not dead, young lady."

"He looked so different," Alana said. "He's no less handsome now, but he's closed off. It's like a light went off behind his eyes."

"His divorce was hard on him," Mrs. Battle said as she looped her purse over her arm, "but he was different before he came back. Whatever happened in Denver changed Lucas Ridgeway, and not for the better."

ALANA'S AUDI ZIPPED past him as Lucas walked along the sidewalk in front of his house. He unclipped Duke's leash and let the dog loose to sniff the squirrel trails in the front yard. Across the driveway, Alana slid out of the car, collecting an assortment of bags from the passenger seat.

"I just need a few minutes," she said with a quick smile. "Mrs. Battle and I just met with Delaney Walker-Herndon about the library renovation proposal. The meeting ran late."

"You should change clothes," he said. "Temps are going to start dropping as the sun sets. Something warm, and wear good shoes."

Her gaze skimmed him, taking in his jeans, uniform polo, windbreaker with *POLICE* in big white letters, and black uniform boots. "Ten minutes," she said.

If she was ready to go in ten minutes, he'd eat Duke's dinner rather than the meatball subs he'd planned to pick up at Gina's, but he let it slide. When she got the door open, Duke pricked his ears and trotted across the driveways to follow Alana into the house. She cooed a greeting, then poked her head out again. "Duke seems to like this house."

"Gran gave him treats all day long," he said, resigned. "Bring him with you when you're ready."

"He's coming?"

"He's coming."

Exactly nine minutes and forty-five seconds later, Alana held the screen door for Duke, then followed the dog out onto the paved strips serving as a driveway. She locked the door behind her, then walked over to Luke's Blazer. He used the excuse of making sure she was ready for a long, cold night to look her over. She wore jeans, a dark gray turtleneck sweater, a peacoat, and a pair of gray hiking boots with a purple snowflake decorating each side, white fur peeking out from the shank, somehow both fashionable and appropriately dressed for the damp chill growing in the air as the sun set. She'd removed her makeup, making it easy for him to watch the heat bloom on her cheeks as he studied her.

"Do I pass inspection, Chief?"

He gave her a single nod. Duke finished his olfactory exploration of her jeans, then sneezed his approval.

She smiled, then bent to scratch behind Duke's ears. "I last wore these when I was at Linda Moore's house for supper. Her cats spent the evening wandering in and out of my lap."

"That's nice," he said, for lack of anything else to say.

"Not really. I'm not a cat person."

He opened the passenger door for her. "You don't like cats."

"I don't dislike cats, but we had dogs growing up. Labs, mostly."

Duke took advantage of the conversation to jump up into

the passenger seat. Alana smiled. "You're in my seat," she said. To Lucas's utter astonishment, Duke turned and wriggled between the two front seats, into the back. "Good dog," she praised. "He's very smart."

"Working dogs have to be. It's not the brains that are a problem. It's the obedience. He usually ignores everyone except me."

"Your grandmother isn't the only person who knows her way around a treat jar," Alana said loftily as she fastened her seat belt.

Duke nosed her ear, then licked her cheek before Alana shooed him back into the backseat. Lucas covered a moment of irrational jealousy with a quick briefing.

"I'll take you out for a few hours. If anything happens requiring lights and sirens, I'm going to put you out of the car at the nearest crossroads. Call county dispatch." He tapped the number, visible on a worn sticker affixed to the visor. She entered it into her cell phone. "They'll send someone to pick you up. You're okay with that?"

"Yes," she said. "What are the odds of anything happening?"

"Probably nothing will happen. I just want you prepared in case a call comes in and I ditch you at the intersection of two gravel roads."

"Nothing's going to happen," she said confidently. "Nothing ever happens to me. It comes with the librarian territory. We're like a spell against excitement."

He shifted into drive and pulled out into the street. After a quick stop at the mini-mart to gas up the truck and pick up coffee, he turned onto the highway leading out of town. Duke curled up on the floor behind Alana's seat. She sipped her cream and sugar with a topper of coffee. "Where to first?"

He pulled onto the county road running parallel to Brookhaven, past the cemetery. "I want to stop by Gunther Jensen's place, give him an update."

"All right." Alana turned to look at Brookhaven, the floor-to-ceiling windows running the length of the enormous house, glazed with the pinkish hue of the setting sun.

"Have you been inside since she left?"

"Yes, for yoga classes and coffee dates, and I went to look at the kitchens. You were at the wedding reception. What did you think?"

"It was nice, but the Walkers wouldn't do anything less." One corner of her mouth lifted. "I meant of the house."

"Unbelievable," he admitted. "I hadn't been inside since the last summer I spent here in high school."

"Were you there that night?"

"No. Still in school in Denver." He glanced over at her. "You know what happened with Marissa and Adam. You had something to do with that."

"I did."

He didn't say anything after that, just parked the Blazer in front of Gunther's house. "Stay," he said to Duke. Alana followed him out of the truck, up to the front steps. They waited while Gunther eased out of his chair and made his way to the door.

"Well, hi, Lucas. This is a surprise. Come in, come in. I've got coffee on. Let me get you some."

He introduced Alana to Gunther. An audiobook droned on while she helped the elderly man bring out coffee and a plate of cookies fresh out of the box.

"House looks back to normal," Lucas commented when they were all seated in the living room. Gunther reached over and shut off the CD player.

"Pastor Theresa and the kids came over that night and helped me set the place to rights," Gunther said.

Lucas set down his coffee cup. "I wanted to give you an update on what we've done. I went into Brookings and gave all the pawn shops a picture of the jewelry that was stolen. They've all got my number so they can call if it comes in."

"Well, thanks, Lucas. You didn't have to do that."

He didn't. He could have faxed a picture, description, and phone number to the pawn shops. But he did have to do it. Rings meant something, and this ring was especially precious. "It's no problem," he said.

"You seen Tanya lately?"

"Not since the day after your break-in," he said. "Has she been back to help you with anything?"

"No," Gunther said. "She said she would, but she didn't show up."

He kept his face expressionless, something he found all too easy to do except when he knew Alana was watching. "When was this?"

"A week or so ago. She was going to help me change out the storm windows."

"And she didn't show?"

"No."

"I think she's using again, Gunther. If she does show up, it's probably best not to let her in."

Gunther nodded reluctantly. Alana shifted beside him to peer over her shoulder and look at the windows. "If you still need help with the windows, Cody Burton would probably be glad for the work," she said.

"I'm not sure that's—" Lucas started.

Gunther was already nodding. "I'll call down there tomorrow," he said.

Lucas slid a look Alana's way. She gave him a quick smile, then returned her attention to Gunther.

"I'm very sorry to hear they stole your wife's engagement ring," she said quietly.

Gunther sat quietly for a moment. "It wasn't worth much, but it's everything to me."

"I understand," she said.

Didn't she see what she was doing, getting involved when all she'd do was leave? As they got up to leave, she tapped her finger on a stack of plastic DVD cases sitting on the table by the door. "Do you want me to take these back to the library for you?"

"Thank you. That's very kind." They declined cookies for the road and got back in the truck.

"Where to next?"

"The Burtons. Colt and Cody both have curfews, Colt because he's on parole and Cody because he's doing community service." He backed down the driveway to the road. "Generally speaking, I don't send suspects back to the scene of the crime."

"Cody didn't break into that man's house and steal his wife's engagement ring. He's got no way to get it to Brookings to pawn it."

"He's got friends with cars. His brother has a car."

"He wouldn't do that. He's not that kind of kid."

"He's working for you because he was convicted of theft."

"Not from someone he cares about, and if he's helping Gunther on his own time, he cares about him."

Steel lay under the pale skin that blushed so easily. "So he's not giving you any trouble?"

She didn't answer right away. "No," she said finally.

"You had to think about that," he said.

"Sometimes trouble is just people being people," she replied.

They bumped up the ruts to the trailer sheltered by budding trees. Music blasted from the bedroom end of the trailer, competing with the dialogue from a kids' show coming from the open living room window. He took the steps to the door and knocked. The door was wide open, and the smell of macaroni and cheese drifted through the open door. Three little boys sat in a row on the sofa, absently eating mac and cheese from mismatched bowls. One of them looked up at the sound of Lucas's knock on the door frame.

"Colt! Run!" the kid screamed.

Adrenaline spiked in Lucas's brain, and before he

registered movement, his hand was on his weapon. "Get behind the truck," he barked at Alana.

Wearing jeans and a muscle T-shirt with the armholes cut to the hem, Colt emerged from the back of the trailer. "What the fuck, little man?"

"Hands!" Lucas barked, keeping the door open with his left hand as he flipped the snap off his holster with his right. "*Hands!*"

Colt's eyes widened, and Cody emerged from the kitchen, the mac-and-cheese pot in one hand and an incongruous blue plastic serving spoon in the other.

"Whoa," Colt said, raising his hands. "Hey, he was just joking. It's a game. It's just a game!"

"Lucas."

Alana's voice, soft and yet commanding, flexed into the air, slicing open space for him to hear the little boy giggling. No danger. No threat here. He lifted his hand from his weapon and watched the tension ease from the situation.

"Not funny," he said to Colt as he stepped into the trailer. "Not fucking funny. That's what you're teaching your little brother? To run from the police?"

Colt's sullen face was his only answer. Cody set the pot on the crate doubling as an end table. "Go into Mom's room," he said to the little kids. "You can watch the rest of the show in there."

"Mom doesn't like it when we get food in her bed," the budding comedian said.

"Sit on the floor," he said with far more patience than Lucas would have shown.

It took a minute to relocate the three imps, but Lucas didn't move. "You stay here," he said, when Colt turned toward the hallway. He glared at Lucas while Cody situated the kids, shut off the music, and came back down the hallway. He pointed the remote at the television and turned off the dancing sponge.

"You said you weren't—"

"Hello, Cody," Alana said with a cheerful edge that cut Cody short. His mouth snapped shut. "This must be your brother. Alana Wentworth. So nice to meet you." She held out her hand to Colt, who stared at her, then at Cody, with an astonishment all too familiar to Lucas, before giving her hand one firm shake.

"What are you doing here?"

Time to get this situation under control. "You both have curfew," Lucas said.

"And we're both home," Cody said.

"Have a seat," Lucas said to Colt.

Colt rolled his eyes. "Jesus fuck," he said, slumping into the sofa hard enough to rock the trailer. "It was just a goddamn game."

Until he found something. Lucas pulled on a pair of latex gloves and searched the trailer from top to bottom, starting with the bedrooms. The three younger boys were lined up on the floor at the foot of their mother's unmade bed, gazes avidly fixed on the television. They ignored Lucas entirely as he methodically took the trailer apart, room by room.

When he shifted his search to the living room, Cody and Alana stood beside the door. Alana held a large sketch pad. Cody's shoulders were hunched over, his attention obviously split between this invasion of what little privacy he had, and Alana's careful examination of the pad's contents.

"You drew pictures," she said.

"I don't think in words."

Both Lucas and Alana looked around at that. "You don't think in words," she repeated.

He shook his head impatiently. "I don't. I think in images, sketches, colors. Lines."

"He always has," Colt added from the couch, without taking his attention from the television. "He learned to draw before he learned to write."

"How do you do in school?" Alana asked.

This forced a laugh from Cody. "How do you think I do?"

The blush flared on her cheekbones. "Stupid question," she said. "I like these."

Lucas peered over her shoulder, blinked, then refocused. The page was rough, like Cody had erased a drawing to make room for this one. The colored-pencil rendition on the page was obviously the library building, but yet vastly different. Where the interior now was an institutional green relieved only by wooden shelves in the front and taller metal stacks at the back, Cody had drawn seating areas, some clustered around tables, others just chairs and pillows on the floor. The industrial carpet covering everything except the entryway was gone, and hardwood floors gleamed in the light pouring down from the Reference balcony. The drawing was as precise as any architectural rendering Lucas had ever seen, but with an astonishing amount of feeling. It held beauty and possibility.

It held hope.

Alana flipped through the pages again, stopping on a picture of the storage room in the basement transformed into a technology center.

"You said it needed to be high tech," Cody said. "I didn't want to put all that stuff upstairs, where the sunlight would glare off the monitors. And once you sell all those books, you'll have space downstairs again."

"Cody, this is spectacular," she said. The admiration in her voice was evident as she once again paged through. "It's amazing. It's exactly what we need for the final proposal."

He shrugged, but even Lucas could see the effect her words had on the boy. He straightened ever so slightly, and tension eased from his shoulders. "It's just a couple of drawings."

"You should see what he can do with a story," Colt said, arms folded across his chest. "He's a word weaver. A dream spinner."

Lucas shot him a look, then strode into the kitchen to finish his search.

"I have seen," Alana said absently as she handed the pad back to Cody. "He does a great story hour at the library."

Cody tossed the pad on the crate next to the mac-and-cheese pot. "Find anything?"

Lucas stripped off his gloves and turned to Colt, who, unlike his brother, had the good sense to keep his mouth shut. "Found a job yet?"

A muscle jumped under the precisely shaved sideburn. "Like I told my parole officer, I've put in applications."

"Where's your mom?" he asked Cody.

Lucas knew the answer to that question, but he still had to ask. Cody knew he knew, so the boy struggled to keep a lid on his temper. "Work. She gets home at eleven most nights."

He nodded, then turned to leave. Alana stopped him with a hand on his arm. She pointed at the discarded sketch pad. "May I take this and scan the pictures?"

Cody blinked. "I'll just tear them out," he said.

"No, don't do that. Your sketch pad is a record of your growth as an artist. I'll give it back to you."

Cody flipped the pad open, sectioned off pages, then ripped them from the spiral binding. "Just take them."

"All right," she said. "Thank you. Bring your notebook with you tomorrow, and we'll tape the pictures back in."

"Forget about it."

Alana looked ready to argue with Cody until daybreak. Lucas put his hand firmly between her shoulder blades and turned her toward the door. "'Night," he said.

The door slammed behind them. They crossed the dirt yard, their breath hanging in the air in glittering clouds until they climbed into the truck. Lucas turned over the engine and shoved the heat to high.

Blond hair with the dull sheen of gold slid free from its mooring behind her ear when Alana bent over the sketches. "I asked him for input on what teens would like from the library," she said distantly. "I thought he'd give me a list of bullet points. A few ideas. Not these." She looked up at the trailer, then down at the sketches again before lifting the pages to the dimming overhead light. "He erased drawings. I can make out the lines . . . it looks like one of his younger brothers. He erased drawings to do this because this is the only sketch pad he has. And I stopped him—oh, God."

The light dimmed to black. "Stopped him from what?"

"Never mind," she said, and lowered the picture. "I'll fix it."

He backed down the dirt ruts to the road. "You're not hearing what I'm saying. Don't get too involved with a kid like Cody."

"Why not? Because he'll fail and let me down?"

"No. Because you're leaving." *Because he'll start to hope. He'll start to need you, and you'll be gone.*

She blinked. "But that's not a surprise. Everyone knows I'm here temporarily."

She really had no idea. She had no idea whatsoever of the impact she had on people. It took a former senator, a political hostess, and her sister the genius to make her unremarkable. In the everyday world inhabited by lesser mortals, she went off like a nuclear bomb.

"That's what you do, isn't it? You come in, you do your thing, and you leave. Do you ever think about what happens after you leave?"

She bristled slightly. "Of course we do! The foundation underwrites and supports local organizations to carry out the day-to-day management of whatever programs we implement," she said.

"What does that mean?" he asked. "It means you leave."

"But other people are there. People from the communities," she said. "I can't be there. I can't be in one place and do what I do."

"Never mind," he said.

"Don't do that. I want to understand."

He shook his head. "I can't explain this."

"Fine," she said. "Where's the nearest art supply store?"

Lucas shook his head. "Don't make Cody hope for something that's not likely to happen."

"Why do you think he doesn't have a chance? Have you seen his work? He's talented enough to get a full-ride scholarship to art school."

"Cody's got ties here. Family. People he's responsible for. You understand that. Trust me on this one. Keep him busy for a hundred hours, then send him on his way."

She went back to flipping through the pages, even though he knew she couldn't see very well by the dim dashboard lighting. He watched her, that hair, her hands, the soft curve of her lips, and very nearly missed the figure stumbling along the dirt road.

"Christ!" he barked, slamming on the brakes at the same time he flung his arm across Alana's chest. Both seat-belt harnesses locked as the truck skidded to a stop, angled across the road. Behind him, Duke scrabbled to his feet on the floorboards.

"Who on earth?" Alana started, but he was out of the truck and running.

Tanya.

He caught her by the shoulders and spun her around, her head tracking a good two seconds after her body. "Christ," he said again, and this time the word was half prayer, half curse. He clapped his hand to her cheek, then looked at her fingers. Her skin was ice under his palm, her fingernails purple in the garish light. She wore a flannel shirt, jeans, and flip-flops. Dirt and blood smeared her feet. She'd been walking for hours.

He tipped her head back, using the Blazer's headlights to get a read on her pupils. "What is it this time?"

"Fuck off," she said. A little shake got her attention, and his. He smelled enough beer to stage a party for the entire football team.

"Are you just intoxicated, or did you take something else?" he demanded.

An angry laugh was her answer, then she sagged in his grip. "Get Duke into the back of the Blazer."

Alana ran around to the passenger door and called Duke out. "Up," she said as she swung open the hatch. The dog's tail had barely cleared the frame before she slammed the door again. She reappeared beside the Blazer with the blanket from the emergency kit. "Do you want my boots?" she said.

She must not have seen the dirt and blood smeared on Tanya's feet. "Her feet are filthy," he said.

"It doesn't—"

"No," he said tersely, manhandling Tanya to the rear passenger door, then into the truck. Once she was inside, the fight went out of her. Alana held out the blanket, and he tucked it around her torso, then her calves and her bare feet.

Duke whined, then clambered over the seat back separating him from Tanya. He sniffed her from her bare feet to her face, then licked her cheek. "Good boy," she murmured. Her reflexes dulled, her hand patting the air where the dog was the moment before. Duke lay down by her feet, and she burrowed her toes into his thick coat.

At the intersection Lucas turned towards town and the hospital. "No," Tanya said. "Take me home."

"Where were you?"

No answer.

"Who let you walk home like that?" As the silence stretched, he snapped, "Goddammit, Tanya."

"I just want to go home, Lucas."

They were three-quarters of a mile from the cabin. She might have made it on her own. Then again, she might not have. "These new friends of yours sure do care about you if they'll let you walk yourself home in your condition. You could have passed out and died of hypothermia."

He saw her fingers tighten in Duke's fur. "Like you care," she slurred.

"I do care," he said. "I would have come to get you. You know that."

Then Alana's quiet voice. "Lucas."

He tightened his grip on the steering wheel and swung the Blazer around, then white-knuckled it the rest of the way to the cabin. "The door's usually open," he said to Alana. She opened it wide as he jockeyed the unresisting Tanya out of the backseat. A light shone dimly from the open front door. Her knees gave way when he put her on her feet, so he slipped his shoulder under her arm and gripped her waist to walk her through the glazed air, into the cabin.

"I couldn't get the overhead light to work, and it's freezing in here," Alana said. "I think she left the windows open when she went out. I closed them, but—"

"Start a fire," he said as he dumped his cousin on the sofa.

"You do that," she replied. "I'll take care of her."

A simmering cauldron of emotions seethed inside him, so he took the prudent step back. "She needs to be on her side in case she vomits."

"I'm aware of the protocol," she replied. She went on her knees next to Tanya and turned her. Tanya's hand grazed Alana's shoulder before flopping to the floor. While Lucas crumpled newspaper for tinder and built up logs and kindling, Alana gathered the blanket from Tanya's unmade bed and a knitted throw from the back of the rocking chair.

"This looks like your grandmother's work," she said as she laid the blankets over Tanya's unconscious form.

"It is," he said.

Alana eased the flip-flops from Tanya's bare feet and considered them for a moment, then went to the kitchen and turned on the water. While it warmed, she went into the bedroom again and returned with two pairs of socks and a tube of antibacterial ointment. After searching the cupboards for a stainless steel bowl, she found a clean cloth and sat on the end of the sofa by Tanya's feet. She immersed the rag, wrung it out, then started cleaning the dirt from Tanya's ravaged feet.

Fear trapped him on his knees by the fire. "I'm sorry you had to see her like this," he said.

"It's fine," she replied softly.

"She used to be amazing. Now I'm afraid someone's going to find her frozen to death in a ditch, and I'll have to zip her into a body bag."

Water dripped into the bowl. "Maybe she will be amazing again someday," Alana said as she drew the cloth between Tanya's toes. The unconscious woman stirred slightly, and Alana stopped. When she settled, Alana continued, that bright shiny hair slipping forward again. "Is she an alcoholic?"

"She's a drug addict. Started with pot and moved on to Vicodin. Percocet. Anything else that dulls the pain. She's been to recovery twice, tried to quit on her own I don't know how many times. Drinking is usually the first sign she's slipping. Drugs come next. Then another trip to recovery." He left out the long, slow trip through the hell of using. "The whole process takes a couple of years because she's tough. Each time she swears she's got it beaten."

Alana made another one of those soft noises. For a stretch of time, the fire cracked and popped, and Alana removed blood and dirt from Tanya's skin. Washing finished, she gently patted Tanya's feet dry, then began dabbing ointment on the cuts. That task done, she pulled the cotton socks over defenseless toes, then worked the wool socks up over those, finally tucking the blanket around her feet.

She carried the bowl to the kitchen, where she carefully rinsed it out. Lucas pushed to his feet, gathered the towels and tossed them in the overflowing laundry basket. "Should we stay with her?"

"No," he said without elaborating. He turned off the

kitchen light and closed the door behind them. They rode in silence back to Walkers Ford. The town was eerily quiet, streets empty.

"Do you do this much?"

"Depends."

"On what?"

He thought about that as he drove, trying to figure out how to distill over a decade as a cop into phrases that would make sense to someone who lived and died by research. "Instinct, mostly. Years of experience gone gut deep."

"And tonight?"

"Tonight I wanted you to see the other side of Walkers Ford." He thought about how to say this. "I have to assume you've failed, that the family, the schools, programs, library, mentors, everything has failed. I can't afford to be a Pollyanna about this. Small-town life is supposedly Mayberry, but there's no cushion when things go wrong. We all know Gunther. We knew his wife, how she wore that ring with pride. Some of us were there when he took it off her finger at the hospital. We were there when he buried her. Now it's gone, probably forever."

"Like your grandmother's."

"That's different."

"But the same, because you lost it and you promised her you'd find it. You were eight years old when you made that promise."

"And now I'm thirty-two, and I still haven't found it."

"Why do you keep looking?"

"Because I made a promise."

"I'd ask you to come in and sit for a while, but something tells me you're going back out to Tanya's."

He looked at her sharply, although perhaps the fact that he'd pulled into her driveway, not his, and left the Blazer running was clue enough.

"She shouldn't be alone," was all he said.

Alana nodded and opened the passenger door. "Do you want me to come with you? You shouldn't be alone, either."

Air huffed from his lungs, although whether from the direct hit to his sternum or her matter-of-fact statement, he couldn't tell. Both, probably. Alana Wentworth packed a punch behind that sleek reserve. He desperately wanted to go inside with her, to lose the day in her quirking smile and soft body. "You've got a big day tomorrow."

She hummed something quick and soft, then stepped back. Duke peered over the backseat and whined, upset that the humans were separating. "It's okay," she reassured him. "I'll see you tomorrow. And you," she said with a quick glance at Lucas.

9

THE DAY OF the presentation to the town council passed in a frantic blur. The library was open and nearly everyone in town seemed to want to take a look around before the presentation, so Alana and Mrs. Battle were busier than usual. Cody was still suspended so Alana put him to work scanning his pictures into her laptop and typing her notes into the PowerPoint presentation. As he worked he downloaded an art application and cleaned up the drawings, teaching himself the software as he worked. Between a constant stream of citizens and Cody's absorption in his work, Alana forgot about her nerves until the last-minute strategy session with Mrs. Battle over supper at her house. Alana flipped open her laptop, then chewed a hasty bite of beef stroganoff while she paged through the presentation.

"You're ready," Mrs. Battle said. "Just remember to slow down and make eye contact."

"I don't talk faster when I'm nervous," Alana said.

"Yes, you do," the old lady said serenely. "And you talk fast anyway, with your city ways. Slow down. Build a picture of what could be."

"Cody's drawings are all they need," she said.

"Cody is a Burton, one step away from juvenile detention or the state penitentiary. His drawings are very, very good, but they're not going to sell the proposal, not like you will."

Alana ate another mouthful of stroganoff and tabbed from the _Final version to the _Rough version. Standing behind her with a pot of steaming corn in her hands, Mrs. Battle watched the slides flicker past. "Slow down," she said. "My eyes don't work that fast."

"What do you think of this?" Alana asked, stopping on the slide that troubled her.

"Well, I don't really know what to make of it."

"Cody drew it."

The whimsical, wistful version of Walkers Ford was visible in the picture to anyone who knew the town. Main Street's brick buildings leaped from the page, flanked by the school, the Y, the restaurant district housing the Heirloom. Houses spread out from the center then lapsed into the surrounding prairie. Brookhaven's sharp edges and gleaming glass marked the farthest edge of town, but what really captured the town's essence was the artfully rendered people. Some were recognizable, like the high school principal, Mr. Walker, and his wife; the town's attorneys, Keith Herndon and his father; police officers gathered around the distinctive Blazer Lucas drove. Gina stood outside her café, and several people strolling on the Main Street carried Heirloom coffee cups. But all motion swirled subtly to the center of the drawing: the library. Alana's heart had seized when she saw the picture, realized the story Cody was using art and passion and feeling to tell. *This is the center of our town. Not the restaurants or the shops or the administrative buildings. This place we need to commit to, or we'll lose our center.*

"The mural's growing on me," Mrs. Battle said grudgingly.

"It's really good," Alana said. "He should have formal training, an opportunity for more exposure. He's a junior, right? I wonder if he's planning to go to art school."

"I'm sure he isn't," Mrs. Battle said.

"He should."

Decisively she dragged the slide into her presentation. She knew exactly where it should go and what it should be. The space between the wood shelves lining the east wall and the windows at the top was bare plaster, occasionally adorned with children's art. Bare plaster, repaired and repainted, would be a perfect canvas for Cody's drawing, reworked into a mural.

"We should go," Alana said as she closed down all her windows except PowerPoint. One embarrassing mistake with a chat program had taught her that the safest bet was to have nothing open on her computer she didn't want shown to a room full of people. "I need to set up the laptop and the projector before people start arriving."

She helped Mrs. Battle tidy the kitchen, then drove them both to the high school. Cars already crowded the parking spaces closest to the auditorium doors. "I'll just stop and chat a little," Mrs. Battle said.

Alana left her to whatever last-minute campaigning she felt necessary and made her way to the front of the auditorium. The technology coordinator had left the projector and a dizzying array of connecting cables, but in a few minutes she had her laptop connected and projecting onto the screen. When she looked up from the keyboard, every seat was taken. People stood in the aisles, with more crowding in the doors at the rear and beside the stage. Mrs. Battle claimed a seat in the front row.

She scanned the sea of faces until an all-too-familiar one caught her attention. Lucas stood at the back of the room. He wore a blazer and jeans, and had his weight braced evenly on both feet, his thumbs stuck in his belt in a universal street-cop stance she found ridiculously endearing. The fire chief, Jackson Marshall, stood at the front of the room in much the same pose. Both men were obviously counting noses, so Alana wasn't surprised when they met in the middle of the packed staircase. A moment of discussion, then Lucas hopped onto the stage.

"Microphone?"

She unclipped it from the edge of her blouse and handed it to him, sat down on the edge of the stage, and turned on the battery pack at her waist.

"Folks, Chief Marshall asks that anyone who doesn't have their backside in a seat needs to move into the class-rooms down the hall. We'll broadcast Ms. Wentworth's presentation to the rooms."

The tide of humanity ebbed back out into the hallway. Lucas handed her the microphone. "Good luck," he said quietly.

You've done the research. You've developed a plan based on that research. Mrs. Battle worked her connections. You will be fine.

Her heart was racing. She cleared her throat as the lights dimmed, then launched into her presentation.

Research, research, research. She laid out the damning statistics on library budget cuts around the country, the com-plex transition into the digital age. She cited the rising number of visits to libraries on a national, state, and local level, contrasted that with the number of libraries closing or slashing hours.

"But the library is crucial to your community," she said, then cleared her throat again. A shift of movement at the edge of the stage caught her eye. Lucas braced his shoulder against the wall next to the door leading to the parking lot. Her brain raced as she sipped from the glass of water; prob-ably the position was strategic. Near the exit in case an emergency call came in. In a split second between drinking and swallowing, his expression when he found Tanya freez-ing and bleeding on the side of a dirt road a mile from home flashed into her brain. He cared. On the surface he was as remote as Chicago or Denver, but that distance only served to wall off how deeply he cared about Walkers Ford.

She'd made a huge mistake, getting involved with Lucas Ridgeway.

But then his lips quirked up in a small smile, and he nodded.

Keep going. You're doing fine.

"But the library is crucial to your community," she said again. "We can talk about what Walkers Ford lacks: a movie theater, a bookstore, a hospital. Twenty percent of Chatham County's residents live below the poverty line and lack access to computers, high-speed Internet, and information. I'd rather talk about what you have, and how to make the most of it. The library already arranges and provides space for free health screenings, but this service could easily be expanded, making the library a vibrant town square. A small investment in e-readers preloaded with books both introduces the technology to residents and reduces the investment in large-print books, as the fonts on e-readers can be adjusted to each reader's preferences. Additionally, adding movie nights, reading groups, and more services for children of all ages will help even more." She clicked through the bullet-point slides to Cody's illustrations. "We can upgrade the computers, and renovate the unused rooms in the basement into meeting rooms that could be booked for business meetings or online classes. Universities around the world are making their classes available via the Internet. Information is now digital and accessible all over the world, but sorting through that information to separate fact from fiction requires a new learning process. The library can work with the school to develop and host technology training programs of all kinds."

She clicked through to the last slide, Cody's drawing of the library as the center of the town. A murmur ran through the crowd. "Cody Burton drew the illustrations and this mural. Young people see the library as vital to the community, as do I."

She outlined a three-phase approach to implementing her

suggestions and a cost/benefit analysis that had kept her up nights, and ended with another slide of Cody's mural. "I think," she said, then paused. This wasn't part of the presentation. "I think you have something wonderful here. In an age of increasing disconnectedness, you have the resources and means to connect with the world beyond Chatham County, but more importantly, with each other. Thank you."

She didn't expect applause as she turned off her microphone, but it came anyway, too enthusiastic to be merely polite. To her surprise, people wanted to talk to her afterwards, make suggestions, offer opinions, thank her for her work. In the front row, Mrs. Battle fielded questions as well. Mayor Turner climbed the steps to the stage.

"Nicely done," he said in a low voice.

"I'm a little surprised to hear you say it."

He gave her a surprisingly impish grin. "This is a contrary bunch. Sometimes I have to be against something to build popular support for it. We do better if we think we've come up with the idea, not had our mayor cram it down our throats."

"Well, it's a beautiful building, and such an important part of the community."

"I'll get back to you about the proposal," he said. "The council will meet and vote soon. Thank you for all your hard work."

A generic brush-off she'd heard a hundred times before. "I'll look forward to hearing from you," she said.

She closed down her laptop and disconnected it from the projector. Lucas still stood by the parking lot exit. "Can I get a ride back to the library?" she asked. "I drove Mrs. Battle home in her car. If you're busy, I can walk."

"I'll drive you," he said. "When are you leaving?"

She blew out her breath. "Day after tomorrow, probably. It's a nine-hour drive."

He held the door open for her. "You're not packed yet."

"It won't take long," she said. "I learned to travel light

before I was ten. It got much easier when I got an e-reader. I always packed more books than clothes, to my mother's total despair."

"Nice job with the presentation," he said. "You made a library sound both necessary and really exciting."

"Libraries *are* both necessary and really exciting," she said. "To me anyway."

He parked in the lot and killed the lights. "This wouldn't have worked, would it?"

"It was temporary," she said. "We both knew that. Besides, we're practically a cliché. Introverted research librarian and a chief of police."

A small breath of laughter huffed from his nostrils as he looked at her. "A cliché," he said.

"You know. Repressed. Sexually adventurous."

"You came on to me," he said with a knowing smile. "Not repressed. Also not really a librarian. Maybe we're not a cliché."

The air in the car should have cooled without the heater running, but little sparking shocks of electric heat crackled between them. "Want to come inside and find out?"

In answer, he opened his door. She left her laptop bag on the floorboard but brought her purse, then went on to unlock the front door with all the casualness she could muster. He stood close enough for her to feel the heat radiating from his body, but not improperly close, and that distance made her heart pound.

Once inside, she snagged a stack of encyclopedias waiting to be reshelved, then led him to the staircase spiraling up to the reference section and unhooked the dusty velvet rope holding the brass *Staff Only* sign. He followed her up the tight spiral, then into the darkest corner of the building.

"Very librarian," he said, looking around, but his voice had dropped a register.

"Very practical," she replied. "My office windows

overlook the parking lot, and the rooms in the basement lack ambiance."

She turned her back on him and set the books on a low shelf and turned on one of the desk lamps illuminating a section of shelving. Without turning around, she turned the books spine out and examined the labels. Behind her Lucas stood quietly. She thought about her skirt and cashmere cardigan over a silk blouse. She even wore a strand of pearls and her brown suede heels. Moving very slowly, she selected the first two books from the stack and turned to shelve them.

Lucas was right behind her. She hadn't heard him move, not a rustle of denim over the beating of her heart. He leaned his body weight against hers and swept aside her chin-length hair. It slithered back, obscuring the kiss he pressed into the skin between her collar and hairline.

"Damn," he growled.

She gave a hiccupping little laugh that cut off abruptly when he repeated the motion. This time he gathered the strands into his fist, then used the pressure to tip her head forward.

Oh. Oh oh oh. The pressure of his knuckles against her skull was an erotic contrast to the teasing, testing brush of his lips against her nape. Hard against hard, soft against soft, the primitive possession of his fist in her hair. His mouth worked over the sensitive patch on her nape, first hot and gentle, then with a scrape of his teeth.

Her hands trembled as she slid one book, then the second, into their proper places, and if she took a minute to double-, then triple-check to be sure they were correctly shelved, well, she was a conscientious librarian.

Lucas turned his head and set his teeth into her nape. She gripped the shelf until her knuckles turned white while sparks skittered along her nerves. Her jaw slackened and a very faint moan sounded in her throat.

"I should . . ." she said weakly.

"You definitely should," he replied.

The laugh edging its way up her throat belonged to another woman. "There are more books to put away. . . ."

With one last hot kiss to her nape he stepped away enough for her to pick up the smaller stack, double-check the spines, then walk to the next row. Lucas leaned against the end of the shelf, watching her.

This time he touched her first, reaching out to trail his fingertips down the length of her arm. "Soft," he said quietly.

She hummed her agreement, then tucked her hair behind her ear.

He stroked the collar of her silk blouse with the back of his index finger. "Warm and soft."

The nerves in her throat tingled a proximity warning. When she nodded, her hair slid free from her ear, against her cheek. She slid the last book into place, then startled when his index finger rose to push the hair back from her cheek.

"Hot and soft," he said as he tucked the strands behind her ear again.

Heat flared stronger in her face. "I can't help it around you," she confessed.

"I can't tell you how hot that makes me," he said.

His finger followed the curve of her jaw to her chin, then tipped her face up to his. For a long moment, his mouth hovered over hers, parted lips to parted lips, nothing more than breath shared before he increased the pressure. The noise she made when his tongue slipped between her lips to slide against hers was positively decadent.

When they broke apart, she was gripping the edges of his shirt in her fists. Without breaking eye contact, he brushed his fingertips against her collarbone, then set his fingers to the buttons of both shirt and sweater.

"Pearls," he said, eyeing her necklace nestled at the base of her throat.

"Cliché," she replied.

A low, rough laugh that cut off abruptly when he saw her lacy bra.

"Skin oil is good for them," she said as he kissed and licked his way down her throat. "I wear them often. They were—oh—my grandmother's . . . oh."

He wrapped his arm around her hips and bumped her back against the shelves.

"No!" she gasped. "They're not secured—!"

He grabbed the long shelf just in time to keep it from thudding over, setting off the shelves like a short row of dominos. The head-high shelf swayed alarmingly, and Alana scurried to grab the far end.

When the danger passed, her gaze met Lucas's. Slightly hysterical laughter burbled in her throat, but he strode down the short aisle in two strides and backed her into the plaster wall with two more. Sandwiched between the wall and his hard-planed chest, she felt the breath leave her in a huff. He gave it back with a kiss he ended only to crouch and run his hand up her leg, gathering her skirt as he went. She wriggled to help him get it up around her hips, even as she unbuttoned his shirt; her panties slid to the floor.

The heel of his hand pressed to her mound and she whimpered when his fingers slid into her folds. His tongue mirrored his fingers as he stroked and circled. Her hands inside his dress shirt, she gripped his sides and held on.

Up against a wall. She was about to have sex up against the library's wall, and all she could think about was *more now please*.

One fingertip dipped inside and drew slick heat up to her clit. She made a high-pitched stuttering noise and dropped her head forward to rest against his shoulder. When she trembled on the edge, he withdrew his hand and stepped back to get a condom from his wallet and smooth it on.

Her heels brought them to almost the right height. He widened his stance and urged his hips forward, seeking the right alignment. Finding it meant he glided into her without any preparatory strokes. She gasped and fisted her hands in his shirt.

"Okay?"

She nodded jerkily. She'd never get used to this, the shocking, stretching glide of him inside her, not even if she had all the time in the world. For a brief moment, her manners ruled; she tried to think of ways to help him hold her upright, but then he leaned his chest into hers, secured her hips with one arm, braced the other by her head, and started to move.

Then she stopped thinking at all. It was hot and fast and relentless, not deep but each stroke worked the sensitive flesh at her entrance. Her head dropped back, thunking against the wall, then turning to the side as pleasure coursed like lava through her veins. Her muscles tightened, inside and out, drawing a low groan from him. The rough rumble eddied against her skin, tightening her nipples and sending a shock wave into her pelvis.

The universe contracted, held for a beat, then flung her out into blackness. She curled into him, seeking the heat and strength and stability of his broad shoulders as the shudders wracked her. With a low groan, Lucas stroked deep and surrendered to his own release.

"Oh, God," she said.

Something in her bewildered tone struck Lucas as funny because he laughed. "Yeah." Tipping her unresisting head on her neck, he nuzzled into her cheekbone, then ear. "Still feel like a cliché?"

"No," she said. She felt like she was home. Like this was so right, so good, so her, that it meant something.

Her heartbeat had slowed to something resembling normal when Lucas stepped away and dealt with the condom. Making herself decent again made her blush twice as hard. Panties up, skirt down, blouse buttoned, sweater buttoned over her blouse. Lucas gave her a crooked little smile, then said, "Let me . . ."

She laughed and pushed her hair out of her face while he rebuttoned both blouse and sweater. "There."

"Do I look presentable?"

"You look like you belong here."

She gaped at him.

"Sorry. I don't know what I was thinking. You look like you just had illicit, very hot sex," he said matter-of-factly.

"Oh my God."

"It's dark and we're going home." He held out his hand, support she appreciated when the danger of navigating a tight spiral staircase in heels with the aftershocks of sex weakening her knees became clear.

Outside, she locked up again, Lucas waiting patiently on the sidewalk leading to the parking lot. He scanned the street, then checked his phone. Subconsciously triggered, she checked her own iPhone for incoming messages as she walked to her car. Two from Freddie, one from her mother, and one from Marissa.

Hi, Alana! Adam proposed last night and I said yes. Neither of us want a big wedding, so we're making plans for this weekend. One of the local wedding package places had a last-minute cancellation. Most of Adam's friends are still stationed here in San Diego. His lieutenant is flying in from Chicago and offered to stop and pick up Adam's mom and anyone else coming from Walkers Ford (Lucas????? Adam invited him!). Will you come? Please say you will. I know your contract is up and your family wants you home, but please take a few more days off and come to San Diego for the wedding.

We wouldn't be having it without you. Please come.

Love, Marissa

She wasn't ready for this to end. "Marissa and Adam are getting married this weekend in San Diego. I'm invited."

"Me, too," he said absently. "It's short notice. I don't know that I can get someone to cover for me. You going to go?"

She looked at him and made yet another impulsive decision. "Yes."

He lifted one eyebrow. "I thought you were due home."

She looked at him over the Blazer's hood, weighing the consequences of postponing her return for a few more days. With the presentation delivered, there was no reason for her not to pack her car and leave as planned, giving her the weekend to unpack. If she went to San Diego, she'd jump right back into foundation work, not to mention wedding planning. Freddie wouldn't like it.

But this was a once-in-a-lifetime event for Adam and Marissa.

Her mother wouldn't like it, either.

Too bad.

"I am," she said. "They'll just have to get along without me for another few days. Come with me. It'll be fun."

He turned to look over his shoulder, and she was sure he would say no, that he was needed here, that their understanding was that this was over and they should keep it that way.

She gripped her iPhone too tightly to pretend this was casual, but couldn't make her fingers relax. *Definitely entangled*, she thought. *And the knots are getting tighter and tighter.*

"You know, I haven't taken a vacation since I was hired," he said conversationally.

His gaze met hers, and she breathed again. "Okay. Good. I'm glad. I'm really . . . I'll coordinate with Marissa."

"Great."

"See you at home."

He shot her an odd look. "See you there."

10

ALANA HAD JUST finished brushing her teeth when two sharp raps came at the kitchen door. She hurried into the hallway and peered around the door frame. Lucas stood in the open door.

"We're due at the Huron airfield in an hour. You almost ready to go?"

She nodded. Duke trotted across the linoleum and nosed at Alana's legs.

"Who's watching Duke?"

"Tanya," he said.

Alana looked up from scratching behind Duke's ears. "Is she . . . ?"

"Capable of looking after him? She heard somehow I was taking a couple of days off and offered to keep an eye on him. She's always had a soft spot for him. She'll let me down, but she'd never let him down. I thought I'd give her a chance. He's pretty easy to look after. I've got to run to the station, then I'll swing by and pick you up."

"Do you mind if Adam's mother rides along?"

Lucas looked at his watch. "Sure. Just call her and let her know we'll be there in fifteen minutes."

She nodded again. Lucas clicked for Duke, who obediently turned and trotted back outside. Alana hastily applied a little mascara and lip gloss, then went into the bedroom to check her luggage one last time. She wore jeans, a white T-shirt, and a fitted brown leather jacket. She wore boots for the flight and had packed a pair of sandals for San Diego's warmer climate. Her dress for the wedding was folded into the suitcase. She'd get it quickly pressed before Saturday evening. A couple of changes of underwear, her laptop, toiletries. Snugged into the middle of the soft clothes was her wedding present to Marissa. She'd purchased a platter composed of fired glass with encased prairie crocuses Marissa loved; it had been made by a fused-glass artist working outside Walkers Ford. It would be a pretty thing to have on the boat and remind her of home, useful to serve bread or cheese and crackers when they hosted little parties in various anchorages. Alana had called the artisan after she got home and rushed out to her studio to pick it up before she went to bed.

Alana zipped the bag closed and carried it down the hallway to wait by the door. She looked around the kitchen. She was leaving so much unfinished in Walkers Ford. The kitchen wasn't done. The proposal for the library renovations was complete, but the renovations themselves and any adjustments that should be made would wait for the incoming permanent hire. And there was Cody, the very definition of an unfinished project. She'd say her good-byes when she got back from San Diego, but somehow it didn't sit right with her, to leave people and work she'd grown to care for.

She tucked her hair behind her ear. How did Freddie do this every few months, commit to a location, to a group of people, learn about their histories and needs, their dreams and ambitions thoroughly enough to make effective recommendations, then move on?

Maybe Freddie's brain was in one place and her heart in another. Chicago, with Alana and Mother and the Senator, and now wherever Toby and the band were. Freddie compartmentalized more effectively. One task accomplished, she moved on to the next, while Alana's brain wandered down rose-strewn paths or academic detours, seeking, seeking, always seeking. Freddie was at home in herself wherever she was, while Alana never quite fit in anywhere but in the stacks of a library.

She stepped outside into the bright spring sunshine that now threatened more than promised heat. The rosebushes lining the driveway positively oozed sap and longing. She crouched and examined the stalks rigidly seeking the light, then tucked a few into the trellis. They bent fairly easily now, but in a few weeks training them would be much harder. Would the next tenant take the time? Would Lucas?

Lucas's truck pulled into the driveway. He'd left the department's Blazer at the station in case it was needed while he was gone, and was driving a green F-150 crew cab. She smiled up at him, then straightened to standing.

"We need to . . ." His voice trailed off.

"We need to what?"

He lifted one hand to her cheek. "I forget what I'm going to say around you," he said quietly. "You look amazing."

"I'm wearing jeans and a T-shirt," she said.

"And that jacket. I like that jacket."

It was a gift from Freddie—purchased at a boutique in Paris after the fashion shows—who had insisted the dark caramel color was perfect for Alana's coloring. "Not a cliché?"

"You're anything but a cliché," he said, and bent his head. "Should you kiss me here?"

"No," he murmured, and did it anyway. Quick and light and sweet, his long fingers gently holding her jaw like he was afraid she'd get away. "Made you blush."

"You always do."

He reached into the kitchen, snagged her case, and set it in the backseat. Alana climbed inside and surreptitiously brushed her fingers over her lips. Five minutes later they

pulled into Adam's mother's driveway. Alana climbed out
to give Darla Collins the front seat for the drive to Huron.

"My suitcase can go in the truck bed," she said. "I'll take
the backseat with this."

She reached inside and removed a white dress sheathed
in two layers of clear plastic, carefully knotted at the bottom.

"What's that?" Alana asked.

"Marissa's wedding dress," Darla said.

Her eyes widened, and she jumped forward to help Darla
and the dress get arranged in the truck's backseat. Lucas
locked up for her. She twisted in her seat, trying to get
details about the dress. Silk, obviously, and she could see
soft folds. Not a Cinderella ball gown. "Did you do the
design?"

"It's based on a Romona Keveza dress, but I worked out
the pattern based on Marissa's measurements. The ruching
gave me fits."

Alana gave up trying to ascertain details through two
layers of thick plastic and looked at Darla's clothes instead.
The woman wore a silk camisole, a tailored jacket with
elements of vintage Chanel made modern, and slacks. "Did
you make your outfit?"

"I did," she said.

"That's gorgeous. Last year's New York show, right? I
was there."

"You were?" Darla's face lit up.

Freddie and Toby had front row seats to all of the major
shows. Alana had made sure Freddie had what she needed,
then had met up with a schoolmate to get a tour of the New
York Public Library's research division on Fifth Avenue.
"In a manner of speaking," she said.

She knew enough to keep the conversation going all the
way to the Huron Regional Airport. When they pulled into
the parking lot, one regional jet sat at the terminal, waiting
for the incoming flight from Denver. Lucas parked his truck
at the back of the lot. Darla carried the dress, Alana

managed her suitcase and purse, while Lucas gathered both his and Darla's cases in one hand.

"Everyone got everything?"

They set off across the lot, through the building, and out the back again, where a small jet waited on the tarmac. A shorter, stouter man in a pilot's uniform chatted idly with a taller man dressed in jeans and a button-down shirt. When he saw them, he ended the conversation and lifted his hand in greeting. Alana's heart sank as he strode toward them.

Lucas was out in front, whether because his legs were longer or because he automatically shifted his body between a possible threat and two women and a wedding dress. Being several feet back with Darla and the dress meant she couldn't whisper anything to Nate, asking him not to say anything about . . . anything.

"Lucas Ridgeway? Nate Martin."

The two men shook hands, then Nate turned to Alana and did a classic double take. "Hey, I know you."

"Hello, Nate," she said, and turned her cheek for his automatic kiss. "How are you?"

"I'm fine. Good. It's all good. You? What are you doing here? Last I heard, you and Freddie were headed to India and Pakistan."

She could have fallen at his feet with gratitude. Nate surely knew about the debacle with David and had the wit not to bring it up. "Slight change in plans," she said with a smile. "Freddie went. She's in Chile now. No, I'm wrong. She's in Brazil, with Toby. What are you doing here?"

He laughed. "I'm your ride to San Diego."

"Wait," Alana said, putting the pieces together. "Marissa said Adam's lieutenant was picking us up. *You* were Adam's commanding officer in Afghanistan?"

"Two tours," Nate confirmed, his smile flashing on. "Small world."

"Well, then, you'll be pleased to meet Adam's mother, Darla Collins."

Without seeming to move, Nate straightened his shoulders and spine. "Mrs. Collins, it's an honor to meet you. Your son is one of the finest Marines I've ever served with, and a good man."

"Thank you," she said, clearly touched by his heartfelt words. "He's spoken very highly of you."

"I'll tell you stories once we get airborne," he said with a smile. "Is that the dress?"

"This is the dress," she confirmed.

"Let's get that stowed."

The pilot took the cases from Lucas and they made their way into the jet. Darla carefully placed the dress in the hanging bag locker. Alana settled into a seat by the window and buckled up. Lucas eased into the seat next to her.

"You know him?"

"Oh, yes," she said as she powered down her phone, laptop, and other electronics. "Let's see. His mother and my mother served on several of the same boards, and his father was a big contributor to the Senator's reelection campaigns. He went to the University of Chicago's Lab School while Freddie and I were at Miss Porter's, then I was at Bryn Mawr while he was at Brown, then he went through Officer Candidate School and joined the Marine Corps. So other than a few social events we've lost touch."

"This is his plane."

She smiled. "You're familiar with Ayrshire Warwick Incorporated?" At his nod, she continued. "That's his family's business."

Lucas's brows lifted. "What exactly are you doing in Walkers Ford?"

The plane taxied down the tarmac to the runway. "Working as a contract librarian," she said lightly.

"Why?"

"I needed a break," she reminded him.

He thought about this for a moment. "A person with your connections would have access to houses all over the world.

You could do anything, go anywhere. But you decided to come to a tiny town on the eastern edge of nothing and redesign a library."

"You sound like my mother," she said.

"Not what I usually want to hear from the woman I'm sleeping with, but I'll take it for now."

The pilot announced takeoff. Nate buckled himself into a seat next to Darla, and for a few minutes the only sound in the cabin was the pilot's voice, describing their route to San Diego and dinging off the Fasten Seat Belt sign. Nate took over his role as host and got everyone drinks and snacks. After carrying a blanket and pillow to the back row, he settled in across from Alana.

"Hi again, stranger," he said with a smile.

She smiled back, enjoying the company of someone she could relax with.

"Mrs. Collins was up until three finishing the dress, so she's going to take a nap," Nate continued, then studied Lucas for a quick second. "Where did you serve?"

Lucas gave him a half smile. "Aurora, Five Points, and Federal Boulevard in Denver. I was a cop in Denver for ten years, and spent six of those on the DEA task force."

"Lucas is chief of police for Walkers Ford," Alana said.

"Your hometown?" Nate said.

"My parents are from there. I grew up in Denver, but spent summers in South Dakota with my grandparents. My parents are musicians, and they toured during the summer. A tour was no place for a young child, they said, and my grandparents agreed."

Nate laughed. "What about as a teenager?"

"No way would they let me come. Besides, by then I wanted to go back to Walkers Ford. It's home."

Alana broke off a section of blueberry muffin. "So when Adam took Marissa sailing in Chicago, it was on . . . no, don't tell me . . . it's in there somewhere . . . the *Resolute*?"

Nate laughed. "Nice memory. The last time you were out on her, we were both still in braces."

"It was a beautiful day," Alana said. "And a beautiful boat. She's a Herreshoff yacht, right?"

"Built in the 1920s, overhauled in the '70s, overhauled again when I got home a year ago." He looked at Lucas. "I'm guessing you didn't do much sailing in Denver."

"Hiking, mountain biking, and rock climbing," Lucas said.

Nate's eyes lit up. "Climbed any of the big peaks?"

"All of them. You?"

Nate shook his head. "If I had leave overseas, I found a boat with a sail."

"So what happened when they came to visit?" Alana asked.

"I took them sailing," Nate said. "Nice day, steady breeze, we beat one of my least favorite people ever in a race with Marissa at the helm, which made the victory all the sweeter. Had some lunch. Got sunburned. I dropped them off at the club, and they left. What was that all about, anyway? Adam called and asked if I could recommend a place for day lessons in Chicago. I could tell this wasn't just any person, so I volunteered the *Resolute*."

Alana laughed, a trill of delight Lucas hadn't heard from her. "So instead of Marissa spending the day tacking around the beaches on a rowboat with a mast, she spent the day sailing a Herreshoff yacht?"

"It was the most use I'd been to anyone in months," Nate said with a shrug. "She was a natural. Lots of reading, not too self-conscious to ask questions and put the answers into practice. What did you know about her interest in sailing?"

"I was her enabler, or maybe her dealer. When I got to Walkers Ford, she asked me to order books through the interlibrary loan for her. All of them were about sailing. She was very quiet about it. Adam took it from there."

"And now they're back in San Diego after six months cruising around the Pacific, about to get married."

Both men got a little quiet then. She had a quick glance at Nate's left hand. Bare. She tried to remember if her mother had mentioned a divorce or even a separation, and came up blank. Freddie wouldn't have bothered to pass on the gossip, even if she knew. But Nate left her relationship status alone, so she didn't bring up his marriage.

The conversation continued until the Rockies rose from the western plains. Rock climbing and other extreme sports took over at that point, carrying on until the western deserts in California appeared below them. Lucas asked questions about Nate's military training and service, and Nate started telling funny stories again, about Adam, then the men they would meet when they landed.

It was easy for Alana to slip back into her lifelong role as the smiling observer.

They landed in San Diego. After the plane taxied to a halt, Alana woke up Darla and helped her get the dress from the hanging cupboard. Nate opened the door to a wave of heat and sunshine so tangible Alana felt her skin soaking up the heat. She slipped her sunglasses from her purse. Nate went down the stairs first, then reached up to help Darla, then Alana from the plane.

"Oh, goodness," Darla said.

At first Alana thought she was commenting on the brilliant blue sky and the hint of ocean breeze, but when a crowd of whooping men engulfed Nate, taking him to the tarmac in a group tackle, she just smiled and stepped back.

"I understand why it was so hard for Adam to come home," Darla said quietly.

The pile of muscles and boots untangled and righted itself, ending with Nate, grinning and cursing under his breath as he brushed dirt from his clothes. As one, the group turned to face Lucas, Alana, and Darla.

"Gentlemen," Nate said. "Ms. Alana Wentworth. Lucas Ridgeway. Mrs. Collins, Adam's mother."

Respectful smiles and handshakes for Darla morphed into something slightly edgier and more inviting for Alana, then the whole group turned for the waiting vehicles, sorting out people and luggage with a fair amount of discussion. Lucas opened the back door of the car for Alana, then slid into the backseat with her. The small convoy headed west, toward the ocean, and came to a halt at one of San Diego's hotel/marina complexes, where Adam and Marissa were renting a slip. Alana eagerly slid out of the car, scanning the sterns for *Prairie Dreams*.

"There she is," Nate said, pointing over her shoulder.

She was used for both women and boats, and in this case could have referred to either Marissa or her sturdy, practical little boat. Alana stopped in amazement, staring at the woman confidently crossing the gap between boat and dock. Her hair streamed down her back, honey streaked in the darker brown and red strands. She wore a pair of khaki shorts and a red halter top. Swimsuit straps clung tight against her shoulders. Every inch of exposed skin was tanned to the color of caramel, but the most shocking change was in her face.

Laughter danced in Marissa Brooks's eyes. She looked gloriously, radiantly happy, deliriously pleased with life. The woman Alana had met in Walkers Ford was pretty, dark, compressed under the weight of over a hundred years of family history and obligation. This was a woman bursting with life, and confidence, and sheer joy.

She loped down the dock to envelop Alana in a hug. "Oh, I'm so glad you're here!" she said.

"Ack!" Alana said, hugging her back tightly. "I'm glad to be here, too. Oh, let me take that!" she said, turning to Darla.

She relieved Darla of the precious dress mere moments before Adam swept his mother into a tight hug. She kissed his cheek, then stepped back to let him greet people he hadn't seen since he left the Corps.

Holding her ground in the milling crowd of big male bodies, Marissa peered at the dress. "I can't believe you made this in time," she said to Darla. "Oh, I can't wait to see it!"

"You should try it on as soon as possible," Darla fretted, twisting and turning to get a better look at Marissa. "Did you lose weight? You look like you lost weight. Tell me you didn't lose weight."

"I sent you my measurements a week ago," Marissa said gently. "I haven't lost weight. I promise. Alana, can I use your room? The boat's barely big enough for the two of us, let alone a dress fitting."

"Of course," Alana said.

Alana found it secretly amusing to watch a dozen Marines part like the Red Sea for Darla and the dress. As they passed, Adam caught Marissa around the waist. "We're going out—"

"No peeking!" she said, covering his eyes and laughing. "You can't see the dress."

"I'm not looking," he said obediently. "We're going down to the beach. We'll pick up everything for the barbeque tonight. Text when you're on your way."

"Anything special you like to drink, ma'am?"

Alana turned to find a very young, very bright-eyed Marine at her left shoulder, attempting to look solicitous and succeeding mostly at leering. What was his name? Garrett? "I'm fine with whatever," she said.

"I know what she likes," Nate replied.

"Oh," Garrett said. "Sorry, sir."

"We're old friends, Bill," Nate said. "Bartles & Jaymes sangria, right?" he said to Alana, completely straight-faced.

Laughter pealed out of her. "See you later."

Lucas's face was completely blank through this exchange. Adam hauled him in for a quick slap on the back, then guided him toward the vehicles.

Inside the hotel, they found Nate had checked them all in, and their luggage was waiting in their rooms. Alana and Darla both had marina views, Darla in a suite, three doors down from Alana. She had no idea if Lucas and Nate were even on their floor.

Marissa took the dress from Darla and disappeared into the bathroom. "Did you have a good flight?"

"I could get used to flying like that," Darla said as she opened one suitcase to reveal a sewing machine, thread, fabric, and assorted needles, zippers, and buttons. "How does it fit?"

"What do you think?"

They both turned to see Marissa standing in the doorway between the bedroom and sitting area. The dress fit her perfectly, rich cream silk folded in tight, flat undulations from the bodice to her flat stomach and hips, then flaring ever so slightly around her ankles. Thin flat straps curved over her tanned shoulders, nearly hidden by her tousled fall of hair.

"Oh, my goodness," Alana said, her throat inexplicably tightening. "Adam's going to go weak at the knees when he sees you."

"That's the plan," Marissa said.

Darla was already by Marissa's side, critically pinching the fabric at her waist, smoothing her hand down the seaming in the back. "It's a little loose."

"It's perfect," Marissa said decisively, echoing Alana's thoughts. "I want to be able to dance and eat and laugh all night. It's absolutely perfect."

Darla already had two pins on either side of the bodice and was adding another to the straps. "I'll just tighten it up a little here," she said distractedly. "It won't take a minute."

"Flowers?" Alana said, thinking about white against that cream fabric.

"Red roses."

"What's Adam wearing?"

"No idea," Marissa said. "Shorts, maybe. Not a tux. We're keeping this as simple as possible."

"My son best not show up for his wedding in shorts," Darla said as she jabbed a pin into one of the shoulder straps.

"Hair?"

"You know that style that looks like you just got out of bed, but really you spent a couple of hours on it?"

"Yes."

"That one." She looked at Darla, then mouthed to Alana, "He likes my hair down."

Alana smiled back. "Perfect."

"Where's the location?"

Marissa moved to the sliding glass doors leading to the balcony, pulled back the drapes, and pointed. A little ways down the beach from the marina was a sheltered sandy cove. Rocks rose on the far side, and the sun gilded the wet stone with afternoon light. At sunset it would be bathed in the same undulating red and orange waves as the stained glass windows at Brookhaven.

"It's beautiful," Alana breathed. "How on earth did you find this place?"

"We were calling around, looking for hotel rooms with a marina. I got to talking with the reservations clerk and she mentioned they had a last-minute cancellation." Her face fell for a minute. "A death in the family. I hate to think of my happiness coming at someone else's expense."

"It's not," Alana said. "That's just the way life works. You've been unhappy long enough."

"Sometimes I can't believe this is real, that this is my life. I wake up next to Adam, and we're moored in some remote bay off the coast of Hawaii, and the stars are so thick I understand why our galaxy is the Milky Way, and I can't believe it."

"It sounds idyllic."

"And then a week later, we're becalmed a thousand miles from land, the sun beating down on us, getting on each other's last nerve because we both smell, and I really can't believe it."

"Take that off," Darla said. "I'm going to make a few adjustments, and then I'm going to bed until tomorrow. You all have fun without me tonight."

Marissa swept the older woman into a hug. "Thank you so much," she said. "It's perfect, and I love it."

"You're welcome."

Alana and Marissa watched her go. "She won't be happy until it's perfect by her standards."

"She could be working as a designer in New York or Chicago," Alana said. "My mother would kill for that attention to detail in her clothes." It made her sad to see that kind of talent languishing in Walkers Ford, and only strengthened her commitment to see Cody get the education and opportunity he deserved.

Marissa changed back into her shorts and halter top in the bathroom while Alana dug her swimsuit out of her luggage and pulled on a tank dress as a cover-up. Together they made their way down to the beach. They spread out the towels the hotel provided, then Alana dashed into the water. She sleeked back her hair then returned to the towel.

"You're not going in?"

"I've been in the ocean every day for the last six months," Marissa said complacently.

One of the things Alana liked so much about Marissa was that she didn't feel the need to fill the air with chatter. Unlike Freddie and her mother, who contributed a running commentary on everything, Marissa could sit in silence. Alana lay back and let the sun warm her bones. She should feel relieved, ready to go home, rejuvenated, like she'd accomplished something that mattered to her. She'd had her time as a librarian. She was going back to something meaningful on a global scale.

So why did she feel so restless? Because she was leaving

behind Cody, who needed her, and Mrs. Battle, who made her laugh and felt like the guide she'd never had?

Or Lucas? She admired him. She liked his company. She loved watching him move. She forgot what she was saying when he walked across a room, loose joints and hard muscles and unshakable confidence.

Whatever she'd started with Lucas two weeks ago wasn't anywhere close to finished.

"Thanks for coming," Marissa said. "I wasn't sure you'd be able to, and it means so much to me, because none of this would have happened without you."

"Oh, I wouldn't say that," Alana demurred automatically. "Adam seemed pretty determined to get you back."

Marissa rolled over onto her stomach. "If you hadn't given him the books I ordered, he wouldn't have known which lever to pull," she said seriously. "I could have held out against him if he hadn't known that secret."

Funny how a person couldn't see what raged like a forest fire to everyone else. "It was obvious to anyone who watched him walk into Brookhaven that something was going to happen between the two of you," Alana said.

"Things happen when Adam's around, but something good? Something life-changing?" She shook her head. "It could have gone either way. It's entirely possible that if you hadn't given him those books, I'd still be in Walkers Ford, and he'd be one semester into grad school in Brookings."

"But you'd be together."

"Maybe." Marissa studied the sand. "But like we are now? That's all you."

"And Nate, for taking you out on *Resolute*. And you, for having the courage to follow your dream. And Adam, for whatever he did to set himself free."

"He did something amazingly brave," Marissa said almost inaudibly. "I don't know if I'm strong enough to do what he did. But you were the catalyst. You set it in motion."

"I really didn't—"

"You did." Marissa's eyes narrowed. "Are you not okay with that?"

"I'm just not used to thinking of myself as a person who makes an impact," she admitted.

Marissa's eyebrows shot up, but before she could respond, they were surrounded by Adam, Lucas, and the rest of the group carrying coolers, lawn chairs, Frisbees and footballs, firewood, and portable speakers for an iPod. Within minutes, a fire burned merrily in a fire pit. A couple of guys traded insults as they took over the cooking, and before long, a half-playful football game was going on in the surf.

Lucas showed up in board shorts and a T-shirt with a faded logo for the Boys and Girls Club of Denver on his chest. Adam called him onto his team.

"Do you know anything about football?" Marissa asked.

"Chicago has a team?" Alana said, a hard lemonade in one hand and a doubtful expression on her face.

She'd seen Lucas naked. She'd seen him in motion. She'd seen him naked and in very dirty motion.

She'd never seen him sprint full tilt through the water's edge, then pivot to catch the ball Adam lofted over the other team's players, right into Lucas's arms. As he caught the ball, one of the young Marines tackled Lucas, pile driving him back into the waves, but Lucas surfaced with the ball in one hand outstretched. He waggled it as the other man came up. Adam whooped, and the soaked Marine said something that made Lucas laugh out loud, then extend his hand to pull the kid to his feet.

"Are you sleeping with him yet?"

Alana startled, and felt heat sweep into her face.

"I'll take that as a yes. You didn't say anything in your e-mails."

"It hasn't been going on long," Alana said. "I'm a private person, and he respects that. Or maybe it just suits him to not get involved."

Marissa tipped back her bottle of beer. "You leave when?"

"As soon as we get home. Back to Walkers Ford, that is."

Marissa didn't say anything else. The game came to an end when the players started to lose the ball in the twilight sky. Everyone settled in beach chairs around the fire, Adam's fingers possessively linked with Marissa's. Alana tried to unobtrusively save a space for Lucas, but two guys settled in on either side of her and spent the rest of the night fetching her drinks, making sure she had enough to eat.

"What's the plan for tomorrow?"

"The ceremony starts at sunset," Marissa said lazily. "It's pretty simple. The hotel takes care of everything. We show up, get married, and then do this again."

Alana thought about the freight train of planning on two continents going into Freddie's impending nuptials, about her role in all of that.

"What's the plan for tomorrow?"

"We're going rock climbing," Adam said. "We'll be back in the afternoon. Plenty of time to get ready."

Garrett, sitting next to Alana, nudged her with his elbow. "You going to miss me while I'm gone?"

"I'll try to keep myself busy," she said mildly.

Across the fire, Lucas's face grew more and more expressionless.

"OH EIGHT HUNDRED in the lobby," Nate said. "We'll pick up the gear on the way out of town."

Lucas gave him a nod, then slid his key card into the lock on his own door. First order of business was a shower. Six hours on the beach and Lucas had sand in places his doctor hadn't seen. He didn't relish waking up in a gritty bed. It was late. Alana had left the beach party half an hour earlier, laughing off an invitation to walk her to her room. Just in case.

Just in case Garrett wanted to get laid. A quiet word from

Nate ended the pursuit, for now. He knew how guys like that thought; he'd been one, a lifetime ago. A woman was an easy mark at a wedding. A beach wedding at sunset with a romantic story like Adam and Marissa's? Candy from a baby.

Garrett didn't know Alana. She was many things, but an easy mark wasn't one of them. Complicated, stubborn, single-minded, capable.

His.

Except she wasn't, or so his mind said. His body, as he stripped and got into the shower, said something entirely different. His body said he'd spent all day watching the woman in his bed laugh and talk with everyone but him. He leaned his head against the tiled wall and let water course over his back. The strength of the emotion, jealousy and anger and a blood-hot lust, washed through him with an intensity that left him breathless. This wasn't like him. Feeling this much. Caring so intensely, about anyone, anything.

You used to care like this.

And now I remember why I stopped. It fucking hurts. Not the pain. The longing.

He twisted the dial to cold, because a case of blue balls was better than taking a step down the slippery slope, but all he got for his trouble was wave after wave of goose bumps. He thought about Alana, about the way her hair looked slicked back from her face after she got out of the ocean, the way it dried in tangled sections around her face, the pink on her cheekbones and her lips from sun and salt spray and laughter.

He thought about her two floors up, alone in a room with a big bed.

Don't go there. Don't think that. She's sleeping.

She's leaving. This is the perfect time for you to just let it go.

Funny how the brain churned until it found a rational explanation. She was leaving. They'd go back to Walkers

Ford, and she'd pack up her sedan and leave town forever.
So why not take one more night?

*Because you're angry and hurt, and it's been a long
goddamn time since you felt anything, let alone anything
that powerful. You're out of practice.*

One more night . . .

He was out the door, in the quiet hallway, before he registered intention, let alone movement. Disdaining the elevator,
he took the stairs two floors up and crossed the hall to her
room. He and Nate by unspoken agreement took the rooms
with the parking lot views so Darla Collins and Alana would
wake up to the sound of waves lapping against the beach.

*Remember that nice guy when you feel like a raging
caveman.*

Silence reigned behind her door. He rapped quietly, using
only the knuckle of his index finger, not all four fingers like
he did when he meant business. If she was asleep, she'd sleep
through the knock. After a few moments he heard the gentle
swish of fabric against skin, then a hesitation he hoped was
her looking through the peephole, not deciding whether or
not to let him in.

The safety chain rattled, then the dead bolt clicked open,
followed by the door opening. She wore a thin cotton nightgown that hung low on her breasts and skimmed the tops of
her thighs. Her pale blond hair held the faint dampness of
a shower. She wasn't wearing any makeup, but the moonlight
caught the blue of her irises and her pink lips nonetheless.

He looked at her, letting anger and confusion and desire
infuse his face, giving her fair warning to shut the door.
Instead she stepped back, wordlessly inviting him in.

"Don't make the mistake of thinking I'm a nice guy," he
said. "I'm not."

She didn't move, didn't close the door or answer him with
anything other than the slight tilt of her head that sent her
hair gliding against her cheekbone.

He stepped through the door, took the handle from her,

and closed it. When the latch snicked into the lock she reached out and fisted her hand in his shirt, pulling him in for a kiss.

He pinned her to the wall with mouth and chest and hips, and cupped the clean line of her jaw with both hands as he ravaged her mouth. She made a whimpering little noise but rather than squirming to get away she tried to climb him, looping one leg around his and keeping him close. He slid one arm under her hips and lifted her; when she locked her ankles around his waist he stepped away from the wall, crossed through the sitting area and bore her onto the bed.

She gasped when he scored her throat with nipping, hot kisses. "Lucas!"

"All day I've watched other men try to get into your pants," he growled, hardly conscious of what he was saying.

"Garrett's already been up here," she gasped.

That explained the careful use of the peephole. He shoved her thin nightgown up to her waist, then bent his head and nuzzled it the rest of the way up past her breasts. He closed one hand over her breast and brushed the nipple with his thumb.

Each rhythmic stroke of his thumb tightened her body ever so slightly. Her eyelids drooped. "Were you wearing that when you opened the door?"

"I didn't open the door," she whispered.

He shut her up in the manner used by lust-crazed men everywhere, with a deep kiss. In the part of his brain still capable of observing, he knew he was being rougher, more passionate than he'd been before. He worked his thigh between hers, pressed against the cotton covering her mound. That wasn't enough, so he rolled half on top of her and he used his greater weight to keep her pinned as he kissed her.

Her fingers laced through his hair, holding his mouth to hers as the kiss turned edgy, lips and teeth and tongue demanding what he hadn't put into words. Completing the movement, he shifted between her legs, raked the edge of his teeth down her throat, and took advantage of the way she bucked to tongue each nipple. When he'd kissed his way down her sternum, her hands shifted to his shoulders, pushing him lower.

He settled between her thighs. She was slick and hot, the lap of waves on the beach an erratic counterpoint to the steady swipe of his tongue. Her hip bones held the sun's heat, the ocean's salt filling his senses as he ruthlessly worked her to the edge, then flung her over.

"Mine," he murmured into her hip bone. Then he sat back, worked his shorts low on his hips, pulled a condom from his pocket and rolled it on, then sank inside her.

He expected to finish fast and furious, but the sound she made, the way she tightened around him, inside and out, sounded extremely promising. So he gritted his teeth and held back, keeping his pace slow and steady and relentless. His reward was her heels in the backs of his thighs and her hands flattening against the small of his back. She gave a devastating little shimmy as she adjusted their alignment to just right. He braced one elbow above her shoulder to hold her in place and clamped his hand on her hip, just to be sure she wasn't going anywhere.

"Oh, God," she sobbed.

Her release happened all at once, shuddering out in her breathless sobs, her fingernails digging into the base of his spine, but it was the rhythmic pulsing around his cock that did him in. He buried himself deep inside her, his vision closing to blackness as he came.

Time passed in a heaving, heart-pounding blur before he registered her palms patting his shoulder blades. "Hey," she said. "Are you still in there?"

He cleared his throat, then braced his weight on his elbows. "Yeah. Are you all right?"

"That didn't actually hurt," she said.

"Give it time. You're riding an endorphin rush right now."

He pushed back to his knees, disconnecting their bodies as he did. In the bathroom he ditched the condom, then forced himself to look in the mirror. His face was as flushed as Alana's, and he spent too much time outside to blame it on a California sunburn. That was emotion, anger and frustration and passion, hot and demanding, staining his cheekbones. The arrangement of eyes, nose, and mouth staring back looked familiar, that odd sense of déjà vu he got when a face triggered something deep in his brain.

He used to look like this all the time. A younger, less-worldly version of himself shifted between skin and bone, striving to surface in his eyes.

"Go away," he said to the image. "Nothing to see here you haven't seen before."

He straightened his clothes and flicked off the light as he left the bathroom. Alana had turned off the lamp on the nightstand. They'd pushed the sheet and covers down to the foot of the king-size bed. She lay curled up on her side with one arm bent under her head, facing the wide-open windows and doors overlooking the ocean. Moonlight striped a path across the carpet, bathing the curve of her waist and hip in colorless light. She'd pushed her nightgown down to a more modest position, but he could see the shadowy curves of bottom and cleft.

He should go, but all he wanted to do was fit himself to her like a puzzle piece.

Then she turned to look at him, a small smile on her face. "Do you hear that?"

He cocked his head slightly. "No."

"Come here."

It was all the invitation he needed. He stretched out behind her, then took a moment to fit his knees to the backs of hers, wrap his arm around her waist and align his chest with her back. She wriggled in his arms, then worked her bare feet between his shins.

"I still don't hear anything."

   "I would swear I can hear the sound of starlight on the waves," she said drowsily.

   He lifted his head and stared down at her. "How hard did you hit your head on the wall?"

   A little laugh. "Not that hard. My ears are ringing a little. That was quite intense."

   "I'm sorry," he said quietly.

   "Why?" she asked.

   "I overreacted. We're not dating. This isn't a relationship. I don't have any right to be jealous."

   After a moment's pause, she said, "You don't have any *reason* to be jealous. He's twenty-one years old. Not to disparage the Marine Corps' ability to transform young men into warriors, but he's still twenty-one."

   "I used to be twenty-one," Lucas said. "I know what he's thinking."

   She reached down and wove her fingers through his. "I can't really imagine you that young. If I hadn't seen pictures in the basement, I'd believe you sprang out of the prairie in uniform at thirty."

   The words hit a little too close to home. "Nate's not twenty-one," he said.

   She peered over her shoulder at him. "Nate's married."

   "He's not wearing a ring."

   "I know." Her brow wrinkled. "I'm sure he's still married. I'm behind on my gossip, but someone would have remembered to tell me if Nate Martin had gotten divorced. My mother certainly would have remembered. A divorced Nate Martin would be the most eligible bachelor east of the Mississippi. She'd shove David in front of a bus to free me up for Nate, who remembers me puking up sangria wine coolers behind the Powers' boathouse on Nantucket when we were seventeen, and would no sooner marry me than he'd marry one of the guys downstairs."

   Something inside him eased a little at this matter-of-fact recitation. "Your mother's the matchmaking type?"

"In rather medieval form, she sees me and Freddie as chattel to be bartered off to the highest bidder. Mother still lives in a world where marriages are alliances. A hundred years of marrying for love hasn't proved any more effective than marrying someone suitable, so why risk getting hurt? Settle for compatibility on as many levels as possible, and turn a blind eye to any indiscretions."

"What kind of alliance does she see in Freddie marrying Toby Robinson?"

Alana laughed. "Not much of one. Freddie said she's holding on to wedding invitations like they're political favors. Toby tours eight months a year, and he flatly refuses to be paraded around like he won Best in Show at Westminster, so Mother's not getting much ground out of bringing him to events." She sighed. "That's my next big challenge when I get home. Once they set the date, whatever time I have after the next big global conference will get sucked up into Freddie's wedding."

"Won't that be Freddie's big thing?"

"I'm her maid of honor, for one thing. Freddie's front-facing, as my IT guy would say. She'll pick and choose from whatever I come up with for caterers, dress, decorations, but I'll do the research. That's my job. Freddie doesn't have the patience for research, and I don't have the aptitude for implementing. She's easy enough to work with. It's Mother who second-guesses things, or asks for just a few more options."

She turned to face him. The moonlight gilded her high cheekbone and ear in silver light. "And then I think about how Adam and Marissa have one parent between them at their wedding, and I feel ashamed for resenting my own mother's involvement."

"I should go," he said.

"Stay," she whispered. She reached up to stroke his cheekbone, her fingers seemingly fascinated by the line where skin gave over to scruff. "You don't have to go home tonight. Stay with me."

He shouldn't. He knew he shouldn't, but rather than getting up, he reached for the alarm clock and set it for seven. Plenty of time to go back to his room, shower, and get ready for a bachelor party of rock climbing.

When he flopped on his back, she cuddled in close. As he drifted into sleep, he thought he heard the stars spangling on the waves.

THE ALARM SHRIEKED to life at exactly seven in the middle of radio personalities shouting over the latest celebrity-breakup scandal. With one hand Lucas scrabbled for the alarm, shutting it off by yanking the cord from the outlet in the wall.

"Don't stop," he growled, and tightened his grip on her hips. "Do. Not. Stop."

Alana gave a throaty little laugh as she lifted herself to the tip of his cock, then glided down. The movement worked the head of his cock and wrenched a groan from his throat. "Like that?"

"Yes. Oh, fuck . . . like that." He dug his heel into the smooth cotton sheet and thrust up.

She gasped, then braced her hands on his chest and rode him in earnest. She could probably feel his heart pounding against his ribs, but he could see her pulse racing at the base of her throat. Her head dropped forward, her hair hiding her expression, but then she tipped back, exposing the long line of her throat. "Oh yes," she whispered. She slumped forward, breathless in release. "Lucas. Yes."

The sound of his name in her mouth snapped his control. He wrapped his arms around her, rolled them, and drove into her once, twice. Again. She gave a satisfied little growl when he came.

"Jesus," he said.

In the aftermath, her hand wound into his hair. "I like sleeping together," she said smugly.

He grunted his agreement, then extracted himself from the tangle of her limbs and the sheets to dispose of the condom. "Christ," he said when he got to his feet.

"Sure you're up for rock climbing today?" she asked when he came out of the bathroom.

He slid her a glance, then snagged his shorts and underwear from the floor. Not even two rounds of sex in ten hours could dissipate his emotions about once again going rock climbing, but Alana didn't know how much he used to love the sport, how a difficult climb took his mind off the stress of the job, how he hadn't planned a trip to the Black Hills or the Rockies in years. "I'll be fine," he said.

She braced her head on her palm and looked at him. "You don't have to go, you know."

"What are you going to do today?" he asked as he buttoned his shorts.

"Help Marissa get ready later this afternoon, but before then, I'm going shopping," she said. "I need to wrap my gift. I had time to pick it up but didn't get it wrapped."

"Would you get me a gift card holder?" He reached for his wallet and pulled out a gift card to an online bookstore. "Adam said in his e-mails they were buying e-books."

"That's thoughtful," she said. "I'll find something."

"Thanks," he said.

"Be safe today," she said.

He stopped with his hand on the doorknob. His ex-wife used to say the same thing every morning. "You never say that in Walkers Ford."

"I guess I think climbing up a forty-foot sheer face is more dangerous than policing Walkers Ford." Her eyes went distant. "I could be wrong, though. I wonder which situation results in more deaths annually, small-town police work or extreme sports."

He huffed out a laugh. "Look it up and let me know when I get back. Because I will come back."

"Good," she said with a soft smile.

He made it back to his room without running into anyone, took a fast shower, and went down to the lobby to have breakfast. Nate was already at a table, the newspaper open beside him as he ate. His cell phone sat on the table beside the paper.

Lucas filled his plate. "Mind if I join you?"

"Please do," Nate said. He gave him a quick, speculative glance that Lucas met with his best expressionless face, then Nate handed over the sections of the paper he'd finished. Nate checked the phone eight times in the ten minutes they sat in silence. Lucas counted, and wondered what was so interesting to the married man who wasn't wearing his ring.

Adam arrived ten minutes early, making his way up from the small marina, past the pool, and into the lobby. "Sleep all right?" he said.

"Like a baby," Nate said lightly.

"Fine," Lucas said. "Ready for your last day as a single man?"

Adam huffed out a laugh. "Is it different? I've been with Ris for six months. I've loved her since we were teenagers. I'm hers. Forever. Vows won't make any difference."

Lucas arched an eyebrow at that rather flowery statement coming from the man who compared loyalty and fidelity to the unbreakable bonds forged in the Marine Corps, but he didn't say anything. Adam was right. Vows didn't make a difference. Vows didn't sustain his marriage as it crumbled under the weight of devastation and failure. They didn't sustain his marriage through a move from Denver to Walkers Ford. But a jaded divorced man didn't say that kind of thing to a man so infatuated he lost his train of thought when his love walked into a room.

Beside them, Nate folded his paper precisely and got up for a second glass of orange juice. When he came back, he pulled printouts of route maps from under the newspaper. "When do you have to be back?"

"I need to pick up the rings before five tonight," Adam said. "The ceremony's at sunset. Get the rings, take a shower, be on the beach a few minutes early."

Nate gave him a crooked smile. "Sounds easy enough."

"Ris wanted a low-key beach wedding, and I wasn't about to argue. The hotel arranges everything—chairs, flowers, the officiant, the cake. We bring in our own food. So it will be just like last night, except for the ceremony."

"Must be nice," Nate muttered under his breath. Lucas could only agree. His wedding had been fourteen months in the planning, a peak too high to sustain for the details of daily life after the honeymoon. He knew his marriage wouldn't make it when his wife wanted to renew their vows two years after the first ceremony.

The rest of the group strolled in a couple of minutes before eight. Lucas found himself fading into the background as the Marines told stories, cracked jokes, and did the whole guy-bonding thing. They convoyed to the climbing shop and picked up their gear. The Marines were comfortable with ropes and rappelling, but none of them had his climbing experience. He quietly made suggestions and double-checked the gear before settling the bill with the shop's owner.

"You're good with them," Nate said. Nate's transition from *Lieutenant* to *Mister* hadn't broken the chain of command. The younger guys all still looked to Nate and Adam for leadership, but both men openly deferred to Lucas's greater experience.

"I used to lead hiking and climbing trips into the Rockies for the Boys and Girls Club," Lucas said. "Fifteen kids from Denver's inner city, me, and a program manager."

Nate's smile actually reached his eyes. "We're in good hands, then."

Mission Gorge was one of the largest urban parks in the country. They parked and hiked up the short trail to the Main Wall Center, where they split up into teams. In Lucas's mind it was too early in the morning for anyone to start in on anything, but he'd forgotten exactly how one-track a twenty-one-year-old jacked-up kid's mind was.

"You'll be the one getting married soon."

"No way, man," Garrett said. "Getting married will interfere with my ability to fuck random women. Starting with the blonde back at the hotel. She'll be an easy mark after the wedding. Sunset, wedding, a little alcohol . . ."

He didn't see the gesture, but the tone of the whistles and catcalls told him enough. He wasn't aware of thought or movement. One minute the conversation was background noise as he coiled ropes and checked harnesses, calmly dispassionate, totally under control. The next minute Bill Garrett was backed into the rock face with Lucas's forearm at his throat. In the back of his mind, Lucas knew he looked like God's own avenging angel because rather than fighting back, both of Bill's hands were held up.

Total silence, other than the ground squirrels racing through the scrub brush surrounding the base of the rock. "Show the lady a little respect," Lucas breathed.

"Yessir."

It was a knee-jerk response trained into a kid by a drill sergeant, not a response to Lucas's overpowering command presence. Lucas let his arm drop and took a step back, then another. Given a little space, Garrett eased away from the rock face, then stepped sideways to check on his gear. Conversation resumed, but quietly.

"You okay?" Adam said.

"I'm sorry," Lucas said. He set his hands on his hips and looked at the dead needles under his feet as he shook his head. "I was out of line."

"Yeah, well, he was over it," Adam said. "Something going on with you and Alana?"

Fuck it. "Yeah," he said. "How did you know?"

"You're the only single man not looking at her," Adam said with a laugh.

"Fuck," he breathed. He tilted his head back and stared at the sky. "It's supposed to be a secret."

"That makes no sense at all."

"It did at the time."

But things had changed. He didn't want them to have changed, but he'd long since given up on life performing to his whims and standards. After last night . . . things were different.

"You and Marissa weren't exactly discreet," he said.

"Ris didn't give a damn what people thought about her. Still doesn't."

"Alana does."

"She's worried about her reputation in Walkers Ford?"

For him. They were different for him. She seemed perfectly happy to carry on exactly as they were. He'd sold himself out. "She's a private person. And she doesn't want to make waves in town. She's going back to Chicago as soon as we get back, and she didn't want to damage my reputation."

Adam's eyebrows shot up, and he turned a laugh into a cough. "Thoughtful of her. And you went along with this . . . why?"

Lucas turned and looked at him because surely Adam got this. If the woman you wanted to sleep with had some random stipulation you didn't give a rat's ass about, why not agree? You got what you wanted. She got what she wanted. Simple enough.

"Okay, I know why." Adam blew out his breath. "Still up for this?"

"Yeah. Give me a second."

He walked over to the kid. "I'm sorry," he said. "I was out of line."

Dull heat infused his face as Garrett yanked climbing gear out of his pack. "Is this some fucking game the two of you play? 'Cause I didn't see a ring, and you didn't talk to her at all last night."

Not until he showed up at her hotel room door. "You didn't miss anything."

"Dude, that's fucked up," Garrett said, clearly aggrieved. "I'd never have said a word if . . . that's not right."

"I know," he said, then held out his hand. "We good?"

Eyeing him warily, the kid shook his hand. "We're good. Just don't drop my ass at the base of this fucking cliff, yeah?"

Lucas smiled. "Don't drop mine, either."

"Deal." Garrett smiled at him. "You're fucking spooky. Like . . . *stealth*. You know that? No idea what you're thinking or feeling. Nice. How do you pull that off, anyway?"

You watch a kid you've mentored through rock-climbing expeditions like this one say good-bye to his mother after he's been sentenced to twenty-years-without-parole for armed robbery.

He tried to find the real smile from just seconds ago. "Let's go."

But if this kid doesn't know how he feels, how would Alana? Did *he* even know how he felt?

11

ALANA SET THE plates holding slices of pound cake on the wrought iron table, then eased into a chair at the food court plaza in the Fashion Valley Mall. Adam's mother set up napkins and silverware, then distributed the plates. Marissa followed with three coffee cups balanced in her hands.

"I'd forgotten how fun shopping can be," Marissa said. "The biggest shopping trips I make these days are to grocery stores to lay in provisions before we leave port."

"You're happy with what you bought?" Alana asked as she squeezed honey packets into her tea.

"I am," Marissa said. "A couple of new bathing suits, new shorts because I ripped my least tattered pair on the dock in Hawaii, and something for tonight."

This last statement came with a sidelong glance at Darla.

"You're very sweet to be so modest, but I am aware that you're sleeping with my son," she said, magnificently unconcerned. "I hope you bought something pretty."

The nightgown was exquisite. Alana had recognized the lingerie brand in the window as one Freddie adored, and she'd firmly guided Marissa inside Henri Bendel. Marissa winced at the price tags, but decided she could set aside low-key for the wedding night. They'd left Darla to move at her own pace, examining fabrics and lines and designs— they bought the nightgown and spent the rest of the day wandering in the open air and sunshine.

"Did you get the ring?"

"I did," Marissa said. She brought a dark blue jeweler's box out of the zippered pocket in her purse and opened it. A simple gold band rested inside. Alana saw the date engraved into the band. "The gold's going to get pretty scratched, but I like it. It's traditional."

"What about yours?" Alana asked. Marissa didn't wear an engagement ring.

"The exact same ring, size four and a half," she said, closing the box and stowing it safely away. "I don't wear much jewelry, and when we're done sailing, I'll probably go back into construction work in one way or another. A setting will just snag on things, so I won't wear it during the workday anyway. The more you take it off, the more likely you are to lose it."

"Very practical," Alana said, thinking of Freddie's six-carat diamond from Harry Winston. Then she thought about Lucas's grandmother's missing ring, and Gunther's stolen one. Tokens of affection given to mark momentous occasions, only to disappear. She'd ask Mrs. Battle to let her know if Lucas tracked down Gunther's ring, but she didn't know if she had the courage to ask Lucas to let her know if he ever found his grandmother's.

Especially after last night—when Lucas appeared at her hotel room door, his mask of silent distance stretched so thin over emotions raging behind his eyes. She'd known he didn't like the other men flirting with her. It made her uncomfortable, but she also didn't know how to stop it. Every year thousands of girls fought for spaces at one of the elite boarding schools around the country. Attending a premier school had given her lots of educational opportunities, but learning how to deal with men on a casual basis wasn't one of them. She'd been at a loss for how to tell Bill Garrett to ease up a little.

As a result, she'd hurt Lucas's feelings because she'd assumed that his affectless face meant he didn't have any for her.

Foolish girl. Foolish, foolish girl.

Now she really didn't know what to do.

"What's going on with you and Lucas?"

Alana's eyes widened, then shot to Darla's face. She smiled back and sipped her coffee. "You girls are really very sweet to be so concerned about my tender ears, but please remember, I became an unwed mother at seventeen. I do know people have sex. I'm very hard to shock."

"But . . . no one in Walkers Ford is supposed to know," Alana said.

"No one in Walkers Ford does know," Darla replied.

"She keeps secrets very well," Marissa said with a little smile.

"Nothing's going on. Nothing permanent, anyway," Alana amended. "I'm leaving as soon as we get back to Walkers Ford. My contract's up, and I finished the work I did for Mayor Turner when I made the presentation to the town council."

"Are they going to renovate the library?" Marissa asked.

Alana shrugged. "To be honest, I don't pay much attention to what happens after I do the research. This is the first time I've pulled everything together to develop a proposal and make recommendations."

"It was a lovely proposal," Darla said. "Cody's drawings really brought to life what you described. I could look at them and see exactly what your changes would do for the county."

"It's hard to believe your job is so specialized," Marissa said.

"It's more efficient. I do one thing, and I do it very, very well. Freddie does something else, and she does that thing very, very well. We have researchers, script writers, proposal writers, event planners."

"Do you like that?"

"I like contributing to what the Wentworth Foundation stands for," Alana said. "We make a difference on a global scale. I'm a part of that."

Marissa made a noncommittal noise and finished her pound cake. "So Lucas was just a sabbatical fling. Do people have flings on sabbatical?"

"I did."

"You don't seem like the type," Marissa said gently.

"And that's why I did it," Alana replied. "We should go."

THEY CAUGHT A cab back to the hotel in plenty of time for a quick nap before Marissa knocked on her door.

"I'm actually getting excited," she said. "Oh. You're already ready."

She'd showered, dressed, and done her hair and makeup shortly after waking up, mostly out of habit. Freddie's routine always took longer than Alana's, and she'd gotten used to keeping her own hair and makeup simple so she could help with Freddie's far more elaborate preparations. She looked at the eye shadow compact in shades of dark blue and gray in her makeup bag. A sunset wedding on the beach was the perfect occasion for smoky eyes, but somehow it didn't feel right. She slid the compact back into her makeup bag and used the more neutral shades of sand and pink she always wore.

Marissa took a shower and styled her hair while Alana double-checked all the arrangements with the hotel's event staff. The sun was a ball of red fire hanging low in the sky when Darla knocked on the door, the dress in hand. Alana watched Darla zip Marissa into the dress, fussing until the folds lay just right. Then the older woman stepped back and swiped under her carefully applied eye makeup.

"What's wrong?" Marissa said. "The dress is perfect. It was perfect yesterday, and it's even more perfect today."

"I'm so happy for you," Darla said quietly. "You and Adam. It took so long for you to get here, but you're here, and I'm happy and relieved and just full of joy for you both."

"Don't make me cry," Marissa said. "Not yet."

Another knock at the door. Alana opened it to take the bouquet of red roses from the event planner, who assured her everything was ready down at the beach. The officiant had arrived. They were ready whenever Marissa was ready.

"Let's go," she said.

Alana stuffed the extra packages of tissues and her travel sewing kit into her purse and followed Darla and Marissa through the corridor, into the elevator, and through the lobby. This wasn't all that different from doing things with Freddie. Heads turned and conversations stopped when Marissa swept through the room, tall and slender and barefoot, her dark hair falling in tousled waves to her elbows, her bouquet of red roses held loose in one hand, Adam's ring on her thumb, her eyes bright with fire and life.

They made their way past the pool, through the gate to the beach, and past the hotel guests packing up as the sun went down, to the event space. It was worth it to be in the background, watching for the moment Adam saw Marissa in her wedding dress. While in the middle of a conversation with Nate, Lucas, and the officiant, he stopped talking mid-sentence, as if seeing Marissa made the air evaporate from his lungs.

Gobsmacked was a term Freddie had picked up since meeting Toby. Adam looked gobsmacked. Nate's smile was a little twist of his mouth.

Lucas was looking at Alana.

The expression on his face was so intense, so full of longing, that Alana almost turned to see who was standing behind her. She wore a very simple linen sheath in the cornflower blue that matched her eyes, and like everyone else on the beach besides the officiant, was barefoot. In keeping with the beach theme, she wore a subtle eye shadow and mascara with a tinted gloss on her lips. Her cheeks she'd trusted to her blushes.

Lucas kept staring. She ducked her head and felt her hair sliding across her hot cheek. When she was close enough, he held out his hand. In a move as natural as breathing, she reached for it, felt his warm, callused palm brush hers as he wove their fingers together. She forgot that they weren't supposed to be doing this.

"Shall we begin?" the officiant asked.

There'd been no rehearsal dinner, no choreography. White wooden chairs and low tables laden with a casual meal and drinks lined the beach. The guests closed in a circle around Adam and Marissa, who stood with their hands linked as the officiant guided them through their vows. Fiery sunset reds, oranges, and pinks bathed their faces as they promised to love, honor, and cherish, until death did them part. The honesty and sincerity lay in every line of their bodies, transforming simple ceremony into powerful ritual, binding blood to blood and bone to bone. Tears welled up in Alana's eyes.

"You may now kiss the bride," the officiant said.

Adam's hand slid under Marissa's hair to her nape, a possessive move mediated by the gentle brush he gave her lips. It was respectful and intimate all at once. Marissa's lips curved into a smile under his, then gave way to a laughing sob as she threw her arms around his neck. A whoop and a round of applause, then the circle closed into handshakes and hugs.

"That's not a gold band," Alana said with a laugh.

A platinum band set with princess-cut diamonds encircled Marissa's ring finger. She stared down at it. "No, it's not."

Adam brushed a kiss on the top of her head. "You thought we should have matching bands. I thought you should have that."

"I love it," she whispered.

"Good," he whispered back.

LIGHT POLLUTION BLANCHED the sky to dusky gray velvet dotted with stars when Alana found herself in one of the chairs, sipping a glass of white wine as Marissa opened presents. Nate had organized a group gift from the marines, a transponder with Wi-Fi, USB, and a GPS that could be run from their phones. Lucas slid into the chair next to hers and held out a plate with a slice of wedding cake.

"Thank you," she said, touched.

He sectioned off a bit of the cake and stared out at the ocean.

"Bill Garrett seems to think I have cooties," she said. "You wouldn't know anything about that, would you?"

"I might," he said, then ate another bite. "Do you want to know?"

"Not really," she admitted. "But thank you."

"I thought you'd know how to handle him."

She let the frosting dissolve on her tongue before she spoke. "I'm a product of eleven years of girls' schools, and Freddie Wentworth's little sister. No one ever notices me."

"I noticed you," he said. "I noticed you right away."

Her cheeks heated at his quiet words. "What did you think of the ceremony?" before she remembered he was divorced. "I'm sorry. Forget I asked."

He shrugged. "We tried. It didn't work."

"They're going to work," she said with a nod at Adam and Marissa.

"They know what they want," Lucas said.

She nodded, but the real difference was that they had the courage to go for it. Marissa had been dreaming of the ocean for years before Adam gave her the impetus to live her dream. As a Marine, Adam had seen death up close. Marissa had lost everyone she loved before she was twenty-five years old. Maybe that's what allowed them to break away and start a new life together, the certainty that death was a heartbeat away.

Watching the wedding, Alana thought that Marissa knew what she wanted. She just didn't think she could have it. She'd been tied to her past in Walkers Ford, weighted down by over a hundred years of history, while Adam carried a terrible burden of guilt. But while all the people Adam and Marissa were beholden to—Marissa's father, the boy who died in a motorcycle race with Adam—were dead, Alana's responsibility was to the living. She couldn't possibly leave Freddie, or the Wentworth Foundation to work as a public librarian in a small town. Could she?

"You look amazing," Lucas said softly.

"No different than I normally look," she said. "The night of the town hall I wanted to get out of my work clothes and put on makeup and a pretty outfit. But I was running late, and you were home early. I missed my chance."

"Probably for the best," he said. "If you'd looked any more seductive, I would have ignored Duke and Mitch and the meeting just to get you under me."

His mild tone didn't match the sexual promise infusing his words. An electric current raced through her, intense and shocking because his tone had deepened, darkened. He was seducing her.

"You're blushing again."

"I'm not."

His breath drifted against her bare shoulder. "I want to take you to bed."

"I didn't mean that as a challenge!"

He went on as if she hadn't spoken. "I want to take you upstairs, and turn off the lights, and watch your skin turn pink as I move inside you. When I've kissed you and your skin's marked by my mouth, you look like a rose in the moonlight. It gets darker when I'm moving inside you, that blood flush." He turned to look at her, and the demand in his eyes halted her breath in her lungs. "I want that one more night before you leave."

Her heart stopped in her chest. Lucas Ridgeway hid a poet's soul under that affectless surface. "Is it too soon?" she whispered, looking around the fire.

"Darla went to bed an hour ago. They'll be telling stories until the sun comes up."

She nodded. He took her hand, and they set off across the sand. She caught Marissa's eye and lifted a hand in farewell. From her position on Adam's lap, Marissa gave her a smile and a finger wave, then leaned her head back against Adam's shoulder.

SHE LEFT THE lights off when they reached her room, but opened the curtains and the sliding glass doors to let in the sound of waves lapping at the sand. She walked through the pale swatch of moonlight back to the bed. Lucas's lips were warm and soft against hers, seeming to memorize the taste and feel of her mouth, letting her do the same. He trailed his mouth down her neck to the juncture of her shoulder, then turned her back to him so he could lower the zipper of her dress. His fingertips skated over her shoulder blades, raising goose bumps and pebbling her nipples as her dress fell to the floor, leaving her in her silk underwear. He unhooked her bra and pushed it off. Her panties slipped from her hips, leaving her bare before him.

She should have felt exposed, standing naked in front of him, but his dark gaze, both reverent and intent, draped her in shadows while she unbuttoned his shirt. Soon he was as bare as she was, reclining on the bed, letting her commit him to memory. She focused on areas where tastes and textures changed, from the scrape of his stubble to the soft skin of his neck, the wiry texture of hair giving way to his hip bones, the taste of sweat rising in the crease of his thigh as he arched and groaned under her hands.

When she smoothed a condom down his shaft and took him inside her, everything changed. Her inner walls softened and stretched to accommodate him, then she bent forward and kissed him. "Lucas," she whispered. "Lucas."

"Shh," he said, and rolled her to her back. Her eyes fluttered closed with the first stroke, but she forced them open, the better to capture every moment, every expression. He drew it out until she ached with desire. "Not yet," she murmured. "Not yet. A little longer."

By the time it ended they were both shivering in the moonlight. She muffled her cries in his shoulder and held him while he came. He left her long enough to get rid of the condom, then slid into the bed and pulled the covers over them both.

She lay awake long after he dropped into sleep. The moon and stars held the space between sunset and sunrise. For the first time, sex with Lucas felt like a good-bye.

THE NEXT MORNING dawned sunny and quiet. Nate set an early departure to get him back to Chicago in time for a family commitment, so Alana, Darla, Lucas, and Nate were scheduled to meet up for breakfast at the hotel's restaurant. Darla was the only person who didn't look like she'd been up all night. Nate declined food, held his head rather carefully, and left his sunglasses on against the light streaming through the floor-to-ceiling windows overlooking the marina.

Alana had showered and dressed in her jeans and jacket again, but didn't feel up to dealing with her contacts this morning, so she wore her blue-rimmed glasses. After a quick glance in the mirror, she decided against any makeup at all. The flush in her lips and cheeks was more than enough color.

Packing took no time at all. She rolled her bag between the tables, said a quiet good morning, then got herself some juice and fruit. "Late night?" she asked Nate.

One corner of his mouth lifted. "I fell asleep on the beach just before sunrise."

"That doesn't sound very comfortable," Darla said.

"It wasn't," he admitted. "I'm out of practice for sleeping on the ground."

"Good thing you can sleep on the plane," Alana teased.

"You look like you need a nap, too," he said, one eyebrow lifted.

There were enough seats on the plane for all four of them to claim a row and curl up, but the thought of spending her last moments with Lucas asleep made her throat tighten. "I might do that," she said, and pushed the rest of her breakfast to the side.

She wasn't ready to leave. *It's just San Diego,* she told herself. *It's warm and sunny and you've had a break from both of your jobs. You've spent all night in Lucas's arms. You have beautiful memories of a romantic wedding in a picturesque setting. It's the perfect way to end things.*

Lucas strolled through the lobby, his duffle in hand, and grabbed a cup of coffee for the drive to the airport. Adam and Marissa dashed up the pier and into the lobby just in time to say good-bye.

Marissa hugged Alana tightly. "Thank you so much for coming," she said.

"It was my pleasure," she said. "Stay in touch."

"We will."

Darla said good-bye to her son and daughter-in-law in a firm voice, despite her trembling chin. "See you soon, Mom," Adam said.

The ride to the airport was a little solemn. "Marissa looked beautiful," Alana said to Darla.

"Happiness does that to a woman," Darla said softly, looking out the window. She turned to Alana and smiled. "Thank you."

They were in the air just minutes after boarding Nate's jet. Alana took one of the window seats and purposely didn't look at Lucas as he boarded. She wouldn't give him longing glances. He might be tired, too. He had a job to do in Walkers Ford when he got home. And she couldn't change the rules of the game on him. She'd made it very clear she wanted nothing more than casual.

He settled into the seat next to hers. "You should sleep," he said. "You've got a long drive ahead of you tomorrow. I don't want you driving tired."

"You should sleep, too," she replied.

"Three hours is good for me," he said. "I shouldn't have kept you up most of the night."

"Yes, you should have," she whispered.

His hand slid over hers, then turned it palm-up so he could lace his fingers with hers. Without any concern at all for Darla or Nate, she rested her head on his shoulder and closed her eyes, soaking her memory with the sensation of his muscled shoulder and the scent of his skin.

ALANA AWOKE WHEN the wheels touched down. Momentarily disoriented, she inhaled shakily as she peered out the window and tried to remember where she was. The sight of the rolling green prairie made her smile. Home.

She was home.

Nate leaned across the aisle. "Why don't you ride to Chicago with me? No point in driving across Minnesota and Wisconsin if you don't have to," he said. "You can hire an exec relo service to pack up your stuff and transport your car. You'd have it in a week, maybe less."

Not home. Walkers Ford.

Her eyes widened, and she glanced at Lucas. "Um, I hadn't even thought about it. I'm not quite done packing. I haven't said good-bye to . . . anyone. Thank you, though."

Nate nodded. "Fair enough."

Their bags were stored in the cabin, so the pilot kept the engines running while Nate escorted them off the plane.

"See you soon," he said as he gave Alana a casual kiss on the cheek. "Nice to meet you. Next climbing trip, you're in."

"Deal," Lucas said as he shook Nate's hand.

They loaded up the truck and headed back into town. When they pulled into Darla's driveway, Alana gave the older woman a hug, then climbed back into the truck. She'd forgotten to turn her phone back on at the airfield, so she did now and waited for the infuriatingly slow network to download the influx of messages, mostly from Freddie, and texts, again, mostly from Freddie. She had a voicemail, too, which surprised her. Very few people in her life actually called her, let alone left a message. She tapped on the message and waited for the playback.

"Ms. Wentworth, it's Mayor Turner. Good news. The council approved the proposal you put together for us. We've got some citizens concerned about the police department funding, not Lucas, mind you, but never mind that. I'm asking you to stay a couple of weeks and get the ball rolling."

"What?" she gasped.

"Mrs. Battle has agreed to help you with everything. Just give her a call when you get this message. Okay. Bye now."

She stared at the phone for a second, trying to sort through her emotions. She always left unfinished business behind her. That was her job, to do research and put together proposals. She almost never pitched the proposal, let alone implemented it. But underneath the shock lay something more primitive she couldn't deny.

She didn't want to leave Walkers Ford with this project unfinished. This was her baby, her library, her renovation, for people who loved their library and appreciated her work.

"Everything okay?" Lucas asked when he got back in the truck.

Freddie would *kill* her. Kill her stone dead, and leave her body for her equally furious mother to dismember and pick over. The Senator likely wouldn't notice. No surprise there.

"Mayor Turner just sandbagged me," she said, fighting

to keep her voice even. "The council voted to go ahead with the renovation."

"That's good," he said.

"They want me to stay for a couple of weeks and help draft the request for bids."

SHE'D BE AROUND for a couple more weeks? Lucas's heart leaped in his chest, but he kept his face even. "Okay."

"I can't, of course," she said.

His stomach dropped six inches. "Right."

"Freddie will kill me. We've got New Delhi and London and the Senator's banquet coming up, plus her wedding, which promises to be either an epic battle between her and Mother or the single biggest social event of the decade on two continents, or maybe both. Oh my God. There's seven hours difference between Chicago and London. I'm going to be making calls at three in the morning for weeks. I can't stay."

He gave himself the duration of time it took to back out of Darla Collins's driveway to feel disappointed. That was all he could handle. Five seconds. He gave himself another two seconds to shift into drive and to call himself an idiot. Which he was, for thinking Alana Wentworth, *the* Freddie Wentworth's sister and closest confidant, the younger daughter of *those* Wentworths, would choose to stick around for the renovation of the Walkers Ford Public Library.

Seven seconds to feel something was the longest he'd felt anything in years. San Diego was an exception. He'd felt furious, jealous, happy, and relaxed, when he wasn't perpetually aroused. Alana in tight jeans and a tight leather jacket, or Alana in a pretty blue sheath, barefoot on the beach, Alana in a thin cotton nightgown a thousand times sexier than satin and lace because he loved the feel of a body under cotton.

She wasn't going to stay for the library, and she wasn't

going to stay for him. She'd wanted to go home different. He was sending her home different.

"I want to stay."

He cut her a glance as they turned onto his street. "You do."

"I do," she said. "God. I can't, but I do. I mean, anyone else can put together a request for bids. It's not what I do. And someone has to talk Cody into doing that mural. Now, before he loses interest, or worse. Whatever happens with the renovation, the mural is the key to the library. Mrs. Battle might be able to convince him to do it."

Lucas couldn't help himself. He laughed.

"Okay, probably not. I'm not sure *I* can talk Cody into doing the mural, but he's going to do it. He's good with the kids, too, so maybe he could draw something and let them paint it, or guide them through something. And the furniture, someone has to—"

She visibly stopped herself. "I can't stay."

"But you want to." He wasn't pleading, or so he told himself. He was just playing devil's advocate, a role that came easily to him.

"Someone else is better suited for this," she said.

"How do you know you're not good at implementing things?"

"I'm just not. I do research, outline proposals. Freddie or someone else polishes them and presents them, then someone *else* implements them."

"That's enough for you?"

She blinked. "Of course. I'm part of something of strategic value on a global scale."

"I don't even know what that means," he said.

A little huff of laughter. "If I'm honest, sometimes I don't know what it means, either."

"You're already working for them while you're here. You can get up at three a.m. and call England from here."

She flicked him a glance. "You're not ready to see me go? You were going to tear out the kitchen."

He shrugged with a nonchalance he didn't really feel. "I'll still tear out the kitchen."

"I'll be in your way."

"You bet your sweet ass you'll be in my way," he said as he pulled into his driveway, "because you'll be helping."

She laughed, and swung those long legs out of the truck. He got out and braced for impact from Duke, who shot out of the screened-in porch to writhe and twist around Lucas's legs. He crouched down and got a snout in his face for his trouble. "Miss me, boy? Did you miss me? That's a good boy. You're a good dog," he said, sending up a flurry of fur as he scratched Duke's neck.

He looked over his shoulder to find Alana watching them. She had her phone to her ear, and the call must have connected because she crossed the driveway and bent over to examine the roses. "It's me. Look—oh, India's hot this time of year, I know—yes, yes, oh, that's good. What else do you need? E-mail me the list. Oh. I was out of town and I didn't check my phone much. Yes, no, I'm home now, I can check on it—no, I'm not in Chicago. I meant I'm home in Walkers Ford. . . . It's kind of home."

Lucas hoisted Alana's suitcase from the truck bed, then crossed the driveway to set it inside the kitchen door.

"Look, Freddie, I'm going to stay here another couple of weeks. The city council approved the renovation project, and they want me to stay on and get the process under way. The mayor promises he's close to hiring someone."

Freddie's unhappy shriek pierced Lucas's eardrum five feet away.

"I'm not—Freddie—please, listen to me," she said. "I'm handling most of my job from here. I can—Mother wants what? That's ridiculous. It's a dinner, not a state funeral. I'll call her later."

Freddie's voice escalated again, but Alana cut her off. "I am—I can still—I am *not playing at Library Director!* I am the acting library director here, and this is my responsibility."

Silence on the other end of the line. Perhaps Alana's indignant tone got through to her sister. Lucas couldn't make out the next words, but the tone was apologetic. "I'm sorry, too. I know it's inconvenient for everyone, but I need to stay just a little bit longer. It's last minute, but isn't that how things always go?"

A question.

"I'll be back for the Senator's party. I won't miss that." She looked across the driveway at Lucas. "I need to go, Freddie. Love to Toby."

"She sounds like a handful," Lucas said.

"She's Freddie Wentworth. She's a racehorse on crack, my sister, and my best friend," Alana said matter-of-factly as she slid her phone into her jeans pocket. "She says I'm playing at being library director."

"We don't think you're playing," Lucas replied. "We can't afford for people to play at their jobs around here. We don't have a depth chart. People serve on the school board and the city council and as church deacons and crossing guards and the library board because we need them. Everyone matters here."

He climbed the steps to the screened-in porch and opened the door. Duke stood by the plastic mat holding his food and water dishes. The food dish was empty, which was odd. Duke didn't scarf down his food the moment Lucas scooped it out for him. The dog grazed on kibble throughout the day, often finishing the previous day's meal just before Lucas dumped the day's portion into the stainless steel bowl.

The water dish was bone-dry. He'd been gone the better part of three days.

Lucas looked at Duke a little more closely, no problem given that the dog was standing over his dish, tail wagging expectantly. His bright blue eyes were cloudy and dim, the first sign of dehydration. Lucas lifted the lid on the plastic tote he used to protect the dog food from marauding squirrels and raccoons. The scoop sat in exactly the same place he'd left it when he fed Duke the morning he left.

He cursed, low and hard and vicious.

"What's wrong?" Alana asked from the driveway.

Still cursing under his breath, he picked up Duke's water dish and held it under the outdoor faucet. The dog stuck his snout between the dish and the water splashing into the bowl, lapping up water, spraying Lucas's shirt with icy cold liquid. "I'm sorry, boy," he said.

The dog braced, gave a tremendous sneeze, then shook droplets from his snout and ears. Lucas set the bowl down, then turned to the food tub.

"What's wrong?" Alana asked more quietly.

"I asked Tanya to take care of Duke for me while I was gone." He dumped a scoop full of food into the bowl and watched Duke tear into it, switching between eating and drinking. "She didn't."

"Oh."

"Slow down there," he said, stroking Duke between the ears. "Slow down. It's okay. I'm back."

At the sound of Lucas's voice, the dog leaned against his legs, easing into the scratch. When he stopped, Duke went back to the food dish, but this time with a little less zeal.

"Maybe she's sick."

Lucas huffed bitterly. "Drunk, you mean. Or high. Or both." He dug his keys out of his jeans pocket.

"I'm coming with you."

He glared at her across the truck's hood. "Why? You think I'll hold back because you're around?"

Her gaze didn't flinch. "No. I don't think you should have to do this on your own."

"I'm never alone," he said again. The ghosts of failures past stayed with him every minute of every day.

She didn't bother to respond, just opened the passenger door to the truck. Duke scrabbled out of the doggie door and hurtled into the backseat. Alana got in and closed the door. That left him with three choices: physically hauling her out, making a huge scene in front of the neighbors until she got out under her own power, or taking her along.

He'd never laid hands on a woman in anger, and Alana wouldn't appreciate being a spectacle in front of the neighbors. He got in and slammed his door.

THE DRIVE OUT to Tanya's cabin passed in silence. He could hear his blood rushing in his ears, and some observing part of him noted his white knuckles on the steering wheel.

"Breathe," Alana said quietly when he turned down the rutted lane leading down to the creek.

"I am breathing."

"You aren't. Exhale."

He did, and realized when he exhaled that he had been all but holding his breath. Nature took over and he drew a full breath at the bottom of the exhale. The fury simmering in his veins dialed down to the upper edge of the red zone. He braked to a halt by the cabin and got out, leaving his door open for Duke to follow.

The cabin had the vast silence of an uninhabited building. The door was locked, but Lucas knew the trick for getting in, a specific twist, jerk, and hoist of the handle that released the aging lock. He pushed the door open and stalked inside.

The main room was empty. Dishes crusted with the remnants of heated-up canned spaghetti sat in the sink. He crouched by the hearth and held his hand over the charred logs and ashes. Stone cold, not even lingering heat held in the rack. Through the back windows he saw Alana walking around the house, the late afternoon sunlight gleaming off her caramel leather jacket, then head down the path to the creek.

She was almost as good as a deputy, he thought, then strode to the closed bedroom door. He stopped with his hand around but not touching the knob, listening for signs of life. Snoring, sheets rustling. Anything could be on the other side of this door. Tanya, fast asleep as her toxin of choice worked its way out of her system. Tanya and a bedmate.

He opened the door. The bed was unmade and empty. The room smelled of stale dirty laundry scattered on the floor, alcohol sweat, and the underlying sweet scent of pot.

"Fuck."

Alana's flats slapped against the floorboard behind him. "I didn't see her out back," she said. "Duke chased a rabbit into the trees."

He blew out his breath. "She's not here. I'd guess she hasn't been here for a couple of days, which means she's partying somewhere."

"Do you want to go get her?" He looked at her, hands on his hips. "I assume you have a pretty good idea where she is."

He did. He knew three or four likely spots in Chatham County alone. "If I go get her, I'm going to have to arrest her and whoever she's with," he said. "She knows that, and she knows I won't do it."

"All right," she said, accepting his answer without questioning it. "Now what?"

"Now I call the station and ask Mary to let the guys know they should watch out for her truck. Then I wait. I'll go get Duke."

He went outside and made the call, then whistled. Duke came trotting out of the tall grass around the creek, tail high, ears perked, gaze alert. When he peered back inside the cabin, he found Alana in the kitchen nook, running water into the spaghetti pot to soak off the crusted sauce and noodles.

"It's a waste of time."

"It's my time to waste," she replied, then dried her hands. San Diego felt like a lifetime away.

They pulled into his driveway after dark. She stopped with her hand on the door handle. "Come over for dinner?"

The idea sounded so good. He could sit in her kitchen and watch her cook, find some of the ease and comfort he felt with her. But the reality was that before she kissed him, he hadn't needed any of what she offered. Being with her made him need to be with her, and there was only one solution to that: cold turkey. They'd said their good-byes in San Diego. Mitch's phone call might keep her in town for a couple of weeks, but it didn't change things between them.

But cold turkey was coming in a couple of weeks, when she went home to her life in Chicago. He'd never binged on anything before, but if all he could get of Alana was the next two weeks, he'd take it.

"Yeah," he said.

And if after dinner he took her to bed and made her shudder and clutch him and beg, well, that was just grabbing what he had left in great big, greedy, dripping handfuls.

12

AT SUNSET THE next evening, Alana's house was near to bursting at the seams with the Walkers Ford library board, and a few more "interested parties" who stopped by to listen in and offer opinions.

Mrs. Battle, Mrs. Walker, and Delaney Walker-Herndon sat on the sofa, a laptop open on Mrs. Walker's lap as they browsed industrial furnishings websites and considered seating arrangements for the children's section as well as tables already wired for laptops. Alana sat on a folding chair in a small group focusing on the specifics of the interior renovation. The request for bids had to be as detailed as possible to ensure the project didn't encounter lengthy delays and cost overruns. So far the document ran thirty-eight pages and counting, and they hadn't even gotten to the electrical and fiber-optics requirements, much less the diagrams. Alana's laptop rested on her knees, heating her legs while the fan whirred. They'd opened the windows and the doors to get a cross breeze two hours ago, when people started showing up with food and drinks, and a hundred competing ideas. The sheer number of bodies strained the tiny house's capacity, and an infectious energy surged in the room.

"I'm listening, Billy," she said absently as she entered the details for the high-speed Internet connection.

Billy Olson had enough construction experience to help her with the details, but wouldn't be bidding on the job. "Once that's done, they'll sand and stain the floors. Keep your fingers crossed for a dry stretch. If we get one, they can open the windows. That'll clear out the stink and the plaster, and the polyurethane will dry that much faster."

Alana worked all of this into the calendar and added the tasks to the action plan, then took the pieces of wood stained to different darknesses from Billy and considered them. "What do you think, Mrs. Battle?" she asked as she offered them across the room.

"I like a natural look myself," she said, looking to Mrs. Walker for confirmation. "Stain might make the room darker and smaller."

"Oh, yes," Mrs. Walker said. "Let's keep it as bright and clean as possible."

She had the right people, the decision makers in the room. There were a dozen other people, including Pastor Theresa who appeared to be Mrs. Battle's and Gunther's pastor. In addition to making decisions rapid-fire for the library, a fair bit of gossip was being traded.

"Alyssa's planning to go to the summer program. Her scholarship won't cover it, but her father insisted—"

"Jeannie's pregnant again. Fourteen weeks. Little Evan's only ten months old, but she wanted to keep them close—"

"—Thought he got snipped, but I guess it didn't take—"

"—Hired me to build four one-room cabins in the meadow behind Brookhaven, and a shelter. I guess she wants to hold yoga classes out there. The cabins are for people who want to do longer, private retreats."

"That sounds interesting," Alana said.

"I never thought she'd get enough business to make a go of it," Billy said. "But Lester down at the market says her grocery orders have doubled since she opened in November.

That's a good sign. Lucky for us I helped Marissa when she redid the plaster out at Brookhaven. I didn't know I'd get a chance to use the skills again so soon."

The room went a little bit quiet at Marissa's name. Delaney Walker-Herndon covered smoothly. "Mom, can I get you some more coffee? Lucinda? Anyone else?"

Alana set her laptop aside and stretched, then gathered plates and napkins. In the kitchen, Delaney poured out the old coffee, then started making another pot. Every available inch of counter space was crowded with veggie trays and ranch dressing, a coffee cake, and cookies. Alana looked around for a place to set the plates and silverware. Delaney combined two half-empty plates of cookies, giving Alana the space she needed.

"Have you heard from Marissa lately?" Delaney inquired. She ran water into the sink and added dish soap.

Alana crumpled the napkins in her fist and tossed them in the trash can. She didn't know the whole history between Adam, Marissa, and Delaney, but keeping Marissa's location a secret was one thing. Outright lying to Delaney's face was something else entirely. "I saw her last weekend. She and Adam got married."

Delaney was too composed, too self-assured to show much reaction. "That's good," she said simply. "I wondered when both you and Mrs. Collins were gone. Was it a nice ceremony?"

"It was beautiful," Alana said. "They got married on the beach. It was a really small ceremony, very informal. Darla made her dress. Adam's friends and their girlfriends and wives from the Marine Corps were there, and me, and Darla, and Lucas."

She said his name as casually as she could, as if it were no big deal that she and Lucas spent the weekend together at Marissa and Adam's wedding. As if she had every right to call him Lucas, not Chief Ridgeway. As if she were a part of the community.

"I thought Adam and Lucas fell out of touch while Adam was in the Marines," Delaney mused. "Maybe he was there because he was close to Marissa. Still, that's nice for Chief Ridgeway. He hasn't taken a vacation the entire time he's been chief here."

"No, he hasn't," Alana said absently. In hindsight, it was a bit odd that he didn't do the kinds of things other men in town did, like take a few days for ice fishing, or to go hunting, or simply disappear somewhere warm in the long stretch between Christmas and the crocuses poking up in late March.

Delaney smiled and shook her head. "I'm happy for them. So they don't plan to come home soon."

"I don't know," Alana replied truthfully. No one needed to know the newlyweds were likely somewhere in the Pacific again by now. "Adam talked about opening a bike shop in San Diego."

"Ah," Delaney said.

The kitchen door opened to admit first Duke, then Lucas. Tail wagging, the dog trotted over to Alana and sniffed her jeans, then her fist. Lucas called him with a soft click, then gave a hand signal. Duke curled up by the back door and tucked his nose between his front paws.

"Impressive. I forget he was a working dog," Alana said.

The coffee had finished brewing. Delaney poured two cups and took them back into the living room.

"What brings you by?" she asked Lucas, trying for the kind of casual conversation that wouldn't alert anyone to their relationship.

"I thought I'd take off the counters tonight," he said wryly.

She looked at the food-laden counter. "Maybe later?"

"I have to be up early. We're doing a burn."

"A what?"

"After the court case clears, we burn any illegal substances no longer needed as evidence."

"Really? Where?" she asked.

"The crematorium in Brookings."

"Oh."

One corner of his mouth lifted. "You didn't think we took it upwind outside the city limits and held a big bonfire, did you?"

"No," she said indignantly, then added, "Fine, I did, but not for long."

She glanced over her shoulder to make sure the conversation in the living room continued without her, then crossed the kitchen to give him a quick kiss. But Delaney's random comment sparked a heated little flare in her chest.

"Can I ask you a question?"

"Sure," he said.

"Were you and Marissa ever dating?"

He cut her a glance, one dark eyebrow slightly lifted. "No. Why?"

Her heart did a funny little thing in her chest. "I've heard the gossip. You've been divorced for a couple of years. You're . . ."

"A man?"

Gorgeous. "Delaney asked if I'd heard from Marissa lately, and I couldn't bring myself to lie to her face. I told her about the wedding and that you were there. She said she didn't think you and Adam were close enough friends that he'd invite you to the wedding. Then she said maybe you and Marissa . . . had a thing. Mrs. Battle said you weren't seeing anyone in town. I know you're good at keeping secrets, even if Marissa wouldn't have cared."

There was a funny little silence between them, one she recognized from conversations between her mother and Freddie. "You think Marissa wouldn't have mentioned if we'd dated? Or hooked up?"

"We mostly talked about Adam."

"You think I wouldn't have told you if I'd dated Marissa?"

"You haven't told me you dated anyone since your divorce."

"Because I haven't."

"You've been divorced for almost three years," she said. "I just didn't think about it, but in hindsight, of course you'd need . . . anyway, it's none of my business."

"A flight attendant who works the Sioux Falls–to-Chicago trip texts when she's got an overnight."

Jealousy seared Alana's skin. "It's *really* none of my business."

Lucas kept his face turned to the crowd in his living room. "You're not the only cliché in this . . . thing," he said. "Cops are dogs, on the lookout to score. Marissa Brooks, however, would cross the street rather than talk to a cop."

"Why?"

"The former chief of police was a right bastard with kids. Hard on them if they made mistakes. Marissa made a really big mistake, and so did Adam. He hauled her down to the station in the backseat of a cruiser, locked her in an interrogation room, and read her the riot act, without her father there, or an attorney."

She thought about Marissa, her dreamer's soul, about family obligations. "Dear God."

"I was there when she came out, and she was white as a sheet, shaking. Some women have a thing for uniforms, but Marissa's not one of them." He gave a small chuckle. "One, I was married when I came back. Two, after the divorce, I wasn't in the right frame of mind to start up with someone in town. And three, Marissa Brooks has been in love with Adam Collins since she was seventeen years old, something even an outsider summer kid like me knew. Relationships are hard enough if both people are committed to them. I try not to get involved with women who have divided loyalties."

For a long moment the air between them vibrated with tension. "This was your uncle. Chief Ridgeway, right?" She ran through her few encounters with Lucas's uncle. The man was as emotionless as they came, an older version of Lucas.

Lucas's grandmother gifted Lucas her house in the hopes he wouldn't follow in Nelson Ridgeway's footsteps. "Tanya's father?"

A frown crossed Lucas's face. "Yeah. Tanya's father."

Duke lifted his head at the knock at the door. Cody stood framed in the screen door. Alana took a quick step back from Lucas, then felt her face heat as the damned blush she couldn't control when he was around bloomed on her cheeks.

She hurried past Lucas and opened the door. Cody ducked his head and stepped inside, his shoulders hunched over. He carried a large sketch pad and his messenger bag. "Come on in," she said.

He glanced warily at Lucas, who gave him an assessing look, nothing more. Duke sniffed the air and whined, then looked at Lucas.

Oh, shit, Alana thought.

Lucas's expression didn't change. "Duke used to work on the drug squad with me in Denver," he said evenly. "Right now he's telling me he smells something he didn't smell thirty seconds ago. I don't smell anything I shouldn't smell, but his nose is better than mine."

Cody flushed as red as Alana, but he didn't say a word.

"Well?" Lucas said.

"Well nothing."

Lucas straightened and braced his weight on the balls of his feet. "Should I take a drive out to your place?"

"No! Don't do that. It scares the little kids."

"That's not my fault," Lucas pointed out. "I'm not the one bringing illegal substances into a house with three kids under the age of eight in it. You remember the conditions of your community-service agreement?"

"Fuck this," Cody said and turned to leave.

"Wait!" Alana lunged for him. He shook off her arm, but didn't open the door. She turned one beseeching look from him to Lucas. "Don't go. Just . . . tell us what happened."

"I got a ride into town with someone."

"Someone who might have a little stash in the glove box?"

Cody's face closed off even more.

"Who?"

"Lucas," she hissed.

"Your brother, who's on *parole*? Or one of his loser friends destined for another trip to the pen?"

"I'm not saying."

Lucas shook his head, then shouldered past Alana to stand in the doorway between the kitchen and living room. "Excuse me," he said in a tone of voice that carried easily.

All conversation halted.

"Did anyone see who was driving the car that just pulled out of the driveway?"

"I didn't recognize the driver," Mrs. Battle said, "but Colt and Cody Burton were in the car."

"Neal Rogers from Hanover was driving." This in Billy's voice.

"Thanks," Lucas said.

Cody seethed beside Alana. A muscle popped in his jaw, but the sheen covering his eyes tore at her heart. "It wasn't Colt's stash," he said in a shaking voice when Lucas turned back to him. "It wasn't."

Alana took Lucas to the other end of the kitchen and lowered her voice. "I believe him," she said, keeping one eye on Cody in case he bolted, and the other on Duke, in case he signaled or pointed or did whatever it was drugs dogs did to indicate the presence of illegal substances.

The look Lucas turned on her made her eyes widen. "Why exactly do you believe him?"

"Because the mural matters to him. This matters to him. He wouldn't jeopardize that."

"If he didn't want to jeopardize his community service, he'd make better choices."

"How? He doesn't have a car. Unless I give him a ride he walks from home to the library for his service hours. It's six miles, one way!"

Lucas looked at her, then at Cody, then finally at Duke, who still lay on the floor by the door. "Duke's not interested, so I'm not, either," he said.

Cody flinched, the movement confined to his eyes and not much more.

"I'll be in the basement," he said, and picked up the toolbox.

"Come into the living room," Alana said as she held out her arm to Cody. "Do you want something to eat first?"

"No," he said, clutching the portfolio to his chest.

In the living room, she made sure everyone knew Cody. He opened the portfolio and took out several exquisitely detailed drawings of the mural, then stumbled through an explanation of what he'd drawn and why he'd drawn it. "I'd been in the library on school visits," he said. "But not at all since grade school. It was just books, you know? I didn't care about books. But then I started my community service there, and I realized it was so much more than that. It's easy to say it's our connection to the world outside Walkers Ford, but the other thing I realized is that it's a place where we connect with each other. We have the community center and the school stuff—sports, the plays, church stuff—but the library is the only place that's open most of the week to anybody. You don't have to be smart, or a jock, or able to buy a soda or coffee to sit in a booth. You just go, and Miss Wentworth makes you feel like you belong there, even when you don't."

Tears sprang into Alana's eyes.

A respectful, slightly shocked silence followed as the drawings made their way from hand to hand around the room.

"That's why the building is the central focus of the mural. It's a visual way of reminding everyone who uses the library what's at the center of our community. Most folks have cable or satellite. Some folks have high-speed Internet access and computers. I don't," he said. Alana wondered what it cost him to admit to a room full of patrons who thought he was a loser and a delinquent that he was one of those people. "But the more we isolate ourselves from each other, the less of a community we are. The library brings us together. Because we all have something to offer."

"These are absolutely gorgeous," Delaney said.

As if everyone was waiting for a verdict from a representative of the town's leading family, the dam opened. To Alana's surprise, Cody didn't blush or downplay his abilities. He talked confidently about the techniques he used, how he'd replicate them on the mural, got into a very technical discussion with Billy about the properties of plaster and when the surface would be ready to receive paint.

Watching him, Alana felt total certainty steal over her soul. *He's good at this. He knows what he's good at, what he's supposed to do. I can't leave him here any more than I could leave Marissa here. He needs training, he needs exposure to other artists, to techniques, to the wider world to nurture a brain that could easily turn on itself with drugs, alcohol, or the sheer devastation of being trapped.*

Mrs. Battle and another older woman were looking over the most detailed rendering of the mural, identifying each of the town's residents. Gina stood outside her diner, and Superintendent Miller stood on the steps of the county's high school, watching the football coach run players through practice on the field. The man who owned the gas station was at his pumps, and the shopkeepers on Main Street chatted or watered the flowers lining the business district. Delaney's father and father-in-law shook hands in the space between the Herndon law offices and the bank. Two uniformed officers were getting into police cars outside the station, but Lucas was nowhere in sight.

Cody had revised the drawings since the first time she saw them. He'd captured the marble steps leading up to the front doors. A blond woman dressed in a tweed skirt and cream sweater stood on the steps. That was her, so the man in a suit jacket and slacks with a gun and badge on his belt was Lucas, one step below her, his dark head level with hers as they surveyed the rest of Main Street. Alana felt heat rush into her face when she recognized herself, and Lucas, in a pose that could either be construed as intimate or attentive, depending on how much the looker knew about their relationship. On the grass in the building's shadow stood a russet-haired boy, his skinniness exaggerated into a looming emaciation. Cody.

Her heart clenched in her chest. She didn't belong in the picture. The attitude of both Cody and Lucas, turned toward her as if they needed her, left an unsettled feeling in her stomach. Cody gave her too much credit. All she'd done was her job, her real job, the one where she compiled information, got buy-in from stakeholders. The picture implied she'd made a difference, when all she'd done was her job.

She cast a quick glance at Cody, and found him watching her. She couldn't tell from his expression what he'd deduced, if anything. "It's sweet of you to put me in the mural," she said. "Can you paint over it when the new library director starts?"

"What do you mean? You're the library director."

"Acting library director," she corrected. "I'm leaving in a couple of weeks."

Shock froze his features. "What?"

Did he not know? How could he not know that she was a contract librarian? "I'm not a permanent hire, Cody," she said gently. "I was only here for a few months while the town conducted a search for a full-time librarian. I should have left yesterday, but Mayor Turner and the council approved the renovation. I'm staying to complete it, but then I'm going home to Chicago."

The room had gone quiet again. Suddenly Cody looked as young as his grade-school brothers. His eyes were bright, and his lower lip softened into a quiver until he got it under control. "Sure," he said. "I knew that."

She pulled him into the kitchen, away from the listening ears, and looked at the mural design as if seeing it for the first time. Who else would get the position of honor at the top of the library steps? The composition wouldn't make any sense to have Lucas gazing ever-so-slightly up at the new hire, especially if the town hired a man.

The drawing only made sense if she stood there.

Don't be ridiculous. One person doesn't make a difference in a place like this. Community matters.

He looked at the rendition as if realizing that his entire worldview was completely wrong, that he'd spent the last few weeks thinking the world was round only to discover it was flat.

"You can redo it," she said encouragingly. "Move Luc— Chief Ridgeway to the station, and add the new library director when he or she starts. These are small changes, easy to do, right?"

But even as she said it, she knew what she suggested changed the entire composition. The color scheme depended on Lucas's dark suit and dark hair against her lighter colors. The whole thing depended on her and Lucas together. Which wasn't going to happen.

He looked at her. "Right. Small changes. I'll just shift some people around."

"Cody, I'm sorry," she said softly. "I thought you knew."

"Don't be stupid," he said. "Of course I knew people leave. It's what people do."

Her heart broke a little more. "Look," she said. "When I get back to Chicago I'm going to talk to a friend of mine who runs the summer program at the Art Institute. It's past the application deadline, but I think I can pull some strings and get you a spot there this summer. That will give you an edge when you apply to colleges in the fall. The school takes quite a few students from their summer programs. You've got the talent to make art a full-time career."

The disbelief in his face held tones of a world-weary cynicism. "I'm not going to art school this summer," he said.

"Why not? There are scholarships—"

"Who's going to take care of the little kids?"

Her mouth shut with a click.

"Mom works nights. Colt's not going to be around for long. That was his stash in the car," he said, magnificently unconcerned about Lucas's presence in the basement. "The little kids love him, and someone has to pick up the pieces when he goes to jail again."

"Surely there's someone who can . . ."

"You're looking at that someone, Miss Wentworth," he said, so gently she wanted to cry. "I'm not going to summer school, or art school. I'll graduate. Probably. Get a job. I'll look after my brothers, and my mom. On the plus side, when I have a job, I'll be able to buy art supplies."

"I'm going to ask anyway," she said. "We can figure something out. There must be something, a program, something through the state."

"You can find day cares that take kids at night," he said. "But we can't afford it, and anyway, I wouldn't put my brothers in one. I appreciate the offer," he said. "But that's not how we do things around here."

His voice was deeper, expressive, an indication of how he'd sound when he made the full transition into adulthood.

"Can your mom go to the day shift?"

"Sure," he said. "But the night shift gets a pay differential. She can afford to do that when I'm working. Until then, it's a choice between feeding us all or being around at night."

Alana looked around the kitchen overflowing with food. Without a word she got up and started packing leftovers into pans and plastic tubs. Macaroni and cheese, pasta salad, a casserole made from tater tots, ground beef, and cream of mushroom soup. "I'll give you a ride home," she said.

"I'd appreciate it," he said in return.

When she got back to the house, the street and driveway were empty of cars, except for Mrs. Battle's. Pastor Theresa helped her into the passenger seat, then waited when Alana called out her name.

She explained the situation as quickly as possible. "Do you know of anything that would help the Burtons?"

"I can look into it," she said. "But I can't think of anything that would let Cody leave for school."

"I'm afraid I just broke his heart," she confessed.

"Are you a person of faith?" Pastor Theresa asked gently.

"We're Methodist," Alana responded tentatively, not sure where this was headed.

"I believe that we all have a purpose in life, that God created us to fulfill a responsibility here on earth. We all have a place to be, where we'll make an impact on the world. We can choose to listen to that call, or we can ignore it. The question is, when you hear the call, will you respond with your whole heart?"

That was easy enough to answer. Her whole heart belonged in Chicago, working for the foundation on issues like global poverty, health care for developing nations. Next year they were focusing on human trafficking, and Freddie was getting married. Chicago was where her family and her work was. It would be selfish to ignore the call of national service just because she felt validated.

What about Cody, so clearly called to art and equally clearly stifled in that vocation?

"Thank you. That's very helpful," Alana said.

Pastor Theresa didn't look like she believed that at all. "You're welcome. Call anytime."

She walked into her house and found Lucas prying up the countertops while Duke watched with interest from his spot by the door. What had happened with Cody was too raw for her to bring up, so she crouched by Duke and scratched the top of his head very gently. He grunted his appreciation.

Lucas spoke first. "For a while, the house sounded like

it did when Gran was alive. She always had people over, planning something."

"Mrs. Battle said the same thing," Alana said. "I don't understand this place," she said finally. "Delaney seemed to genuinely care that Marissa and Adam were happy, even after everything that happened between her and Adam. Even though I stood up for Marissa, she wants to do the right thing for the town and the library."

"Delaney's a good person. A kind person. People saw her as wronged when Adam broke off their engagement. Loyalty matters in a community like this. In the end, all we have to depend on is each other. You saw Walkers Ford at its worst with Marissa. You're seeing them at their best now. If you were staying, you could give it a few weeks and you would see them at their worst again."

"Like the weather. Wait five minutes and it changes." She sat down in a chair and put her head in her hands.

"You take Cody home?"

"I did."

"Was it Colt's stash in the car?"

Grateful her face was hidden from him, she said, "Please don't ask me that."

"I'm asking."

"Lucas. Don't do it. Don't go search that trailer."

He tossed the pry bar on the counter. "That's my job. That's what it's like when you stick with one place long enough to learn each other's secrets. You hurt people. They hurt you. You have to do hard things, like sending a twenty-year-old kid to jail because he's hurting other people in the community, or take kids from their meth-addicted parents. You send some to jail and you bury some. That's life, when you're not avoiding every goddamn thing by skimming the surface."

For the first time in Lucas's presence, she felt the blood drain from her face.

"That's not what I do. That is *not* what I do."

He looked down, swallowed hard. "I'm sorry," he said gruffly.

"It's fine."

"I don't have probable cause to search the trailer," he said finally. "Even if you tell me what I already know."

She looked at Duke, dozing on the floor. She understood why men preferred dogs. Duke's loyalty was unquestioningly to Lucas. He felt no qualms about searching out the drugs and giving Lucas the answers that could tear Cody's family apart.

"I have some work to do," she said finally. "I'll be in the office, unless you need me to help with something."

One hand on his hip, he looked like he was being ground between two stones. "Demo's easy," he said. "It's the rebuilding where I need another set of hands."

She went into the office and closed the door, then pulled up her e-mail and prioritized the work she needed to do in the next two weeks. The Senator's party. Preliminary calls around Freddie's wedding. Research for Freddie's upcoming trip. Project management for the library renovation.

Find a way to say good-bye to Lucas that would show him exactly what he'd meant to her.

13

SHE WAS ASLEEP when he pushed open the bedroom door. The light from the kitchen illuminated the curve of her cheek, reassuringly flushed again.

Watching Alana Wentworth go white with shock slid an ice pick under his sternum. He'd apologized, and despite his brutal, uncalled-for words, she'd carried herself with considerable grace, offering to help him destroy the kitchen she was still using, then holding her head high as she walked down the hall to the bedroom she used as an office. She'd worked until after midnight, then asked him if he needed anything before taking herself to bed. He'd worked long past the point of exhaustion, going through the motions of stripping linoleum and plucking staples from the subfloor.

Eventually the noise got to Duke, and he walked past Lucas into the living room. But when his eyes began to sting from exhaustion and he went to claim his dog, Duke wasn't asleep in front of the fireplace. Or the office.

The damn dog was asleep in a tight ball on the braided rag rug, nose tucked under his curled front paw, by Alana's side of the bed. She was asleep, too, covers pulled up around her ears, blond hair gleaming in the moonlight.

His throat tightened. Add another emotion to the list of things he felt around Alana Wentworth. Regret for his harsh words. Shame for lashing out at a woman who'd made him no promises and done nothing but care about the people he was supposed to care about.

"I'm sorry," he murmured again to the moonlight.

At the sound of his voice, Duke's eyes opened. He studied Lucas without moving, waiting to see if he needed to get up or not before committing energy to the action. Alana didn't move.

He crossed the walnut floor to stand at the foot of the bed. "I'm sorry," he said a third time.

No response. Duke closed his eyes, apparently deciding that neither he nor Lucas were going anywhere tonight. How did he know what Lucas didn't know himself, that he wouldn't be going home to his own bed once again? Was it some signal in his body language the dog picked up on before Lucas's brain recognized the decision?

He was too tired to bother undressing, but the demo work had coated his clothes with a layer of dust and shards of debris, so he stripped off his shirt and shoved jeans and socks to the floor. Then he lifted the sheet, blanket, and chenille spread just enough to slide into the bed and curl up around Alana.

Her body was warm and soft from sleep, her hair as cool as the moonlight. She made a little noise when he tucked her into the curve of his body, and turned, nuzzling in search of his mouth.

"I'm sorry," he whispered.

She hummed, the uptick at the end asking a question.

"For what I said in the kitchen. For calling you shallow."

A little smile curved her lips. "'S okay." She rubbed his hip. "Go to sleep."

He closed his eyes and dropped into the blackness, only to dream of dead-eyed teenage boys hanging off sheer cliff faces, then of Tanya, sprawled on the road. He was in his

Denver PD uniform but on the county road leading to the cabin, and his cell phone was ringing. He fumbled at his hip until he woke up enough to realize the phone was actually ringing from his jeans pocket on the floor.

He lurched out of the bed. Duke pushed up on his front legs, ears alert. Alana struggled to one elbow.

The caller ID showed Matt Linden, one of his youngest officers and therefore stuck on the night shift.

"Ridgeway," he said.

"Chief, sorry to wake you up, but I've got a situation with your cousin out on CR-46. I think you'd better come out here."

The road to Tanya's cabin. "On my way."

"What's going on?" Alana asked.

He thought about lying to her, about hiding whatever was coming with Tanya from her, but lying felt like an admission he'd rather not make. Lying insinuated that he had something to hide, that he felt one way or another about what happened in his life. "Something's going on at Tanya's place."

She shoved the covers back and scrambled out of bed, nearly stepping on Duke in the process. "I'm coming with you."

"This is police business, not a social call."

She tucked her hair behind her ear and shot him a narrow-eyed look. "I heard CR-46. That's the road to Cody's home. His mother's working. If anything's going on with him, I'm coming along."

He yanked his jeans over his ass and swiftly fastened zipper and belt. Duke stood at his calves, ears and tail perked expectantly, waiting for a hand signal to send him into action. "It's not Cody."

She stopped dressing. "Oh," she said, clearly relieved.

"Go back to bed," he said through his shirt.

Her eyes narrowed again. "It's Tanya, isn't it?"

If she'd phrased the question as a statement he could have ignored her long enough to get out the door, but ignoring the question answered it. "Yes," he said, and gave Duke the signal to release him.

He had to give her credit. She dressed faster than any woman he'd ever known. Barefoot, wearing jeans under her nightie, carrying her sweater and shoes, she followed him through the kitchen.

"Ouch," she muttered as she stepped on the staples he hadn't pulled yet.

He stopped at the door so abruptly Duke crashed into the screen and Alana crashed into him. "If you come with me, Tanya and Matt will know we were together."

She stepped back, but then her chin lifted. "I don't care. Having another woman along might help."

In his experience, introducing another woman into situations like these very rarely helped. Matt Linden didn't say there was a car accident, or a traffic stop. He said *situation*, which meant it walked that fine, shifting line in the sand between official police business and family circumstances. "Fine, but you do exactly what I say, when I say. Got it?"

"Like the ride along. Got it."

The trip out took fifteen minutes. He kept the lights and sirens off. No need to announce his breakneck trip out of town to every citizen of Walkers Ford. Matt had called his cell rather than use the radio, which meant none of this was on the scanner. The windows of Cody's trailer were dark when they blew past, no car parked out front. Alana's head turned to examine the scene.

"It's a school night," she said to no one in particular.

Cody had made sure the kids were fed, in bed, before doing his homework and going to bed himself. Taking on a father's job before he was old enough not to need a father himself.

He didn't take on other people's problems anymore. He did his job, and yet here he was, worrying about Cody on his way to get Tanya out of whatever *situation* she'd stumbled into this time.

The road surface transitioned abruptly from blacktop to

gravel. He let up on the gas until the balding tires caught in the dirt, then he braked when they crested the hill. Matt's squad car, one of the newer, nimbler Dodges, was angled across the road in a textbook-perfect slant to prevent another car from taking off. He braked to a halt behind and to the right of Matt's car and hurled himself out of the Blazer.

Tanya rambled in and out of the squad car's headlights. She looked like hell, blond hair matted and hanging in snarls around her face. She wore a black men's tank top with a flannel shirt over it and jeans that hung on her frame. Her face, starkly illuminated by the harsh headlamps, had the shrunken look of dehydration. She'd stop eating before she stopped drinking, which explained the skeletal look of her shoulder, bared when the flannel shirt slipped. She was barefoot again.

It was maybe fifty degrees out.

"Jesus Christ," he said.

"Sorry, Chief," Matt said. "I was driving around when I saw her crossing the field."

Lucas spun and looked in the direction Matt pointed, but didn't see Tanya's truck. "She was on foot."

"On foot," Matt confirmed. "She's obviously under the influence, but she wasn't driving. Since she's your cousin and Chief Nelson's daughter, I figured I better call you before I did anything else."

"She try to run?"

Matt shook his head. "She's just wandered around, muttering to herself."

Lucas watched Tanya bite at her nails and roam in and out of the lights like a moth attracted to a light. She was agitated, shaking.

"Shut off your lights," Lucas said quietly. "She's high on painkillers. Normal activity makes them agitated. The flashing lights are worse."

Matt reached into his open window and turned off the red-and-blue lights. "What do you think we should do?"

Lucas stepped forward, into the headlight's beam. Tanya looked up, blinking rapidly. Her eyes were feral in her paper-white face, all humanity leached from her expression. She jerked her head back and her hair slipped enough to reveal a livid bruise on her cheekbone.

"Well, hey," she drawled. "What brings you out this way?"

"You," he said.

She laughed. "It's always me, isn't it? A thorn in your side. The black sheep. The prodigal daughter."

If he remembered his Bible verses correctly, the prodigal son returned home, ashamed of his behavior, but he doubted Tanya would appreciate the correction. "Let's get you home. It's cold out here."

"Not as cold as it is at home."

Her sad tone twisted something deep in his gut. "We'll start a fire," he said and reached for her as she shambled past.

She twisted away. "You call him, Mattie? You call my cousin and tattle on me?"

"I was worried about you, Tanya," Matt said.

"You didn't used to worry." She laughed, low and mean, her eyelids drooping in a parody of seduction. "No, sir. You didn't used to worry at all."

The tips of Matt's ears reddened in the high beams. "I'm worried now," he said evenly.

Lucas gave the kid credit for holding on to his temper, because Tanya was working his last nerve. "You worried about anyone lately, Tan? Anything other than yourself?"

She looked at him, blinking. Maybe it was the edge in his tone, maybe it was his position with the lights at his back, shadowing his face.

"Remember Duke? You were supposed to keep an eye on him for me. Instead I come home and he's got no food, no water."

"That was . . . I thought that was next . . ."

"Lucas."

Alana's voice. She stood by the driver's door of Matt's patrol car, in the darkness, but there was no mistaking that voice.

Matt's gaze flicked from Tanya to Alana, then to Lucas in an expression of utter shock before it closed off again. He'd have to explain this away somehow, after this was all over. Alana had helped Tanya before, that was a good start, except it didn't explain why Alana was with him that time, or this time.

Alana stepped forward. Tanya reeled on her feet, then an awful smile grew on her face. "Wow, Lucas. The town librarian? I didn't know. Did anyone know? Are you having a secret affair with *the town librarian*? Because I can't think of any good reason for you to bring her out here unless she was in bed with you when Mattie here called."

He stared impassively at Tanya, knowing better than to get sucked into an argument with a drunk addict. Alana stayed where she was. She probably didn't see too many mean drunks at the Wentworth Foundation, unless her stepfather had a drinking problem. Or her mother. Or Freddie, for that matter.

She knew everything about him, and he knew nothing about her.

Alana walked into the bright headlights. "Tanya, let's get you home. It's cold out here."

"Do you know him at all, sweetie pie? Do you know what he's really like?"

"Yes," Alana said steadily, demonstrating no self-protective instincts at all. "I do."

"So you know he's a right bastard." She looked at Lucas, and the anger and helplessness in her eyes tore right through him. "He didn't used to be. He used to be my big brother. We were just cousins, but I didn't have a brother. He was my big brother. He was going to help me get through my criminal justice degree, then get a job on the police force. So I could be like my dad."

"I'm sorry things didn't work out like you planned," Alana said.

"Oh, I'm fine," Tanya said. "I'm just fine. He's the one who's changed."

Alana blinked.

"He used to be a nice guy. Did he tell you what happened? Why he left Denver and came back here?"

"No," Alana said.

"Not talking much, huh?" She swayed. "A kid he was supposed to help died, and he gave up. He took the kid on climbing trips, helped him get into a magnet high school for the arts. And when the kid ended up dead, Lucas gave up on people. That's what Lucas Ridgeway does. He quits on people. He came back here so he could be a fucking little dictator in a tiny little town in the middle of fucking nowhere, because he couldn't hack it in Denver. It's a good thing you're leaving, honey. He'll always pick the job over you. That's why his wife left him. He couldn't leave the job at work. He's the job, and nothing but the job."

The way she said it, you'd never know that all her life she had wanted nothing more than to be a cop.

Alana cocked her head ever so slightly to the right. "How interesting," she said politely. "Let's get you home. You'll feel better after a hot shower and a change of clothes."

Tanya stared at Alana. "Did you hear me?"

"I heard you. Which car should she get in?"

"Matt's," Lucas said. If she got in his car, he couldn't be held responsible for his temper.

Matt opened the back door to his vehicle. Tanya, deprived of a target to lash out at, slid into the backseat. Matt closed the door. The parody of chivalry would have been hilarious if Lucas had been in any mood to laugh. Without looking at Lucas, he got into the driver's seat and turned down the road to the cabin.

Alana climbed back into the truck. Lucas shut his door and shifted into drive. "You handled that well."

"My mother would be pleased to hear it," she said. "She spent a fortune on comportment and cotillion classes." There was a moment of silence, then she added, "You should stop underestimating me. I may lack experience with men, but a shrieking catfight is right up my alley."

She wasn't looking at him as she said it. Lucas knew she was using the same polished etiquette to smooth over what had happened.

They pulled up next to Tanya's cabin. Matt handed her off to Lucas and Alana without the slightest hint of regret, and drove away.

"I don't need a shower," Tanya mumbled.

"You're going to take one anyway," Alana said.

"Fucking bossy bitch."

"It's part of my job title," Alana shot back.

Lucas turned on the water in the flatly filthy shower.

"Get out," Tanya said. "You know what, Lucas? I might be a drug addict, but at least I'm not like you."

"I'll stay with her," Alana said.

He went into the living room and built a fire in the fireplace. Newspaper, logs, a few sticks for kindling, but he didn't light it. He stayed on the floor, head bent, trying to process the emotions flaring like fireworks within him.

No one in Walkers Ford knew what had happened with Derik. No one. It wasn't official police business tracked under his badge number. His involvement with the Boys and Girls Club was sanctioned, of course, but what happened slipped through the cracks. How had Tanya known?

Leanne, his ex-wife. She and Tanya had always been close. Back when she'd been angry with him for caring too much about everyone else and not enough about her, Leanne must have told his cousin, and Tanya had nursed it, waiting for the right moment to slip it between his ribs.

How had she known the person he'd hate most to know about his failure was Alana Wentworth?

Alana emerged from the bedroom and closed the door.

"I treated her feet again. She's asleep. On her side," she added. "She's going to have quite a headache when she wakes up."

He couldn't meet her eyes. "Let's go."

"Is what she said true?"

"Why wouldn't it be true?"

"Drunk addicts say hurtful things when they're under the influence."

"It's true."

"Would you tell me what happened?"

He shrugged as they turned onto the paved county road into town. "Derik was a kid I met when I was volunteering at the Boys and Girls Club. Smart kid. Rising rapidly through the ranks in his gang because he had a head for numbers. Shit home life. Mother in jail, father gone since he was a baby, being raised by a grandmother too old to keep him in line and with four other kids in the house. I'd take him and other kids on climbing weekends. I did what I could to help him."

He remembered his uncle laughing at his involvement, at his naivete. *You'll learn, boy. You'll learn.* But he had thought he could make a difference. If he just got Derik through high school, he'd be okay. But then he'd joined the task force and gotten married, and had less time to spend with one kid. He returned phone calls later and later, canceled lunch dates. Forgot his birthday.

Two years later, Derik was dead.

Duke leaned over the passenger seat and laid his snout on Alana's shoulder. She reached up to idly scratch behind his ears. "What happened?"

"He died. Some stupid feud over a corner. Another kid pulled out a Glock and shot him six times at close range. He was dead before the ambulance was dispatched."

The failure destroyed him, destroyed his marriage. Nelson was right. One person couldn't stand against the tide of drugs and poverty and hopelessness. All he could do was clean up afterwards.

"Interesting," she said.

"That's what you said when Tanya shouted it to the sky."

"I was at a loss for words," she admitted.

"This isn't Denver," he said.

"I'm aware of that."

"It's not Chicago, either."

"Also aware of that."

"People matter here."

She turned to look at him.

"People matter. Cody's getting attached to you. So is Mrs. Battle. Her kids and grandkids are scattered all over the country. You're making them care about you, and you're going to leave."

She gaped at him. "Lucas, everyone knew I was leaving. I can't possibly matter that much to any one resident of Walkers Ford."

You do. You matter that much to me.

"What about you? Do I matter to you?"

"You've been handy to have around," he said offhandedly.

She lifted her eyebrows. "Handy."

"You're good with a flashlight."

"I'm sorry for what happened with Derik," she said finally.

"It was a lesson every cop learns eventually. You can't save them." Or Tanya. He couldn't fight off poverty and drugs and hopelessness. He couldn't fight off failure.

"That's not what I mean," she said. "I mean I'm sorry for Derik. For how you must have felt when he died."

He shrugged. "I didn't feel anything at all."

HE DROVE HER back to her house just before dawn, then went into his own house to catch a couple of hours of sleep before starting his day officially. His phone rang as he crossed the driveways to his truck. He'd spent so much time in Alana's rented house that he'd started parking in Alana's driveway as if it were home.

"Ridgeway."

"Uh, Chief Ridgeway? This is Lee from the pawn shop down in Brookings. You were in a couple of weeks ago asking about a ring. I think I've got it."

"I'll be there in an hour," he said.

When he pulled into the parking lot, the shop was nearly empty. Two kids perused the pawned games and consoles. They looked at Lucas, then sidled out the front door.

"What do you have for me?"

He removed the ring from an envelope stored in a drawer behind the counter. "I didn't want to take a chance one of the other guys would sell it," he explained as he opened the flap and upended the envelope over his palm.

A tiny ring dropped out, making no sound as it hit the clerk's palm. Lucas picked it up and studied it. The gold, none too substantial to begin with, was worn thin at the shank. Eight diamond chips almost invisible to the naked eye surrounded a ninth. All were set in white gold shaped like a round flower. He recognized the ring. He'd seen it on Gunther's wife's finger often enough.

"I gave the guy twenty bucks for it," the clerk said. "I'm not supposed to buy stolen property, but you said you were looking for it. My girlfriend said sixty-two years is a long time to be married. I didn't want it to disappear again."

Lucas pulled out his wallet and withdrew two tens. "Thanks."

"No problem," the clerk said.

"Let's take a look at your footage," Lucas said.

"Cameras are just for show," the clerk admitted. "They've been broken for weeks."

He showed the clerk the pictures he'd copied at the station

before coming down to Brookings. "Any of these guys the ones who pawned the ring?"

The clerk shook his head to the first three pictures, all known meth addicts and small-time losers. He studied the next picture more closely. "Almost, but not quite," he said. "Like, that could be the guy's brother."

Lucas slid the final picture to the top of the pile.

"That's him," the clerk said. "That's the kid who pawned the ring."

His heart sank. "Thanks. I'll be in touch if this goes to court."

He tucked Gunther's ring carefully into the breast pocket of his shirt and headed out the door, into the sunshine.

WHEN HE PULLED off County Road 46 into the ruts that led to the Burton trailer, Alana's Audi was already parked by the front door. She stood on the rickety steps leading into the trailer, holding the door open for Cody.

"Lucas," she said. "What are you doing here?"

"Get away from the door," Lucas said, striding up the dirt path.

She blinked, her eyes going wide as he reached behind him for his handcuffs, then hurried down the steps to stand on the bedraggled grass beside the stairs. Cody appeared in the door.

"Come here, Cody," Lucas said evenly.

"What are you doing here?"

"Now."

Cody hitched his long, skinny body down the steps. "What?"

"Where's your mother?"

"Yesterday was payday. She took the little kids to McDonald's for breakfast."

"Your brother inside?"

Cody blocked Lucas. "He's sleeping."

Lucas heard scuffling at the back of the trailer, then the sound of a door slamming. With a muttered curse, he leaped off the stairs and sprinted past Alana, gaining speed and traction as he rounded the corner of the trailer. Colt Burton was running flat out through the field, toward the creek.

It was pointless. There was nowhere to go. Colt had built up some muscle in prison, but Lucas had speed and endurance on him. He brought him down in a flying tackle a few yards from the slope to the creek bed. The impact knocked the wind out of Colt, giving Lucas enough time to get him cuffed.

He hauled him to his feet. Colt doubled over again, the panic on his face no doubt a mixture of an inability to breathe and being back in police custody. This didn't stop him from trying to twist out of Lucas's grip.

Cody and Alana stood side by side at the end of the trailer, watching all of this. Alana held one arm across her stomach while the other hand covered her mouth. Cody's hands were fisted impotently.

"What the fuck are you doing to my brother?"

"Your brother just pawned Gunther Jensen's ring at a pawn shop in Brookings," Lucas said.

Cody looked at Colt, who was still gasping for air. "Is that true?"

Colt refused to look at his brother. "Fuck, no."

"Did you break into Gunther's house?"

"Fuck off."

"He didn't," Cody said, half-pleading, half-asserting. "He didn't. He's met his curfew. He's seeing his parole officer. He's looking for jobs. He wouldn't do that to us."

Alana's face was a frozen mask, but Lucas could see the sorrow and horror in her eyes.

"Where'd you get the ring?"

"I didn't pawn any damn ring!"

"The clerk identified you."

"He's lying."

"Was he home last night?" Lucas asked Cody.

"Yes," Cody said defiantly. Color stood high on his cheekbones.

"Don't lie to me," Lucas said. "I will arrest you for obstructing justice and lying to a police officer. Do not fucking lie to me."

"Lucas," Alana said quietly.

Eyes locked on Cody's, Lucas held up one finger. He wasn't pointing at her, just reminding her that this was police business, not hers. "Was your brother home last night?"

Fury and shame and sheer hatred shifted across Cody's face, aimed at Lucas because he couldn't aim it at his brother. "He came home an hour ago."

"Oh, God," Alana said.

"You little fuck," Colt said, twisting in Lucas's grip. "Way to look out for your family."

"Don't go anywhere," he said to Cody. He got Colt into the backseat of his Blazer, then shut the door.

When he turned back to Cody, the boy was standing at the foot of the stairs, his arms folded over his stomach, shoulders hunched. Alana stood next to him, her expression worried, her hands fluttering as if she wanted to comfort Cody but knew he'd just shake her off.

"What are you doing here?"

"Picking Cody up so he can start working on the mural," she said.

"I'm not working on any fucking mural," he spat.

Lucas put his hands on his hips and shook his head. "Don't do that," he said resignedly.

"You think I'm going to go down there and paint a picture on the wall like I'm some kind of trained performing dog?" he screamed. "You . . . this fucking town . . . you have to take him away again? He didn't steal that ring. The clerk's an idiot. He's got the wrong guy."

"He almost identified you," Lucas said.

Cody's eyes widened.

"That's the thing about hanging out with people who make stupid choices," Lucas went on. "Sometimes you get caught up in their bad shit."

"I didn't pawn that ring," Cody said.

"I know you didn't. You were here with your little brothers. But Colt wasn't. Colt violated his parole. Selling stolen goods is a parole violation. He's going back to jail."

"Maybe he didn't know the ring was stolen," Cody said, his voice shaking.

"He knew," Lucas said.

"Fuck you."

"Cody," Alana said quietly. "Come with me. We'll get something to eat before we get started."

"Fuck you, too," he snarled at her.

Lucas saw her eyes widen. He took a step forward, intending to put himself between them. "Watch your mouth," he said to Cody.

Things were escalating, but Alana was somehow now the one between him and Cody.

"I know you're angry. Staying here alone won't make that any better. Come with me and we'll—"

"What the fuck do you know about staying anywhere? You're leaving. You can go fuck yourself, your fucking mural, and your fucking art classes, too. Just fucking leave me alone." He dashed up the stairs into the trailer and slammed the door so hard the flimsy metal rocked on its foundation.

For a long moment Alana stood beside Lucas. Then she turned and got into her car.

14

THE NEXT WEEK was one of the busiest in Alana's life. Finishing the request for bid document, and fielding questions, comments, and concerns from the public via newspapers, radio, and the Internet consumed most of her time. She was up early most days, talking to Freddie, but having one foot in both worlds was taking its toll. A steady stream of residents came to the library with ideas for the renovation, leaving Alana in the uncomfortable position of explaining that yes, the building renovations and technology upgrades were exciting and would be well worth their investment, but no, she wouldn't be around to oversee or enjoy them.

She was going home tomorrow morning.

"You've done this place a world of good," Mrs. Battle said as Alana locked the front door. Outside the building, traffic at the Spring Fling Carnival was picking up. The library would be open all day tomorrow, staffed by Mrs. Battle and some handpicked friends. Mayor Turner still hadn't made an offer to any of the library director candidates, but he promised he would pick a candidate soon.

"I just did some research," Alana said, pacing herself to match Mrs. Battle's careful steps.

"Don't downplay your role in all of this, young lady," Mrs. Battle said. "It's a very bad habit of yours, pushing your accomplishments and efforts into the background. That's not where you belong."

Alana blinked, because the background was where she'd lived her whole life. "Thank you," she offered instead. "I was happy to do it."

She was, she realized. She was happy doing this. Not just content, but happy. The realization startled her, because she didn't come to Walkers Ford to learn to be happy. She came to be different.

Was she unhappy in Chicago? Six months ago she would have said *Of course not.* Now . . . ?

"You're welcome. Cody's still refusing to paint the mural?" Mrs. Battle asked.

Alana nodded. She'd been out to Cody's trailer twice in the last week. Both times he refused to open the door to her. His sullen face and broken eyes scared her. "I don't know what to do," she admitted. How did she frame this question to develop the appropriate search terms?

How to heal a broken heart
How to give someone reason to live
Ending hopelessness
Giving life meaning

She wished she knew the answer to that question for herself, for Cody, for Lucas.

"We'll have to find something else to put on the wall," Mrs. Battle said. "The historical society will have some pictures. That will do. Anchor the room in our past while we look to the future." They paused in front of the beer garden. "You're sure you can't stay?"

"I'm positive. If I'm not back in Chicago by Saturday for my stepfather's awards banquet, my mother will have my head on a pike."

"This is very important to your family."

"Six hundred people are flying in from all over the

world," she said. "It's being held at the Palmer House, with a four-course meal, wine, and speeches by some of the most powerful people on five continents."

"That sounds much more delightful than a little country carnival."

"I don't know about that," Alana said. "You got the funnel cake machine. I love funnel cakes."

"They're delicious. Completely outside my diet, of course."

"I'd share one with you," Alana said.

Tears shone in Mrs. Battle's eyes. "I'm going to miss you."

"I'm going to miss you, too."

"We'll all miss you. Including Chief Ridgeway."

Alana laughed lightly. "Oh, he'll be happy to get me out of his house so he can finish the kitchen renovation."

Mrs. Battle studied her. "I'm old and my eyesight's not what it used to be, but I'm not blind yet, my dear. He's going to miss you."

"I don't think he feels much of anything anymore," Alana said.

The hug surprised her. Mrs. Battle barely came up to Alana's chin, but she turned and hugged her with a ferocity that nearly stopped her heart in her chest. Just as quickly she stepped back. "You drive carefully," she said.

Alana swallowed the lump in her throat. "I will."

She was going home heartbroken, leaving things unfinished. That wasn't in the cards. But neither was not going home. And she always left things unfinished. She had her job, her tasks in the project plan. Other people carried on in their wake. But this time the people carrying on weren't strangers, or nongovernmental organization workers. They were friends, and more.

SHE WALKED BACK to her house—Lucas's house—through a warm spring evening. A month made such a difference.

The flowerpots were in full bloom, and the air was actually warm. She would open the windows when she got home.

Lucas's truck popped and cooled in his driveway. Duke trotted out of the doggie door when she walked up the driveway, sniffing at her skirt and wagging his tail. "Hey, big dog," she said. "Where's Lucas?"

"Hey."

She looked up to see him standing in his doorway, one shoulder leaning against the frame, a bottle of beer in his hand. A lump swelled in her throat as she looked at him, so handsome and strong and holding so much inside. She had to go. She had to. She had no business getting attached to people. Her life was elsewhere, and thanks to Lucas and the library renovation project, she was ready to go back to it.

Falling for her rebound guy wasn't in the project plan.

"Come over for dinner?" she asked.

He studied her for a long moment. "You didn't blush that time."

She had nothing more to hide. "Please?"

He nodded and reached back to shut the door behind him. They crossed the driveways, Duke trotting beside Alana to the screen door and waiting until she opened it. She didn't care if the neighbors were watching. She didn't care if people gossiped. She had one more night with Lucas, and she intended to wring every moment out of it with both hands.

She set her bags down in the living room. Lucas surveyed the boxes and suitcases. "You're finally packed."

"I am," she said lightly as she walked down the hall to her bedroom. Her last suitcase lay open on the neatly made bed. She swapped her skirt and sweater set for the pair of jeans and long-sleeve T-shirt she'd make the drive in the next day.

Duke was nosing around the suitcases, his tail drooping.

"Does he know what suitcases mean?"

Lucas nodded, then clicked softly to call Duke to him.

In the kitchen, Alana unpacked the take-out pork chops and dirty rice she'd picked up from the Heirloom Café on her way home.

"Need any help?" Lucas asked. He was sprawled on the bare plywood kitchen floor, Duke nosing around him before he curled up at Lucas's chest. "We could go over to my place."

"I'd like to stay here," she said.

NPR filled the silence in the room. Alana mixed up a quick salad to finish off what was left in the fridge. Braced on his elbow, Lucas scratched behind Duke's ears, then the dog's broad chest, finally rubbing his belly. The dog let out a grunt and rolled onto his back. Lucas stroked his belly.

"That's one happy dog," she commented.

"He's comfortable here."

He wasn't the only one. Alana looked out the kitchen window at the rosebushes growing persistently toward the sun, buds forming on the stalks. The grass was spring green, just waiting to darken in the summer sun. The kids who lived in the house behind her played on the swing set in the yard across from her picket fence. Their laughter reached through the open window.

"Good traffic at the carnival?"

"Yes," she said. "I left Mrs. Battle there. It looks like fun. Aren't you working?"

"I'm on call both nights."

He gave Duke one last pat and got to his feet. The dog rolled on his side and closed his eyes again. Lucas washed his hands, took down plates, and got silverware from the drawer.

"You want to finish off this wine?"

"Please," she said.

He poured her a glass and set his beer bottle on the table.

It felt so natural, so right to sit down with Lucas to a meal after a long day.

"How was work?" she asked.

"I took Gunther's wife's ring back to him," he said.

"He must have been so happy to get it back," she said.

"He was. He kept saying thank-you, saying how much it meant to him to have it back. It can't be worth more than a couple hundred dollars. There's almost no gold left in the shank, and the diamonds are too small to be chips. You'd think I'd given him a Kardashian's engagement ring."

"That makes me happy," she said quietly. "When is his granddaughter's sweet sixteen?"

"Next month. You?"

She lifted an eyebrow before she realized he was asking about her day. "Wrapping things up, mostly, which was harder to do than I thought."

He gave her a sharp look.

"Twenty people must have stopped by the library to say good-bye and thank me. It was . . ." Her voice trailed off. To cover her emotions, she swallowed the last of her pork chop. "It was very nice."

"Freddie will be glad to get you home."

"I'll be glad to see her."

"There's so much energy in Chicago," he added. "You can see Nate again."

She flicked him a glance through her lashes. "Unless he's planning to relocate Martin Industries to Mumbai or London, I don't think I'll see much of him this year."

"That's where you're headed?"

"The day after the Senator's party. I'll be lucky to get my boxes out of the car before I have to leave. Freddie's speaking at a global human-trafficking initiative in Mumbai next week. Then it's on to London for the first round of wedding planning."

He set his silverware neatly on his plate and pushed it aside. "You'll forget all about us in no time," he said easily.

"I won't," she whispered. "I won't forget. Mrs. Battle's going to send me pictures from the carnival, and I'm not

giving up on Cody. There's no law that says if he doesn't go
to art school at eighteen, he can't ever go. Maybe when the
little kids get a bit older . . . or he can do something long
distance. I'm not giving up. I'm not walking away from him.
He has family responsibilities now, but he won't always."

Lucas just looked at her. "He'll come around."

"He thinks I'm abandoning him."

"He's seventeen. Everything is drama at that age."

"I'm not. I'm not abandoning him," she said firmly. Her
eyes stung. "I'm not. I did what I could. It's a good start.
Someone else can carry it through."

The legs of Lucas's chair scraped against the subflooring.
"Come here," he said gently.

She stepped over Duke on her way to Lucas's lap. The
dog peered up at her, then seemed to think Lucas had things
under control because he slumped back to the floor with a
grunt. Lucas stroked her hair and let her cry herself out.

"I never meant to hurt him," she said finally. "Or Mrs.
Battle."

He was quiet for a long time, his hand curved around her
shoulder, one finger stroking at her nape. "No one ever
does," he said finally.

AS THE SUN set, they cleaned up the kitchen, which meant
throwing away take-out containers and disposable cutlery.
Then Alana reached for Lucas's hand and drew him down
the hallway. In the dim light of her bedroom, she stripped
off his shirt, then his jeans, and pressed her mouth to all the
parts of him she wanted to remember. His forehead, so she
would remember the way it wrinkled when he smiled. His
eyelids, so she would remember the way he looked at her
under his lashes when he thought she wasn't looking. His
cheekbones, so she'd remember the angles of his face.

His mouth. So she would remember his rare smiles, the
way he whispered to her.

His shoulders and collarbone and chest, so she would remember how strong he was. His abdomen, so she would remember the first six-pack she ever saw on a live man. His hip bone and his shaft, jutting hard and heavy from his pelvis, so she would remember the way making love really felt. She pressed her mouth to his thighs and his knees and his insteps. When he glided inside her, moving slowly so it would last and last, she closed her eyes and committed his back to her tactile memory. The way his shoulder blades jutted, his spine between the thick muscles on either side. The nape of his neck, so vulnerable and strong all at once.

"Alana," he murmured against her throat. "Alana."

She didn't expect to come. While always present between them, the line between the pleasure of intimacy and the anguish of leaving had never been so fine, so easily crossed. Tears welled in her eyes and spilled down her temples, even as her hips lifted to meet his steady thrusts. He licked away the tears, murmuring nonsense words as he slid his hand under her hips and lifted her closer. The angle narrowed and pleasure coursed along her nerves until her fingers tightened on his shoulders and she cried out.

Holding him while he shuddered out his release was almost unbearable.

She fell asleep in his arms.

THE NEXT MORNING while Lucas was walking Duke, she said good-bye to the house. It was as difficult as she'd thought it would be. The walk around in the backyard was even worse, until she saw a single pink bloom on the bush at the corner of the house. After getting the scissors from the kitchen, she snipped off the bloom, then turned over the dirt at the bush's base to add more fertilizer. The cement poured into the cinder blocks in the foundation was cracked, and when Alana's hand trowel scraped against it, a glint of gold caught her eye.

Her heart tripped, then picked up to double time as she carefully cleared dirt away from the crack, then reached into it. The ring was dulled from years of exposure and scratched from the freeze-thaw cycle contracting the cement around the soft gold, but it was clearly the ring she saw sketched in the rose-care book. Carefully molded petals unfurled around a small diamond. Even dirty and scratched, the craftsmanship was evident.

It was the perfect way to say good-bye, and thank-you. She rinsed most of the dirt from the ring, and used a tooth-brush to gently scrub the ring clean, then took a quick shower and didn't bother with her contacts. She dressed quickly and zipped her suitcase. When she reached the living room, she found it empty of boxes or cases. The door to her Audi slammed, then Duke and Lucas came into the house.

"How long's the drive?"

"Nine hours, not including stops," she said. "I'll be home by six or so."

He didn't offer to get breakfast with her. She didn't offer, either. There was no point in prolonging this, and based on what had happened last night, she didn't trust herself not to cry in the middle of the Heirloom. Better to make the break now and get a couple of hours of road behind her before stopping.

"You'll take what's in the fridge, right?"

He nodded. Duke, sitting at Lucas's feet, whined as he looked between the two of them.

"I left the project plan with Mrs. Battle, but I found the building plans in my laptop bag. Can you take them to her?"

"No problem."

"When you see Cody again, tell him I'll be in touch. Tell him . . . tell him I'm sorry."

She ran out of things to say, so she crouched down to give Duke a quick hug. He licked her cheek then whined again, peering anxiously up at Lucas.

Lucas took her case and carried it out to her car. There was room for it on the floor behind the passenger seat. He'd set her purse and laptop bag on the passenger seat. "Cover that with your coat when you're at a rest stop or a restaurant," he said.

"I will," she promised.

The morning air held a little chill. She wrapped her arms around her abdomen and told herself the cool air caused her shaking. "Well, then," she said, and opened her arms.

He wrapped her in tight. "Take care of yourself," he said.

"You, too."

"Let me know when you get there."

"I will." She swallowed hard. "I have to go."

He opened the door for her, waiting until she'd buckled her seat belt before giving her a quick kiss on the lips. "Bye," he said, and closed the door.

She started the car. As she backed out of the driveway, Duke barked once, a sharp sound in the early morning air. When she was safely in the street, she rolled down the passenger window.

"Look on the ledge in the kitchen," she said, but her voice caught as she said it.

His brow wrinkled, but he lifted a hand in acknowledgment and a parting wave.

DUKE WHINED AT his feet, then set off down the driveway, his plume of a tail waving back and forth determinedly. Lucas clicked for him, then said, "Duke. Come!"

The dog stopped, then looked at Alana's disappearing car, then back at Lucas. He could see the confusion in the dog's face. *She's my person. Where is my person going? Why are you not with her? Why am I not with her? We should be with her.*

"She's gone, boy," Lucas said when the dog walked back to him, stopping every few steps to peer over his shoulder. "I knew she was leaving, but you didn't."

She'd told him to look on the kitchen window ledge, but he couldn't bear to go back in the house right away. She'd likely left him a note, and he didn't feel like reading her elegant good-bye, written in her decisive, angular hand. She'd say she had enjoyed his company, appreciated the time they'd spent together, thanks for the memories.

Best to just get it over with and keep moving. He walked back into the kitchen and looked at the ledge. A single rosebud, small and tightly furled, lay in the sunlight streaming through the window. When he picked it up something gold slid off the stem to clatter into the sink. He reached down and picked up his grandmother's ring, lost for decades.

Found.

Sunlight glinted off the small diamond. He opened the note:

Lucas—

I found this while you were walking Duke this morning. I went out to the rosebush to cut the first bloom for you, and when I loosened the dirt worked into the foundation, there was the ring, glinting in the dirt. The gold is a little scratched, but a jeweler can polish that out and check the prongs to make sure the diamond is secure.

You and Duke just turned the corner onto this block, so I don't have much longer here with you. I'm fairly sure we're both going to be grown-ups about saying good-bye. After all, this was a contract position for me, a short-term lease for you. You helped me find the strength I needed to go back to my life stronger, more confident, better able to hold my ground against other people's expectations. I'm glad to have found something of yours in return.

Alana

She thought he'd helped her find something? That strength was there all along. All he did was give her sex and sleepless nights chasing Tanya all over the county. He'd given her a troubled boy and a fixer-upper rental house.

She'd found something much more valuable.

He looked at the ring, then at the bloom, and for a moment longing swelled inside him, pushing at the edges of his skin. He wanted to get in his truck and follow her, chase her down on the interstate and pull her over, and beg her not to leave. He wanted to tell her how she made the house feel like a home again, with her books and her simple homemade meals, how Duke ignored the other tenants, how he checked to see if a light was on every time he pulled into his driveway.

His fist curled tight around the ring. The pain of the sharp edge of the petals cutting into his palm brought him back to reality. He had nothing to offer a Wentworth. He had two houses in a small town in South Dakota. At thirty-two, he'd reached the pinnacle of his career in law enforcement. He had an aging dog, and a police vehicle he drove because it was so old and battered he wouldn't send another officer on patrol out in it. He had a failed marriage, a failed effort at mentoring, and a family that was falling apart in slow motion.

He had a heart that had been broken so many times, the pieces weren't even worth offering to someone else. Especially not to Alana. Who would soon be in India, and then in London.

There was one thing he could give her, something that would make her happy, because it wouldn't just be for her.

THE NEXT DAY, Lucas locked Duke in the screened porch and headed down County Road 46.

The trailer's front door was wide open when he pulled off the road and onto the dirt tracks leading to the front door. The little kids were playing in the turtle sandbox. Cody sat on the steps, a sketch pad balanced on his knees. Lucas almost didn't recognize him without the hoodie, but the way his shoulders hunched under the T-shirt when he saw Lucas's truck tipped him off.

The little kids perched on the edge of the sandbox turned to stare when Lucas got out of the truck.

"What do you want?" Cody said. "I finished my community-service hours. Mrs. Battle signed my form on Friday. We're done."

Okay, they'd skip the pleasantries. "Is your mother home?"

"Yeah," he said. "She just got up."

Mrs. Burton appeared in the doorway. She wore a pair of sweatpants and a tank top, and her hair was pulled back in a loose ponytail. "What did you do?" she hissed at Cody.

"Nothing!"

"He hasn't done anything," Lucas said. *That I'm aware of and I want to keep it that way.* "I'd like a minute of his time, ma'am."

Mrs. Burton gave Cody a little shove down the stairs. The boy crossed the lawn at a lope, resentment clinging to him like the faded jeans and T-shirt.

"What?"

"You're going to paint the mural in the library," Lucas said.

"You can't make me do something I don't want to do," Cody said.

"No, but I can help you do something you *do* want to do," Lucas replied.

"I don't want to do it."

"You wanted to hurt Alana. You wanted to withhold the only thing you had to give her. But she's gone, and the only person you're going to hurt if you don't do this is yourself."

"She lied to me."

"We all knew she was leaving, Cody. It just didn't occur to us that you didn't know. I'm sorry about that. Alana's sorry about that."

"You knew?"

Lucas nodded.

"What's the point of painting the mural if she's not here to see it?"

Lucas tipped his head toward the little kids, playing in the sandbox under their mother's watchful eye. Between her and Cody, those kids might have a chance at something. It was a brutal sacrifice to watch Cody make, but he was making it, without complaint. "They'll see it," he said. "They'll see it every week and know their big brother did that. So will everyone else who uses the library, and everyone in town's going to be using that library."

Cody shoved his hands into his pockets. "It doesn't matter."

"You know what matters? What you decide matters, and that you choose something. Anything. Anything positive, not destructive," he added hastily. "It's a really nice design."

"I've never done anything that big before," Cody admitted. "Or worked on that surface. I've done canvases in art class. I drew a sketch, a stupid sketch, with colored pencils. That's it."

"It's okay to be afraid of what you're going to try," Lucas said. "It's not okay not to try it."

Cody stared off into the distance for a while. Lucas watched him waver, then decide to fight off the cynicism and apathy. "Okay," he said. "I'll do it."

Together they crossed the grass to Mrs. Burton. "Cody's going to paint the mural," Lucas said. "With your permission, I want to take him into Brookings to buy the supplies."

A smile of pure delight flashed across Mrs. Burton's face. "Oh, Cody, honey. I'm so glad. You'll do just fine," Mrs. Burton said.

Lucas looked at his watch, thinking about the second shift at the plant. "Are you working today?"

"It's my day off."

"I'll have Cody home in time for supper," Lucas said.

Neither of them said much on the drive into Brookings. Lucas called Mrs. Battle and told her about the mural; Cody's shoulders hunched at the delight in her voice. At the art supply shop, they filled a cart with cans of paint and brushes, tape and charcoal and pencils. Lucas didn't say a word about Cody's selections, just pulled out a credit card when the cashier rang up his purchases. When they'd loaded the bags into the back of the truck, Cody paused to thumb through his thin wallet.

"Gunther paid me to plant his garden," he said defensively.

The kid had every right to assume Lucas would jump to conclusions. "You forget something?"

"Yeah," Cody said, "give me a second," and he trotted back into the store.

Lucas waited outside, the spring sunshine warming his face and shoulders. Cody returned with one more bag.

"Sketch pads and crayons for the little kids," he said. "I'll have to bring them with me when I'm working at the library. They want to do what I'm doing."

Cody shrugged, as if this kind of planning to keep his little brothers entertained while he worked wasn't the foundation for keeping kids out of trouble, as if he wasn't modeling hope and positive choices and community engagement, all before he could vote. In that moment Lucas remembered why he did this job.

He did it because he cared.

"GOOD THINKING," LUCAS said. The library was controlled chaos, and Lucas was glad he wasn't the one in charge. He found Mrs. Battle in the library director's office. She'd quickly dispatched work crews to tape plastic to protect the floor. "You have what you need?" Lucas asked Cody.

"Yeah," Cody said absently. "I'm good. Whatever."

Lucas lifted an eyebrow, then went back to Mrs. Battle's office. "He's good to go."

"I'll make sure he's fed," Mrs. Battle said. "He'll forget to eat if I don't."

HE WENT HOME through the twilight, driving under the banner the town council was erecting over Main Street announcing the library's grand reopening. When he pulled into his driveway, a blond woman was sitting on his porch steps, her arm around Duke. For a moment his heart stopped dead in his chest, but his brain noted that the hair was too long to be Alana's.

So much for not missing her.

"Tanya," he said when he got out of the truck.

She'd been crying, and crying hard. Duke's fur was wet. Her hands were shaking and she was gaunt to the point of skeletal. "Hey, Lucas," she said shakily.

"What do you need?" Money, he thought. She needed money to get the utilities turned back on, or maybe for groceries. He'd buy the groceries for her, or pay the bill, but he wouldn't give her cash—

"A ride to rehab," she said. She swiped at her damp cheeks. "Please. Will you take me?"

"Sure," he said. "I'll take you. Let me make some calls."

He helped her inside and got her a glass of water after she washed her face and hands in his bathroom. While she sipped the water, he made a couple of calls and found her a bed at an inpatient facility in Brookings.

"Why?" he asked as they headed out of town. Duke sat in the backseat with his chin resting on Tanya's seat back. "I'm not complaining, but why now?"

She stared out the window. "I failed Duke. What kind of

person can't take care of an animal? Even animals take care of other animals. I couldn't even do that." Tears trickled down her cheeks, but she didn't seem to notice them, just lifted her hand to pat Duke's head. "I can't be a cop anymore. I've screwed that up forever. But I can be something. Somebody. I can be somebody."

They pulled up in front of the treatment center. Tanya got out and smoothed her hands down the fronts of her jeans. "I'll bring your stuff out tomorrow," Lucas said.

She gave him a wry smile. "Best to get me here in case I change my mind."

She wouldn't change her mind this time. It would be tough, every day, for the rest of her life, but something inside her was different. Inspired, he reached into his pocket and pulled out the lost ring, the one Alana found, the one he'd been carrying around since she left, and held it out to Tanya.

"Grammie's ring," she said. Her hands flexed as if she'd reach for it, but then she folded her arms. "I thought it was gone."

"Alana found it worked into one of the cracks in the foundation."

"I can't take it, Luc," she said. "I can't. I don't . . . Grammie wouldn't want me to have it."

"Yes, she would," he said. He tapped it on her forearm. "Grammie never gave up on anyone. She didn't give up on you. I'm not giving up on you, either. Take it."

Tears were rolling down Tanya's cheeks. She unhooked the gold chain she wore around her neck, slipped the ring on, and refastened the chain. She gave Lucas one last hug, and walked down the hall.

IF TANYA COULD admit herself to rehab knowing she'd fight the addiction every day of her life and never get the job she always wanted . . . if Cody could agree to paint the mural knowing it might be the biggest project he ever took on . . . if Mrs. Battle and Mitch and Delaney Walker-Herndon could do the right thing for the town and the library, then Lucas could join the fight.

He knew what he had to do. He had to go get her. He had to bring her home.

15

ALANA PULLED INTO the driveway of the Senator's house in Kenwood well after five. The Secret Service security detachment hadn't changed in her absence. After a friendly wave, she parked behind the house, snagged her overnight bag, then walked up the landscaped patio to the back door.

Freddie stood in the kitchen, wearing a robe, her six-carat yellow-diamond engagement ring, and the fuzzy troll slippers Alana had gotten her as a gag gift three Christmases earlier. She had her iPhone in hand and her hair coiled into a knot at her nape. She squealed when she saw Alana and practically leaped across the kitchen to envelop her in a huge hug.

"You're here! You're finally here!"

"I'm here? You're finally here. You're the one who flew in from New Delhi for this party."

Freddie pulled back and looked at her. "Are you okay?"

No. She hurt worse with every day she put between herself and Lucas, and Cody, and Mrs. Battle. "I'm fine. Just tired."

The house felt too big. Everything about it felt wrong,

the size, the gleaming modern kitchen, the view through the windows to the professionally landscaped backyard. Her apartment, dusty from disuse, felt equally wrong. No roses, no detached garage, no shared driveway that a battered Blazer would pull into for the sweetest reunion.

Freddie was staring at her. "Oh, God. You got entangled."

"I did not get entangled."

"Oh, honey," Freddie said quietly. Her sister's blue eyes, the mirror image of her own, showed a genuine concern. "Oh, honey."

"Who's entangled?"

Her mother appeared in the doorway leading to the parlor. She wore Chanel and had obviously just come from the salon. Alana tugged out of Freddie's hug and crossed the slate floor to give her mother a kiss on the cheek. "You look lovely," she said.

"Thank you," her mother said, and eyed her jeans. "You've just enough time for a shower. Frederica and I chose a dress for you—"

"Jason Wu, very chic, perfect for your coloring," Freddie added as she thumbed away at her phone.

"It's upstairs in your room. Try to be ready in an hour, dear."

Freddie gathered the folds of her silk robe in her hand and followed her up the stairs. "Spill."

"There's nothing to tell," Alana said as she opened the door to her childhood bedroom. A midnight blue dress hung from the back of the door to the bathroom. She set her bag down and looked at the dress so she didn't have to look at her sister. It had a fitted bodice and a gorgeous raw silk skirt. "It's lovely, Freddie," she said. "Where's Toby?"

"Halfway between Sao Paolo and London."

"So you'll meet up with him again in Mumbai?"

"Lannie," Freddie said quietly. "Talk to me."

"There's nothing to talk about," Alana said. "We should be talking about your wedding. You can get Westminster

Abbey if you want it. The bishop's secretary was very accommodating—"

"Alana."

Her sister never called her by her first name. Never. Alana looked at her, and swallowed hard. She wouldn't cry over this. She wouldn't. "Okay. I got entangled."

"What's his name?"

"Let's see. There's Cody Burton. He's seventeen, and he's got three younger brothers he's helping his mom raise, and an older brother who's going back to jail for breaking and entering and stealing Gunther Jensen's dead wife's engagement ring."

"He's *seventeen*?" Freddie said, for once shocked into looking up from her phone.

"Or do you mean Mrs. Battle? She's seventy-seven, and she's got macular degeneration, and her kids all left Walkers Ford, so she doesn't have anyone to drive her to doctors' appointments. She taught English and physics at the high school for forty years. She's amazing."

Freddie's lips shaped into a soft *Oh*.

"Then there's Tanya. She's addicted to prescription painkillers, and she's probably also an alcoholic. She needs rehab, but we both know you can't make someone go to rehab."

Freddie backed up to Alana's brass bed and sat down on the edge. "Go on."

"There's Carlene, and the moms with their kids who come into the library for the backpacks, and the home-schoolers who need extra resources, and . . ."

"And?"

"And Lucas Ridgeway. He's the chief of police."

"Your landlord?"

Her landlord, her lover. Her everything. "He's renovating the kitchen in the house I rented, and he's got this dog, and he's just . . . he's just . . ."

Hot and distant and wounded and willing to keep her

secrets and possessive and not at all interested in telling her who or what she should be. He let her just be.

"That blush says it all," Freddie said.

"He liked the way I blushed," Alana said. She sat down on the floor with her back to the closet door. "He liked me."

Freddie held her tongue. More important, she dropped her phone on the bed behind her. "Of course, he did. You're very likable."

"David didn't actually like me. David saw me as a fixer-upper."

"David is a brown-nosing ass," Freddie said. "Anyway, you didn't see yourself that way."

"No," she agreed. "I didn't really see myself any particular way. But after the marriage proposal debacle, I realized that if I didn't, someone else would always define me. Mother or David or someone like him."

Freddie studied her. "You're not a pushover, Lannie. You stand your ground when it matters most. Especially when it matters most. You didn't say yes to David."

"It's not enough to know what I don't want," she said. "I need to know what I do want. You know what you want."

"Sure," Freddie said as she leaned back, lifted her feet, and studied her pedicure. "But that's easy because what I want fits in with what the family needs and can use."

"Me, too," Alana said automatically.

"I call bullshit," Freddie sang out. "Bullshit, bullshit, bullshit, bullshit . . ."

"Oh, God," Alana said. "Stop that. Mother will have a fit if she hears you."

Freddie lowered her voice but continued to sing. A knock came on her bedroom door. "Alana? I don't hear the water running."

"I'm starting it now," Alana said. She clambered to her feet and turned on the shower in the bathroom.

"What do you think of the dress?" her mother called.

She looked at it while Freddie continued to sing *bullshit* to the Barney song sotto voce.

"Stop it," she hissed at Freddie. "It's gorgeous. The embroidery is exquisite." Now that she looked, she could see delicate vines of roses in a thread only slightly lighter than the blue of the dress. They clustered deeply around the hem, then curled around the skirt to coil and burst into bloom at the edge of the bodice.

Roses. She shook her head. Never again would she be able to look at a rose without thinking of Lucas, of gleaming walnut and old-fashioned roller shades, of everything she'd left behind to come home.

Had Lucas found the ring? If so, he hadn't bothered to text or e-mail or call her. So many ways to get in touch, but without emotion they were meaningless.

"We leave in fifty minutes, Alana. Frederica, stop singing foul language at your sister and get dressed, please."

"Told you so," Alana whispered.

Freddie stuck out her tongue, grabbed her phone, and slid off the bed. "Don't go anywhere."

She wasn't going anywhere. That was the point. She was home, and needed here. This was her life, her family.

She stripped and got into the enormous shower, shivering from the cold air that collected in the corners of the stall. She applied lotion, dried her hair and spritzed it with shine spray, then shimmied into her underwear. When she opened the door to put on her ball gown, Freddie was waiting in her own dress in a brilliant shade of ruby red. She turned her back to Alana.

"Zip me up."

"So you're wearing red and Mother's wearing white, and I'm wearing blue," Alana said as she ran up the zipper. "We're the Senator's living flag."

Freddie squirmed and wriggled the tight bodice into place, then smoothed the skirt with her hands. "What do you think? Alexander McQueen."

"It's beautiful. It's the perfect color for you, too."

"I'm thinking about getting married in red," Freddie said nonchalantly. "This shade. It's Toby's favorite color. Red for love. Red for power. Red for passion. Red for blood of my blood and bone of my bone. God knows I'm hardly able to wear white."

"Have you told Mother?" Alana asked as she slid the dress from the padded hanger.

"Hmmm . . . no," Freddie mused.

Alana hummed the Barney song under her breath as she took the gorgeous blue dress from the hanger and stepped into it. Freddie zipped her up. "It fits perfectly," she said. "I'll do your makeup."

"Smoky eyes," Alana said. She dug through her makeup bag until she found the right compact.

"Really? You usually never like that. You want modest and understated and demure."

"Tonight I want smoky eyes," she said.

Freddie applied eyeliner and shadow in shades of blue and gray, smudging both together, then touched up the tips of her lashes with mascara. "This isn't about David, is it? Go with a pale lip gloss. Shine, not color."

"I know that. This is about me," she said as she uncapped the lip gloss.

She let her heels dangle from her fingers as she followed Freddie down the curving staircase to the entry hall. Freddie braced herself on Alana's shoulder first to step into her stilettos, then stood still for Alana to do the same. Their mother hurried around the corner, issuing last-minute instructions to Nancy, her assistant

"You both look lovely," her mother said. "It's good to have you home, Alana."

The correct answer to that was she was glad to be home, but somehow she couldn't make herself say the words. "I missed you," she said instead, because that was true.

But a truth was growing inside her, one she couldn't ignore. This wasn't home anymore. Walkers Ford was.

"Where's the Senator?" Freddie asked.

"He's meeting with David. They'll join us at the hotel."

They followed their mother out the front door and into a limousine. Inside, Freddie kicked her heels off. Alana watched the city slide by as they made their way to the Palmer House Hilton. She'd lived here off and on for her whole life, always considered it home, a place of possibility and opportunity, of change and industry and significance. But today the buildings hemmed her in. She missed the endless arc of sky. She missed the prairie, undulating to the horizon. She missed the wind buffeting the grasses into endlessly changing patterns and cross-hatching.

She missed the people. She missed Lucas so badly, she ached inside.

Her mother was preoccupied with her phone.

"You okay?" Freddie asked quietly.

"It's been a very long day," Alana said.

"You always feel something when you leave," Freddie said finally. "It's perfectly normal to like people, enjoy their company, feel sad when you move on to the next project."

"You get entangled?"

Freddie shrugged. "Not really. That's just what people say."

"Don't you ever want to just stay and make a difference in one place, to one group of people?"

"I never really thought about it," Freddie admitted. "I like what I do. I like the pace, the dialogues, the global scale. I like knowing I've made a difference to thousands of people."

"I know," Alana said. *But that's not what I like. I liked seeing Cody come alive at the library. I liked sitting with Mrs. Battle at her doctor's appointment. I liked making dinner for Lucas. I liked peeling back his layers, watching him struggle with who he was and what his life meant.*

I needed him. But he doesn't need anyone.

"Lannie," Freddie said quietly.

"Not now, girls," their mother said. "Freddie, you go first. Alana, smile."

The limo pulled to a halt in front of the hotel. A red velvet rope kept the press back, and flashbulbs exploded as the doorman helped first their mother, then Freddie, then Alana from the limo. They smiled but kept moving up the red carpet. In addition to the standard gauntlet of political reporters were photographers and stringers from the more avaricious tabloids, all in search of a good shot of Freddie. She obligingly stopped and smiled, then reached for Alana. Her arm went around Freddie's waist and her sister tipped her head to hers.

"Love you," Freddie whispered.

"Love you, too," Alana replied.

This was enough. This was more than enough.

THE HOTEL WAS absolutely packed. Freddie and their mother moved through the crowd with the confidence that nothing would start without them, so they could take their time. Alana kept an eye on her watch and played her role, murmuring quietly to disengage them from conversations and keep them somewhat close to the schedule. They were united with the Senator at the head table, where Alana collected her perfunctory welcome-home kiss, then took her place beside Freddie. Everyone was seated only thirty-five minutes behind schedule—not bad, all things considered.

Speeches, toasts, more speeches, then a luxurious dinner. Alana picked at her food and refused a second glass of wine in favor of water. After dessert, the servers opened the dance floor, and the real business of the night began, the backroom conversations and negotiations that would grease the wheels of the next round of policy talks.

Alana made the rounds, then found herself in a group of people she'd known casually since childhood. One level of her brain tracked the conversation, filing away gossip and updates that her mother or Freddie might find useful. They'd compare notes later, sifting through the social strata, always searching for ways to tighten the connections that would advance the foundation's interests.

Another level, very quiet, very calm, and very, very unshakable, said that *enough* wasn't enough anymore. Before her time in Walkers Ford, it was enough to work for the foundation. It was good work, interesting, important. But she'd made the life she always wanted in Walkers Ford, a life rich in the meaning and connections she never found in Chicago. Tomorrow morning, she'd get back in her car, drive back to Walkers Ford, and apply for the permanent library director position. Period. End of story. The town needed a librarian, and she wanted the job. Cody needed a mentor, and she wanted to watch him grow into the man he would become. Mrs. Battle needed a friend.

Lucas needed a lover.

They all needed her. Not for what she could do, but for who she was. Now she knew what she wanted. She knew where she belonged. She knew who she should be with, forever.

The conversation stuttered, then halted as all eyes turned to Alana. "I'm sorry," she said, startled out of her reverie. "You were saying?"

They weren't looking at her. They were looking over her shoulder. She turned around to find Lucas standing behind her. He wore a dark suit and tie, with his too-long hair neatly parted and combed. His face was unreadable, but in his eyes flickered something that made her hope.

"Ms. Wentworth," he said. "A moment of your time?"

SHE LOOKED BEAUTIFUL. He should have more eloquent words to describe Alana Wentworth dressed in a gown the color of the night sky strewn with roses. Her slender shoulders and neck gleamed like cream above the dress, but when her gaze met his, his heart nearly stopped beating. She looked mysterious, untouchable, as out of his reach as the sky, and for a moment, Lucas regretted getting in his car and driving nine hours after her.

"Of course," she said. "Excuse me, please," she said to the group of women she stood with. All of them were taller or thinner, wearing flashier dresses or more makeup, but they all disappeared into the background next to Alana. He didn't fit into this world, and he'd come here thinking she didn't either.

He now realized that was a big, big mistake.

Alana's eyebrows drew down. "Why are you calling me Ms. Wentworth? We've been naked together. Many times."

A laugh huffed from his chest. "Given the circumstances, I'm being professional," he said.

"How did you get past security and the Secret Service?"

He pulled back his suit jacket just enough to show her his badge, clipped to his belt. "I bluffed my way in. Don't give me away."

"Why are you here? Did something happen? Is everyone okay?"

"Everyone's fine. Better than before. Tanya's in rehab, and this time I think it will stick. Cody's working on the mural," he said, and pulled out his phone to show her the pictures he took while Cody worked.

"How did you do that?" she asked as she scanned through the pictures on his phone.

"I told him it was a nice thought that he'd do the mural for you, but that he should do it for himself, and for his brothers. Then I drove him into Brookings to get supplies."

"Lucas," she said quietly.

"You gave us all so much. The momentum to renovate the library. The roses. The ring. I gave it to Tanya before she went into rehab."

Alana's eyes filled with tears. "Your grandmother would have wanted her to have it."

Lucas nodded. "Engagement rings are about hope," he

said. "Wedding rings are about commitments, but engagement rings are about hope for a future together. That ring is a reminder that we can find things we thought we'd lost forever. Tanya needs hope right now."

"I'm so glad," she said.

"It reminded me that I found what I thought was gone forever, too," he said. "Letting you leave was the biggest mistake I've ever made, and God knows I've made plenty."

"Because you cared and tried and wanted to do something good for people," she said staunchly. "Because you got involved."

"Because *you* got involved," he said.

"So . . . you're here for me," she said.

"I'm here for you."

"You drove a long way for nothing," she said.

His face went blank again.

"No! No, I don't mean it that way," she hurriedly added, and felt the blush climbing her neck, into her cheeks. "Oh, God. I meant I'd already decided to leave tomorrow. This isn't home anymore. Walkers Ford is. You are. You are my home."

He bent his head and kissed her, full of heat and promise lingering warm and purposeful against her lips.

"You must be the entanglement."

They broke apart to find Freddie standing beside Alana. She held out her hand. "I'm Freddie Wentworth."

"Lucas Ridgeway," he said, and shook Freddie's hand. "What entanglement?"

"I told her not to get entangled out there on the prairie because we needed her here," Freddie said. She gave Lucas a considering look. "She's amazing, and she's been my best-kept secret for a long, long time. But I can see she's not just my secret anymore."

"I don't need to be here, Freddie. I can do my job for you and the foundation from Walkers Ford. But I need to be there. They need me, and I need them."

"I need her," Lucas said.

"We need her, too," Freddie said. Alana straightened her shoulders in anticipation of an argument, but then Freddie surprised her. "But she knows what she needs. I wouldn't let her go for anything less."

Lucas stared at Freddie for a long second. He'd thought Alana's sister would be a diva. And she was, but a completely different kind of diva. Instead of demanding her younger sister's constant presence to smooth her way through life, she demanded Alana get nothing less than what she deserved. Someone who loved her for her. Nothing more. Nothing less. He reached for Alana's hand. "How much longer do you need to stay?"

Alana didn't hesitate. She didn't think about who she should talk to, or what people would think, or what her mother would say. "I can leave right now," she said firmly.

Freddie laughed out loud. "I'll tell Mother you're going home."

Alana looked at Lucas, and wove her fingers more tightly with his. "Tell her I'm already there."

ONE YEAR LATER . . .

"Tell it again! Tell it again!"

Cody Burton hunkered down among the little kids clustered at his feet. "I can't right now," he said gently. "The library is about to close, but if you come back next week, I'll be here and I'll tell you another story about Growler. What do you think he has to carry next time?" Little eyes widened expectantly. "Watermelons."

He detached himself from the crowd of kids and parents sprawled on beanbag chairs in the newly renovated children's section and made his way past the touch-screen computers to Alana. It had taken nearly a year of work to complete the renovation from the building's framework to the exterior, but it was the most rewarding year of Alana's life. The children's section had been freshly painted in a pretty pale yellow, and murals by the high school students lined the wall above new shelves. Low, brightly colored chairs surrounded circular rugs to create seating areas for kids to read. Origami cranes and elephants, created in an art workshop earlier in the month, hung from the ceiling and danced gently in the warm breeze.

The circulation desk marked the transition to the adult shelves and reading area. Mission-style chairs covered in a subtle print were grouped in front of the fireplace. A whole wall of shelves held DVDs for checkout. Alana stopped to straighten the furniture and reshelve the day's newspapers. All of the e-readers were checked out, with forty-one names on the waiting list, but she checked the lock on the storage cabinet out of habit.

"Thanks for coming," she said to the parents as they collected their children and escorted them out the front door. Cody snagged his bag from her office and turned out the lights. He'd filled out a little in the year she'd been back, but it would still be several more years before he gained his adult weight. He had a girlfriend now, a sweet, shy young woman taking nursing classes in Brookings who loved his younger brothers almost as much as he did.

"Nicely done," she said when he came up beside her. "How's the book coming?"

"Almost done painting the final sketches," he said. "The little kids have so many ideas about what Growler should look like, whether he should be tomato red or fire engine red or black. I sent the proposals to the agents and a few of them have asked to look at it."

"Good."

The Chatham County Spring Fling Carnival was in full swing as people made their way to the food tent for a barbecue dinner before the dance started up. Cody waited at the bottom of the steps while Alana locked the library door behind her.

"I'm meeting Jodi at the food tent after she finishes her shift at the nursing home. You want to join us?"

"No, thanks," she said. "I'm headed home first. Duke needs a walk, and Lucas had court today. We're going to meet there and walk over together."

"He's not such a bad guy, once you get to know him," Cody admitted.

"I like him," Alana said with a smile.

"I guess you do," Cody replied. "See you there."

She tipped her face to the setting sun, then set off for home, making her way slowly through the people crowding Main Street. She knew almost everyone by name now, and was slowly learning the family connections stretching back nearly a hundred and fifty years. Lucas would be waiting for her. There was no need to rush, no need to worry. The Spring Fling celebrated the completed library renovation. In a few weeks, Mrs. Battle and Lenore would staff the library while she flew to England for Freddie's wedding.

Then she'd come home.

When she rounded the corner to her block, Lucas's truck was parked in the driveway. Her steps quickened as she looked forward to her own reunion with the man she loved. Duke always stepped aside and watched the hello kiss with his tail wagging. It had taken months before he stopped getting worried when Alana got in her Audi alone.

She took a few moments to check the rosebushes for blooms. The canes had buds on them, but while several showed promise for blooming, so far none of them had. Tomorrow, she thought. If not tomorrow, the next day. She would be here to see them. Every spring for the rest of her life, she'd watch these roses bloom.

Lucas stood at the sink, washing his hands. She gave a happy little sigh and dropped her bags by the door. Duke scrabbled to his feet on the slick hardwood floors and came over to nose at her skirt. "Hello, stranger," she said.

"I've been gone twelve hours," he said with a smile as he dried his hands.

"Twelve hours, but there was the four-day hiking trip last

weekend . . ." she murmured, and tipped her mouth up for his kiss.

"That's better," he said, and slipped his arm around her waist.

"I still love it," she said. She studied the cream-painted beadboard cabinets and sage green walls. The color scheme soothed Alana's soul every time she walked through the door. The kitchen renovation took a fair bit of the fall and turned into a total replumbing of the house, but Alana figured if their relationship could survive a kitchen reno, it could survive anything.

"Even if it took longer than it should have?" Lucas asked. He wore a navy suit and red tie suitable for a court appearance, and an American flag pin on his lapel.

"Unplanned delays here and at the library gave us a good reason to take a weekend off to go camping. All work and no play makes for tired cops and librarians."

Mayor Turner rehired her as the contract librarian, then formally offered her the library director position after finishing the search process. She'd thought she'd known what she was getting into, but after a particularly contentious board meeting in November, Alana announced she couldn't face another weekend of taping and painting, and they both needed a break. Lucas packed climbing and camping gear for a three-day trip to the Black Hills. Alana spent her days sitting under pine trees by a lake, drinking tea and reading thrillers while Lucas scaled rock faces. On the drive home Lucas looked like the boy she'd seen in the pictures. Happy. At ease. Alive.

He'd started taking groups of kids on snowshoe, cross-country skiing, and rock-climbing trips, and loved every minute of it. She loved seeing him back in the sports that meant so much to him. They'd both come back refreshed and ready for the next set of challenges.

"With the grand opening over, you're due for a climbing trip," he reminded her.

"You can take the girl out of the library, but sending her up a rock face isn't a good idea," Alana said with a laugh.

"I'll be your anchor," he said.

"I just might do it, then," she said.

Duke sat at their feet and looked at them expectantly.

"What's that all about?" she asked.

Lucas tipped his head toward the kitchen window. She followed his glance and saw the bud vase on the shelf. A single pale pink rose bloom leaned against the edge.

"The first bloom! I thought it might open today, with the sunshine and nice weather." She reached for the clear vase. Lucas turned her so she leaned back against his hard chest, and he bent to nuzzle in her hair as she examined the flower. "It's perfect," she murmured as she turned it in the small vase. "The new fertilizer really . . ."

Her voice trailed away when she saw the single loop of green wire wrapped around gleaming gold. Lucas's arms tightened at her waist as she carefully unwrapped the wire. A ring dropped into her palm. It was an old-fashioned setting updated for the modern era, a center diamond surrounded by tiny diamonds that winked in the twilight.

Or maybe it was the tears in her eyes. She turned to face him, her heart pounding in her chest.

"Marry me?" he said quietly.

She looked out the window at the backyard, at the promise of spring in the greening grass and the rosebushes bursting out of the cold winter earth toward the sun. She looked at Duke. "You knew about this, didn't you?"

He shifted on his haunches and looked at her, ears perked expectantly. *Of course I did! Say yes!*

She lifted her gaze to Lucas, to the man who'd opened his heart and life to her when he'd thought he'd never feel again, who'd given her the thing she'd wanted most. She held her palm open to him, offering him the ring. He picked it up. She held her left hand out in front of her.

"Yes," she said, and watched as he slid the ring onto her ring finger. "Always yes."

He kissed her, slow and sweet. She threw her arms around his neck and hugged him. "I love you," she whispered.

"I love you, too," he whispered back.

Familiar female voices sounded in the driveway. "Look at the sky. Really look at it. Have you ever seen anything that spectacular in your life?"

"Mother, when have you not seen a spectacular sky? The sky is, by definition, spectacular."

Alana peered up at Lucas. "That sounds like—"

A delighted squeal shocked Alana nearly out of her skin. Freddie hauled open the kitchen door, tears in her eyes, her hands clasped together under her chin. Her mother stood slightly behind Freddie. Tears gleamed in her eyes as she watched Freddie leap across the kitchen and engulf Alana in a huge hug.

"What are you doing here? You're supposed to be in Dublin!" Alana said as she automatically hugged her sister.

"It's a surprise! You didn't think we'd miss the Walkers Ford Spring Fling Carnival and library grand reopening, did you? You did," Freddie said, answering her own question.

"There was a conference," Alana protested. "I booked hotel rooms. I booked plane tickets. I researched the impact of economic austerity programs on poverty."

"The conference is going on without us," Freddie said. "I lied about the rest of it. You aren't the only person who can book plane tickets."

Lucas stifled a laugh. "I won't forget that," Alana said, regaining her footing. "You knew about this," she said to her fiancé.

He gave her a smug smile as he loosened his tie. "I picked them up in Sioux Falls on my way back from court."

"Hello, Mother," Alana said, leaning forward to kiss her mother's cheek. "I hope you had a good flight."

Her mother lifted Alana's left hand and looked at the engagement ring. "Congratulations, darling," she said quietly.

Not exactly the enthusiastic response she hoped for, but Freddie was more than making up for it, and genuinely, too. "It's beautiful. Perfect for you," she said, turning Alana's hand so the diamond caught the light.

"I'm going to get changed," Lucas said, edging away from the all-girl reunion. Duke followed him.

"I want to take them on a tour of the library," Alana said. "Meet us at the beer garden."

"Hallelujah," Freddie said. "My two favorite words. Beer garden."

"I thought your two favorite words were on-time departure," Alana said.

"Nope," Freddie said. "Beer garden ties for first with cheese curds, funnel cake, and corn dog, courtesy of all of those campaign stops at the Illinois State Fair."

Alana poked her. "Where are you staying?"

"We're staying out at that huge house on the prairie. Brookhaven. Chloe had space, and my God, it's gorgeous. The sunset through those windows . . . unbelievable. You know the former owner, right? She renovated the house herself? I want to talk to her. We've got our eye on a town house in Chelsea but it will need to be gutted to the rafters. Coming, Mother?"

"I'll be right behind you," her mother said. "I want to look at those roses."

Freddie brought her up to speed on the gossip from home as they strolled toward the street fair. "Nate's divorce will be final in a few weeks," she said confidentially. "They just never recovered from him being gone for so long. His wife—what's her name—"

"Miranda," Alana supplied.

"—says he isn't the same since he came back."

"Nate seemed the same to me, but she sees him more than I do, obviously. Post-traumatic stress disorder?"

Freddie shrugged. "If that's the case, no one's talking about it, not even Miranda."

Alana peeked over her shoulder and found her mother studying the houses, the gardens beginning to bloom, the sky. "What does Mother think about all of this?"

"Ask her yourself," Freddie said with a smile.

The sound of laughter and music reached them well before they crossed Main Street. Alana gave them the tour, mildly amused at the way her sister switched off Freddie and turned on Frederica Wentworth to ask questions about the architecture, the renovation project, the number of people served, the budget, and the mural. "That's quite good," she said absently. "I love the lines. It's surprisingly sophisticated and unsentimental, given his age."

"He's got so much talent," Alana agreed. "He just needed a way to express it."

Freddie wandered off to examine the framed pictures from the historical society. Her mother joined her in front of Cody's mural. "Very nice," she said.

"Nice." Wounded, Alana turned to look at her. "I know it's not what you imagined for me," she said quietly. "But I love it here. I'm happy. For the first time in my life, I've found where I belong."

"That makes me a little sad, dear," her mother said.

Her heart sank. "I won't apologize."

"Nor should you." Her mother's eyes followed the subtle swirling motion of the mural, spiraling from the edge of the prairie to the library at the center of the painting. Alana stood there, with Lucas at her side. "I'm disappointed in myself. A mother shouldn't fit her children into a mold. I wanted the wrong things for you. I wanted my dreams and Freddie's dreams for you. I should have been thinking about what you wanted. I kept you on the periphery of Frederica's life, rather than helping you find your own center. I'm glad you found this, despite me."

Alana blinked. "It wasn't despite you," she said valiantly.

Her mother's lips curved in a smile. "It certainly was,

Alana. I promise not to make the same mistakes going forward. Where will the wedding be?"

No hesitating. No waiting for someone else to weigh in. "In the backyard," Alana said. "Next June when the roses are blooming. Family and close friends only. If she's got time, a local seamstress will make the dress. I'll have to ask Lucas about all of this, but I can't imagine he'll mind."

"Perfect," her mother said without batting an eyelash. "That's absolutely perfect. It will be exactly right for you."

"Why don't I have a corn dog in my hand?" Freddie asked from the foyer, where she was looking at pictures of the town circa 1908. "I smell fried food in every variation, and yet I have none. No corn dogs, no funnel cakes, no cheese curds. It's tragic."

Alana laughed.

"What? I live for cheese curds," Freddie said.

"I desperately want a beer," her mother added fervently, which made Alana laugh even harder.

"Let's eat," she said.

They stopped to load up on fair food, then found seats in the beer garden, where Freddie picked up three cups brimming with a local microbrewery's spring ale.

"Oh, that's good," her mother said, then took another sip. "That's very good. Hand me a corn dog, Freddie."

The band was on a break when Lucas, dressed in jeans, boots, and a long-sleeve policeman's polo shirt, slid onto the picnic bench beside Alana and snitched a cheese curd. Tanya sat down next to him, still wearing her Bureau of Land Management uniform. Her eyes were clear, her skin tanned, her grandmother's engagement ring on her right hand. She'd been out of rehab and drug-free for almost a year, and she'd quickly become one of Alana's close friends. Before long, Cody and his starstruck girlfriend joined them, but Freddie's status rose from celebrity to goddess with every question she asked Cody about the mural and his art.

"Scoot over, Cody," Mrs. Battle said imperiously.

Cody obeyed, making space between him and Alana. They helped her distribute paper plates laden with funnel cakes to the table. Mrs. Battle sat down next to Alana, did a double take at the ring on her hand, then looked at Lucas. "It's about time," she said.

The news spread quickly once Mayor Turner got hold of the band's microphone; before long she and Lucas were shaking hands and giving hugs. Freddie was working on her second funnel cake while the band warmed up for their second set. "The town's chief of police getting engaged to the town's librarian is a big deal," Freddie noted. "It's kind of a cliché, you know."

"We are nothing of the sort," Alana said firmly. "We're a once-in-a-lifetime love."

"That you are," Freddie said, shaking extra powdered sugar onto the funnel cake.

"You have to fit into an Alexander McQueen dress in three weeks," Alana reminded her.

"That's why you're eating half of this."

"I'm not eating another funnel cake. I have to fit into an Alexander McQueen dress in three weeks, too."

Cody snitched half of the cake and took a huge bite. "Problem solved," he said to laughter.

Lucas shook his head, then held out his hand to Alana. "Dance with me?"

The band started their second set with a cover from The Band Perry. She took his hand and followed him onto the dance floor. It was such a relief to settle her head against his shoulder and close her eyes.

"This is nice," she said.

"Uh-huh."

"We're getting married next June in the backyard."

"Sounds good to me."

"Let's wait to take our honeymoon. Go somewhere warm in January. Last winter was horrible."

"Okay."

"You don't care?"

"I'd go anywhere with you. Live anywhere to be with you," he said.

"That's a lovely sentiment, but this is home. So we'll travel, but we'll always come back here."

"Home," he murmured into her hair. Alana closed her eyes and rested her cheek against his shoulder as they turned in a slow circle. "We'll always come home."